PENGUIN BOOKS

THE PENGUIN BOOK OF
SOUTHERN AFRICAN VERSE

Stephen Gray was born in Cape Town in 1941 and educated in England and the United States. His books include *John Ross: The True Story* (1987) and his latest novel, *Time of Our Darkness*, published in 1988. He has edited, for Penguin Books, Herman Charles Bosman's *Makapan's Caves and Other Stories* (1987) and *The Penguin Book of Southern African Stories* (1985), to which this collection is a companion. He lives and works in Johannesburg.

D0197464

THE
PENGUIN
BOOK
OF

SOUTHERN AFRICAN
VERSE

EDITED BY
STEPHEN GRAY

Penguin Books

PENGUIN BOOKS

Published by the Penguin Group
27 Wrights Lane, London w 8 5 TZ, England
Viking Penguin Inc., 40 West 23rd Street, New York, New York 10010, USA
Penguin Books Australia Ltd, Ringwood, Victoria, Australia
Penguin Books Canada Ltd, 2801 John Street, Markham, Ontario, Canada L 3 R 1 B 4
Penguin Books (NZ) Ltd, 182–190 Wairau Road, Auckland 10, New Zealand

Penguin Books Ltd, Registered Offices: Harmondsworth, Middlesex, England

This selection first published 1989
10 9 8 7 6 5 4 3 2 1

The Acknowledgements on pages 394–9 constitute an extension of this
copyright page

Made and printed in Great Britain by
Cox and Wyman Ltd, Reading, Berks.
Filmset in Linotron Sabon by
Rowland Phototypesetting Ltd, Bury St Edmunds, Suffolk

CONTENTS

CONTENTS

INTRODUCTION

———— ~ ————

The anthologizer's task of selecting from a large library of literature sufficient to fill only a single volume is an over-responsible one. Always one has too much power in terms of setting trends. Many readers will take the cross-section for a profile of the whole. The work is assumed to be representative, a quick rich route through an arduous, time-consuming and probably otherwise unreachable terrain. The labour having been done, readers can all too conveniently take the part for the whole.

The dangers inherent in contriving this metonomy can at least be minimized with some setting out of the ground rules of anthology-making: the editor's principles, procedures and preferences. In compiling this collection of *The Penguin Book of Southern African Verse* I have been guided by the following criteria. Other criteria would release other anthologies.

The scope of this collection is a literary subcontinent rather than any political nation-system. It concerns that wedge of countries at the base of Africa, distinct from West, Central and East Africa. Currently this region comprises 'South Africa' and the 'Frontline States'. The last bastion of racism – in a word, apartheid – South Africa dominates the region, but the point here is that it does not entirely control it, nor ever has; Southern Africa as a literary system has flourished in spite of South Africa, not because of it.

The poets of this conglomeration of geography, for those who prefer such discriminations, are classified by modern nationalities in the index at the end. But the grouping of the literature by nation – 'South African poetry', 'Zimbabwean poetry', 'Swaziland poetry' – is, at present and at best, an arbitrary process which can drive poets into having identities which are not primary with them. The notes on contributors reveal that as many as half the poets here have not written about their birthplaces, or alternatively do not – often cannot – live in them. This is pre-eminently a literature firstly about adoptive countries and then of loss of them. This may pose problems for the bibliographer, but for the poets themselves the very issue of nationality is still open. An editor should reflect this situation, not force it into a configuration it does not have.

The language of the original work is another defining organizer – there is 'Shona literature', 'Afrikaans literature', 'Lusophone literature' and so on, each the subject of specialist studies. The predecessor of this anthology, *The Penguin Book of South African Verse*, edited by Jack Cope and Uys Krige in 1968, although limiting itself to the poets born and bred in South Africa only, for its time made a considerable breakthrough in this regard. Cope and Krige wisely included all the major languages of South Africa, beginning with an 'English' section (187 pp.), followed by translations under the following headings and in this order: 'Afrikaans' (51 pp.) and 'African', subdivided into 'Bushman' (6 pp.), 'Hottentot' (6 pp.), 'Sotho' (19 pp.), 'Xhosa' (12 pp.), 'Zulu' (18 pp.). To considerable controversy they did invite comparison between these sub-literatures of their system. But the arrangement of their material actually inhibited comparison by keeping the works to be compared poles apart. 'English' was privileged, and then 'Afrikaans', while 'Zulu' – possibly because of the unfortunate circumstance of its name beginning with the last letter of the alphabet – came in last, inevitably implying a slide in quality.

Today the meeting place they offered, organized by simple language origins, seems outdated, even offensive. In the darkest days of apartheid a mere methodological rule had divided the poets further still. They may have all been in the same bus, but white English-speakers drove it while blacks had the seats reserved in the back.

My own objection to their arrangement is more than the obvious one. Hardly any of Cope and Krige's poets were in fact the unilingual purists their division into language camps implied. Like landscape, language is not a simple issue in the literary system of Southern Africa. Class indeed conditions mother-tongue use, for most English-speaking white writers have tended to be monolingual, Afrikaners bi-, and 'Africans' have frequently, possibly owing to the harassed nature of their experience, been multilingual. While acknowledging that this pyramid has existed, my impulse is not to read it Cope and Krige's way. There, from Douglas Livingstone you had to go back to Eugène Marais, and from Marais go back to Xaa-ttin. Here these three reappear in the reverse order, which is all the more democratic as it reflects their actual chronological sequence.

In other words, instead of enforcing distances between languages, I insist on their proximity. For example, take the Second World War sequence here, from Van Wyk Louw's *Raka* to Krige the Afrikaner's own English poem, through Zuma's Zulu praises and Makabo's Sotho ones on to Butler's 'Stranger to Europe', to which Chipasula's 'Tramp' of a later period should be added. Read in comparative and contrastive terms this sequence reveals far more than keeping them apart by language does. All were involved in the same episode, and made poetry out of it.

Using this comparative method, our indebtedness to translators becomes substantial. They are the ones who must have felt that a poem was worth hearing in another context. In Southern Africa where so many languages live shoulder to shoulder in the marketplace, yet are so segregated from one another in the institutions of literature, translation itself is more than the technical transposition of a work across from one language to another. It is an act of unblocking channels of communication to insist on the reciprocity of human feelings.

Fortunately for us, and on account of its power in international forums, English has been the major recipient of this heritage of translation. Rather than commission too many new translations for this collection, I have decided to use the existing legacy, often obscurely hidden, and to honour it. Many translated pieces are historic in their own right (Fanshawe's Camoens is one example, Pringle's Ntsikana another). The index of translators shows that in the past they have overwhelmingly been poets themselves, often operating with little institutional support.

Instead of implying that translations are somehow second-hand, the arrangement of this work foregrounds translation itself as a major, life-sustaining activity within the system. Because translations are read for the original behind them – which is not the same process as reading an original directly – I have labelled each translation in an obvious way, so that the necessary adjustment can be made before interpretation and judgement. This should alert us to a deeper characteristic in the system. Many Southern African poems are internal translations themselves (the Khoikhoi hyena into human speech, Scully's ''Nkongane', Smith's 'Katisje's Patchwork Dress' and Battiss' 'Limpopo' are examples). Patel's 'Haanetjie's Morning Dialogue' at the end, which by all the rules is untranslatable, is actually about (mis)translation.

The proximity of writers arranged in this way tends to stress the importance of common, public events over individual biographies. The comparative approach is usually more sociological and historical than aesthetic, and certainly I have chosen more poems which record group, communal, national and international happenings than private aches. But Camoens' 'Canto V' is as much a historical document as part of a great and influential epic poem; Schreiner's 'The Cry of South Africa' is as much a gesture of protest, fixed for all time, as a competent lyric in the imperative; Serote's 'The Breezing Dawn of the New Day' is as much a programme of policy and a statement of intent as a rhetorical tour de force.

To expect poets to give systematic testimony of their times, at the one extreme, is as unjust as to expect them always to be superb technicians at the other. Nevertheless, many anthologies have been formed from these two points of view: Barry Feinberg's *Poets to the People: South African Freedom Poems* (1974) is hyper-activist and technically banal, while D. J. Opperman's perennial *Groot Verseboek* is an utterly gutless trove of the finest writing. Here I have tried to remain flexible without making this separation between content and form decisive – there is, to quote Timothy Holmes, room for all.

Other anthologies have divided the system along colour lines. For example, Frank Chipasula's *When my Brothers Come Home: Poems from Central and Southern Africa* (1985) includes blacks only, specializing in the poetry of black statement. In the deep past anthologies like Francis Carey Slater's *The Centenary Book of*

South African Verse (1925) set the precedent by admitting the white interest only. Because the intention here is to reflect the long and complex story of what poetry has done, and is doing, in Southern Africa, such exclusivity is neither desirable nor sound. The principle is: poems first.

Another imbalance I have tried to correct, although not with much success, is that between men and women represented. Afrikaans-language poetry at least offers us a tradition where women have been major figures in each decade of its development. With other languages this is not so, and the field to date remains male-dominated. That is the history that arrives at our present.

To the chagrin of an editor trying to maintain a sense of the historical background of a collection aimed at a reader who may have no knowledge of it, though, the event all too often does not occur neatly on schedule in the poetry. 'Boer War poetry', that unfashionable grouping in the system, is a case in point. The war of the combative poets during 1899 to 1902 left many casualties – see Kipling through to Greene here, and their work is a mere fraction of the outputs triggered. But it took Leipoldt until 1911 to take stock of the same events.

In occasional poetry event and poem nearly coincide, although we have inherited a great prejudice against occasional poetry for its being too quickly reflexive. Yet many poems here are keyed to the datelines beneath them in an urgent and impressive way and no one, I am sure, would call a poem like Craveirinha's 'Ode to a Lost Cargo in a Ship Called *Save*' suspect because it is written right out of the headlines of the day. Nor for that matter are John Campbell's 'I'm far from what I call my home' and Mqhayi's 'The Pleiades', which also spring from particular moments, any the less efficient and effective for that.

Beyond the occasional use of events in poetry there appear to be two further possible uses – history as recollection made subsequently, and then cold-blooded historical reconstruction of events taken place before the poet's lifetime. Bessa Victor's 'That Old Mulemba' and Mattera's 'The Day They Came for Our House' are recollections; Couzyn's 'World War II' and Cullinan's '1818. M. François le Vaillant Recalls . . .' are reconstructions. Mothibi's 'Speech' about the Mantatee invasion of the moment eventually becomes Matshoba's 'The Mantatee Horde', its reliving. In a content-orientated anthology 'The Day They Came for Our House' would have to go under 'Demolition of Sophiatown, 1950–60' and, even more extremely, Cullinan's poem under the eighteenth century. But obviously it is the time of composition which decides the ordering here. Both Mattera's and Cullinan's style is of their dates of publication in the 1980s.

The sequence as a whole develops more or less as its own literary history does. Camoens' epic of discovery gives way to Pringle's domestic account of settlement; Bain's 'Address' gives way to Brodrick's record of colonizing tactics in 'Joe's Luck'; Ntsikana's 'Great Hymn' of conversion gives way to Sontonga's 'Lord Bless Africa' – a song for re-unification – and Ndlovu's 'Elegy for the Dead of Soweto' to the vatic prophecy of Wakolele's 'Southern Africa'. The sweep of a literary history is resonantly there.

The smaller unit of organization is the period. Jolobe, Vilakazi, Plomer, Pessoa and Swart are essentially of the 1930s, just as Brettell, Kumbirai, Mutswairo and Hodza are of the 1960s of pre-Zimbabwean Rhodesia. The 1970s – the best-represented period in this collection – stretches from Breytenbach through to Mapanje, not that either of these two poets has ceased publishing. Poets with lengthy productive careers like Plomer's (1923–73) present special problems, but within their space their development is clear from the way their poems are dated.

If those are the principles on which this collection is assembled, these are some of its procedures. In selecting from the work of a poet I have not gone for any time-hallowed 'best poems' that in some unshakeable, absolute way are meant to represent the height of that poet's achievement. Then we would be back to an alphabetical listing, or one ordered by date of birth, and yet another accretion of anthology favourites; and besides, Southern Africa is notoriously quick to break reputations and make new ones overnight. My obstinacy in avoiding most of the chestnuts is deliberate, because chestnuts have often become favourites for reasons not really connected to their inherent quality, even if there is such a thing. Space restrictions in anthologies often insist that 'best poems' be short ones, and in the end for reasons of expediency the compact lyric becomes the quality form in which to write.

For example, Roy Campbell's 'The Zulu Girl' and 'The Serf' – at best uneven and certainly uncharacteristic works – have come to seem his only certified masterpieces. My procedure in a case like this is to cease perpetuating the way anthologies cannibalize anthologies, and to force a reassessment of the otherwise lost corpus. For the purposes of this anthology a sizeable portion of a Campbell book-length satire of the 1920s seemed more useful in the sequence. Then Plomer, through an accident of birth Campbell's junior by a few months, always seemed in the old model to follow him, like some influenced brother, with a lesser selection. I have revalued that relationship, separating them as they were irreconcilably separated in life and for sound, important political reasons, and given the technically younger room enough in the forms in which he did excel.

Where I have included some poets and inevitably left others out, a value-judgement may only partially be implied. Where there is a density of working poets, one may sometimes stand in for another. The proportions of pages given to the nineteenth century, or to 'post-independent Zimbabwean' or 'Mozambican' poetry may also be hotly disputed. But I cannot claim representativeness, still less authority, in the grouping of the pages. In the end this is the list of poems of Southern Africa that I admire, find memorable, and for many reasons feel are irreplaceably valuable. Above all, for me they interact well. There is a tissue of sources and influences, culminations and re-emergences, connecting them, which is greater than the sum of its parts and which is my main concern.

In assembling the sequence, certain characteristics of the whole from which it comes did begin to emerge. Many Southern African poets, for example, like to pay generous homage to their predecessors (Kunene towards Vilakazi, Stockenström towards Jonker and Nakasa), and they certainly enjoy answering one another back (Abrahams to Wright, Zimunya to his white poetess). The dramatic monologue is a prevalent form (Leipoldt's Oom Gert, Hunter's Rand miner, Hodza's slighted wife and Ndebele's spokeswoman in 'The Revolution of the Aged'). The choric, first person plural is used exceptionally often when the voice is communal rather than individual (Small's 'What abou' de Law?', De Sousa's 'The Poem of João', Mtshali's 'The Removal of Our Village, KwaBhanya', Manaka's actual choruses).

Poems discussing the purpose of poetry are quite frequent, as if redefinition of its function needs constantly to be undertaken (Gwala's 'In Defence of Poetry' and Mann's 'The Poet's Progress' are two examples). Because of the Southern African's frequent need to explain to outsiders, epistolary poems are a favourite form (Pringle's 'The Emigrant's Cabin', Brooks' 'A General Description of Men and Things in Cape Town', Driver's 'Letter to Breyten Breytenbach from Hong Kong', Wright's to Isabella Fey and Mungoshi's 'A Letter to a Son'). Because of recurring anxieties over the shape of the future, the form of the lullaby – hardly ever reflected in 'best poem' anthologies for its association with childishness – is obsessively present here (Pringle's Ghona widow's song, Marais' ferocious cradle-song, Small's 'Brown Lullaby', Breytenbach's and Cronin's). Since much of the poetry is forward-looking, rather than nostalgic, a form like the lullaby becomes crucial.

To an outsider familiar with Western European and North American poetry it can only prove distressing to find the major role played by the lament in Southern Africa. An anthology of its own could well be devoted to the dirges of the Southern African people of the past and the present. Funeral-songs, elegies, commemorations of sorrow and loss abound. Here 'The Broken String' of the San does indeed set the tone for Vilakazi's fearsome grief, Butler's 'In Memoriam, J. A. R.', Paço d'Arcos' 'Re-encounter' and Mapanje's epitaphs, through to Malange's dedication to the late Brother Andries Raditsela and the final poem of this collection, which is about the practice and purpose of the lament.

Battle-songs are also actively composed, and the praise-poem – that most malleable form, which has accumulated a literature of its own – is hardy and enduring. Here I have not attempted to represent these adequately, or even partially, but have inserted a few examples at points as reminders. The praises of Mbuyazi of the 1820s, of the eland, of his chief in Mqhayi's poem and of J. C.

Smuts are included, and of the old comrades for good measure. The not so distant form of the ballad also persists, and well beyond its time in Europe or America. Animal poems are also found, although I have not stressed these, with birds, possibly because of their connotation with freedom, being most popular.

Satire and parody are most widely practised, although, thanks possibly to the marketing of books where it is often difficult enough to have a general collection published, few books of satire and parody as such have appeared. (Brooks' and Campbell's are the only ones represented here.) But in Southern Africa satire and parody are more frequently integrated into other modes, and have been since the first recorded poems (Shaka's heroic piece is an example). To Westerners this is one lead to follow, showing that Southern African poetry in general is different in kind from their own, and follows its own set of conventions.

If there is one central image of the poet in this anthology, for me it is Mtshali's in his 'Farewell to My Scooter', despite the fact that it appears there in comic terms. It is the poet as messenger. The poet as 'been to' is chronically returning with news: Eglington from Maputo to Johannesburg (1940s), Knopfli from Johannesburg to Maputo (1950s), Jensma from Maputo to Johannesburg (1960s), Mhlongo from Johannesburg to Zululand (1970s), and so on. These messengers are often quite unambiguous about their message, for much of Southern African verse is unashamedly didactic. Saying it well is often predicated on having something to say.

And not many of these poets feel library-bound – elitist, privileged and effete. The dominance of voices over written characters shows that poetry is still felt to be living communication rather than bookish exercise. Yet, of the poets alive today, very few have direct access to their audiences. There are few court-poets left and even fewer courts worth singing for. Most of the living poets have been displaced into exile, as well, so are forcibly removed from their hearers. Readership is all-important, then, and publication becomes an urgent means to an end. Censorship and banning have tried to control this for a long time. But the switch to print does not mean that oracy has given way in any new literacy; it has merely refined its medium.

For me four poems in particular symbolize the Babel that is sprawling Southern Africa: Bain's 'Polyglot Medley' – the title of which would serve well as a subtitle here; Jacinto's 'Poem of Alienation', cataloguing the city-cries of pre-liberation Luanda; the unstoppable voice of Chipasula's hanged man; and triumphantly the multiple speakers of Craveirinha's soaring praise of the human spirit, 'The Tasty "Tanjarines" of Inhambane'. (Like the majority of the rest of the contents, both the Bain and the Craveirinha are anthologized here for the first time.)

But there are about 120 poets here, with some fifty-five translators, making a total of 224 items. To single out further pieces for admiration is hardly my job – it is now the reader's. I hope whoever enters this labyrinth – which is only one route through the whole, and which is presided over by that recurring symbol of the Southern Constellation – will find it a rewarding pleasure.

STEPHEN GRAY, 1989

LUIS DE CAMOENS
(c. 1524–80)

The Lusiads, Canto V

Translated from the Portuguese by Sir Richard Fanshawe (1655)

1

The rev'rend *Father* stood inculcating
These *Sentences*; when *Wee* to a serene
And gentle Gale expand our Canvas wing;
When from the loved Port our selves we weane:
And sayles unfurling make the *Welkin* ring
(After the manner of *Sea-faring* Men)
> With BOON VOYAGE. Immediatly the *Wind*
> Does on the *Trunks* his Office and his kind.

The old man has prophesied disaster, but the armada of caravels sails from Lisbon. Vasco da Gama continues addressing the King of Malindi in East Africa. July 1947

2

The ever burning *Lamp*, that rules the day,
In the *Nemean Bruite* began to rage;
And the *great world* (which doth with time decay)
Limpt in his *Sixt* infirm and crooked *Age*:
Thereof (accompting in the *Church* 'is way)
Of *Sol's* incessant *Race* the THOUSAND stage,
> *Four hundred, Ninetie Seav'nth*, was running, whan
> In all their *trim* the *Shipps* to saile began.

3

Now by degrees out of our sight did glide
Parts of our *Countrey*, which abode behind.
Abode deer TAGUS: and we *then* did hide
Fresh SYNTRA (About *this* our eyes did wind).
In the *lov'd* Kingdom likewise did abide
Our *Hearts*, whose strings could not be thence untwind;
> And, when as *all* the *Land* did now withdraw,
> The sea and *Firmament* was *all* wee saw.

4

Thus went we opening those seas, which (save
Our *own*) no *Nation* open'd ere before:
See those new *Isles*, and clymates near; which brave
PRINCE HENRY shewd unto the *world* before:
The *Mauritanian Hills* and *Strand*, which gave
ANTEUS birth, who *there* was King of yore,
  Upon the *left hand* left (for there is none
  Upon the *right*, though now suspected, known).

5

We the great *Island* of MADERA pass,
Which from its *Wood's* abundance took the name;
The first which planted by our *Nation* was,
Of which the *worth* is more than the great *fame*;
Nor (though the last place in the *world* it has)
Doth any, Venus loves, excel the same:
  Who (rather) were it *Hers*, would lay aside
  For *This*, CYTHERA, CYPRUS, PAPHOS, GNIDE.

6

We leave adust MASSILIAS barren Coast,
Where AZENEGUES's lean *Heards* take their repast;
A People, that want *water* to their *Roast*;
Nor *Herbs* it self in any plenty tast:
A LAND in fine, to bear no *Fruit* dispos'd:
Where *Birds* in their hot stomachs Iron waste:
  Suff'ring of all things great Necessitie:
  Which ETHIOPIA parts from BARBARIE.

West of the Sahara
which divides the
Maghreb from
black Africa

7

We pass the *Bound* that hedges out the *Sun*
When to the frozen *North* he bends his way:
Where *People* dwell, whom CLYMENE's rash Son
Deny'de the sweet Complexion of the *day*.
Here NATIONS strange are water'd one by one
With the fresh Currents of black SENEGA.
  Here ARSINARIUS Aloof is seen,
  That lost his name: *confirmed* by us CAPE GREEN.

8

CANARIAN ISLES (the same men call'd of old
The FORTUNATE) declined: After *These*
Among the *Daughter-Islands* we did fall
Of aged HESPER, term'd HESPERIDES:
(*Locks* in the which the *Fleets* of Portugal
To *wonder* new before had turn'd the *Keys*).
        There did we touch with favourable wind,
        Some *fresh provisions* for our *Ships* to find.

9

It's *Name* the *Isle* on which we Anchor cast
Did from the warlike St IAGO take,
The *Saint* That holp the SPANIARD in times past
Such cruel havock of the MOORS to make.
Thence, when the *North* renew'd his kinder blast,
We cut again the circumfused *Lake*
        Of the salt *Ocean*; And that *Store-House* leave,
        From which Refreshment sweet we did receive.

10

Winding from thence about your *Affrick shore*,
Where to the EAST (like a *half-moon*) it bends
About JALOFO's Province (which doth store
The *world* with BLACKS, whom, forc't Aboard, it sends),
The large MANDINGA that affords the *Ore*
The which doth make Friends Focs, and of Foes Friends
        (Which suck't GAMBEA's crooked water laves
        That disimbogues in the *Atlantic* Waves),

11

We pass the GORGADES, peopled by faire
Sisters, in ancient time residing *there*:
Who (rob'd of *seeing*) did amongst them share
One onely *Eye*, which they by turns did weare.
Thou onely, *Thou* (the *Net* of whose curld Haire
Caught NEPTUNE, like a Fish, in his own *Were*)
        Turn'd of them all at last the ugliest *Lout*,
        With *Vipers* sow'dst the burning sands about.

12

Ploughing in fine before a *Northern* Wind
In that vast GULPH the *Navy* went embayd;
LEONA'S craggie mountains left behind,
The CAPE OF PALMS (so call'd from *Palmie* shade)
And that great RIVER, where the *Sea* (confin'd)
Against the shores, which we had planted, bray'd:
    With th'*Isle* that boasts *his* name, who would not trust
    Till in the side of GOD his Hand he thrust.

13

There lyes of CONGO the wide-spreading *Ream*,
By *Us* (before) converted to CHRIST'S Law;
Through which long ZAYRE glides with crystal stream:
A *River*, this, the Ancients never saw.
In fine through this vast *ocean* from the Team
Of known BOOTES I apace withdraw:
    Having already past upon the *Maine*
    The BURNING LINE that parts the *World* in twain.

14

There we before us saw by its own light
In this new EPICICLE a *Star* new,
Of which the other *Nations* ne're had sight,
And (long in darkness) no such matter knew.
The world's *Antartick* Henge (less gilt, less bright,
For want of *Stars*, than th'*Artick*) we did view:
    Beneath the which, a question yet depends,
    Whether more *Land* begins, and the *Sea* ends.

15

Past in this sort those *equinoxiall* clymes
By which his steeds *twice* yearely drives the *sun*;
Making two *Summers, Winters, Autumns, Primes,*
Whilst he from one to t'other *Pole* doth run:
Now *tost*, now *calm'd* (A *sufferer* in all *Times*:
By *want*, and *plenty*, equally undone)
    I saw both BEARES (the *Little* and the *Great*)
    Despight of JUNO in the *Ocean* set.

4

16

To tell thee all the *dangers* of the DEEP
(Which humane Judgment cannot comprehend)
Suddain and fearfull *storms*, the *Ayres* that sweep;
Lightnings, that *with* the *Ayre* the *Fire* doe blend;
Black HURRACANS; thick *Nights*; THUNDERS, that keep
The *World* alarm'd, and threaten the last *End*:
      Would be too tedious: indeed vain and mad,
      Though a *brasse* Tongue, and *Iron* lungs I had.

17

I *saw* those things, which the rude *Mariner*
(Who hath no *Mistresse*, but *Experience*)
Doth for unquestionable *Truths* aver,
Guided belike by his *externall* sence:
But ACADEMICKS (who can never err,
Who by pure *Wit*, and LEARNING's *quintessence*,
      Into all NATURE's *secrets* dive and pry)
      Count either *Lyes*, or *coznings* of the *Eye*.

18

I saw (as plain as the *sun's* midday light)
That *fire* the *Sea-man* saints (shining out faire
In time of *Tempest*, of feirce *winds* despight,
Of *over-clowded* Heavens, and black despayre):   St Elmo's fire
Nor did wee *all* lesse wonder (and well might,
For 'twas a *sight* to *bristle* up the Hayre)
      To see a *sea-born Clowd* with a long *Cane*
      Suck *in* the *sea*, and spout it *out* againe.

19

I *saw* with these *two eyes* (nor can presume
That *these* deceiv'd mee) from the *Ocean* breathed
A little *Vapour*, or aeriall *Fume*,
With the curld *wind* (as by a *Turnor*) wreathed.
I *saw* it reach to *Heaven* from the salt *spume*,
In such thin *Pipe* as *those* where *springs* are sheathed;
      That by the *Eye* it hardly could be deemed:
      Of the same substance with the *Clowds* it seemed.

20

By little *this* and little did augment,
And swell'd beyond the Bulk of a thick *Mast*.
Streightning and *widening* (like a *Throat*) it went,
To gulp into it self the water fast.
It *wav'd* upon the *wavy* Element.
The top thereof (impregnated at last
 Into a *Clowd*) expanded *more*, and *more*,
 With the great load of *Water* which it bore.

21

As a black *Horse-leech* (mark it in some *Pool*!)
Got to the *Lip* of an unwary *Beast*,
Which (*drinking*) suck't it from the *water* cool,
Upon *another's* blood *itself* to feast;
It swells and swells, and feeds beyond all Rule,
And stuffs the paunch; a rude, unsober *Guest*:
 So swell'd the *Pillar* (with a hideous Crop)
 It self, and the black Clowd which it did prop.

22

But, when that now 'tis full, the *Pedestal*
Draws to itself, which in the *Sea* was set;
And (flutt'ring through the Ayre) in show'rs doth fall:
The *couchant* Water with *new* water wet.
It pays the waves the *borrow'd* Waves, but all
The *Salt* thereout did first extract and get.
 Now tell me, SCHOLARS, by your Books; what skill,
 Dame NATURE us'd these *waters* to distil?

23

If old PHILOSOPHERS (who travayld through
So many Lands, *her* secrets out to spye)
Had *viewed* the *Miracles* which *I* did view,
Had sayled with so many *winds* as *I*;
What *writings* had they left behind! what new,
Both *Starres*, and *Signs*, bequeath'd to *Us*! What high
 And strong *Influxes*! What *hid Qualities*!
 And all pure *Truths*, without *allay* of *Lyes*!

24

But when that *Planet* (which her *Court* doth keep
In the *first sphere*) five times with speedy Race,
Had, since our *Fleet* was wand'ring on the DEEP,
Shew'd sometimes *half*, and sometimes *all* her *Face*:
A quick-eyd *Lynx* cryes, from the *Scuttle* steep,
LAND! LAND! With *that*, upon the *decks* apace
    Leaps the transported *Crew*: their *Eyes* intent
    On the *Horizon* of the ORIENT.

25

At first the *dusky Mountains* (of the *Land*
Wee *made*) like congregated *Clowds* did look:
Seen *plain*, the heavie *Anchors* out of hand
Wee ready make: *Approach'd*, our *sailes* we strook:
And (that we might more cleerly understand
The parts *remote* in which we were) I took
    The ASTROLABE, a modern *Instrument*:
    Which with sharpe Judgement SAGES did invent.

26

We disembarke in the most open space:
From *whence*, themselves the rasher *Land-men* spread
(Greedy of Novelties!) through the wyld Place:
Which never *Stranger's* Foot before did tread.
But I (not passing the *Land's* sandie Face),
To find out where we are, with *Sea-men* bred
    Stay taking the *Sun's* heighth by th'OCEAN curld;
    And with my *Compasse* trace the *painted* World.

St Helena Bay,
November

27

We found, we had already wholly past
Of the *half-Goate*, half *Fish*, the noted *Gole*:
Between the *same* and *that* cold *Countrey* plac't
(If such there *be*) beneath the SOUTHERN POLE.
When, loe! (lockt in with my *Companions* fast)
I see a NATIVE come, black as the *Cole*:
    Whom *they* had took perforce, as in the *Wood*
    Getting out *Honey* from the *Combe* he stood.

Encounter with San

28

He comes with *horrour* in his *looks*: as *Hee*
Who of a *snare*, like this, could never dreame.
Hee understood not *Us*, neither *Him Wee*:
More savage than the brutish POLYPHEME.
Of COLCOS'S glistring Fleece I let him see
The *mettle* which of *mettles* is supreme:
    Pure *Silver*; sparkling stones (continuing suite);
    But in all *these* was unconcern'd the *Bruite*.

29

I bid them shew him lower prized Things,
Beades of transparent crystall; a fine noyse
Of little *Bells*, thridded on *tawdry* strings,
A red Cap, Colour which Contents, and joys.
Streight saw I, by his *looks* and *beckonings*,
That he was wondrous taken with these *Toys*.
    Therewith I bid them they should set him free:
    So to the *Village* nigh away went *Hee*.

30

But the next *morn* (whilst *yet* the skyes were dim),
All *naked*, and in colour like the *shades*,
To seek such *Knacks* as had been given to *Him*,
Loe, by the *Craggs* descending his *Camerades*!
Where now their carriage to us is so trim,
So tractable, and plyant; as perswades
    VELOSE with them to venture through the *Cover*,
    The Fashions of the *Countrey* to discover.

31

VELOSO says, his Pass shall be his *Blade*,
And walks secure in his own Arrogance;
But, having now away a good while stayd,
And, I out-prolling with my countenance,
To see what *signs* for our *Advent'rer* made,
Behold him comming with a vengeance
    Down from the Mountain-top towards the *shipps*!
    And faster homeward, than he went, he skips.

32

The *long-boate* of COELLIO made hast
To take him in: but, ere arrive *that* could,
An ETHIOPIAN bold his weapon past
Full at his bosome, least escape he should.
Another, and *Another* too: Thus chac't
VELOSE and *those* farr off That help him would,
  I run, when (just as I an Oare lift up)
  A Troop of *Negroes* hides the mountain-top.

33

A Clowd of *Arrows*, and sharpe *stones* they rain,
And hayle upon us without any stint:
Nor were *These* uttered to the Ayre in vain,
For in this leg I *there* receiv'd a dint.
But *wee* (as prickt with *smart*, and with *disdayne*)
Made them a ready answeare, so in print,
  That (I believe in earnest) with our Rapps
  Wee made their *Heads* as *crimson* as their *capps*.

34

And now (VELOSO, off, with safety brought)
Forthwith repayre we to the *Fleet* agin,
Seeing the ougly *Malice*, the base Thought,
This false and brutish people hid within:
From whom of INDIA (so desired) nought
Of Information could we pick, or win,
  But that it is remote. So once more *I*
  Unto the *Wind* let all the *Canvas* fly.

35

Then to VELOSO said a Jybing lad
(The rest all laughing in their sleeves) 'Ho! Frend
'VELOSE, the Hill (it seems) was not so bad
'And hard to be come down, as 'twas t'ascend.'
'True (quoth th'*Advent'rer* bold) howe're, I had
'Not made such haste, but that the DOGGS did bend
  'Against the *Fleet*; and I began to doubt me
  'It might go ill, that you were here without me.'

36

He tells us then, he past no sooner was
The *Mountain's* top, but that the people black
Forbid him any farther on to pass
And threat to kill him if he turn not back;
And (turn'd) they lay them down upon the grass
In *Ambuscade*, whereby they *Us* might pack
    To the dark Realm, when we in haste should sally
    To rescue *Him*, before we well could rally.

37

The *Sun* five times the *Earth* had compassed
Since *We* (from thence departed) *Seas* did plough
Where never Canvas-wing before was spred,
A prosp'rous Gale making the *top-yards* bow:
When on a *night* (without suspect, or dred,
Chatting together in the cutting *Prow*)
    Over our Heads appear'd a sable *Clowd*,
    Which in thick darkness did the *Welkin* shrowd.

38

So big it lookt, such stern *Grimaces* made,
As fill'd our Hearts with horror and appall;
Black was the *Sea*, and at long distance bray'd
As if it roar'd *through* Rocks, *down* Rocks did fall.
'O *Pow'r* inhabiting the *Heav'ns*, I said,
'What divine threat is this? What *mystical*
    'Imparting of thy will in so *new form*?
    'For this is a Thing greater than a *Storm*?'

39

I had not ended, when a *humane* Feature
Appear'd to us ith'*Ayre*, Robustious, ralli'd
Of *Heterogeneal* parts, of *boundless* Stature,
A *Clowd* in's *Face*, a *Beard* prolix and squallid:
Cave-Eyes, a *gesture* that betray'd ill *nature*,
And a worse mood, a clay *complexion* pallid:
    His crispt *Hayre* fill'd with *earth*, and thick *as Wyre*,
    A *mouth* cole-black, of *Teeth* two yellow Tyre.

40

Of such *portentous* Bulk was this COLOSSE,
That I may tell thee (and not tell amiss)
Of that of RHODES it might supply the loss
(One of the WORLDS *Seav'n Wonders*). Out of this
A *Voyce* speaks to us: so profound, and grosse,
It seems ev'n torn out of the vast ABYSS.
      The *Hayre* with horror stands on end, of *mee*
      And all of us, at what we *hear*, and *see*.

41

And *this* it spake, 'O *you*, the boldest Folke
'That ever in the world great things assayd;
'Whom such dire *Wars*, and infinite, the *smoke*
'And *Toyle* of GLORY have not weary made;
'Since these *forbidden* bounds by *you* are broke,
'And *my* large Seas *your* daring *keeles* invade,
      'Which *I* so long injoy'd, and kept *alone*,
      'Unplough'd by *forreign* Vessel, or our *owne*;

42

'Since the hid secrets you are come to spye
'Of NATURE and the *humid* Element;
'Never reveal'd to any MORTAL'S Eye
'*Noble*, or *Heroe's*, that before you went:
'Hear from *my* mouth, for your presumption high
'What *losses* are in store, what *Plagues* arc mcant,
      'All the wide OCEAN over, and the LAND,
      'Which with hard *War* shall *bow* to your command.

43

'*This* know; as many *Ships* as shall persever
'Boldly to make the Voyage *you* make now,
'Shall finde this POYNT their enemie for ever
'With *winds* and *tempests* that no bound shall know:
'And the first FLEET OF WAR that shall indeaver
'Through these inextricable Waves to go,
      'So fearful an *example* will I make,
      'That men shall say I *did* more than I *spake*.

44

'*Here* I expect (unless my hopes have ly'de)
'On my *discov'rer* full Revenge to have;
'Nor shall *He* (onely) *all* the Ills abide,
'Your *pertinacious* confidences crave:
'But to your Vessels *yearly* shall betide
'(Unless, provoked, I in vain do rave)
  '*Shipwracks*, and *losses* of each kinde and Race;
  'Amongst which, *death* shall have the lowest place.

45

'And of the first that comes this way (in whom
'With heighth of *Fortune*, heighth of *Fame* shall meet)
'I'll be a new and everlasting Tomb,
'Through GOD's unfathom'd judgment. At these Feet
'He shall drop *all* his *Glories*, and inhume
'The glitt'ring *Trophies* of a *Turkish* Fleet.
  'With *me* conspire his Ruine and his Fall,
  'Destroyd QUILOA, and MOMBASSA's Wall.

46

'Another shall come after, of good *fame*,
'A *Knight*, a *Lover*, and a *lib'ral Hand*;
'And with him bring a fair and gentle *dame*,
'Knit *his* by LOVE, and HYMEN's sacred Band.
'In an ill hour, and to your loss and shame,
'Ye come within the *Purlews* of *my* land;
  'Which (kindly cruel) from the *sea* shall free you,
  'Drown'd in a *sea* of miseries to see you.

47

'Sterv'd shall they see to death their *Children* deare;
'*Begot*, and *rear'd*, in so great *love*. The black
'Rude CAFRES (out of *Avarice*) shall teare
'The *Cloathes* from *Angellick Lady's* back.
'Her dainty limbs of *Alabaster* cleare
'To *Heate*, to *Cold*, to *Storm*, to *Eyes's* worse *Rack*
  'Shall be laid *naked*; after she hath trod
  '(Long time) with her soft Feet the burning Clod.

48

'Besides all this; *Their Eyes* (whose happier lot
'Will be to scape from so much miserie)
'This *Yoake* of LOVERS, out into the hot
'And unrelenting *Thickets* turn'd shall see.
'Ev'n *there* (when *Teares* they shall have squeez'd and got
'From *Rocks* and *Desarts*, where no *water* be)
        'Embracing (*kind*) their *souls* they shall exhale
        'Out of the faire, but miserable, *Jayle*.'

49

The ugly *Monster* went to rake into
More of our *Fate*; when, starting on my feet,
I ask him, '*Who art Thou?* (for to say true
'*Thy hideous Bulk amazes me to see't*).'
HEE (wreathing his black mouth) about him threw
His sawcer-Eyes: And (as his soul would fleet)
        Fetching a dismal groan, *replide* (as *sory*,
        Or *vext*, or *Both*, at the *Intergatory*),

50

'I am that great and secret HEAD of LAND
'Which *you* the CAPE OF TEMPESTS well did call;
'From STRABO, PTOLOMEE, POMPONIUS, and
'Grave PLINY hid, and from the ANTIENTS all.
'I the *but-end* that knits wide AFFRICK'S strand;
'My *Promontory* is her *Mound* and *Wall*,
        'To the ANTARTICK POLE: which (ne'erthelesse)
        '*You*, only, have the boldness to transgresse.

51

'Of the rough *sons* oth'Earth was *I*: and *Twin-*
'*-Brother* to *Him* that had the hundred Hands.
'I was call'd ADAMASTOR, and was in
'The *Warr* 'gainst *Him*, that hurls hot VULCAN'S Brands.
'Yet Hills on Hills *I* heapt not: but (to win
'That *Empire*, which the SECOND JOVE commands)
        'Was GENERALL at *Sea*; on which did sayle
        'The *Fleet* of NEPTUNE, which *I* was to quayle.

Adamastor, the
Titan

52

'The *love* I bare to PELEUS's spouse divine
'Imbarqu'd mee in so wild an *Enterprize*.
'The fayrest GODDESSE that the *Heav'ns* inshrine
'I, for the *Princesse* of the *Waves* despise.
'Upon a day when *out* the *Sun* did shine,
'With NEREUS's daughters (on the Beach) these eyes
 'Beheld her *naked*: streight I felt a *dart*
 'Which *Time*, nor *scorns*, can pull out of my *Heart*.

53

'I knew't impossible to gain her *Love*
'By reason of my great deformitie;
'What *force* can doe I purposed then to prove:
'And, DORIS call'd, let *Her* my purpose see.
'The *Goddess* (out of feare) did THETYS move
'On my behalfe: but with a chaste smile *shee*
 '(As *vertuous* full, as she is *fayre*) replide:
 '"What NYMPH can such a heavy love abide?

54

'"However *Wee* (to save the *sea* a part
'"In so dire *War*) will take it into thought
'"How with our *honour* we may cure his smart."
'My *Messenger* to *mee* thus answer brought.
'I, that suspect no *stratagem*, no *Art*,
'(How easily are purblind *Lovers* caught!)
 'Feel my selfe wondrous light with this Return;
 'And, fann'd with *Hopes*, with fresh *desire* doe burn.

55

'Thus fool'd, thus cheated from the warr begun,
'On a time (DORIS pointing where to meet)
'I spy the glitt'ring forme, ith'*evening* dun,
'Of snowy THETYS with the silver feet.
'With open Armes (farr off) like mad I run
'To clip therein my *Joy*, my *Life*, my *Sweet*:
 'And (*clipt*) begin those orient *Eyes* to kiss,
 '*That* Face, *that* Hayre, *that* Neck, *that* All that is.

56

'O, how I choake in utt'ring my disgrace!
'Thinking I *Her* embrac'd whom I did seek,
'A *Mountain* hard I found I did embrace,
'O'regrown with Trees and Bushes nothing sleek.
'Thus (*grapling* with a *Mountain* face to face,
'Which I stood pressing for her *Angel's* cheek)
 'I was no *Man*: no, but a stupid *Block*,
 'And *grew* unto a *Rock* another *Rock*.

57

'O *Nymph* (the fayrest of the OCEAN'S Brood)!
'Since with my *Features* thou could'st not be caught,
'What had it cost to spare me that *false* good,
'Were it a *Hill*, a *Clowd*, a *Dreame*, or *Thought*?
'Away fling I (with *Anger* almost *wood*,
'Nor lesse with *shame* of the *Affront* distraught)
 'To seek *another* World: that I might live,
 'Where *none* might laugh, to see me *weep*, and *grieve*.

58

'By this my *Brethren* on their Backs were cast,
'Reduc'd unto the depth of misery:
'And the *vain Gods* (all hopes to put them past)
'On *Those*, That *Mountayns* pyl'd, pyl'd *Mountains* high.
'Nor *I*, that mourn'd farr off my deep distast,
'HEAV'N, (Hands in vain *resist*, in vain FEET *fly*)
 'For my *design'd* Rebellion, and Rape,
 'The vengeance of pursuing *Fate* could scape.

59

'My solid *flesh* converteth to *tough Clay*:
'My *Bones* to *Rocks* are metamorphosed:
'These *leggs*, these *thighs* (behold how large are *they*!)
'O're the long *sea* extended were and spred.
'In fine into this CAPE out of the way
'My monstrous *Trunk*, and high-erected *Head*,
 'The GODS did turn: where (for my greater payn)
 'THETYS doth *Tantalize* me with the MAYN.'

60

Here ends. And (gushing out into a *Well*
Of *Tears*) forthwith he vanisht from our sight.
The black *Clowd* melting, with a hideous yell
The OCEAN sounded a long way forthright.
I (in *their* presence, who by *miracle*
Had thus far brought us, ev'n the ANGELLS bright)
    Besought the LORD to shield his *Heritage*
    From *all* that ADAMASTOR did presage.

61

Now PHLEGON and PYRÖUS pulling come
(With other *Two*) the *Charet* of the Day:
When that *high* LAND (to which this *Gyant* grum
Was turn'd) doth to our Eyes it self display.
Doubling the point, we take another *Rumb*;
And (coasting) plough the *Oriental* Sea.

Rounding the
Cape, their second
landfall is at Mossel
Bay

    Nor had we plough'd it long, when (underneath
    A little) in a *Second Port* we breathe.

62

The *People* that this *Countrey* did possess
(Though they were likewise ETHIOPIANS All)
Did more of *humane* in their *meens* express,
Than *Those*, into whose hands we late did fall.

Encounter with
Khoikhoi

Upon the sandy *Beach*, with cheerfulness
They meet us, and with *Dances* Festival.
    With *them*, their *Wives*: and their mild Flocks of
        Sheep,
    Which *fat* and *faire*, and *frisking* they did keep.

63

Their *Wives* upon straw-Pillions (black as *Jet*)
Slow-paced *Oxen* (like EUROPA) ride:
Beasts, upon which a higher price *they* set
Than all the *Cattle* of the *Field* beside.
Sweet *madrigalls* (in *Ryme* or Prose compleat,
In their own *Tongue*) to *rustick-Reed* apply'de,
    They sing in *Parts*, as gentle *Shepherds* use,
    That imitate of TYTIRUS the *Muse*.

64

These (and no less was written in their *Faces*)
Love and *Humanity* to Us afford:
Bringing us *Hens*, and *Muttons*, in the places
Of *Merchandizes* which *we* had Aboard.
But, for (in fine) our men could spye no traces
(By any *Sign* they made, or any *word*
From their dark *Tongue*) of what we wisht to know:
Our *Anchors* weigh'd, to *Sea* again we go.

65

Now had we giv'n the other demi-wheel
About black AFFRICK, and (the burning Hoope,
That girts the *World*, inquiring with my Keel)
To the ANTARTICK POLE I turn'd my *Poope*.
By that small *Isle* (such emulous Thoughts we feel)
Discover'd by a former *Fleet*, we Soope;
Which sought the CAPE OF TEMPESTS, and (*that* found)
Pitcht *here* a CROSS: our *then* DISCOV'RIES' Bound.

Kwaaihoek
where in 1487
Bartholomew Diaz
laid a padrao

66

Thence, many *nights*, and many sadder *days*,
Betwixt rough *Storms*, and languid *Calmes*, we grope
Through the great OCEAN, and explore *new* ways:
No *Lanthorn* to pursue, but our high *Hope*.
One time above the rest (as *danger* Plays
At *Sea* the PROTHEUS) with strange Waves we cope.
So strong a *Current* in those parts we meet,
As ev'n obstructs the passage of our *Fleet*.

67

More violent without comparison
(As our *reculing Vessels* plain did shew)
The *Sea* was, that did there *against* us run,
Than the fresh *Gale*, that in our *favour* blew.
NOTUS (disdaining much to be out-done
By *That*; and, as he thought, on purpose too
To affront *Him*) puffs, blusters, reinforces
His angry Blasts: and so we pass THE COURSES.

68

The *Sun* reduc'd the solemnized *Feast*,
On which, a King laid in a *Cratch* to find,
Three *Kings* did come *conducted* from the EAST,
In which ONE KING, *three* KINGS at once are joyn'd.
That day took *we* another *Port* (possest
By *People* like to *Those* we left behind)
  In a great *River*: Giving it the Name
  Of that *great day* when thereinto we came.

Nguniland named
Natal to celebrate
Christmas Day

69

Here *fresh Provisions* of the *Folks* we take:
Fresh-water from the *River*. But, in summ,
No guess concerning INDIA could we make,
By *People* unto *Us* as good as dumb.
See (*King*) how many *Countreys* we did rake
Without a *door* found *out* from that *rude scumm*,
  Without descrying the least *Track*, or *Scent*,
  Of the so much desired ORIENT!

70

Imagine, *Sir*, in what *distress* of *mind*,
How *lost* we went, how much *perplext* with *Cares*,
Broken with *Storms*, and *All* with *Hunger* pin'd,
Through *Seas* unknown, through disagreeing *Ayres*,
(So far from *hope*, the wished LAND to find,
As, *ev'n* with *hoping*, plung'd into *despaires*)
  Through *Climates* rul'd by other heav'nly SIGNES;
  And where no *Star*, of our *acquaintance*, shines.

71

The food we have, too, spoyl'd; and what we crave
As *nutriment*, ev'n turn'd into our *Bane*:
No *Entregens*, no *news*, to make us wave
Our *Griefs*, or feed us with a *hope*, though vaine.
Think'st *Thou*, if this choyce *band* of *soldiers* brave
Were *other* than of *Lusitanian* straine,
  They had obedient held to this degree
  Unto their *King*, and his *Authoritie*?

72

Think'st *Thou*, they had not risen long ago
Against their GEN'RALL (cross to their desire)
Turning *Free-booters*, forced to be so
By black *despair*, by *Hunger*, and by *Ire*?
If ever *Men* were *try'de*, These are: since *no*
Fatigue, no *suff'rings*, were of force, to tyre
      Their *great* and *Lusitanian* excellence
      Of *loyalty*, and firm *Obedience*.

73

Leaving, in fine, the sweet fresh-water Flood,
And the salt Waves returning to divide;
Off from the *Land* a pretty space we stood,
Our whole *Fleet* bent into the *Ocean* wide:
Lest the cold *Southern* wind, increasing shou'd
Impound us in the *Bay* and furious *Tyde*
      Made in that *Quarter* by the crooking shore,
      Which to SOFALA sends the *golden Ore*.

74

This past (and the swift *Rudder* up resign'd
To good St NICH'LAS, as in case deplor'd)
Towards that *Part* we steered, where the *Wind*-
Possessed *Waves* against the Beaches roar'd:
When the 'twixt *hope* and *fear* suspended mind,
And which confided in a *painted Board*,
      (Faln from *small hope* to *absolute dispaire*)
      Lookt up again by an *Adventure* rare.

75

'Twas *thus*. When to the *Coast* so nigh we drew
As to see plain the *Countrey* round about:
A *River* broacht into the *Sea* we view,
Where *Barks* with *Sails* went passing *in* and *out*.
To meet with Men That *Navigation* knew
Surpriz'd us with great *joy*, thou canst not doubt:
      For amongst *Them*, of things from *Us* so hid,
      We hop't to hear some *News*: and so we did.

76

These too are ETHIOPS: yet it should appeare
They had in better company been bred.
Arabick words we pickt out here and there,
By which was reacht the scope of what they sed.
A kind of *Terbant* each of them did weare,
Of *Cotton* fine, pres't close unto his head:
    Another Cotton-cloth (and *this* was blew)
    About those-parts that should be kept from *view*.

77

In the *Arabick-Tongue* (which *They* speak ill,
But FERNAND MARTYN understandeth though)
They say: in *Ships* as great as these *we* fill,
That *Sea* of theirs is travers't to and fro;
Even from the rising of the *Sun*, untill
The *Land* makes *Southward* a FULL POINT, and so
    Back from the *South* to *East*: conveying, *thus*,
    Folks, of the colour of the DAY, like *Us*.

78

If with the *sight* of *These* so joy'd we were,
The *news* they give us makes us much more glad.
This (for the *signes* by *us* collected *there*)
We call THE RIVER OF GOOD SIGNS. We add
The *Land-mark* of A CROSS, the which we reare,
Whereof some number in our *Ships* we had
    For such Intents: *This* bare the fair *Guide's* name
    Who with TOBIAH unto GABAEL came.

79

Of Slyme, scales, shell-fish, and such filthy stuff,
(The noysome Generation of the DEEP)
The *Ships* (that come therewith sordid, and rough,
Through so *long* Seas) *there* do we cleanse, and sweep.
From our kind *Hosts* we had supply'de enough
Of the *Provisions* usual (as *sheep*,
    And *other* things) with smooth, and jocund *meen*,
    And as cleer *hearts*: which through their *eyes* were
      seen.

80

But the high pregnant *Hopes*, we *there* embraced,
Bred not a *joy* unmixt with some *Allay*.
To *ballance* it, in t'other *scale* was placed
A new *disaster* by RHAMNUSIA.
'Thus gracious HEAV'NS their *Boons* have interlaced:
'*These* are the *interfearings*, *This* the way,
 'Of *humane* Things. *Black sorrow* holds the *Dye*:
 '*Light joy* fades in the twinkling of an Eye.'

81

And *this* it was. The loathsom'st, the most fell
Disease, that ever these sad eyes beheld,
Reft many a *life*, and left the *Bones* to dwell
For everlasting in a *forreign* Field.
Who will believe (*unseen*) what I shall tell?
In such dire manner would the *gumms* be swell'd
 In our mens *Mouths*; that the black flesh thereby
 At once did *grow*, at once did *putrifie*.

82

With such a horrid *stench* it *putrifide*,
That it the neighb'ring *Ayre* infected round.
We had no circumspect PHYSITIAN try'de:
No *Lady*-handed SURGEON was there found,
But by a CARVER might have been supply'de
The *last*. 'Twas handling of a *dead-mans wound*.
 The rawest NOVICE with his *Instrument*
 Might *cut*, and never *hurt*, the PATIENT.

83

In fine, in this wild LAND *adieu* we bad
To our *brave* Friends (never to see them more)
Who in such *Ways*, in such *Adventures* sad,
With *Us* an equal burthen ever bore.
'How easily a burying place is had!
'The least wave of the *Sea*, any strange *shore*,
 'Serve, as to put *our Fellows's Reliques* in,
 'So of the bravest *Men* that e're have bin.'

84

Thus, from this fatal *Haven* we disjoine
With *more* of joy than what we brought, and *less*:
And (coasting upward) seek some farther *signe*
Of INDIA, to make out our present guess.
At MOZAMBIQUE we arriv'd in fine;
Of whose *false* dealing, and *hard*-heartedness,
  Thou must have heard: as also of the *Vile*
  And *barb'rous* dealing of MOMBASSA'S *Isle*.

85

Then to the *Sanctuary* of thy *Port*
(Whose soft and Royall *Treatment* may suffice
To *heale* the *sick*, to *cheer* the *Alamort*),
We were conducted by *propitious* Skyes.
Heer sweet Repose, *Heer* soveraign support,
Heer Quiet to our Breasts, Rest to our Eyes,
  Thou doest impart. Thus (if thou hast attended)
  Thou hast thy wish; my NARRATIVE is ended.

86

Camoens resumes in his own voice, addressing the King of Portugal

Judge now (*O King*) if ever *Mortalls* went
Upon so *long*, upon so *desp'rate* ways.
Think'st Thou ENEAS, and the eloquent
ULYSSES travayl'd so much *World*, as *These*?
Durst *either* (of the *watry Element*,
For all the *Verses* written in their prayse)
  See so much through his *Prowesse*, through his *Art*,
  As I *have* seen, and shall, or the *eighth* part?

87

THOU, who didst drink so deep of HELICONE,
For whom *sev'n Cities* did contend in fine,
Amongst themselves, RHODES, SMYRNA, COLOPHONE,
Wise ATHENS, *Chyos*, *Argos*, SALAMINE;
And THOU, whom ITALY is prowd to owne,
Whose *Voyce*, first *low*, then *high* (always *divine*
  And *sweet*) thy native MINCIUS (hearing) fell
  Asleep, but TIBER did with glory swell:

88

Sing, and advance with praises to the skye
Your DEMI-GODS, stretching your twanging lungs
With WITCHES; CIRCES; GYANTS OF ONE EYE;
SIRENS, to rock and charm them with their *songs*:
More, *give them* (both with *Sayls*, and *Oars*) to fly
CICONIANS; and that *Land*, where there *mates'* Tongues
      With LOTO toucht, makes them forget they're *slaves*;
      Give them, to drop their *pilot* in the waves:

89

Project them *winds* (carried in *baggs*) to take
Out, when they list, Am'rous CALYPSOES bold;
HARPIES, their *meat* to force them to forsake;
Hand them to the *Elysian* shadows cold:
As *fine*, and as *re-fin'd*, as ye doe make
Your *Tales* (so sweetly *dreampt*, and so well told)
      The *pure* and *naked Truth*, I tell, will git
      The hand, of all the *Fabricks* of your Wit.

90

Upon the *Captain's* honeyed lips depends
Each gaping *Hearer* with fresh Appetite;
When his long *Story* he concludes and ends,
Fraught with *high deeds*, with *Horror*, and delight.
The vast *Thoughts* of our KINGS, the *King* commends:
And their *Warrs*, known where're the *Sun* gives light.
      The NATION'S ancient *Valor* he extols:
      The *loyalty*, and *Brav'ry*, of their *Souls*.

91

The PEOPLE tell (with *admiration* strook)
To one another, what they noted most.
Not one of them can *off* those People look,
That came so *far*, That such dire *Seas* have crost.
But *now* the *Youth* of DELOS, who re-took
The reins which LAMPETUSA'S Brother lost,
      Turns them to sleep with THETYS in the DEEP:
      The KING leaves *that*, in his *own* House to sleep.

92

How *sweet* is Prayse, and justly purchas't GLORY
By one's *own Actions*, when to *Heav'n* they soare!
Each *nobler Soul* will strain, to have his story
Match, if not *darken*, All That went before.
Envy of other's *Fame*, not *transitory*,
Screws up *illustrious* Actions more, and more.
    Such, as contend in *honorable deeds*,
    The *Spur* of high *Applause* incites their speeds.

93

Those glorious Things ACHYLLES did in *War*
With ALEXANDER sank not half so deep,
As the GREAT TRUMPET That proclam'd them, far
And neer; He envies *this*, *This* makes him weep.
The *Marathonian* Trophies *Larums* are,
Which suffer'd not THEMISTOCLES to sleep:
    He said, no *Musick* pleas'd *his* ear so well
    As a *good Voyce*, that did *his* prayses tell.

94

VASCO DE GAMA takes great payns, to show
Those NAVIGATIONS which the *World* up-cryes
Deserve not in such gorgeous Robes to go,
As *his*, which doth astonish *Earth*, and *Skyes*.
True: But that WORTHY (who did foster so
With *Favours*, *Gifts*, *Rewards*, and *Dignities*,
    The MANTUAN MUSE) made *that* ENEAS sing,
    And set the ROMAN GLORY on her wing.

95

SCIPIOS, and CAESARS, *Portugal* doth yeild;
Yeilds ALEXANDERS, and AUGUSTUSSES:
But with those *lib'ral Arts* it doth not guild
Them though, which would file off their roughnesses.
OCTAVIUS made compt *Verses* in the Feild,
Filling up so the *blanks* of *Business*.
    Forsaken FULVIA will not let me lye
    Through CLEOPATRA'S charms on ANTHONY.

96

Brave CESAR marches conquering all FRANCE;
Nor was his *Learning* silenc't by his drumme:
But (in *this* hand a *Pen*, in *that* a *Lance*)
To th'*eloquence* of TULLY he did come.
SCIPIO (whose *Wit* in other's *Socks* did dance)
Wrote *plays*, ev'n with that *Hand* which had sav'd Rome.
    On HOMER doted ALEXANDER so,
    That th'ILIAD was his constant Bedfellow.

97

All, That have ere been *famous* for COMMAND,
Were learned too; or lov'd the Learned *All*:
In Latium, Greece, and the most *barb'rous* Land,
But only in unhappy PORTUGALL.
I speak it to our shame; the cause no grand
POETS adorn our *Countrey*, is the small
    Incouragement to such: For how can *He*
    Esteem, That *understands not* POETRIE?

98

For *This*, and not for want of *Ingenie*,
VIRGIL and HOMER are not born with *Us*:
Nor will ENEAS, and ACHYLLES, bee,
(This *Brave*, Hee *pious*) if the World hould *thus*,
But (which is worst of all) for ought I see,
FORTUNE hath shapt our *Lords*, so *boysterous*,
    So *rude*, so carelesse to be *known*, or *know*,
    That they like well enough it should be so.

99

Thankt let the *Muses* be, by our DE GAME,
To my deer *Countrey* that my zeale was such,
As to commend her *noble Toyles* to FAME,
And her great *deeds* with a bould hand to touch:
For *Hee*, That's like him (only in his *name*)
Deserves not of CALIOPE so much,
    Or TAGUS's Nymphs, That They their golden Loom
    Should leave, to carve his ANCESTOR a *Tomb*.

100
Love to my *Brethren*, and to do things *just*,
Giving all *Portingal-Exploits* their dues,
To serve the *Ladies*, to procure *their gust*,
Are th'onely *spurr*, and *int'rest* of the MUSE.
Therefore, for fear of black *Oblivion's* Rust,
Herroick Actions let *no* man refuse:
    For by *my* hand, or some *more* lofty strain,
    VERTUE will lead him into HONOUR'S *Fane*.

One of ten cantos, this extract is the central sequence of *Os Lusíadas*
(*The Lusiads*), the Portuguese national epic. Modelled on the *Odyssey*
of Homer, the *Argonautica* of Apollonius of Rhodes, and particularly
Virgil's *Aeneid*, which all offered the classical themes of sea-discoveries
and merchant expansionism, Camoens' Renaissance epic – first pub-
lished in Lisbon in 1572 – chronicled the establishment of the Portu-
guese empire and its heroic achievements when it was, in fact, in decline.
Fanshawe's translation, the first of some ten made into English,
maintains the ottava rima stanza of the original. See Camoens and
Fanshawe in the Notes on Contributors for further information.

On a Shipmate, Pero Moniz, Dying at Sea
Translated from the Portuguese by Roy Campbell

My years on earth were short, but long for me,
And full of bitter hardship at the best:
My light of day sinks early in the sea:
Five lustres from my birth I took my rest.
Through distant lands and seas I was a ranger
Seeking some cure or remedy for life,
Which he whom Fortune loves not as a wife,
Will seek in vain through strife, and toil, and danger.
Portugal reared me in my green, my darling
Alanguer, but the dank, corrupted air
That festers in the marshes around there
Has made me food for fish here in the snarling,
Fierce seas that dark the Abyssinian shore,
Far from the happy homeland I adore.

ANON.

The First Stone of the New Castle

Den Eersten Steen Van't NIeuwe CasteeL Goede Hope
Heeft Wagenaer gelecht Met hoop van goede hope
Ampliatie

Soo worden voort en voort de rijcken uijtgespreijt,
Soo worden al de swart en geluwen gespreijt.

Soo doet men uijtter aerd een steene wall oprechten,
Daer't donderend metael seer weijnigh can ophechten.

Voor Hottentosen warent altijts eerde wallen,
Nu comt men hier met steen voor anderen oock brallen.

Dus maeckt men dan een schrich soowel d' Europiaen,
Als voor den Aes- Ameer- en wilden Africaen.

Dus wort beroemt gemaeckt 't geheijligst Christendom,
Die zetels stellen in het woeste heijdendom.

Wij loven 't groot bestier en seggen met malcander,
   Augustus heerschappij, noch winnend Alexander,
Noch Caesars groot beleijd, zijn noijt daermee geswaerd
   Met 't leggen van een steen op 't eijnde van de Aerd.

Translated from the Dutch by H. C. V. Leibbrandt

Thus more and more the kingdoms are extended,
Thus more and more are black and yellow spread.

Thus from the ground a wall of stone is raised,
On which the thundering brass can no impression make.

For Hottentots the walls are always earthen,
But now we come with stone to boast before all men,

And terrify not only Europeans, but also
Asians, Americans and savage Africans.

Thus holy Christendom is glorified,
Establishing its seats amidst the savage heathens.

We praise the great director and say with one another,
    Augustus' dominion nor conquering Alexander,
Nor Caesar's mighty genius has ever had the glory
    To lay a cornerstone at earth's extremest end!

Transcribed by George McCall Theal, in his *History of South Africa
before 1795*, in his summary of the year 1666, as reflected in the journal
of the Dutch East India Company. Theal notes of the laying of the
foundation stone of the Castle in Cape Town, 'A holiday was not
properly kept in the opinion of the people of the Netherlands without a
recitation of poetry specially composed and containing allusions to the
event which was being celebrated. Such a time-honoured observance in
the fatherland could not with propriety be omitted in its South African
dependency. Accordingly, some lines had been prepared – by an
amateur poet, says Commander Zacharias Wagenaer, without men-
tioning his name – which were considered so appropriate that after they
were recited a copy was placed for preservation with the records of the
colony.' Ingeniously the occasional poet works the date into his title.
Wagenaer was Commander Van Riebeeck's successor. The poem was
reprinted in the *Precis of the Archives* at the turn of the century by their
keeper, Leibbrandt, with his own translation.

LADY ANNE LINDSAY
(1750–1825)

Auld Robin Gray

When the sheep are in the fauld, when the kye's come hame,
And a' the weary warld to rest are gane,
The waes o' my heart fa' in showers frae my e'e,
Unkent by my gudeman, wha sleeps sound by me.

Young Jamie lo'ed me weel, and sought me for his bride,
But saving ae crown-piece he had naething beside;
To make the crown a pound my Jamie gaed to sea,
And the crown and the pound – they were baith for me.

He hadna been gane a twelvemonth and a day,
When my father brake his arm and the cow was stown away;
My mither she fell sick – my Jamie was at sea,
And Auld Robin Gray came acourting me.

My father couldna wark – my mither couldna spin –
I toiled day and night, but their bread I couldna win, –
Auld Rob maintained them baith, and, wi' tears in his e'e,
Said, 'Jeanie, O for *their* sakes will ye no marry me?'

My heart it said na, and I looked for Jamie back,
But hard blew the winds, and his ship was a wrack;
His ship was a wrack – why didna Jamie dee,
Or why am I spared to cry wae is me?

My father urged me sair – my mither didna speak,
But she looked in my face till my heart was like to break;
They gied him my hand – my heart was in the sea –
And so Robin Gray he was gudeman to me.

I hadna been his wife a week but only four,
When, mournfu' as I sat on the stane at my door,
I saw my Jamie's ghaist, for I couldna think it he
Till he said, 'I'm come hame, love, to marry thee!'

Oh sair, sair did we greet, and mickle say of a',
I gied him ae kiss, and bade him gang awa', –
I wish that I were dead, but I'm na like to dee,
For though my heart is broken, I'm but young, wae is me!

I gang like a ghaist, and I carena much to spin,
I darena think o' Jamie, for that wad be a sin;
But I'll do my best a gude wife to be,
For, O, Robin Gray, he is kind to me.

JOHN CAMPBELL
(1766–1840)

I'm far from what I call my home

I'm far from what I call my home,
In regions where no white men come;
Where wilds and wilder men are found,
Who never heard the gospel sound.
Indeed they know not that there's one
Ruling on high, and GOD alone. –
In days and nights for five months past,
I've travell'd much; am here at last,
On banks of stream well named Great,
To drink its water is a treat. –
But here to have the living word,
Enriching treasure! Spirit's sword,
A favour this that can't be told,
In worth surpassing finest gold.
May Bushmen and the Bootchuanas,
The Namacquaas and the Corannas,
All soon possess this God-like feast,
And praise the Lord from west to east.

30

From Campbell's journal, 18 July 1813; on his first seeing the Orange River. He notes: 'After our worship, I went to a retired eminence on the banks of the river. The views to the N. E., E., and S. E. were very extensive. The reflection that no European eye had ever surveyed these plains, and mountains, and rivers, and that I was ten thousand miles from home, made a solemn impression on my mind, which was deepened by the stillness which at that time prevailed. I snatched a scrap of paper from my pocket, on which I wrote these lines.'

TRADITIONAL (SAN)

The Broken String

(Dictated in July 1875, in the Katkop dialect, by Dai-kwain, who heard it from his father, Xaa-ttin)

ǀk'é kăṅ ddóǟ ē,
ǀkaṅ́n ǀkwā kā ǀnṻïṅ.
Hé tíkẹn ē,
Tí ǀnĕ ( ) ǀkwĕ úä̈ kkā,
Ī̈,
Ŏ ǀnṻïṅ a ddóä̈ ǀkwā kā.
Hé tíkẹn ē,
Tí-g ǀnĕ ɣáuki ttăṅ́-ă kkā,
Tí kă ssïṅ́ ǀkwéï̈ ttā kkā,
Ī̈.
Tā,
Tí ǀkŭ-g ǀnĕ ttă̌ bbōkẹn ǀkhéyă̈ kā,
( ) Ŏ ǀnṻïṅ ā ǀkwā kkā.
Hé tíkẹn ē,
Tí ɣáukï ǀnĕ ttă̌ ‡hă̌ṅnṻwă̈ kkā,
Ī̈.

Translated by W. H. I. Bleek

People were those who
Broke for me the string.
Therefore,
The place ( ) became like this to me,
On account of it,
Because the string was that which broke for me.
Therefore,
The place does not feel to me,
As the place used to feel to me,
On account of it.
For,
The place feels as if it stood open before me,
( ) Because the string has broken for me.
Therefore,
The place does not feel pleasant to me,
On account of it.

The system of orthography is Bleek's own; for example, I represents the dental click, ! the cerebral click, = under vowels represents a deep pronunciation, n indicates a ringing pronunciation of the n, as in 'song' in English. His informant, the poet's son, came from north of Calvinia and the poem, with several others, was recorded in Cape Town. Bleek's notes are: 'The above is a lament, sung by Xaa-ttin after the death of his friend, the magician and rain-maker, Nuin-kui-ten, who died from the effects of a shot he had received when going about, by night, in the form of a lion. Now that "the string is broken", the former "ringing sound in the sky" is no longer heard by the singer, as it had been in the magician's lifetime.'

Translated by W. H. I. Bleek

The Hyena

Thou who makest thy escape from the tumult!
Thou wide, roomy tree!
Thou who gettest thy share (though with trouble!),
Thou cow who art strained at the hocks!
Thou who hast a plump round knee!
Thou the nape of whose neck is clothed with hair!
Thou with the skin dripping as if half-tanned!
Thou who hast a round, distended neck!
Thou eater of the Namaqua,
Thou big-toothed one!

The Hyena Addressing Her Young Ones

*(On her return from a marauding expedition,
with regard to the perils she has encountered)*

The fire threatens,
The stone threatens,
The assegais threaten,
The guns threaten,
Yet you seek food from me.
My children,
Do I get anything easily?

The Giraffe

Thou who descendest river by river,
Thou burnt thornbush (‡*aro*)!
Thou blue one,
Who appearest like a distant thornhill
Full of people sitting down.

The Zebra

Thou who art thrown at by the great (shepherd) boys,
Thou whose head the (kirrie's) throw misses!
    Thou dappled fly,
    Thou party-coloured one,
    Who spiest for those,
    That spy for thee!
    Thou who, womanlike,
    Art full of jealousy.

The Horse Cursed by the Sun

It is said that once the Sun was on earth, and caught the Horse to ride it. But it was unable to bear his weight, and therefore the Ox took the place of the Horse, and carried the Sun on its back. Since that time the Horse is cursed in these words, because it could not carry the Sun's weight:

'From today thou shalt have a (certain) time of dying.
This is thy curse, that thou hast a (certain) time of dying.
And day and night shalt thou eat,
But the desire of thy heart shall not be at rest,
Though thou grazest till morning and again until sunset.
Behold, this is the judgment which I pass upon thee,' said the
    Sun.

Since that day the Horse's (certain) time of dying
commenced.

Bleek's Note: 'The original, in the Hottentot language, of this little Namaqualand Fable, is in Sir George Grey's Library, G. Krönlein's Manuscript.'

THOMAS PRINGLE
(1789–1834)

The Emigrant's Cabin
(An Epistle in Rhyme)

Where the young river, from its wild ravine,
Winds pleasantly through Eildon's pastures green, –
With fair acacias waving on its banks,
And willows bending o'er in graceful ranks,
And the steep mountain rising close behind,
To shield us from the Snowberg's wintry wind, –
Appears my rustic cabin, thatched with reeds,
Upon a knoll amid the grassy meads;
And close beside it, looking o'er the lea,
Our summer-seat beneath an umbra-tree.

This morning, musing in that favourite seat,
My hound, old Yarrow, dreaming at my feet,
I pictured you, sage Fairbairn, at my side,
By some good Genie wafted cross the tide;
And after cordial greetings, thus went on
In Fancy's Dream our colloquy, dear John.

P. – Enter, my friend, our beehive-cottage door:
No carpet hides the humble earthen floor,
But it is hard as brick, clean-swept, and cool.
You must be wearied? Take that jointed stool;
Or on this couch of leopard-skin recline;
You'll find it soft – the workmanship is mine.

F. – Why, Pringle, yes – your cabin's snug enough,
Though oddly shaped. But as for household stuff,
I only see some rough-hewn sticks and spars;
A wicker cupboard, filled with flasks and jars;
A pile of books, on rustic frame-work placed;
Hides of ferocious beasts that roam the waste;
Whose kindred prowl, perchance, around this spot –

35

The only neighbours, I suspect, you've got!
Your furniture, rude from the forest cut,
However, is in keeping with the hut.
This couch feels pleasant: is't with grass you stuff it?
So far I should not care with you to rough it.
But – pardon me for seeming somewhat rude –
In this wild place how manage ye for food?

P. – You'll find, at least, my friend, we do not starve;
There's always mutton, if nought else, to carve;
And even of luxuries we have our share.
But here comes dinner (the best bill of fare),
Drest by that 'Nut-Brown Maiden,' Vijtje Vaal.
[*To the Hottentot Girl.*] Meid, roep de Juffrouwen naar 't
    middagmaal:
[*To F.*] Which means – 'The ladies in to dinner call.'

[*Enter Mrs P. and her Sister, who welcome their Guest to Africa.
    The party take their seats round the table, and conversation
    proceeds.*]

P. – First, here's our broad-tailed mutton, small and fine,
The dish on which nine days in ten we dine;
Next, roasted springbok, spiced and larded well;
A haunch of hartebeest from Hyndhope Fell;
A pauw, which beats your Norfolk turkey hollow;
Korhaan, and guinea-fowl, and pheasant follow;
Kid carbonadjes, à la Hottentot,
Broiled on a forkèd twig; and, peppered hot
With Chili pods, a dish called Caffer-stew;
Smoked ham of porcupine, and tongue of gnu.
This fine white household bread (of Margaret's baking)
Comes from an oven too of my own making,
Scooped from an ant-hill. Did I ask before
If you would taste this brawn of forest-boar?

    Our fruits, I must confess, make no great show:
Trees, grafts, and layers must have time to grow.
But there's green roasted maize, and pumpkin pie,
And wild asparagus. Or will you try

A slice of water-melon? – fine for drouth,
Like sugared ices melting in the mouth.
Here too are wild-grapes from our forest-vine,
Not void of flavour, though unfit for wine.
And here comes dried fruit I had quite forgot,
(From fair Glen-Avon, Margaret, is it not?)
Figs, almonds, raisins, peaches. Witbooy Swart
Brought this huge sackful from kind Mrs Hart –
Enough to load a Covent Garden cart.

But come, let's crown the banquet with some wine.
What will you drink? Champagne? Port? Claret? Stein?
Well – not to tease you with a thirsty jest,
Lo, there our *only* vintage stands confest,
In that half-aum upon the spigot-rack.
And, certes, though it keeps the old *Kaap smaak*,
The wine is light and racy; so we learn,
In laughing mood, to call it Cape Sauterne.
– Let's pledge this cup 'to all our friends,' Fairbairn!

F. – Well, I admit, my friend, your dinner's good.
Springbok and porcupine are dainty food;
That lordly pauw was roasted to a turn;
And in your country fruits and Cape Sauterne,
The wildish flavour's really not unpleasant;
And I may say the same of gnu and pheasant.
– But – Mrs Pringle . . . shall I have the pleasure . . . ?
Miss Brown, . . . some wine?—(These quaighs are quite a
    treasure.)
– What! leave us now? I've much to ask of *you* . . .
But, since you *will* go – for an hour adieu.

[*Exeunt Ladies.*]

But, Pringle – 'à nos moutons revenons' –
Cui bono's still the burthen of my song –

Cut off, with these good ladies, from society,
Of savage life you soon must feel satiety:
The MIND requires fit exercise and food,

37

Not to be found 'mid Afric's deserts rude.
And what avail the spoils of wood and field,
The fruits or wines your fertile valleys yield,
Without that higher zest to crown the whole –
'The feast of Reason and the flow of Soul?'
– Food, shelter, fire, suffice for savage men;
But can the comforts of your wattled den,
Your sylvan fare and rustic tasks, suffice
For one who once seemed finer joys to prize?
– When, erst, like Virgil's swains, we used to sing
Of streams and groves, and all that sort of thing,
The spot we meant for our 'Poetic Den'
Was always within reach of Books and Men;
By classic Esk, for instance, or Tweed-side
With gifted friends within an easy ride:
Besides our college chum, the Parish Priest;
And the said *den* with six good rooms at least. –
Here! – save for Her who shares and soothes your lot,
You might as well squat in a Caffer's cot!

　　Come now, be candid: tell me, my dear friend,
Of your aspiring aims is *this* the end?
Was it for Nature's wants, fire, shelter, food,
You sought this dreary, soulless solitude?
Broke off your ties with men of cultured mind,
Your native land, your early friends resigned?
As if, believing with insane Rousseau
Refinement the chief cause of human woe,
You meant to realise that raver's plan,
And be a philosophic *Bosjesman!* –
Be frank; confess the fact you cannot hide –
You sought this den from disappointed pride.

P. – You've missed the mark, Fairbairn! my breast is clear.
Nor wild Romance nor Pride allured me here:
Duty and Destiny with equal voice
Constrained my steps: I had no other choice.

　　The hermit 'lodge in some vast wilderness,'
Which sometimes poets sigh for, I confess,

Were but a sorry lot. In real life
One needs a friend – the best of friends, a wife;
But with a home thus cheered, however rude,
There's nought so very dull in solitude, –
Even though that home should happen to be found,
Like mine, in Africa's remotest bound.
– I have my farm and garden, tools and pen;
My schemes for civilizing savage men;
Our Sunday service, till the sabbath-bell
Shall wake its welcome chime in Lynden dell;
Some duty or amusement, grave or light,
To fill the active day from morn to night:
And thus two years so lightsomely have flown
That still we wonder when the week is gone.
– We have at times our troubles, it is true,
Passing vexations, and privations too;
But were it not for woman's tender frame,
These are annoyances I scarce would name;
For though perchance they plague us while they last,
They only serve for jests when they are past.

And then your notion that we're *quite* exiled
From social life amid these mountains wild,
Accords not with the fact – as you will see
On glancing o'er this district map with me.
– First, you observe, our own Glen-Lynden clan
(To whom I'm linked like a true Scottish man)
Are all around us. Past that dark ravine, –
Where on the left gigantic crags are seen,
And the steep Tarka mountains, stern and bare,
Close round the upland cleughs of lone Glen-Yair, –
Our Lothian Friends with their good Mother dwell,
Beside yon *Krantz* whose pictured records tell
Of Bushman's huntings in the days of old,
Ere here Bezuidenhout had fixed his fold.
– Then up the widening vale extend your view,
Beyond the clump that skirts the Lion's Cleugh,
Past our old camp, the willow-trees among,

Where first these mountains heard our sabbath song;
And mark the Settlers' homes, as they appear
With cultured fields and orchard-gardens near,
And cattle-kraals, associate or single,
From fair Craig-Rennie up to Clifton-Pringle.

    Then there is Captain Harding at Three-Fountains
Near Cradock – forty miles across the mountains:
I like his shrewd remarks on things and men,
And canter o'er to dinner now and then.
– There's Landdrost Stockenström at Graaff-Reinet,
A man I'm sure you would not soon forget,
Who, though in this wild country born and bred,
Is able in affairs, in books well read,
And – what's more meritorious in the case –
A zealous friend to Afric's swarthy race.
We visit there; but travelling in ox-wagon,
(And not, like *you*, drawn by a fiery dragon)
We take a month – eight days to go and come –
And spend three weeks or so with Stockenström.
– At Somerset, again, Hart, Devenish, Stretch,
And ladies – whose kind acts 'twere long to sketch;
The officers at Kaha and Roodewal,
Bird, Sanders, Morgan, Rogers, Petingal;
All hold us with right friendly intercourse –
The nearest thirty miles – five hours with horse.
– Sometimes a pleasant guest, from parts remote,
Cheers for a passing night our rustic cot;
As, lately, the gay-humoured Captain Fox,
With whom I roamed 'mid Koonap's woods and rocks,
From Winterberg to Gola's savage grot,
Talking of Rogers, Campbell, Coleridge, Scott,
Of Fox and Mackintosh, Brougham, Canning, Grey;
And lighter themes and laughter cheered the way –
While the wild-elephants in groups stood still,
And wondered at us on their woody hill.
– Here too, sometimes, in more religious mood,
We welcome Smith or Brownlee, grave and good,

Or fervid Read, – to Natives, kneeling round,
Proclaiming the GREAT WORD of glorious sound:
Or, on some Christian mission bravely bent,
Comes Philip with his apostolic tent;
Ingenious Wright or steadfast Rutherfoord;
With whose enlightened hopes our hearts accord.

And thus, you see, even in my desert-den,
I still hold intercourse with thinking men;
And find fit subjects to engage me too –
For in this wilderness there's work to do;
Some purpose to accomplish for the band
Who left with me their much loved Father-Land;
Something for the sad Natives of the soil,
By stern oppression doomed to scorn and toil;
Something for Africa to do or say –
If but one mite of Europe's debt to pay –
If but one bitter tear to wipe away.
Yes! here is work, my Friend, if I may ask
Of Heaven to share in such a hallowed task!

But these are topics for more serious talk,
So we'll reserve them for an evening walk.
Fill now a parting glass of generous wine –
The *doch-an-dorris* cup – for '*Auld Lang Syne*';
For my good Margaret summons us to tea,
In her green drawing room – beneath the tree; –
And lo! Miss Brown has a whole *cairn* of stones
To pose us with – plants, shells, and fossil bones.

[*Outside the Hut.*]

F. – 'Tis almost sun-set. What a splendid sky!
And hark – the homeward cow-boy's echoing cry
Descending from the mountains. This fair clime
And scene recall the patriarchal time,
When Hebrew herdsmen fed their teeming flocks
By Arnon's meads and Kirjath-Arba's rocks;
And bashful maidens, as the twilight fell,

Bore home their brimming pitchers from the well. —
— But who are *these* upon the river's brink?

P. — Ha! armèd Caffers with the shepherd Flink
In earnest talk? Ay, now I mark their mien;
It is Powána from Zwart-Kei, I ween,
The AmaTembu Chief. He comes to pay
A friendly visit, promised many a day;
To view our settlement in Lynden Glen,
And smoke the Pipe of Peace with Scottish men.
And his gay consort, Moya, too attends,
To see 'the World' and Amanglezi friends,
Her fond heart fluttering high with anxious schemes
To gain the enchanting beads that haunt her dreams!

F. — Yet let us not these simple folk despise;
Just such *our* sires appeared in Caesar's eyes:
And, in the course of Heaven's evolving plan,
BY TRUTH MADE FREE, the long scorned African,
His Maker's Image radiant in his face,
Among earth's noblest sons shall find his place.

P. — [*To Flink, the old Hottentot Shepherd, who comes forward*]
Well, Flink, what says the Chief?

Flink.   'Powána wagh
Tot dat de Baas hem binnenshuis zal vraagh.'

P. — [*To F.*] In boorish Dutch, which means, 'Powána waits
Till Master bid him welcome to our gates.'
[*To Flink.*] — We haste to greet him. Let rush mats be spread
On th' cabin-floor. Prepare the Stranger's bed
In the spare hut, — fresh-strewn with fragrant hay.
Let a fat sheep be slaughtered. And, I pray,
Good Flink, for the attendants all provide;
These men dealt well with us at Zwart-Kei side:
Besides, you know, 'tis the Great Guide's command
Kindly to treat the Stranger in our Land.

[*Exeunt.*]

42

L'ENVOI

Fairbairn, adieu! I close my idle strain,
And doff wild Fancy's Wishing Cap again,
Whose witchery, o'er ocean's wide expanse,
Triumphant over adverse Circumstance,
From Tyne's far banks has conjured you away,
To spend with me this summer holiday;
Half-realising, as I weave these rhymes,
Our kind companionship in other times,
When, round by Arthur's Seat and Blackford Hill,
Fair Hawthornden and homely Hyvotmill,
(With a dear Friend, too early from us torn!)
We roamed untired to eve from early morn.

Those vernal days are gone: and stormy gales
Since then on Life's rough Sea have tossed our sails
Far diverse, – led by Fortune's changeful Star,
From quietude and competence afar.
Yet, Comrade dear! while memory shall last,
Let our *leal* hearts, aye faithful to the Past,
In frequent interchange of written thought,
Which half the ills of absence sets at nought,
Keep bright the links of Friendship's golden chain,
By living o'er departed days again;
Or meet in Fancy's bower, for ever green,
Though 'half the convex globe intrudes between.'

(Glen-Lynden, 1822)

The Caffer Commando

Hark! – heard ye the signals of triumph afar?
'Tis our Caffer Commando returning from war:
The voice of their laughter comes loud on the wind,
Nor heed they the curses that follow behind.
For who cares for him, the poor Caffer, that wails
Where the smoke rises dim from yon desolate vales –

43

That wails for his little ones killed in the fray,
And his herds by the Colonist carried away?
Or who cares for him that once pastured this spot,
Where his tribe is extinct and their story forgot?
As many another, ere twenty years pass,
Will only be known by their bones in the grass!
And the sons of the Keisi, the Kei, the Gareep,
With the Gunja and Ghona in silence shall sleep:
For England hath spoke in her tyrannous mood,
And the edict is written in African blood!

Dark Katta is howling: the eager jackal,
As the lengthening shadows more drearily fall,
Shrieks forth his hymn to the hornèd moon;
And the lord of the desert will follow him soon:
And the tiger-wolf laughs in his bone-strewed brake,
As he calls on his mate and her cubs to awake;
And the panther and leopard come leaping along;
All hymning to Hecate a festival song:
For the tumult is over, the slaughter hath ceased –
And the vulture hath bidden them all to the feast!

The Ghona Widow's Lullaby

Utiko Umkulu gozizuline,
Yebinza inquinquis, Nozilimele,
Umzi uakonana subiziele,
Umkokeli ua sikokeli tina,
Uenze infama zenza ga bomi.

The storm hath ceased: yet still I hear
    The distant thunder sounding,
And from the mountains, far and near,
    The headlong torrents bounding.
The jackal shrieks upon the rocks;
    The tiger-wolf is howling;
The panther round the folded flocks
    With stifled *gurr* is prowling.

But lay thee down in peace, my child;
God watcheth o'er us midst the wild.

I fear the Bushman is abroad –
   He loves the midnight thunder;
The sheeted lightning shows the road,
   That leads his feet to plunder:
I'd rather meet the hooded-snake
   Than hear his rattling quiver,
When, like an adder, through the brake,
   He glides along the river.
But darling, hush thy heart to sleep –
The LORD our Shepherd watch doth keep.

The Kosa from Luheri high
   Looks down upon our dwelling
And shakes the vengeful assagai, –
   Unto his clansmen telling
How he, for *us*, by grievous wrong,
   Hath lost these fertile valleys;
And boasts that now his hand is strong
   To pay the debt of malice.
But sleep, my child; a Mightier Arm
Shall shield thee (helpless one!) from harm.

The moon is up; a fleecy cloud
   O'er heaven's blue deeps is sailing;
The stream, that lately raved so loud,
   Makes now a gentle wailing.
From yonder crags, lit by the moon,
   I hear a wild voice crying:
'Tis but the harmless bear-baboon,
   Unto his mates replying.
Hush – hush thy dreams, my moaning dove,
And slumber in the arms of love!

The wolf, scared by the watch-dog's bay,
   Is to the woods returning;
By his rock-fortress, far away,
   The Bushman's fire is burning.

And hark! Ntsikana's midnight hymn,
 Along the valley swelling,
Calls us to stretch the wearied limb,
 While kinsmen guard our dwelling:
Though vainly watchmen wake from sleep,
'Unless the Lord the city keep.'

At dawn, we'll seek, with songs of praise,
 Our food on the savannah,
As Israel sought, in ancient days,
 The heaven-descended manna;
With gladness from the fertile land
 The veld-kos we will gather,
A harvest planted by the hand
 Of the Almighty Father –
From thraldom who redeems the race,
To plant them in their ancient place.

Then, let us calmly rest, my child;
 Jehovah's arm is round us,
The God, the Father reconciled,
 In heathen gloom who found us;
Who to this heart, by sorrow broke,
 His wondrous WORD revealing,
Led me, a lost sheep, to the flock,
 And to the Fount of Healing.
Oh may the Saviour-Shepherd lead
My darling where His lambs do feed!

The epigraph is ll. 5–9 of Ntsikana's hymn (see next item).

NTSIKANA GABA
(c. 1780–1821)

———— ❦ ————

Great Hymn

Translated from the Xhosa by Thomas Pringle (1827)

O thou Great Mantle which envelops us,
Creator of the light which is formed in the heavens,
Who framed and fashioned the heavens themselves,
Who hurled forth the ever-twinkling stars;
O thou Mighty God of Heaven,
Who whirlest round the stars – the Pleiades,
In thy dwelling place on thee we call,
To be a leader and a guide to us,
O thou who to the blind givest light.
Our great treasure, on thee we call;
For thou, O thou art the true rock;
Thou, O thou art the true shield;
Thou, O thou art the true covert.
On thee, O holy Lamb, we call,
Whose blood for us was sprinkled forth,
Whose hands for us were pierced;
O be thou a leader and a guide to us,
Creator of the light which is formed in the heavens,
Who framed and fashioned the heavens themselves.

(later version)

Translated from the Xhosa by John Knox Bokwe (1876)

He, is the Great God, Who is in heaven;
Thou are Thou, Shield of Truth.
Thou are Thou, Stronghold of truth.
Thou are Thou, Thicket of truth.
Thou are Thou Who dwellest in the highest.
He, Who created life below, created life above.
That Creator Who created, created heaven.

47

This maker of the stars, and the Pleiades.
A star flashed forth, it was telling us.
The Maker of the blind, does He not make them on purpose?
The trumpet sounded, it has called us.
As for his chase He hunteth, for souls.
He, Who amalgamates flocks rejecting each other.
He, the leader, Who has led us.
He, Whose great mantle, we do put it on.
Those hands of Thine, they are wounded.
Those feet of Thine, they are wounded.
Thy blood, why is it streaming?
Thy blood, it was shed for us.
This great price, have we called for it?
This home of Thine, have we called for it?

CHIEF MOTHIBI

Speech

(Of His Majesty, at the opening of the Great Pietshow
or Bechuana Parliament held at New Lattakoo, in the
month of June last, on the invasion of the Mantatees.

Done into English, from the short-hand notes of the
Hottentot Hatta, Prince Peclu's sworn interpreter, now
in the Cape.)

Bechuanas – Matclapees –
Dare ye meet the Mantatees?
Bamacootas – Baralongs –
Dare ye front the hostile throngs?
Myrees, Matcloroos and Briquas,
Dare ye mingle with the Griquas?
Dare ye face with noble Moffat
These savage hounds and sons of Tophet?

I know ye well – ye Matclapees!
Your bloodless hearts are soft as cheese; –

48

Before the women always bragging,
Near the foe, your courage flagging,
Ye scamper off like scar'd jackalls
To your coverts or your kraals,
Where with heads between your knees
Ye skulk like dogs, and kill – the fleas!
Dastard dogs, that merit not
To eat – even from a broken pot!

Bechuanas! – Matclapees! –
Dare ye face the Mantatees?
Shall we muster to the battle?
Will ye fight or lose your cattle?
Lose your cattle – kraals – and wives –
To cannibals with crooked knives!

But hark, ye women – hold your shrieking –
At least till we are done with speaking –
I say, abate your senseless squalling,
Or I will give your hides a galling!
Provoking pests of womankind!
With fear or fury always blind –
The secrets of our COURT revealing, –
Ever scolding – often stealing –
In some mischief, aye, delighting,
And hindering the men from fighting; –
Such milky-liver'd sneaking things,
Are men who make their wives their kings!
A husband who can't use the *sambok*,
Has less discretion than a ram, bok,
Baboon or jack-ass! – take for sample,
My recreant brothers' late example –
Which, if *you younger ones* shall follow,
And I be left *solus cum sola* –
I say no more – but wish that Evil
May catch you, – which the whites call *Devil!*

And tho' we sore might feel the want
Of females born to build and plant,

And dig, and do domestic duties –
(Not done so well by Cape Town beauties,)
Yet, by the head of Mallahavlin,
I swear I will not shake a javelin,
Nor draw an arrow from my quiver,
To save the carcase, limbs, or liver,
Of women that shall scold and squall,
From the ravenous maw of the Cannibal!

Keep silence, too – ye kidney-eaters,
Coward, cunning, canting cheaters!
Oft incog. upon my rambles,
I've found you near the royal shambles,
Hanging round, like gaunt hyenas,
Of the guts and grease to drain us –
Think, if foes our cattle *did* seize,
Where would ye get tripe and kidneys?

But listen to your king's command,
Ye chiefs and champions of the land! –
To your wives no more be trucklers,
Seize your kirries and your bucklers;
Smear your limbs with melted lard,
Let your hearts be great and hard!
Banish fear and faint demurrage,
Strike your shields and rouse your courage;
Rouse yourselves for feats uncommon,
Curse the Bushmen and the foemen!

Lo, MELZIL, Lord of Griqua – Bastards,
Hastes to help ye, heartless dastards!
And, eke, upon his fiery steed,
A trusty friend in time of need,
Call'd Captain TONSON of Cape Town,
Comes to ride the rascals down;
From Cape-land Chiefs he kindly greets you –
And *here* he's! – present at our Pietshow,
Noting down, with pen and ink,
All that now we say or think –

Consider, then, how ye shall look,
When put into a printed book;
And how white Captains that wear breeches,
May criticise black Captain's speeches!

Rouse up for shame, ye warriors, then!
Up and quit yourselves like men.
Like heroes now, and Mallahowans,
Give to vengeance full allowance! —
Fight not as ye use to do — as
Children fight — but like Macooas;
Make your bull-hide targets stronger,
Your battle-axes sharp as hunger!
In their faces howl defiance,
Gnash your teeth and roar like lions!
Point your arrows at their eyes,
Pin them with your hassagais!
Drive them back to whence they came,
And blast their nation and their name!
Then to your kraals return in glory,
While HATTA shall rehearse our story
To the Captains of the Cape,
Who at our daring deeds shall gape!

Up Teysho, Issita, Moshuma!
Up Incha! Dleeloqua, Ranyuma!
Semeeno, Mongual, and Bromello!
Each wary sage and warlike fellow;
Up and arm you for the battle —
We must fight, or lose our cattle!

Recorded in the fourth number of the weekly *South African Commercial Advertiser* (21 January 1824), edited by John Fairbairn, and occasioned by a delegation from Kuruman to Cape Town of dignitaries, including the son of Chief Mothibi of the Tlhaping and his Khoikhoi amanuensis, led by the missionary, Robert Moffat. The poem appeared after the combined Tswana-Griqua alliance had in fact repulsed the Zulu Mantatees. The versifier is unknown.

FREDERIC BROOKS

(dates unknown)

A General Description of Men and Things in Cape Town

Churches, Chapels, Stores, and Houses,
Jealous wives, and antler'd spouses:
Folks of all hues mix'd together,
Streets unpleasant in all weather;
Prisons, offices contiguous,
Broken roads, streams irriguous.
Gaudy things enough to tempt ye,
Showy outsides, insides empty;
And for the neat mechanic arts,
Old Dutch coaches, and cover'd carts.
Troops of Slaves cag'd like canaries,
To breed and bring forth Dolls and Marys;
Cellars full of *human* pelf,
To increase the dealer's wealth.
People bawling in every lingo,
Auctions in the streets by jingo;
Men of Vendue folks afraid,
Warrants, Deaners, bills unpaid;
Goods *zonder reserve* a going,
Smouchers looking very knowing;
To see all's right Ladies handling
Manly Slaves 'pon a table standing.
Taps which in vice and iniquity,
With fam'd *St Giles'* cellars vie;
Fiddles squeaking, people dancing,
Dogs a barking, horses prancing;
Sland'rous dames all day backbiting,
Blacks, like rams, with their heads fighting;
Malays all day busy gambling,
Passengers thro' the town a rambling.

Taudry, vain, slip shod Dutch wenches,
Piles of filth, various stenches,
Burgher carts thro' the streets trotting,
Leaving the dirt behind a rotting.
Jehus eight in hand a driving,
Some folks failing, others thriving;
Waggoners with tremendous whips,
Almost as long as masts of ships.
Dashing Bells, and amorous Sparks,
Bulls, Bears, and Pigeons, lots of Sharks;
Stiff Rumps, Merchants, Pedlars, Knaves,
Soldiers, Sailors, Jews, and Slaves.
Adventurers, both good and bad,
Stage-struck Heroes acting mad;
A useless *Head* devoid of brains,
Numerous losses, little gains.
Impertinent Coolies 'pon the beach,
Trying their employers to o'erreach;
Idle puppies each other *shaving*,
Politicians like mad men raving;
Noble, simple, all conditions,
And the *turpentine* Physicians.
Little folks striving to be great,
Great folks in a tottering state;
Lawyers, Poets, and *Priests* for *sartain*,
With all my Eye and Betty Martin.
Hypocrites, charity ever preaching,
But, by example, never teaching;
Worth beneath a thread-bare cover,
Bedaub'd with villainy all over.
Women, black, red, fair, and grey,
Prudes, and such as ne'er say nay;
Handsome, ugly, noisy, still,
Some that won't, and some that will:
Many a Widow not unwilling,
Many a Clerk without a shilling,
Making as grand an outside show,
As a first-rate Bond-street beau.

Noble grooms, exalted lackeys,
Lots of misbegotten Jackeys;
Demireps, Pimps, and Panders,
Geese, and sapient *Africanders*.
Young beardless boys keeping wenches,
Public Gardens depriv'd of benches;
Thanks to – but stay, I'll say no more,
Press restrictions are a cursed bore:
Therefore, as the post is waiting,
For the present I'll cease prating;
So, now, my worthy friend, adieu!
I'm thine for ever,

Saucy Q.

From 'A Fragment Letter, to a Correspondent in the Country, who
requests me to write him a Descriptive Epistle in Verse' in the fourth and
last of a series of anonymous satirical pamphlets entitled *South African
Grins; or, the Quizzical Depot of General Humbug*, printed by W.
Bridekirk in Cape Town in 1825.

KING SHAKA
(c. 1787–1828)

Battle Song
Translated from the Zulu by Henry Francis Fynn

Zhi, zhi, zhi, zhi, zhi, zhi, zhi, zhi,
    We never heard of wars like those of the Bathwas and the
       Jayis,
Also that of Mlotshwa, son of Vezi,
    All enemies indeed,
They ran off with Phunga's cattle,
    And threw in their lot with the Swazis;
So too, Mlotshwa, who likewise stole from Ntombazi;
    Though we at first were his protectors
And put ourselves betwixt him and the foe.

We removed Mlotshwa from the stump behind which men
    are wont to hide,
Oh, Swazis and Mthethwas, how have we offended you?

Give ear, oh people!
    The honey's been eaten by the ratel,
The bees have flown and quite deserted you.
    You turned from the path without even trying it.
Not by word of mouth are arguments decided,
    But by facts being put to the practical test.
You drove them away there, o'er Nhlokonhloko hills,
    Raising great dust in the land,
Who dare now take and slaughter them.

Fynn's note on the poem, composed after battle against the Pondos
during Shaka's abortive invasion of the Cape in 1828, is as follows:
'After the cattle taken had been sorted, the army formed up in
the centre of a plain, where it went through the usual ceremonies at
the hands of the doctors. The whole of it then proceeded by order of the
King to wash in the sea. When the troops returned from the sea a song,
which had been composed by Shaka during their absence, was sung.
'The interjections Zhi, zhi, zhi . . . are exclamations of triumph. The
Bathwas and amaJayi were two tribes; Umlotshwa the chief of yet
another. These three tribes were continually at war with Shaka, though
at length he defeated them. At first he had invited them to become his
subjects, but they declined. Mlotshwa subsequently stole a lot of cattle
belonging to Shaka (inherited by the latter from his great grandfather,
Phunga), joined the Swazis (other enemies of Shaka), and then took
refuge in their caves. After this he joined Shaka's most formidable foe,
the Ndwandwe tribe, only, however, to be put to death by Ntombazi,
Zwide's principal wife. It is this that makes Shaka say that he was, at
first, Mlotshwa's protector and offered him peace. For the Zulu army,
when attacking Zwide, at the time hostile to Mlotshwa, passed by
Mlotshwa, i.e. beyond where he was living. It is the same incident which
makes him say further that he put him (Mlotshwa) in the rear, i.e. set the
Zulu army between him and his enemy.
'The association of the names Swazis and Mthethwas is deliberate.
The latter, of course, were, by this time, Shaka's subjects, but, owing to
having recently offended him, he here uses their name in conjunction
with that of the former to show his great displeasure at their conduct.
'The latter portion of the song beginning "Give ear, oh people!"
alludes to the Zulu army's dilatoriness in attacking the Pondos so much
as to afford the latter an opportunity of running off with the greater part
of their cattle. This made it possible for any other tribe but the Zulus to
capture them. The word honey means cattle, and being eaten by the
ratel refers to those who might have seized them as the Pondos were

making off with them helter-skelter. Ratel is the Cape badger, an animal very fond of honey. The two lines about arguments mean that all the Zulu army says in defence of their conduct is of little avail, as, after consideration of actual circumstances, Shaka is convinced of their being unsound.

'The driving them over the hills of Nhlokonhloko merely refers to the cattle fleeing over the hills with their owners, the Pondos. There is no such hill as Nhlokonhloko in those parts. The word Nhlokonhloko is a fictitious term used in derision of the Pondos, who are accustomed to wear their hair extraordinarily long (*inhloko* means a head). The plural *inhlokonhloko* might be said to mean a mass of heads or many head-dresses. Raising a great dust refers to the clouds of dust caused by so many cattle fleeing in all directions. The last line, "Who dare now take and slaughter them," means that, having succeeded in escaping him (Shaka), what other person could possibly capture and enjoy them.'

ZULU PRAISE-SINGERS
(1820s)

─────── ◄► ───────

Mbuyazi (Henry Francis Fynn)
Translated by Daniel Malcolm

Mbuyazi of the Bay!
The long-tailed finch that came from Pondoland,
Traveller who was never going to go home,
Hungry one who ate the scented reed of the river,
The finch that never begged, unlike the 'kaffirs';
Deep-voiced speaker like rumbling thunder,
Bull-calf with the capacious paunch,
Feathers that grow and then moult,
Tamer of the intractable elephant.
He who became pregnant with many children,
They multiplied as river after river was crossed,
And then they became dogs and barked at him;
He who when he turned his back looked like the tail of an
    antelope;
Great swaying frame, he ran heavily but fast,
Running away from Zululand he made haste.
Back with thorns on it like a mamba,

Beauty like the mouse-birds of Manteku
That are yellowish on their wings.
Our white man whose ears shine in the sun;
Long snake that took a year to pass by
And eventually passed in another year.
Protector of orphans;
Pusher-aside of elephants so that they fall,
He who points with a stick and thunder and lightning come
   forth,
Everything that he points at falls and dies.
Our egret that came out of the sea;
Elder brother of Shaka whom he raised from the dead.
He took refugees out of the forests and nourished them,
So that they lived and became human again.
Hurrah! Hurrah! Hurrah for the Rescuer!
Wild animal of the blue ocean.

HENRY FRANCIS FYNN
(1803–61)

Adieu to Fortune

Adieu, blind fortune, with thy miserable purse.
To some you're generous, to others you're a curse.
Glittering with Hope, Ambition in your train,
both poor and rich, they follow you in vain.
For while to some you give with generous hands,
you drag your votaries from their native lands,
destroy their happiness and content of mind,
ill-health and discontent is all you leave behind.
'Twas in youthful age I heard thy wondrous charms,
when I had hardly left my nurse's aged arms.
'Twas then I fancied you could not be found
but in some secret isle or on foreign ground.
Then far I voyaged, left my native shore,
to barbarous lands to man unknown before.

Twelve years I sought thee in wild Africa's coast
but saw not your face amidst the savage host.
But now, terrestrial imagination's queen,
while these your deeds engross my present theme,
how can I rise from this, my hapless state?
Must poverty ever be my destined fate?
If so, adieu to all imaginary races
to Fortune and such other gods and graces.
Content at home shall rather be my aim
than in foreign lands to follow you again.

JOHN WHEATLEY
(d. 1830)

The Cape of Storms
(Written at sea)

Poet's own notes:

Spirit of Gama! round the stormy Cape,
Bestriding the rude whirlwind as thy steed;
The thunder cloud, thy car, – thy spectre shape
Gigantic; who upon the gale dost feed
And drink the water spout; – thy shroud, the skies; –
Thy sport, the South and vast Atlantic sea; –
Thine eye, the light'ning's flash! – Awake! arise
From out the deep, in dread and awful sov'reignty!

Now hast thou risen! By heaven it is a sight
Most God-like, grand, and glorious to behold;
Three elements contend, and fierce in fight

The Titans

As those who warr'd with mighty Jove of old.
Oh, God! if any doubt thy being, or rate
With vain and impious mind, at nought thy pow'r,
So may it be such daring sceptic's fate
To pass the Cape of Storms, when angry tempests lower.

Do'st note the gath'ring clouds, as on thro' heav'n
They speed their midway flight 'twixt sea and skies?

58

Like to the first-born by the Archangel driv'n
On earth, with flaming sword from Paradise.
Do'st mark the spirit stirring of the deep,
As onward sweeps the stormy hurricane;
Rous'd like a roaring lion from his sleep,
That wildly stares around, and shakes his shaggy mane?

Nor doth he wake in vain. From his abode
Hath ocean risen in terrible array,
Magnificent as when the voice of God
Call'd forth the world, from chaos, into day!
'Tis night; and now the tempest shrouded bark
With surge lash'd crest, upborne aloft, doth ride
Upon the heaving billows, vast and dark –
And braves, as did the Patriarch's ark, the whelming tide.

Oh, God! it is a fearful sight! and all around
Is dismal, drear, and dark, both near and far, –
Save, when to make the darkness more profound
And visible, some pale and twinkling star
Peeps for an instant forth, and then, as 'twere,
In fear recedes, – or the phosphoric dash
Of wild long sweeping waves, with horrid glare,
Lights up the dread abyss, and shines along the splash,

And waste of waters, like to the pale horse
Whom death shall ride upon that awful day,
When sun, and moon, and stars have run their course,
The world and time itself be swept away! –
And now the waning moon would fain forth shine,
And thro' the heav'ns pursue her wonted track;
But three wild warring elements combine
At once in unison, and drive her rudely back!

Did'st hear that crash – tremendous as the roar,
Which burst on Sinai's summit, touching heav'n,
When by the Lord, on that all-sacred shore,
To man in thunder were his mandates giv'n?
Did'st mark of that destructive element
Promethean nam'd, the fork'd and lurid light,

With vivid flash, from heav'n directly sent,
Like the lit flame which struck the apostate Saul in night!

Hark to the rending of the storm split sail,
And mark the reed-like quiv'ring of the mast;
List! list ye to the howling of the gale,
Dreadful as the Archangel's trump its blast! –
On such a night, the twelve Disciples cried
In fear, and rous'd the Saviour from his sleep!
Jesus arose, the elements to chide,
'Silence, ye angry winds, and peace, thou troubled deep!'

So spake the Son of God! and thus allay'd
The storm which howl'd upon the Assyrian shore;
Prompt at his call, the tempest's rage obey'd;
The winds were hush'd – the waters ceas'd to roar!
When Royal Canute once, with scepter'd hand,
And rob'd in pride of earthly majesty,
Forbade the sea to dare to lave the land,
The wild waves rose in sport, and roll'd all heedless by!

Jehovah! what is man compar'd with thee –
Or son of man – in mockery of sense,
That he should dare assume the Deity?
Oh, Man! would'st learn to know thine impotence,
Thy littleness, and inferiority,
Come hie thee to these regions of the storm,
Behold the face of God upon the sea,
And worship in the gale, his dread Almighty form!

But see the darkling spirit of the night,
That brooding sate upon the wat'ry plain;
Flies at the approach of thee, Ethereal Light!
Awaking now the universe again!
The sea-boy wet, rude nursling of the blast,
Whose sleep was cradled in the dashing spray,
And rock'd upon the high and giddy mast,
Regardless of the storm – unseals his eyes with day!

Ye who would further seek to know of Light,
Go read it as recorded in the page

Milton, Book iii

60

Of that immortal bard, bereft of sight
Himself – the god-like Homer of his age!
Oh! for one spark of that celestial flame,
That inspiration once to Milton giv'n,
Which lit his way to never dying fame;
The fire – 'the pomp, and prodigality of heav'n!'

In dread magnificence, the lurid sun
Now pierces thro' the tempest troubled sky,
And drives the thunder clouds dark rolling on,
As Satan and his rebel tribe were seen to fly
Before the red right arm of God! – No streaks
Of orient purple tinge, announce his rise,
In solitary splendour he awakes,
And seizes, as by storm, at once on all the skies!

Did'st mark the whale that dash'd along the deep,
'Hugest of all the ocean born that roam'   Milton, Book i
Like that Leviathan, whom once asleep,
The mariner (as on through Norway's foam
He steer'd his rude and shatter'd skiff) at night,
Mistook for land, so vast and still he seem'd,
And anchor'd thus – then rose in wild affright,
When morning's dawn upon the mighty monster beam'd.

Again he comes! gigantic as the beast
Of old, that God in mercy sent to save
The prophet Jonah, from the foamy yeast
Of waves, his else unknell'd – unshrouded grave!
Three days and nights, the slimy monster sped
His way, as thus the chos'n of God he bore,
By 'raging floods' and 'seas encompassed,'
Then cast him all unscath'd upon the Syrian shore!

Hark to the sea-mew's wild and piercing shrieks
As round the strong ribb'd bark they hover nigh,
Now o'er the waves' white foam they skim their beaks –
Now far away they speed, and seek the sky!
– But mark the might and majesty of motion
Of him, who sweeps cloud cleaving from the height   The Albatross

Of heav'n – it is the Condor of the ocean,
So nobly doth he soar aloft – so bold his flight!

The aspirations of this bird arise
Above those eagles that are seen afar,
O'er Chirombazo, loftiest in the skies –
Of Andes, 'Giant of the Western star!'
From mountain on to mountain let them urge
Their narrower flight, and habitations change,
His resting place the South Pacific surge –
All heav'n his Eyrie, and Immensity his Range!

Against the conquest crown'd Dictator's sway,
From Sardis, when the noble Cassius drew
His legions forth, in battle's stern array, –
E'en such a bird it was, that hov'ring flew
Upon his 'former ensign,' – then would feed
From out the soldier's hands, and flapping fly
His broad extended wings, that seem'd to lead
The embattled Romans on to certain victory!

But at Philippi sought, he then was gone –
And vultures, crows, and kites, were seen instead
For those whom hope of conquest had flush'd on,
Now vanquish'd lay, the dying and the dead!
– 'Twas such a bird, all wild and young that rose,
When Swedish Charles, with 'soul of fire' went forth,
And 'frame of adamant,' 'mid polar snows,
To plant his standard on the steeple of the north.

But when the fickle fortune of the war,
As history tells, on dread Pultowa's day
Forsook the warrior king, and woo'd the Czar,
The bird had wing'd his eagle flight away! –
On daring pinion borne – 'twas such that o'er
The modern Hannibal was seen to fly,
Above Saint Bernard's Alpine snows, to soar
To Fame's proud Temple, and 'unutterably high!'

There were, who said o'er Lybia's arid waste,
And chief the Pyramid's dim solitude,

The self-same bird, his flight had boldly trac'd,
And once before on Lodi's bridge been view'd –
To sweep Marengo's field, he left the Alps,
A laurel wreath inscrib'd he waved on high,
Then gain'd with nobler speed, their 'snowy scalps,'
The wreath enroll'd, Napoleon and Victory!

By Danube's darkly rolling tide, and o'er
The field of Austerlitz – on Eylau's plain
At Friedland – Jena – Berlin – Ulm – once more,
All splendid did he re-appear again!
On Moscow's conflagration – when the sun
Turn'd ghastly pale, and sicken'd at the sight,
The eagle saw his race of Glory run,
He tried in vain to soar – then shriek'd and sunk in night!

Oh! haste and look upon yon glorious zone,
The bow of God, which girdles half the sky,
The heav'nly arch, by the Almighty thrown
In vast and infinite variety
Of tints most beautiful, – th' Immortal's span
To mortal sight display'd in time of yore
The great Creator's covenant with man,
That whelming waters should o'er land prevail no more!

Thou pledge redeemed of the Deity!
To man below, in consolation sent,
Thou fairest, brightest vision of the sky,
I hail thee! Dolphin of the firmament!
For each succeeding varied change imbues
Thee with a magic colour, that doth shine
More splendid than before – till all thy hues
Proclaim the God at once, – like him, thy form divine!

And if on earth thy beauty be extreme,
When view'd o'er mountain height, or level plain;
Far, lovelier far, thy variegated beam,
Expanded o'er the surface of the main,
With either horizon thy resting place,
Thou mak'st the sea the mirror of thy light;

The ocean back reflects thy radiant face —
Like lovers, each belov'd — both gazing with delight!

Jehovah! with thy name commenc'd my strain!
Jehovah! with thy name it shall conclude,
By those alone who track the dark blue main,
The grandest of thy wond'rous works are view'd;
I envy not the man, whose inward fire
Of soul, expands not, riding o'er the deep,
Whose mental aspirations soar not higher
With the wild waves, 'ere night behold him laid in sleep!

For me! whatever dangers yet may lower
Upon my life, or errors be my fate —
So shall it soothe me, in my latest hour,
That once, at least, I tried to celebrate
Thy praise; and in Thy temple of the sea,
Its canopy, the clear and cloudless sky,
That thus I struck the lyre, and bent the knee,
Oh, God! in homage to Thy pow'r and majesty!

With love of fame, my dawn of life awoke,
And hopes of honours that ambition fired;
Too soon the demon disappointment broke
Upon the day-dreams which those hopes inspir'd.
And be it so — yet, haply, if I dare
Uplift a suppliant's voice to heav'n 'twould be,
That God in mercy might accord my prayer
To die a hero's death in planting Freedom's tree!

I little reck what soil it be upon,
So danger lead, and point to glory's star
In fighting on the plains of Marathon,
Or 'neath thy banners, noble Bolivar!
For since young Freedom's standard is unfurl'd,
On Atho's crags, and Pernambuco's shore,
Alike to me, the east or western world,
So that my soul escape amid the battle's roar!

When life from selfish joys is disallied —
If callous gloom succeed to cherish'd hope —

'Twere nobler far to fall by Freedom's side,
Than on to live a moody misanthrope,
Or die a heartless suicide — If life
Hath ceas'd to please — what higher aim can be
Than in the glorious rapture of the strife
To breathe our last upon thine altar — Liberty?

But 'circumstance' is, aye, one's blight and curse,
It mars our best and brightest hopes — since then
It may not be my lot to spur my horse
In Freedom's ranks, and aid my fellow men
(Embattled in her sacred cause,) in rending
A tyrant's chains, a bigot's iron crown —
The patriot's and the martyr's laurel blending,
And dying, strike some Selim, or Pizarro down.

Perchance the grandest boon to be bestow'd
By heav'n on man — the shortest, best relief
From all his mortal sufferings, and load
Which life entails of misery, and grief —
The termination of his woes, might be
As now he braves the billows of the Cape,
To grapple with grim Death upon the sea,
The whirlwind for its courser, and the storm its shape,

So might the bark become his coffin's shell,
The murky cloud enshroud him as his pall,
The roar of distant thunder ring his knell,
The lightning's flash illume his funeral!
His winding sheet the wild white curling wave,
The rolling billow as his bier, be lent,
The rain his tears! the ocean for his grave,
The Cape of Storms itself his mighty Monument!

First published in *The Cape of Good Hope Literary Gazette* (No. 4) of 15 September 1830. In No. 8 of 5 January 1831, John Wheatley is reported as 'died at sea, on his passage to England from the Cape of Good Hope'.

ALLEN F. GARDINER
(1794–1851)

The Natal Hunters

In olden times we oft have heard,
Though many deem those tales absurd,
   Of half-tamed men called Buccaneers
Who scoured the sea, and oft the land,
On plunder bent, with sword in hand,
   Cutting off noses, sometimes ears.

Now these men, as the story runs,
Were strangely garbed, though armed with guns,
   And blunderbluss, and spear;
All men of wild terrific mien,
The fiercest that their foes had seen,
   Transfixing all with fear.

Now just such men as these I've seen,
As wild to view – on slaughter keen;
   But, perhaps, you'll think I'm jesting;
'Twas but the other night I found
The ruffians seated on the ground,
   Each from his labours resting.

White, brown and black, of varied hue,
Composed this strange – this motley crew,
   The sullen Hottentot and blithesome Kali;
So long unshaved the whites had been,
Thick bristles stood on every chin;
   Despised the toil of washing daily.

Each proud Incosi stood erect,
Which added much to the effect,
   The rest like monkeys crouched behind;
It would not many words require,
To give an inventory entire,
   Of all their habiliments combined.

Four leathern trowsers duly worn
With woollen frocks, some badly torn,
    Two bonnets rouge – a hat crowned,
Three shoes that ne'er had covered hose,
With openings wide t'admit the toes,
    Were all the four white people owned.

In suits of ditto, *closely fitted*,
The natives never can be pitied,
    One garment lasts them all their days;
But Hottentots on finery bent,
Are not so easily content,
    And ape their moody masters' ways.

The lip moustached – the sallow face,
Denote that haughty, thankless race,
    They'd sell their skin for brandy;
E'en Erin's sons they far eclipse,
In placing goblets to their lips,
    Whene'er they find them handy.

A few I marked with strange attire,
While crowding round a blazing fire,
    Some sea-cow fat devouring.
Red caps and tattered frocks they wore,
With brigantines besmeared with gore,
    Like border bandits lowering.

In strange confusion, round them strewed,
Muskets and powder-horns I viewed,
    With skins, and fat, and dogs, and game;
For neither elephant nor buffalo
They ever leave in peace to go,
    But fell with deadly aim.

I've seen the savage in his wildest mood,
And marked him reeked with human blood,
    But never so repulsive made;
Something incongruous strikes the mind,
Whene'er a barb'rous race we find,
    With shreds of civil life displayed.

There's more of symmetry, however bare,
In what a savage deigns to wear,
   In keeping with the scene;
These, each deformed by what he wears,
Like apes that dance at country fairs,
   Seemed but a link between.

'Twould puzzle poet – painter too –
In vivid colours bright and true
   That living chaos to pourtray:
The twilight shed a ghastly glare
On all the group assembled there,
   As round the flick'ring fires they lay.

The Zoolus' song, the white men's cheers,
With grating Dutch, assailed our ears,
   As we approached their lair;
E'en faithful Echo stood amazed
At the wild Babel they had raised
   Upon the evening air.

E'en now the image haunts my brain!
Those hideous forms and shouts remain,
   Like fever'd dreams on restless nights;
And perhaps 'twere better here to end
These sorry rhymes, lest I offend
   By painting such outlandish sights.

TRADITIONAL (SOTHO)

The Praises of the Canna
*Translated into French by Thomas Arbousset (1833) and
into English by John Croumbie Brown (1846)*

Brown-coloured Trotter!
Sprout of the mountains!
  It cannot gallop;
  It goes as its sides go.

It is a cow that conceals its calf in the unknown fords of the
    rivers;
It is the cow of Unkonagnana.
      The heigho! of the mountain,
      The heigho! amongst the rocks.
Its two horns,
Perhaps they are two reddish feathers!
An ox which one presents as food to his uncle or his aunt
Although it has eaten a woeful plant.
Let fly! – It trots no more!
      It has stopt to weep!
      Or is it that the leader of the herd thirsts for delicious
          waters?
These weapons, they are the darts!
The piercers of the white ant hills!
– Already the old men at the kraal are sharpening their knives!

Arbousset's note: 'The Sotho word *litoko* has a more extended signi-
fication than the word *praises*, by which we have translated it. It
embraces all that is worthy to be narrated on the subject of the song, –
every thing remarkable that is known; and in this narration the above
piece answers to its title. It takes up all the notions of the Basutos on the
eland, with an economy of words indispensable to a people who have
no other means than memory for preserving their traditions. The word
mathlethla (trotters), in which the *th* is pronounced as in English, is a
beautiful ontomatopy which well expresses the clumsy movements of
the eland, when it is large and fat. The words *thloro thloro einchueng*,
imperfectly translated by *heigho! heigho!*, represent so admirably the
sigh of the animal in laboriously clambering up the steep rocks when it
is pursued by the huntsmen, that they always excite in the Basutos a
noisy cheerfulness. This phrase, "These weapons, they are the darts!
The piercers of the white ant hills!" will not be understood without
explanation; it implies that the assegais of the Basuto are going to pierce
the eland, as they pierce the hills of white ants – hills, which rising
sometimes to the height of three feet, frequently serve the Basutos for a
mark when they practise throwing the assegai.
    'The Basutos give to the herds of these animals an imaginary
shepherd, whom they call Unkonagnana (*little nose*). He lives in the
Malutis, and is never seen by human eye. They also pretend that the
canna has, between the two horns, and hid in its hair, a very dangerous
yellow viper. For this reason, when the canna is brought to the ground,
they strike it with a stick with heavy blows on the top of the head, before
stabbing it to the heart. They purify themselves before eating the flesh,
because of the venomous juices with which they believe it to be
charged. The natives say that it eats bitter and poisonous plants, which

communicate to its entrails a nauseous and sometimes poisonous odour; and they refuse to eat them. The flesh of the canna is good, and almost equal in quality to beef; it has a slight taste of venison. The flesh of the male is preferable to that of the female, because it is generally fatter. The hide of the male is also more esteemed for its strength and its thickness; lashes, bridles, harness, saddles, native cloaks, and shields are made of it.'

A War Song of the Basotho
Translated by Daniel P. Kunene

A male child – ox abandoned to the vultures!
Twice we are governed: We're endlessly slaughtered,
And, being slaughtered, we're apportioned to the eagles!
We're apportioned to the pied crow and the vulture.

O vulture, cease hovering above us, we're burying a man!
He who falls by the spear is not buried at home;
A man who falls by the spear is buried in the mountains,
The grave of him who falls by the spear – the tall *seboku* grass!

We men are oxen abandoned to the vultures.
Men, for their part, call death upon themselves,
They call it when spears are being brandished,
And the young brave his mother mourns him.

And the little girl, the youthful maiden, cried,
She cried when the sun moved on towards the setting.
– When you were told to stay you said you'd go –
O vulture, let me be, that I go to see the courtyards at home.

O woman, say not your man has lived,
We go once again upon the morrow.
O woman, give me to eat, I'm going to battle,
This night I'll spend kneeling upon one knee!

There they go *qu! qu! qu! qu!*
There are the owners of the cattle, they're coming!
Thunder out the song, all you men;
Why so sullen, being man-eaters?
You thunder not, for you thunder with reluctance.

According to Kunene, recorded by A. M. Sekese in *Leselinyana la Basotho* (1 February 1891), the newspaper initiated at Morija in the 1860s. A full account is given of this war song or *mekorotlo* in Kunene's *Heroic Poetry of the Basotho* (1971).

WILLIAM HENRY
(dates unknown)

Verses

(On the Wreck of the Convict Ship *Waterloo*, in Table Bay, on the Morning of Sunday, August 28, 1842)

1

Come, all ye men of England, and listen unto me,
While I relate the hardships we've met upon the sea,
When sailing from Old England, as you shall understand,
According to our sentences, bound for Van Diemen's Land.

2

'Twas on the first of June our ship from Sheerness did set sail,
And through the Downs away we bore with a sweet pleasant
  gale.
We left our friends all weeping, not knowing what to do,
While we did cross the Ocean wide in the ship called *Waterloo*.

3

Two hundred and twenty convicts in her did sail away,
Who for their wives and families dear most earnestly did pray,
Still hoping to return again unto Old England's shore,
Then from their friends and country dear they never would part
  more.

4

We had a pleasant passage for twelve long weeks or so,
But to the famed Cape of Good Hope we were obliged to go;
When safe arrived at Table Bay we thought all perils past.
On the 24th August our anchor it was cast.

5

For fresh water and provisions we called at the Bay,
And lay in perfect safety until early the fifth day,
When a thunder-storm did then arise, which caused us to fear,
And think upon our homes and friends and those we held most
    dear.

6

The rain it fell in torrents – the thunder loud did roll,
The lightning from the elements did flash from pole to pole.
Just at this time, our cable chain on the starboard side gave way,
The wind blew hard, which caused our ship on her larboard side
    to lay.

7

The soldiers on the quarter-deck did then begin to fire,
As signals of distress; to land our Doctor did desire;
But nothing could be done for us by those upon the shore,
The morning being very dark, and thunder loud did roar.

8

Here we did lie till six o'clock, and sorely we were tossed;
It being about half-past four, our anchor it was lost;
But another was got ready, and overboard was cast.
We then thought all our sufferings were at end at last.

9

'Twas nearly ten o'clock our ship did strike against the sand,
And hundreds of the inhabitants were gathered on the land,
For to do all lay in their power, our precious lives to save,
Not thinking that so many would have met a watery grave.

10

And all this time we, poor convicts, were locked down below;
The striking of the ship caused us to stagger to and fro;
And many upon their knees, that never did expect
The doors would e'er be opened for us to get on deck.

11

But, by the assistance of the Lord, a hammer soon was got,
One of our men got hold of it, and soon did break the lock;
Then quickly upon the deck we men by men did go.
A scene to us there did appear, which filled our hearts with woe:

12

Both men, women and children were lying on the deck,
And calling for assistance to take them from the wreck.
The main and mizzen-mast were sprung, and overboard did fall,
And o'er the starboard side the waves like mountains they did
    roll.

13

And many men jumped overboard, the wished-for shore to gain;
And many more that could not swim did on the deck remain,
Until assistance by a boat did reach us from the shore;
But by this time many had sunk, and never did rise more.

14

There were three hundred souls on board when we left England's
    shore,
But very near two hundred sunk, and rose with life no more.
Of two hundred and nineteen convicts, just seventy-six remain,
Who hope and trust that such a scene they'll never see again.

15

Ye inhabitants of Cape Town, long happy may you be!
Which will be our earnest prayer, when far across the sea,
For the kindness that you showed to us when we in need did
    land.
Your praises loudly we'll proclaim, when in Van Diemen's Land.

16

So, to conclude, and make an end of this imperfect rhyme,
May God above reward you well in his own way and time;
For when we were upon your shore, we had no cause to rue;
But still we'll think on Table Bay and the old ship *Waterloo*!

ANDREW GEDDES BAIN
(1797–1864)

———— •~• ————

Polyglot Medley

Oh what a gay, what a rambling life a Settler's leading
Spooring cattle, doing battle quite jocose:
Winning, losing – Whigs abusing, shopping now, then mutton
    breeding,
Never fearing – persevering, on he goes

When to the Cape I first came out in days of Charlie Somerset
My lands were neatly measured off and reg'larly my number set
I strutted round on my own ground, lord of a hundred acres, Sir
I said I'd plough – I'd buy a cow, the butcher's cut and baker's
    Sir

Oh what a gay, what a *rambling* life a Settler's leading
Spooring cattle, doing battle quite jocose
Winning, losing – Whigs abusing, shopping now, then mutton
    breeding
Never fearing, persevering –

    Deep in a vale, a cottage stood
      Oft sought by travellers weary
    And long it proved the best abode
      Of Edward and of Mary,

    For her he'd chase the mountain goat
      O'er Alps and glaciers bounding;
    For her the Chamois he would shoot
      Dark horrors all surrounding.

    But evening came, he sought his home,
      Where anxious lovely woman;
    She hail'd the sight, and every night
      The cottage rung as they sung –

Oh! dulce, dulce Domum; dulce dulce Domum;
The cottage rung as they sung –

My name is Kaatje Kekkelbek, I come van Kat Rivier
Daar is van water geen gebrek, but scarce of wine and beer:
Myn A.B.C. at Flippes School I learnt een kleine beetje
But left it just as great a fool as gekke Tanta Meitje!

(*Spoken*) Regt dat's amper waar wat Oúwe Moses in de Kaap segt
– hy segt –

> Du du liegst mir im hertzen!
> Du du liegst mir in Sinn;
> Du du machst mir viel Schmertzen,
> Weist ja wie gut ich dir bin,
> Ja, ja weist ja wir gut ich dir bin. –

Come bustle neighbour Prig, Buckle on your Sundays wig:
In our Sunday cloths so gaily, let us strut up the Old Bailey
Oh, the devil take the rain – we may never go again
    See the Shows have begun oh rare oh!

When the fair is at the full, in gallops a mad bull:
Puts the rabble to the rout, and lets the lions out:
Down tumbles Mrs Snip with a monkey on her hip
    We shall see her swallowed up I declare oh!

Roaring boys – gilded toys: Lollypops, shilling hops,
Tumble in, just begin – cups and balls, wooden walls,
Shins of beef – Stop thief! lost shoes, kangaroos,
O Polly, where is Molly – Bow wow, what a row
    Is kicked up in Bartlemy Fair oh! –

(*Spoken*) Here valk up ladies and gentlemen! Here is the wonderful kangaroo from Bottomhouse Bay – The wonderful Bengal tiger from the Westindees. Here is the astonishing hanimal called by the Dutch Boers of South Hafrica the Seacow, and the 'ouse where he lives in the Seacow gat. This here creature was known to the hancient Greeks, who called it the River 'oss because it had the resemblance to that noble hanimal – but the naturalists of hour enlightened day calls it the 'Ipperpothamouse, because it can't live on the land and dies in the vater. Here is the wonderful Sun Heagle – the 'otter the sun the 'igher he flies. And here is the Mighty Skeleton of the self-same whale that swallowed up Jonah. But the

wonderful wonder of all is the beautiful 'Ottentot Wenus from the
Cape of Good 'Ope – measures three yards and three quarters
round her.

> Heigh down, ho down, derry, derry down
> Oh the humours of Bartlemy Fair oh! –

Pypje gy zyt alles woord, gy, gy zyt het troost van 't leven
Als ons ramp of kwelling baart, kunt gy ons genoegen geven.
Kwelt ons soms het huywilyks juk; gaat U vrouwtje ant raasen;
Stop een lekker pyp tabak, ga op U gemak maar blaazen!
Stop een lekker pyp tabak ga op U gemak maar –

> Drink of this Cup you'll find there's a spell in
> Its every drop gainst the ills of Mortality,
> Talk of the cordial that sparkled for Helen
> Her cup was a fiction but this is reality.

> Would you forget the dark world we are in,
> Only taste of the bubble that gleams on the top of it:
> But would you rise above earth till akin
> To immortals themselves you must drain every drop of it.

> Send round the Cup and – but this is –

Partant pour la Syrie le jeane et beau Dunois
Venoit prier Marie du benir ses exploits.
Faites Reine immortelle, lui dit il en partent
Que jamais la plus belle, et soit le plus vaillent –

> Barney Bodkin broke his nose,
> Want of money makes us sad,
> Without feet we can't have toes –
> Crazy folks are always mad.

> We all shall live until we die
> Barney leave the girls alone – for –

Brave Somerset's coming a ho! a ho!
The Kafirs are running a ho! a ho!
The Cape Mounted Rifles who stick at no trifles
Are charging like teufels a ho! a ho!

O'Reilly and Bisset have paid them a visit
Which doubtless elicits their blessings again
While the brave little Tot now begins to get hot
In pursuit of his vrot savage foes o'er the plain

Brave Somerset's coming and – are singing like teufels –

Come cheer up lads 'tis to glory we steer
To add something new to this wonderful year
To honour we call you, not press you like slaves
For who are so free as the sons of the waves

Hearts of oak are our ships, jolly tars are our men
We always are ready – steady boys steady!
We'll fight and we'll conquer again and again

Old King Coul was a merry old soul, and a merry old soul was
        he
Old King Coul was a merry old soul, and he had fiddlers three –

When Britain first at heaven's command
Arose from out the azure main
This was the charter, the charter of the land
And guardian angels sang this strain –

Rule Britannia, Britannia rules the waves
For Britons never shall be slaves.

Bain's selection of comic and patriotic pieces, including quotations
from his own works. The opening stanzas are from 'The British Settler'
(to the tune of 'Oh what a row'), first sung by him at a dinner in 1844
commemorating the Queen's Road engineered by him along the Cape
frontier, from Grahamstown to Fort Beaufort, and reminiscing about
the tribulations of the 1820 settlers. The Kaatje Kekkelbek sequence
is from his dramatic sketch, 'Kaatje Kekkelbek, or Life among the
Hottentots', first performed in Grahamstown in 1839, and reprinted
as a broadsheet in *Sam Sly's African Journal* in 1846. The barker's call,
among other African marvels, introduces the Hottentot Venus, the
origin of the above sketch. From the arranger's own manuscript,
uncorrected.

Address

(On the Second Anniversary of the Graham's Town
Scientific, Literary and Medical Society)

Well here we are! – and don't you think we're looking quite
  respectable?
What change appears in two short years, from nought to what's
  delectable!
Look round our walls and see what calls we've for your
  admiration;
And all should know our minutes show a wise administration.

Our first attempt, two years ago, was meek and unpretending,
But now our cup is filling up and circumstances mending:
Some six or seven Medicos our Institution founded,
While now with more than seven score we're firm and stably
  grounded.

Don't say our views are narrow, as we for the Million labour,
Imparting all our knowledge to th'advantage of our neighbour;
Our Essays have been various, no lack of brain demanding,
And they'll be more varied still as our means go on expanding.

The Science of Anatomy we've certainly advanced,
And Botany its value too materially enhanced;
In marvels of the microscope our boys and girls are knowin'
And deeply read in Ehrenberg, in Hooker and in Owen!

We cultivate Belles-Lettres, but we don't despise bell metal,
When Metallurgic differences by Chemistry we settle:
Zoology and all the other *ologies* we handle,
And none can in Geology to us e'en hold the candle!

In Mathematics and the Classics our ladies are *au fait*,
While Hydrostatics and Pneumatics they study every day;
Besides they're such Astronomers they lead you up to Heaven,
And hard 'tis to get down again, such powers to them are given.

Hence some complaining husbands say – but they are stupid
  varmints –

That now their wives begin to wear improper nether garments,
For they conjecture every lecture's so replete with knowledge
That we're laying the foundation of a true *Blue-stocking*
 College.

'Tis a disgrace and out of place – I'd banish them to Delhi –
Those wicked swells who'd make their belles with us a *casus*
 belli,
So let the dears dispel their fears and show us oft their faces,
Their tyrant lords must sheathe their swords and take their
 proper places.

We'll go ahead depend upon't too rapidly I fear,
As some want Anniversaries in future twice a year;
With other sprees and novelties all precedent quite scorning
As monthly meetings once a week and Soirées every morning.

THOMAS PHIPSON
(1815–76)

The Press

All honour to the persevering toil
That mines the earth or ploughs the fallow soil,
Flings the swift shuttle, tends the whirling wheel,
Moulds the rough orc, or bends the stubborn steel,
Hews the hard mountain, rears the lofty dome
Or builds, or decorates, a humble home;
But hath the 'noble art' no power to bless?
Is the hand useless that controls the Press?

See the quick finger and the practised eye
Make the loose types in well-drawn order lie
Till word by word and line by line expand
The pages that shall cheer or curse the land;
The sparkling wit, the truth, the warm appeal,
The poet's tones, the tale of woe and weal
On the blank sheet receive their varied dress
And greet the anxious reader from the Press.

LANGHAM DALE
(1826–98)

Prejudice against Colour

Candida de nigris, et de candentibus atra. – OVID
Black sheep among the white, and white among the black.

'Ne crede colori,' the Poet erst sang,
 Appearances ever delude;
But white is the hue, that to us is genteel,
 The black one, of course, is tabooed!

Jan Wit-schijn, – he ranks with the favour'd race,
 Though conscience by vice is long sear'd:
To him virtue's a stranger, and honour unknown;
 What matter? He's duly veneer'd!

Poor Zwart-kleur's an honest and truly good fellow,
 Fears, honours, and humbly obeys;
But still, 'mid the fold of the black sheep, he's spurn'd;
 'Tis colour, not merit, that pays!

ANON.

The Concert

Translated by Stephen Gray

A Griqua describes in the Taal the first concert held in the
schoolroom, Kokstad, 1876

 A concert's what the English like,
  Their best clothes they put on;
 Never mind if it's day or night,
  They're always game to have some fun.

 With wife and child that's where he'll trot,
  For talk and laughing and to sing;

They like their kind of sport a lot,
    It goes on and on without ending.

So I was very keen to see
    What type of show makes them swarm;
That they can spend such good money
    To hear a Rooinek perform.

With a swallow-tail a big black coat
    I borrowed from Brother Sem,
From Uncle Gert a shilling, a shirt –
    Then I was just like them.

Now in I go with a proud tread,
    I sit on the foremost bench,
Of the local whites I am never scared,
    So what do I owe to them?

The house was full. Ah, it was grand
    To see such happy settlers here;
Gents and girls sit hand in hand.
    All I lacked was an interpreter.

They played and sang with wild applause,
    Each minute something fresh and fit;
They improvised with never a pause –
    Not that I grasped a word of it!

Then came an item that I confess
    Put me in great apprehension –
Ten black fellows in fancy dress
    Each with a kind of violin

Entered and lolled upon a stool,
    Their hair frizzed out in great display,
Rowdy and ugly and each a fool –
    I shivered on the spot, I say.

I thought to myself, what's going to be,
    From where are they appearing?
Are they Negro folk from oversea,
    Or are those masks they're wearing?

Well, masks they certainly were not;
    It was bootblack on their skin;
Where one had wiped his lips all hot
    I saw the jaw of Sergeant Glynn.

So they dance and play the stupid coon,
    Ten creatures on a spree;
When all at once I almost swoon –
    They point and wink at me:

The brown man! Oh, in my own hall,
    To be the object of their laughter!
In all the noise my bitter gall
    Was going to boil for ever after!

We laboured hard to build this school
    Where all our children can learn;
Now there seems they've made a rule
    To drive us from our home again.

Well, blood is thicker than water once more,
    For darkies as well as for fair,
If you scratch too much an open sore
    The pain is hard to bear.

So 'Christy Minstrels' is what they're called;
    Don't they have any shame? –
To give such a really godless act
    Such a very lovely name?

Appears in *The Early Annals of Kokstad and Griqualand East* (1902)
by William Dower (1837–1919). The 'Afrikaans'-speaking Griquas
had been forced to remove to Nomansland on the Transkei–Natal
border, where they were annexed by the Cape in 1874. The incident
described here thus precedes the Griqua rebellion against the garrison
in 1878. It is not clear if the poem was written by its anonymous
spokesman, or a satire devised by the missionary to the Griquas, Dower
himself. The first stanza of the original reads:

    Veel hou de Engelsch van CONCERT,
        Hij trek de best aan.
    Laat staan, al is 't de ergste smert,
        Is 't licht of donker maan.

The translation is based on a literal rendering by Wilma Stockenström,
Tobie Cronjé and William Pretorius.

W. C. SCULLY
(1855–1943)

'Nkongane

Old – some eighty, or thereabouts;
  Sly as a badger alert for honey;
Honest perhaps – but I have my doubts –
  With an eye that snaps at the chink of money;
Poor old barbarian, your Christian veneer
  Is thin and cracked, and the core inside
Is heathen and natural. Quaint and queer
  Is your aspect, and yet, withal, dignified.

When your lips unlock to the taste of rum,
  The tongue runs on with its cackle of clicks
That like bubbles break as their consonants come,
  For your speech is a brook full of frisky tricks.
You love to recall the days of old –
  That are sweet to us all, for the alchemist, Time,
Strangely touches the basest of metals to gold,
  And today's jangled peal wakes tomorrow's rich chime.

But not like the past in a moony haze,
  That shines for us sons of old Europe, is yours –
You glow with the ardour of bloodstained days
  And deeds long past – you were one of the doers –
Of spears washed red in the blood of foes,
  Of villages wrapped in red flame, of fields
Where the vultures gorged, of the deadly close
  Of the impi's horns, and the thundering shields.

Strange old man – like a lonely hawk
  In a leafless forest that falls to the axe,
You linger on; and you love to talk,
  Yet your tongue full often a listener lacks;
Truth and fiction, like chaff and grain
  You mix together, and often I try

To sift the one from the other, and gain
  The fact from its shell of garrulous lie.

You were young when Shaka, the scourge of man,
  Swept over the land like the Angel of Death;
You marched in the rear when the veteran van
  Mowed down the armies — reapers of wrath!
You sat on the ground in the crescent, and laid
  Your shield down flat when Dingaan spake loud —
His vitals pierced by the murderer's blade —
  To his warriors fierce, in dread anguish bowed.

And now to this: to cringe for a shilling,
  To skulk round the Mission-house, hungry and lone;
To carry food to the women tilling
  The fields of maize! For ever have flown
The days of the spear that the rust has eaten,
  The days of the ploughshare suit you not;
Time hath no gift that your life can sweeten,
  A living death is your piteous lot.

ALBERT BRODRICK
(1830–1908)

On a Government Surveyor

Death roodly knocked him off his perch;
  He cares no more for sluit or dam —
No more with paint and deep research —
  He'll frame the dainty diagram.

All earthly boundaries are passed,
  His beacon's fixed on Hope's high crest;
And freed from worldly chains, at last —
  He'll taste the od-de-lite of rest.

84

Epitaph on a Diamond Digger

Here lies a digger, all his chips departed –
A splint of nature, bright, and ne'er down-hearted;
He worked in many claims, but now (though stumped)
He's got a claim above that can't be jumped.
May he turn out a pure and spotless wight,
When the Great Judge shall sift the wrong from right,
And may his soul, released from this low Babel,
Be found a gem on God's great sorting table.

Shu' Shu' of Delgo

(Jim's yarn)

Beautiful maid of Delgo, I liked your face so black,
'Twas in a storm I met you, just close to Mac-a-Mac,
I asked your birth and parentage, I did it half in lark,
You seemed a little reticent, and kept it very dark.
You lived upon the coast, you said, and since you were a child
Had watched the surf upon the beach, in foaming fury wild.
You loved a bold young digger, had followed him thro' mire,
And swamp, and stream, and wastes of sand, to see your heart's
    desire;

And when you found him near his claim, his looks were stern
    and cold:
His love had faded in the fierce relentless lust for gold!
Splashed was your graceful agile form, your feet showed signs of
    squash,
I sheltered you from wind and rain with half my macintosh,

And as we sat down side by side, your dark expressive eyes
Gazed sometimes on my pensive face, and sometimes on the
    skies.
I thought: 'Here is a denizen of Nature's solemn ways:
She wears no flounce, nor frill, nor ruff; she scorns a Polonaise;

85

Untouched by laws and social shams that make most women
    stiff.
She even takes my pipe a bit, and has a friendly whiff!
How far superior is she to women white and wan,
Who faint beneath a sack of meal, their figure quickly gone!

How much above her sisters pale, who give themselves such airs,
And can't sit gently on the grass, but must have stools and
    chairs.'
I placed a kiss upon her brow – 'twas shining yellow, flat,
And had been just anointed with a little strongish fat.

I gave her some tobacco, an inch or two, enough
To last her down to Delgo – when pulverised to snuff.
I shook her hand and kissed her – the storm was really o'er –
I said: 'Go back, dark sister, tap at your parent's door,
And cast yourself upon the mat, and ask forgiveness sweet,
And marry one of your own race – a man in the same street.'
Then shaking her round shiny hand with gentle force again,
I gave her a small locket that was hanging to my chain.

'Take this,' I said, ''twill soothe your heart when in your hut you
    lie,
To open it and look upon my physiognomy.'
For in it just behind a glass (a very natural place)
There was a coloured miniature of my illustrious face.

She raised the locket to her lips, and thanked me with a smile.
I walked to Mac-a-Mac that night, a matter of a mile,
And at my favourite Spotted Dog I stopped to take a wet,
And there the shock I got, I think I never shall forget.

There stood the barman smiling – bland – and I felt as if shot –
My locket hanging to *his* chain – she'd sold it *for a tot!*
Since that unhappy eve, I meet a black and pass her by,
I dimly see, as if I had a half-*caste* in my eye.

But still at times sweet Shu' Shu' my memory will recall –
I wonder if she creeps or walks, I know she has a kraal;
And whether she has dusky sons, who roam the veld and shy –
Or 'hurl their lances at the Sun' – (for 'lance' read 'assegai'.)

Joe's Luck

Pros-pectin' round about one day,
  I saw a little fairy;
Her father's name was Jan Marais,
  Her front name, it was Mary.*

She stood upon the stoep, her face
  With feathers she was fanning,
And showed a lot of colour when
  She watched our first outspanning!

Down where the Aapjes river flows,
  Between its willow fringes,
Just where some quartz makes two queer blows,
  My heart went off its hinges!

I traced the reef right past her door,
  Then in the dip I lost it,
Just where a heap of broken slate
  Like some old school had crossed it.

Her hair was gold, of various sorts,
  I saw *that* in a minute;
Her skin was white as *Tati* quartz,
  With purple veins run in it.

I'd cleaned up for the week, and dressed
  (I do on such occasions);
My general show had what we call –
  'Aurif'rous indications.'

I'd got a pin stuck in my tie,
  I won it at a raffle –
A whip and jockey cap entwined
  With bridle, and a snaffle.

I'd got a chain, of nuggets made;
  I'd got a watch – (a Lever);
In fact, I looked, as Blazes said,
  'A reg'lar Gay Deceiver!'

* It was Saartje, really; only it won't rhyme.

Oh! Lord, I thought, if I can slide
    Into this gal's good graces,
And work her father's reef beside –
    With Kreer I won't change places.

She asked me in. Her Ma was there,
    In silky, black alpakker;
She asked me then to take a chair,
    And coffee, and tobaccer.

I spoke, with rough and reddy tongue,
    Of Gold, while Mary listened;
Of Gold in quarts – for I was young –
    Till both her peepers glistened.

I spoke of most *gigantic* piles –
    And then I gave some figures;
And Mary said with many smiles –
    'Ik heb groot leef voor Diggers.'

That fetched me – what more *could* she say?
    It came so natural, pretty,
(For let a gal try how she may,
    She *never* can be witty).

And then the old Man came, and we
    Made then and there Agreement
To work on halves upon his reef
    (He knew what I meant – *he* meant).

It went five ounces to the ton,
    That reef did, till it slided,
And every week, sure as a gun,
    The profits we divided.

Of course for extrys I went in,
    And first all costs reduced,
For really brains was bound to win,
    And wit did more than luck did.

So then I up and spoke to *her*;
    I said on her I doted –

(In Dutch) she murmured, 'Thank you, Sir.'
    That's how my love was floated!

I kissed her o'er and o'er again;
    She tried to hide her blushing;
I hugged with all my might and main –
    And that was Love's first crushing.

I told her, as a Digger should,
    When I grew sort of 'boulder':
'There ain't no syndicates in love,
    Only one Baas – one holder!

And if she had another chap,
    And if her love – was *not* meant;
She'd better let him join the Board
    'Fore going to allotment.'

We went to Church, and were made one,
    No Man could do it straighter;
The Reverend Mr Constant Dun
    Was our amalgamator.

And if we have a Boy, by Joe!
    Sure as my name is Dixon,
Of all the names that you can show,
    Digg'ry's the one I'll fix on!

(After six months, statuary meeting)

Now when at dinner-time I'm late,
    She gives ten stamps a minute;
Like quicksilver I clear my plate,
    Then her retort comes in it!

EDGAR WALLACE
(1875–1932)

The Song of the Bounder

My father left his English home
On board a Union liner,
With vague ideas that o'er the foam
He'd be a kind of miner,
And though he thought that he'd go forth
To regions wild and merry,
He never got much further north
Than Maitland Cemetery!

    Though there are northern woods to hew
    And northern towns to founder,
    I much prefer the Avenue,
    Since I've become – 'twixt I and you,
    A first-class Cape Town bounder.

At home we always 'grubbed' at one
On mutton hash and sauces,
But now we dine with setting sun
On six or seven courses:
Upon my genealogy
I lecture to the boarders,
And tell them that my ancestry
Were Norman Duke Marauders!

    (If mother only heard me fix
    These yarns, they would astound her,
    For every day from six to six
    My father used to carry bricks
    To help support this bounder.)

In first-class carriages I sit
(A third *was* more the figure),
But thirds out here would only fit
A soldier – or a nigger;

And though I was but Board School bred,
To advertise my knowledge
I always wear upon my head
The colours of the College.

I wear pince-nez upon my nose,
Though sight was never sounder,
But when the wild south-easter blows,
I find I cannot manage those,
I'm but a mortal bounder.

ANON.

A War (?) in the Desert

Afar in the desert I love to ride,
    While the manacled Bush-boy to my stirrup is tied,
Away from the haunts of civilized men;
    Away from the fear of the journalist's pen;
In places remote, where reporters are not,
    And the captured Bechuana may safely be shot.
With my Burgher contingent I daily patrol,
    And search every cranny, every bush, every hole;
And woe to the 'rebel' whose spoor we can trace,
    For we'll treat and maltreat him and spit in his face;
Then his handcuffs are loosened, he's told to 'voetzak,'
    But he's almost immediately shot in the back.

Afar in the desert I love to ride,
    With the captured Bush-boy no more by my side.
O'er the brown burnt veldt, where his pleading cry
    Went up to his Maker so plaintively;
We were deaf to his cries, nor thought it a sin
    To blow him to bits and his skull to smash in.
To see him lie there, a mere human mess,
    Was to us first-class sport, no more, and no less.

Our thirst for the blood of the nigger is strong,
　　And a sharp look-out's kept as we canter along;
Lest by untoward chance we should fail to descry
　　The spot where a possible victim may lie.

At night in the desert I love not to ride,
　　And think of the Bush-boy no more by my side;
Like the fleet-footed ostrich over the waste,
　　I race for the camp, thoughts of spooks make me haste;
I remember the vultures how they wheeled overhead,
　　Greedy to scent and to gaze on the dead.
The fiend-like laugh of hyena grim
　　Seems to say (*pace* Barham), 'That's *him*! That's *him*!'
I shake with dread as the lines I reach,
　　The Bush-boy's cry's in the wild-dogs' screech,
I lie as one dead on the dusty plain,
　　And feel on my forehead the brand of Cain.

Signed 'Gibbet', 'with apologies to Pringle the poet'. Published in No.
50 of the satirical and social weekly, *The Owl* (18 December 1897) in
Cape Town, edited by the redoubtable cartoonist, Mrs C. Penstone,
about whom, in the best tradition of anonymous journalism, little is
known. This is a parody of Pringle's 'Afar in the Desert', the poem
which opens many anthologies of South African English poetry, and
which begins:

> Afar in the Desert I love to ride,
> With the silent Bush-boy alone by my side:
> When the sorrows of life the soul o'ercast,
> And, sick of the Present, I cling to the Past . . .

and continues:

> There is rapture to vault on the champing steed,
> And to bound away with the eagle's speed,
> With the death-fraught firelock in my hand –
> The only law of the Desert Land!

and concludes:

> 'A still small voice' comes through the wild
> (Like a Father consoling his fretful Child),
> Which banishes bitterness, wrath, and fear, –
> Saying – MAN IS DISTANT, BUT GOD IS NEAR!

Stellenbosch

The General 'eard the firin' on the flank,
  An' 'e sent a mounted man to bring 'im back
The silly, pushin' person's name an' rank
  'Oo'd dared to answer Brother Boer's attack.
For there might 'ave been a serious engagement,
  An' 'e might 'ave wasted 'alf a dozen men;
So 'e ordered 'im to stop 'is operations round the kopjes,
  An' 'e told 'im off before the Staff at ten!

      And it all goes into the laundry,
      But it never comes out in the wash,
      'Ow we're sugared about by the old men
      ('Eavy-sterned amateur old men!)
      That 'amper an' 'inder an' scold men
      For fear o' Stellenbosch!

The General 'ad 'produced a great effect,'
  The General 'ad the country cleared – almost;
The General ''ad no reason to expect,'
  And the Boers 'ad us bloomin' well on toast!
For we might 'ave crossed the drift before the twilight,
  Instead o' sitting down an' takin' root;
But we was not allowed, so the Boojers scooped the crowd,
  To the last survivin' bandolier an' boot.

The General saw the farm'ouse in 'is rear,
  With its stoep so nicely shaded from the sun;
Sez 'e, 'I'll pitch my tabernacle 'ere,'
  An' 'e kept us muckin' round till 'e 'ad done.
For 'e might 'ave caught the confluent pneumonia
  From sleepin' in his gaiters in the dew;
So 'e took a book an' dozed while the other columns closed,
  And De Wet's commando out an' trickled through!

The General saw the mountain-range ahead,
  With their 'elios showin' saucy on the 'eight,
So 'e 'eld us to the level ground instead,
  An' telegraphed the Boojers wouldn't fight.
For 'e might 'ave gone an' sprayed 'em with a pompom,
  Or 'e might 'ave slung a squadron out to see —
But 'e wasn't takin' chances in them 'igh an' 'ostile kranzes —
  He was markin' time to earn a K. C. B.

The General got 'is decorations thick
  (The men that backed 'is lies could not complain),
The Staff 'ad D. S. O.'s till we was sick,
  An' the soldier — 'ad the work to do again!
For 'e might 'ave known the District was a 'otbed,
  Instead of 'andin' over, upside-down,
To a man 'oo 'ad to fight 'alf a year to put it right,
  While the General went an' slandered 'im in town!

      An' it all went into the laundry,
      But it never came out in the wash.
      We were sugared about by the old men
      (Panicky, perishin' old men)
      That 'amper an' 'inder an' scold men
      For fear o' Stellenbosch!

Half-ballad of Waterval

      When by the labour of my 'ands
        I've 'elped to pack a transport tight
      With prisoners for foreign lands
        I ain't transported with delight.
        I know it's only just an' right,
          But yet it somehow sickens me,
      For I 'ave learned at Waterval
          The meanin' of captivity.

      Be'ind the pegged barb-wire strands,
        Beneath the tall electric light,
      We used to walk in bare-'ead bands,

94

Explainin' 'ow we lost our fight.
An' that is what they'll do tonight
  Upon the steamer out at sea,
If I 'ave learned at Waterval
  The meanin' of captivity.

They'll never know the shame that brands –
  Black shame no livin' down makes white,
The mockin' from the sentry-stands,
  The women's laugh, the gaoler's spite.
  We are too bloomin' much polite,
    But that is 'ow I'd 'ave us be . . .
Since I 'ave learned at Waterval
  The meanin' of captivity.

They'll get those draggin' days all right,
  Spent as a foreigner commands,
An' 'orrors of the locked-up night,
  With 'Ell's own thinkin' on their 'ands.
  I'd give the gold o' twenty Rands
    (If it was mine) to set 'em free . . .
For I 'ave learned at Waterval
  The meanin' of captivity!

OLIVE SCHREINER
(1855–1920)

The Cry of South Africa

Give back my dead!
They who by kop and fountain
First saw the light upon my rocky breast!
Give back my dead,
The sons who played upon me
When childhood's dews still rested on their heads.
Give back my dead
Whom thou has riven from me

By arms of men loud called from earth's farthest bound
To wet my bosom with my children's blood!
Give back my dead,
The dead who grew up on me!

(Wagenaar's Kraal, Three Sisters, 9 May 1900)

F. W. REITZ
(1844–1934)

The Proclamation, or Paper Bomb
Translated from the Afrikaans by the poet

I undersign'd *Lord Kitchener of Karthoum*
   (For all my other titles there's no room)
In the King's name, at least we call it so,
   But really meaning Chamberlain & Co.,
Hereby proclaim and solemnly declare,
   And this is final – so let all Beware!

Whereas I with a quarter-million men,
Can't beat you, though you're only one to ten,
   And flying columns answer just as well
Or just as little – as a lyddite shell,

Whereas by setting fields and homes a-flame
I have but added to my former shame,
   And catching women really shows no true sense,
Since it has only proved a dreadful nuisance,

Whereas it's now more than a year ago,
Since we annexed you – Roberts did you know –
   Yet, notwithstanding this illegal Fiction,
Where big guns fail there ends my jurisdiction,

Whereas Cape rebels still continue rising
In numbers both alarming and surprising

And Kritzinger with Scheepers and Fouché,
Are causing French so much anxiety,

Whereas the war-costs that we have to pay
Run to a quarter-million pounds per day,
And things have now already gone so far
That even the Funds are falling below par,

Whereas my horses ridden to and fro
But serve to feed the vulture and the crow,
And that in spite of all my plans and schemes,
Ending the war is harder than it seems,

Whereas no other means I can conceive,
Than just to bluster and to make believe,
I have resolved this paper bomb to let off
To try if that perchance may make you 'get off.'

So I proclaim – that if there's any Judas
Who has no wish to go to the Bermudas
Let him lay down his arms – but then remember
The day I fix is Fifteenth of September.

Generals and Officers I hereby warn,
That if they treat these liberal terms with scorn,
Their goods will all be forfeit to the state,
They'll bitterly repent it when too late,

Now therefore come up Burghers one and all
'Tis for the sake of Peace I make this call,
Oh! come to me and then you'll quickly feel
How a Boer's neck fits to a British heel.

Oh! come to me! oh! come and do surrender
Then Chamberlain's hard heart may yet grow tender,
And p'rhaps he'll send you one of his old shoes,
That you may kiss as often as you choose.

Then all men shall the Great Millennium see,
Then Boer and Briton both shall equal be,
The British lion will no longer sham
For he will swallow th' Africander lamb.

Thus given under my own hand – and so
Long Live the King! and long live Pushful Joe!
Signed Kitchener – dated – and to be of use
To be sent under a *Private* flag of *Truce*!

(Athole, 8 October 1901)

The parallel text begins:

Ik *Lord Kitchener van Karthoem*
(Om andere titels niet te noem)
Krachtens machtiging gegeve
Door mij Koning *Etwart zeve*
Maak bekend en proklameer
– D'is nou voor di laaste keer! . . .

ALICE GREENE
(1858–1920)

The Four Roads

A young Dutch lady from one of the midland towns of
Cape Colony said recently to the writer: 'We have had
four sets of executions in our town. They always made
known the sentence on Saturday and carried it out on
Monday. Sunday was a terrible day. A great black cloud
seemed to hang over the town, and at church our hearts
were filled with prayer for the dying men. The executions
were carried out at earliest dawn, before the town was
awake, and the bodies were buried in the four roads
leading out of the town, so that we shall always have to
tread on their heads. The exact spot where they lie is
unmarked in any way, and is never made known.'

Fourie, one of 'the rebels three,' was a farmer of 50,
who was much respected as a good and kind man, and
left behind him a wife and eight children. The youthful
'rebel' of the third execution was said by the authorities
to be 20, but is known to have been only 16, as is proved
by the birth register of his own village.

Four roads lead out of the town,
    And one of them runs to the West,
And there they laid the rebels twain
    With the bullets in their breast.
And the English Commandant laugh'd low,
    As he looked at the sleeping town,
'Each road shall bear its vintage soon,
    And your feet shall tread it down!'

Four roads lead out of the town,
    And one of them runs to the East,
And there they laid the rebels three,
    When their stout hearts' life-beat ceased.
They had looked their last at the bright, bright sun,
    As he rose o'er the eastern hill,
They had prayed their last for the wife and babes
    Who are weeping and praying still.

Four roads lead out of the town,
    And one of them runs to the South,
And there they led the 'rebel bold,'
    With a smile on his gay young mouth.
Sixteen years he had lived on earth
    When they led him forth to die,
And there he lies, with his white young face
    Turned upward to the sky!

Four roads lead out of the town,
    And one of them runs to the North,
And there they led the dying man
    In the Red-Cross wagon forth.
And a bullet has stopped the glorious life,
    And stayed the gallant breath.
And Scheepers lies 'neath the road that leads
    To the land he loved till death.

Four roads lead out of the town,
    And for ever and for aye
Our feet must tread on the noble dead
    Till the trump of the Judgment Day.

But the blood of martyrs is still the seed
    Of the Church that is to be,
And rebel blood still bears the fruit
    Of a nation's Liberty!

Four roads lead out of the town,
    — God's sun shines on them still,
Though our brothers' blood cries from the ground,
    And echoes from hill to hill.
And our hearts cry out to the quiet dead,
    Where they keep safe watch and ward,
'Blest are the dead, the noble dead,
    The dead who die in the Lord!'

(Cape Colony, 17 April 1902)

C. LOUIS LEIPOLDT
(1880–1947)

Oom Gert's Story
Translated from the Afrikaans by C. J. D. Harvey

My boy, what do you think that I can tell you?
You want to hear the story of our death?
All right!
        It never is too late to learn
More about that, if you can use the knowledge,
Especially for you youngsters. Just hold tight
To what we have, stand on your feet and take
Your part in this our nation.
                But you've come
To the wrong man; there must be many others
Who'd tell the story straight, in the right order
And with a moral too, and better grasp
Of all the politics than I could have:
My only knowledge comes out of my soul,

I can delve only into my own heart,
And it is very old and almost dead –
My heart, I mean. Truly, if you yourself
Had been through what I've been through, seen as much,
And struggled as I've struggled – what's more, seen
So many things that you would rather not have –
Your heart would also not be free of cracks.
But come – let's see what I can tell you of.
It's a long story! And a sad one, too,
Shot through with tears and sobs, my boy. All right?
You want to hear it? Good!
                                    But sit, man, sit.
How can I talk while you stay standing up?
Sit there. (And, Gerrie, fetch something to drink!
Your Dad could use a cup of coffee, too.)
Right. Now, you know, my boy, that when our people
Round here were all dumbfounded by the war,
A troop of khakis occupied the town
And 'Martjie Louw', as usual, was proclaimed.
Old Smith, the magistrate – he is a man
For whom I have respect although he's English:
He always acted like a gentleman
And got on with our people very well;
But he was quietly removed from office
And sent off to East London. This because
He wouldn't glibly dance to all their tunes.
And in his place a colonel was appointed,
His name – say Gerrie, now, what was his name?
Jones? No, child, *he* was just an underling,
You know, that ape with chevrons on his sleeve,
Ah! that's it, Wilson, that was the chap's name –
A big, fat bloke with yellow-grey moustaches,
And great, long eye-teeth and a bright red face;
They said he drank; I must say, though, I never
Saw him the worse for drink and don't now want
To slander him behind his back. Although
He was indeed a swine, one must be fair.
He really ground us down; his hand was hard:

We weren't allowed to light the lamps at night,
And had to be indoors by eight o'clock.
He kept us under constant watch and even
Came nosing through our houses to make sure
That none of us were hiding arms or powder,
Cartridges, caps or anything like that.
He thought we had collected stocks of food
In order to supply the Boer Commandos.
Yes, he was hard all right! (Sweetheart, pass back
The sugar, please! Two lumps are not enough:
You know Dad likes his coffee sweet.)
                                        And we
Were all confused and in a state of panic,
And not one of us knew from day to day
What to expect or what was going to happen.
The town was seething with rebellious murmurs,
Like dough in which the yeast has been well kneaded;
You've seen it rise? Well, we were just like that!
Yes, all our people. But, what could we do?
The younger ones, especially, were so restive
That we could hardly keep them all in check,
And, without warning, two of them cut loose.
(Young Klaas's cup is empty again, sweetheart.)

One evening Bennie Berends came to me,
With him was Johnnie Hendriks, old Saarl's son.
They'd skipped across the street so quietly,
The sentry didn't even get a glimpse –
Else Saarl and I would have known all about it!
And had to pay a fine into the bargain! –
Old Saarl and I had always been good friends;
But that same month, alas, he died of cancer –
A cancer of the stomach – God's hand there,
For thus he didn't live to see the day . . .
But wait, I go too fast, we'll come to that.
Yes, I was sitting here in my own chair
And Bennie sat right there where you are now,
And Johnnie there. Yes, I can see him now,

At that time, just an adolescent kid,
Not wholly dry behind the ears, in fact,
Though he'd a pretty sharp tongue in his head.
Confirmed only that year. (Gerrie, my child,
Fetch me the album!) – Here's a snap of him
And this is one of Bennie; that's the line
That his late mother wrote on the day after . . .
After his er . . . er . . . death. You read it, son,
My glasses don't fit well, and in the smoke
I can't see properly. Yes, read it out:
'Barend Gerhardus Berends' – Right! and then?
'Born on the sixth of May' – That's how it goes!
'Ha –' No, shut up the book, I know it all!
(Take it away, please, sweet. Don't stand there frozen
Just like a frightened rabbit. Pour some coffee!
We should have enough milk, and sugar too,
Seeing it isn't 'Martjie Louw' here now!)
Yes, Bennie was a real born gentleman,
My godson, and, though I say it myself,
The sort to be a favourite with the ladies,
With his straight back and smooth, clean-shaven face –
I don't suppose he'd even started shaving.
(Sweetheart, please go and see if Leentjie has
Brought all the wood into the kitchen.)
                                                          Yes,
My boy, he courted Gerrie here, and I
Was not against the match, because he seemed
Cut out for her, somehow – just the right lad.
You see she's still not quite got over it;
But all of us have crosses we must bear,
Yes, even when it seems our hearts must break.
My darling, too, will, with our dear Lord's blessing,
Surmount her sorrow and forget the pain,
However hard it seems, that's how things go,
Though when we talk about him it seems better
To send her out on some pretext or other.
Now where was I?
                              Oh, yes, the night they came

To ask for my advice. Ben's plan was this:
Johnnie and he would make for Witkransspruit,
Where, so they understood, Smuts was encamped
With his commando.
               When they told me this
I nearly fainted. Then I reasoned with them,
But, no!
          Oh, dear, youth is so obstinate!
And Ben was always headstrong: as a child
He often got a whacking just for that!
They had made up their minds and they would go.
I had two horses at my house just then –
The khakis hadn't taken them as yet –
I don't know why, but I can tell you this,
It wasn't my fault that the animals
Just happened to be there, but there they were!
Nonnie, my wife and Gerrie's mother, she
Who died that very year down at Goudini
Of heart disease, but, also, by the war
Broken in soul and body – Nonnie, too,
Added her pleas to mine, but all in vain.
'We can't take any more of this, Oom Gert;
A man must *do* something to aid his nation!'
'Do? Do? Do something! Ach, what can you do?
Or what can any of us do?'
                   In vain.
So Nonnie packed my knapsack full to bursting
With lots of rusks and biltong. As for me
I filled the saddlebags with hard-boiled eggs
And other edibles. For, after all,
He was my godson, and then Johnnie, too,
Was old Saarl's son, and Saarl and I were friends.
So nobody could say I acted wrongly,
Although, it's true, I was a British subject.
Could I stand by and see my own flesh suffer
Whilst I had food? No, I was right, my boy,
And conscience since has never bothered me.
So, in a word, the two were off. Of course,

Next morning the whole mob came swarming round;
The colonel buzzed around us like a horsefly
And swore, and made a fuss, but I stood firm:
It wasn't my fault that the horses were
Still in my garden, and I told him so:
That it was his fault, certainly not mine!
Of course, about the eggs and rusks and biltong,
I thought it better not to mention them!

Don't ask me how we lived through all those months.
A dark cloud seemed continually to hang
Above us, and not just above our town,
But over the whole country, our whole nation.

Then one day came the news . . . (Wait, here she's back. –
Please, sweetheart, chase the chickens off the stoep.
Look at that rooster scratching up the flowers!)
Right, one day came the news – and what a shock!
Johnnie and Ben had both been captured and
Been slapped in gaol. A military court –
You know the rest! And then a further blow:
The sentence was – that both were to be hanged!
And what a dreadful blow, God knows, that was!
We did our best, but all in vain; the rabble
Were shrieking for revenge and they must hang.
That morning the head constable arrived:
'The colonel sends his compliments.' My God,
His compliments! – you hear? You understand?
You understand, boy, *compliments*!
                                        Oh, no,
Be still, be still, my heart, or you'll break too!
Our crosses we must bear whate'er the cost.

And please would I present myself next morning
To see the treatment meted out to rebels,
Otherwise . . . The head constable was human
And certainly was very ill at ease
At having to deliver such a message.
The khakis, too, I must say, behaved well,

But had to do their duty. I was grateful
They did it without added insolence.
The policeman, Nichols, yes, that was his name –
He, later, in the Free State, got a dose
Of lead he couldn't stomach – told me, too,
That others had got similar commands
And there'd be quite a crowd of us to witness
The – you know – at the gaol, and also warned me
I'd better come, however sick I felt!

We didn't sleep that night, Nonnie and I.

Yes, I remember well. The day was cool –
You don't forget a day like that so quickly! –
With just a slight east wind – a little cold –
For it brought on Nonnie's rheumatic pains –
She always suffered quite a lot from them
And never could bear cold. Well, as I said,
The day was cool and so I had my jacket
Well buttoned up. You know I always liked
To have my waistcoat show. What is the point
Of wearing waistcoats if nobody sees them?
However, that day it was really fresh,
And so I had my jacket buttoned up.
Down at the bend there, just below the mill,
I met the others in the early morning,
For, as I said, all of us were commanded.
The minister was there, and Albert Louw –
You know old Cock-eye Louw, Klaas? Yes, of course,
And Michiel Nel, and Gys van Zyl, and Piet –
No, you, of course, wouldn't remember Piet;
He was before your time; but that chap was
As strong as Samson – gee! but he was strong!
And just as restive as a scorpion, too.
But droll, my boy, and one who could laugh even
When clouds were dark and stormy and the thunder
Rumbled among the clouds. I know, of course,
We all of us have faults and I don't really
Hold it against Piet Spaanspek that he always

Had to be making jokes, though all the rest
Of us were feeling queer and sick at heart.
'This wind bites shrewdly, Cousin Gert,' he said,
'You'd better lend your overcoat to Ben
In case the weather's bad upstairs!' He laughed,
But I was glad the minister was there
To reprimand him on the spot, and, neatly,
He put him in his place.
                              'Is this the time
For jokes, Mr Van Ryn?' he asked him coldly.
'For shame! For shame! How dare you say such things
Today, when all our hearts are full, our eyes
Half-dimmed with tears for our beloved country?'
(Sweetheart, do chase those chickens out! They make
The yard so dirty. We can help ourselves.)
But Piet Spaanspek was never at a loss
For words and, not put out, he carried on
His little jokes, although the rest of us
Pretended not to hear and took no notice.
I think he felt as sick at heart as I
But didn't want the rest of us to see.

We walked up to the forecourt of the gaol
And it was full of khakis. At the gates
They made us come in slowly, two by two.
And there in the back yard the gallows stood,
Beside them Ben and Johnnie, hand in hand,
For they were not in chains. We got permission
To go up close to them and talk to them
But only for five minutes.
                              I was speechless,
Completely tongue-tied with embarrassment.
But Bennie took me by the hand and said:
'Oom Gert, it's all up now. Goodbye, Oom Gert!
Just tell Aunt Nonnie, and tell Gerrie – no,
Don't tell them anything, they'll understand.'
And Johnnie also took my hand and said,
A smile around his lips: 'Good morning, Oom.

No, Oompie, don't you cry!' Yes, as I've said,
He always was inclined to be precocious
And cheeky, too. 'No, Oompie, don't you cry!
We did our duty, and it's over now.'

And then they both talked to the minister,
And I, as Bennie's nearest blood relation,
Accompanied him to the gallows, there . . .
No, boy, it's just the smoke. I'm getting old
And your tobacco is too strong for me.
I smoke it mild myself. Because, you see,
It doesn't make my eyes so sore.
                                    Where was I?
Oh yes. Then all of us shook hands with them.
We couldn't speak and even Piet was dumb
And just as sick as I, and one of us –
I don't know who it was – began to sob.
They wanted to pull over Bennie's face
A handkerchief or scarf or something, like
A sort of hood. But Bennie bravely asked,
In English too, yes, he could speak it well –
Whether they couldn't hang him, please, without it?
The colonel nodded; then . . .
                              No, boy, let go!
Why do you grab my hand again? Let go!
Confound it! How can I tell you the story
When you will put me off my stroke like that?
And, blow your smoke out on the other side!
My eyes have got too old for your tobacco.
(Sweetheart, fetch me a handkerchief.)
                                        Well, now,
There's nothing more to tell. We came on home
And here in this same room we all knelt down.
The minister conducted a short service
For us here on our knees – then – it was finished.

That night, though, Cousin Piet and Cock-eye Louw
Left town and set out for the nearest farm,
And afterwards they joined up with our people.

(Sweetheart, just pass me back the sugar-bowl,
And pour another cup for Cousin Klaas!)

Translator's notes: 'Although oom is the ordinary Afrikaans word for
uncle, there is really no English equivalent for its use as a familiar yet
respectful title for any older man. Oompie, the diminutive, is somewhat
disrespectful. Martjie Louw is the colloquial term for martial law.'

PERCEVAL GIBBON
(1878–1926)

Mooimeisjes

I mind me of a morning while the mountains yet were grey,
And the fetlocks of our horses splashed in dew along the way,
Ere the sun was in the saddle for the half-way house of day,
    And we rode to Mooimeisjes in the morning.

There was Jim and I and Kafir Jack and all the other boys,
And we waked the kloofs in echo to our laughter and our noise,
For we sloughed the cares of living as we doffed our corduroys,
    To ride to Mooimeisjes in the morning.

Oh, the little sun-swamped hollow where the little village lay!
Mooimeisjes, where we are gathered, workers all, to take our
    play;
And it lent its patch of purple to our leaden everyday,
    When we rode to Mooimeisjes in the morning.

But I mind me of a morning that was misty-like and drear,
When the earth was sick with sadness, and there droned upon
    the ear
The rumble and the thunder of the gun-wheels in the rear,
    As we rode to Mooimeisjes in the morning.

There was Jim and I and Kafir Jack and each one did his share,
Till we saw the rooftrees blazing where our gentle memories were;
And I know, despite our handiwork, our hearts were over there,
    With crippled Mooimeisjes in the morning.

An Answer

Yesterday you had a song
I could not but choose but hear,
'Twas *Oh, to be in England
Now that April's there!*
But I have found a new refrain
I cannot choose but sing,
'Tis *Oh, to be in Africa
Now Summer's on the wing!*

Yesterday we languished
For loaded boughs of may,
And largesse of the hawthorn
That April flings away;
But foundering in the sunset,
To watch the kopjes melt,
And see the wacht-a-bitje bloom
That gleams across the veldt.

Yesterday we yearned for
The breath of English fields,
The note of life triumphant
That English April yields.
But I've a longing for the kloofs
Where red-plumed aloes stand,
And calling to my heart I hear
My Foster-Mother-Land.

(1903)

IAN D. COLVIN
(1877–1938)

The Flying Dutchman

When they sailed out of Amsterdam
'Twas Christmastide, and now 'twas June;

For seven long weeks they had not seen
   Nor any star, nor sun nor moon.

When they put out of Amsterdam
   A hundred women waved goodbye;
Now scarce two score could handle a rope,
   The others were dead or like to die.

The watch lay on the after deck,
   Longing amain for the night to pass.
'Oh, would that we might make the Cape!
   Our very bones yearn for the scurvy grass.'

Their eyes glowered out like fire from a pit,
   They scarcely looked like mortal men.
'If I press my fingers into my skin,'
   Said one, 'it will not rise again.'

'My flesh is sodden like salted meat,'
   Another said, 'See that running sore!
'Tis black and livid a span around,
   'Twas a little scratch that a handspike tore.'

They were beating up against the wind,
   With the great seas smashing under the prow.
'I fear me much,' the Captain said,
   'The timbers will start at the weather bow.'

'Oh, Van der Decken,' the boatswain cried,
   'With this contrary wind we make no speed.
When all things fail, I have heard men say
   That a prayer is good in the hour of need.'

Old Van der Decken looked stark and black.
   He said: 'I know not how that may be;
I have sailed with Masters that sang and prayed,
   But they never did good that I could see.

'I have seen men pray in the Church at home,
   Fat and black like penguins they stood;
They had everything that their hearts could wish,
   But they whined by the hour for their daily food.

'If I had been master of such a crew,
 I'd 'a laid about with a stout rope's end.
If a man is a man he will stand and take
 With a laugh or a curse what God may send.'

But the boatswain rose and prayed aloud,
 And the men all struggled upon their knees.
'Oh, God, make an end of storm and cloud!
 Let the stars shine out and the tempest cease!'

As he prayed a squall came along the sea,
 And struck the ship like an open hand.
The topmast split and swung by the shrouds,
 Like the broken top of a fishing wand.

And a racing wave came over the ship,
 From the poop to the bows there was nothing seen
But the white sea washing round the masts.
 There were twelve men now where a score had been.

The good ship staggered and stopped awhile,
 And then she rose and shook herself free.
'All hands on deck,' the Master cried,
 'To cut the wreckage into the sea.

'See now how your prayer has served, ye fools!
 To swear in fine weather and pray in a gale
Is a coward's game that God sees through.
 Never tempest was brewed that would make me quail.

'A curse is as good as a prayer they say;
 Now hear, Oh God, now mark me well!
I'll bring this good ship into the Bay
 In spite of the power of heaven and hell!'

Then the clouds were drawn from off the sky,
 As a fisherman draws his net from the sea.
Lo, the dawn had broken! Lo, and was nigh!
 And the waves were sparkling merrily.

'See the long black mountain round the Bay!
 See Van Riebeeck's fort and his garden green!

Now, listen, I hear a pealing bell,
'Tis the holy Sabbath morn I ween.

'And look, the folk are going to the Church!
What think ye men, have I brought ye in?'
The boatswain clutched the Master's arm,
'Now Christ forgive us for our sin!'

'Why look ye strange?' the Master cried;
'Why cover your eyes like a man struck blind?'
'Look, look, how the square sails bear on the mast!
God's wounds! We are sailing against the wind!'

The ship was sailing out to sea,
The wind was blowing upon the land;
'Now, bring her round,' cried Van der Decken.
She heeded not the helmsman's hand.

Now the gardens green were far away,
And faintlier sounded the Sabbath bell;
Never a word the mariners spoke,
As one by one on the deck they fell.

And still in the storm, as sailors say, –
Sere and worn and white as a bone,
The phantom ship drives against the gale,
And an old man stands on her poop – alone.

Tristan da Cunha

Living in honesty, sobriety and harmony, free apparently
from all crime, vice, dissension or double-dealing, they
seem to have unconsciously carried out the purpose
entertained by the original settler in 1811, Mr Jonathan
Lambert, by keeping themselves 'beyond the reach of
chicanery and ordinary misfortune'; but they must also
have lost the instincts of suspicion and circumspection,
which, unfortunately in less-favoured countries, are

necessary in order to carry on successfully the struggle for
existence.
— *Mr Hammond Tooke's Report on Tristan da Cunha,*
1904

I'm tired of town and suburb life,
　　Of sermons dull and dinners witty,
I loathe the bustle and the strife
　　And strain of this infernal city —
The bolted breakfast and the run,
　　The morning trains, the evening papers,
The listening when the day is done
　　To Mrs Rip van Winkle's vapours.

What matters that the sea is blue,
　　What skills it that the sun is shining,
I only know that bills are due,
　　That trade is dull and stock declining,
And if I breathe the word 'advance,'
　　Or overdraft I dare to mention,
My bankers look at me askance,
　　Or feign abstracted inattention.

But sometimes when a good cigar
　　Has charmed my fancy into dreaming,
I see a little isle afar,
　　In sparkling sea and sunshine gleaming.
Tristan da Cunha! Had I wings
　　Like the proverbial dove's, I'd hurry
To thee, where life has got no stings
　　And duns and debtors do not worry.

There (*vide* Mr Hammond Tooke),
　　The people live in peace together,
Their sermon is the running brook,
　　Their sole anxiety the weather;
Their only altar — to the sky
　　The hearths smoke upward like a censer,
Their only law the family tie,
　　As taught by Mr Herbert Spencer.

For if there ever are disputes
    Amongst this happy little nation,
They never think of bringing suits,
    But settle them by arbitration;
And if a whale is washed ashore
    They do not fight about the blubber,
But pool it in the general store,
    So no one loses in the rubber.

In politics this pleasant place
    Has got no Merriman or Sauer;
There are no jealousies of race,
    There is no rivalry for power;
There argument is not abuse,
    Nor obstinacy resolution;
For treason they have no excuse –
    You see they've got no constitution.

They dress exactly as they please,
    Flannels are *de rigueur* on Sunday;
And lovers wander at their ease,
    Without a thought of Mrs Grundy,
For spite and slander are not known,
    And no one thinks of asking whether
There's an attendant chaperone
    When Jack and Jill go out together.

There gossips are not heard to say
    That 'Mr Brown is blind and stupid,
Or he would surely see the way
    His wife goes on with Captain Cupid.'
There ladies do not draw aside
    And murmur with an air of mystery:
'You see that person on the ride,
    Hers is a sad and shocking history.'

There charity is not for show,
    And friendship does not rest on money,
And there the people do not know
    The art of catching flies with honey;

They have no Ghibeline nor Guelf,
    Nor class nor clique nor clan nor party;
Their welcome's simply for yourself,
    And 'tis invariably hearty.

I see thy cliffs, thy shining sand,
    Thy long fields sloping to the ocean!
O, happy people, happy land,
    Far from the world's insane commotion!
Thy seabirds wheel, thy grey rocks gleam
    Soft as the shades of evening falling –
Am I awake, or do I dream? –
    Yes, yes, my dear, I hear you calling!

JOHN RUNCIE
(?1864–1939)

A Slumber Song of the Gardens

I'se gwine home to Dixie,
I'se gwine no more to wander.
    – Old plantation ditty

Soft haze upon the mountain and a haze upon the sea,
    High noon above the Gardens and shadows on the way;
And twenty weary people slipping out of time awee, –
    Out of time and out of trouble, on a hot midsummer's day.
Blow softly, silver trumpets, in a fairy serenade,
Ye lilies of St Joseph, swinging lightly overhead.

In the shadows of the Gardens the wearied come to rest,
    In the spacious dusk and quiet the fevered blood is stilled;
While sleep, on tiptoe stepping, lays aside the hopeless quest,
    Takes away the fag of travel and the promise unfulfilled;
In white and gold and purple the wondrous petals gleam;
In white and gold and purple is the wondrous slope of dream.

Here be ever Jew and Gentile, Briton, German, Dago, Pole, –
   Mostly young and mostly reckless, some unkempt or
      liquor-stained;
Here and there a grizzled hobo, or bepainted, draggled troll;
   Here and there an eager seeker for the labour yet ungained;
Not alone for rank or station may Titania's maidens bring
Happy dreams of happy Dixie to the people slumbering.

Here's a lad – and ne'er a razor licked the smoothness of his
      chin, –
   Curly-headed, slim and supple, coiled within a corner seat,
Worn at heel, and frayed at elbow, blistered foot, and roughened
      skin –
   God! how far we have to wander for a little bread to eat!
Puck, who puts on mortal eyelids filmy cobwebs, – hither, quick!
Take the boy across the water, he is ill or mammy-sick.

Fires of life among your ashes, what have ye to give or gain,
   In that haggard shell and ancient, snoring on with mouth
      agape?
What among your outworn pleasures hold ye now, and what
      remain
   Heartsome still, – a rank old cutty and a little juice of grape?
Still, with these a man may travel to the last foot-weary mile,
Halting for a dream of Dixie in the Garden depths awhile.

In the mine's untrammelled shanty or Johannesburg caboose
   O'er the cards and vicious whisky, men may query in a jest,
How she struck the trail to Cape Town in her paint and
      lacquered shoes,
   With her skirt's pathetic draggle, hopeless, weary like the rest.
Here, within the pure bright Gardens, let the fairy folk undo
What the mortal folk have made her, for a blissful hour or two.

Evermore through sun and shadow wefting down upon the grass,
   Take the dreamers back to Dixie – wheresoever that may be, –
To the lost hearth and the mother, to the lost youth and the lass,
   Over all the plains and mountains, over all the leagues of sea:
All roads but lead to quiet, though the heat and noise be long, –
Grace for the sleepers, by your leave, and this their slumber song!

KINGSLEY FAIRBRIDGE
(1885–1924)

—————— ~ ——————

Magwere, Who Waits Wondering

I

Among the smooth hills of Manika,
Near the edge of the big swamp where cane rats live,
Grew Magwere the mealie.

The crows who nest on the Peak,
And the striped field-mice from underground,
And the thin-nosed shrew that dies on footpaths,
Had miss'd Magwere when she was sown.

Therefore the mealie grew
In the moist earth on the swamp edge
With many of her sisters;

And threw up gay leaves, yellow-green,
That glitter'd brightly in the sunshine,
And always laugh'd when the wind blew,
And lisp'd, day long, in the ears of her sisters.

And Madongwe, the red locusts,
Found not the green leaves of Magwere,
Who flourish'd on the swamp edge.

Kwagudu, the old wife, with her hoe
That was worn blunt-nosed with use,
Weeded all day the fields of her husband,
And hoed the weeds from the roots of Magwere.

And Wanaka, the young mother,
Left her baby in the shade of Magwere,
While she pick'd mowa for the pot.

And the fat baby laugh'd greatly
At the green leaves that waved so, –
So gaily in the cool wind
That set all the mealies a-rustling.

II

But Dzua the Sun, who lives beyond the sky line,
Laugh'd in the sky, and sent words by the wind,
And the Wind whisper'd in the ear of Magwere.

'O Magwere,' the Wind said, 'thus says the Sun: –
"Ha, ha, Magwere, by the swamp edge!
Smile now, Magwere, while you can,
For the time of harvest is very close.

"Then will your flowers die, Magwere,
Your brown leaves sing only of death,
And your shiny beard will wither and turn brown.

"Madzua Nipi, or some other maiden,
Hot and hard-handed, from the kraal,
Will pluck you from your stalk, and tear your sheath
That hides the softness of your golden grain.

"What will Madzua Nipi do with you?
Roast you upon the coals, and shred your grains
Into her hand, and throw them in her mouth!

"Or will Marumi come, the husbandman,
Saying, 'This cob is good,' – and put you by
To sleep awhile and wake again in Spring,
To blossom gloriously an hundred-fold?"'

III

Magwere answer'd nothing, standing still
And very rigid in the mocking sun;
And knew not any answer for the wind.

And very dry her leaves grew in the sun,
And very brown her stalk, her sheath, and beard;
And all her joy drew back into her heart
That swell'd so sorrowful beneath its sheath.

South African Exhibition, 1907

Here in the middle of London,
Here on the heart of the world
Grey hang the skies in smoke-wreath
And the sun sinks fog-enfurl'd;
Without is the slush and the traffic –
Within, for an hour or two,
Is the sun on the aloed kopje
And the sweep of the great Karroo.

Here is the toil of the winepress,
And the golden yield of the Rand;
The golden fruit of the cornfield,
And the fruit of the orchard-land;
The baled white snow of Rhodesia,
The baled grey snow of the Cape;
The sheen of the piled karosses
And the purple glow of the grape.

Here, cheek by jowl with locusts
(Red flame-dried food of the wild)
Is the price of a dozen princes
In the size of the hand of a child;
And here by the priceless feathers
Gold-chased for the hand of a Queen
Are the bark of the wild mimosa
And Boer-wrought cloth-stuffs seen.

Fibre of ramie and buckhorn
At 'thirty seven a ton';
Pines from Natal and the coastline,
And forage still warm with the sun;
Coal from Dundee and the Wankies,
Tobacco and mealies and soil;
Silk, and asbestos sheeting,
From the worm and the workman's toil.

Yea, there is wealth in Ophir;
But here is a greater sign

Than the mere gain of the gold-reef
Or the mere fruit of the vine:
For Briton and Boer are brothers
(With the yield of their toiling hand)
In the fear of a Common Peril,
And the love of a common land.

For a brother is good to a brother,
He sees the fault but allows;
And the hate dies with the gun-smoke,
And the love grows with the ploughs.
And mightier ties are bounden,
And keener efforts spring,
When the fruit of his toil is honour'd
At the hands of the Human King.

WILLIAM ELIJAH HUNTER
(1839–1913)

Monologue in a Rand Hospital

Poor chum, dear chum, so here you lie at rest,
In the same bed where by my side you watched
When the fierce fever brought me nigh to death.
The tools have fallen from your listless hands,
Your shift is done, and in the weltering mine
Another takes your place. – How quiet it is,
Shut in from all the tumult of the Rand.
The nurses pass like shadows silently
From bed to bed, oft lingering here and there
To smooth a pillow or to catch a word,
Whispered by dying lips for their beloved,
In rugged cottages far off, where breaks
On Cornwall's coast the vast Atlantic wave.
Thanks, nurse, I shall be going soon! But yet,
If not against the rule, a little while
I'd hold his hand remembering other days;

Chiefly that day when on a mound of slain
We lay in touch upon Tugela's bank,
And words of cheer and comfort passed along
To comrades helpless as ourselves. At length
Swooning I heard a voice, 'He looks like dead,
But yet he bleeds. I do not like to pry
Into a dead man's secrets, though a foe's,
But he may have a mother or a friend
To whom 'twould bring some comfort just to know
He died in honour, foremost at the pits
Where we had lain in wait, as in old times
For lions. Turn out his pockets! Matches, pipe,
A letter, that may tell us who he is.
Stephanus you can English read, read out.'
Here is the letter that Stephanus read,
Please fold Jack's hands around it at the last,
So Heaven may succour him as did the Boers.
'Dear Jack, I have not heard from you for months,
Not since you landed safely at the Cape;
And you remember how you promised me
No week should pass without at least a line.
And now the weeks run on, and no line comes,
Though never day dawns but I pray for one;
Doubtless from victory to victory
You pass by marches long and wearisome;
And in the fountain-pen I filled, the ink
Is long since dry, 'neath Afric's burning sun.
But O my boy, remember our last words,
Sealed with that lingering kiss; abstain from drink,
And in the hour of triumph and hot blood
Respect the captive women, and keep bright
Their honour and your own,
And to the children act a brother's part,
So God will bless you and your mother too.'
No more Stephanus read; the commandant
Held up his hand, as I have heard, and cried:
'Enough! Enough!
The man with such a mother shall be saved

If we can save him. Feel his heart. It beats!
Plug up the gash and bear him to my tent.
My doctor shall attend him.' All that day
And half next night I lay in agony
Of thirst, then over us a black cloud rose
And broke; it seemed all heaven came down in rain,
And ever and anon the lightning fell,
Fell red and staggering like a wounded thing,
And all the horror of the field lay bare
In sudden flame where raging torrents swept
The dead and dying to the Indian Sea;
Then the great storm was shattered in a crash
Of thunder, and from cloudless skies the night
Held forth a shining cross of silver stars.
Day dawned, a British ambulance drew near,
And I remember clearly nothing more
Of all that followed while dark months stole by.
At last I woke to consciousness and knew
Myself on ship-board, homeward bound, unfit
For active service. – Yes, and there was Jack!
Of whom no single thought had come to me
Since we in blood lay side by side athirst
Upon Tugela's awful bank, and saw
The bounteous river sweeping on and on,
The bounteous river that we could not reach.
The commandant had kept his word, and proved
A man of men, full of humanity
From rough brown schoon to crown of his slouched hat.
He nourished Jack as if a household guest,
And when his wounds at length were fully healed
Passed him in safety into Buller's camp.
But there the fever that repulsed returns
Came on him, and he too was shipped for home,
But found no home. The village churchyard held
All that had loved him, all that he had loved.
Amongst the fisher-folk some friends were mine
Who gave us shelter 'neath their roof awhile,
Till one June morning in my pulsing veins,

At a canary's loud glad-hearted song,
The tide of life surged back exultingly.
English and Dutch had now again joined hands,
The great Boer War was ended, and we yearned
For brighter skies, the veld,
And freedom from the narrow ways, shut in
By walls and gates a poor man may not pass.
A speedy voyage and the Cape was reached,
And then the Golden Reef,
Where ten long years we laboured in the mines
And shared our luck. But now I work alone.
Why should a man work on, just for work's sake,
When none of all he loved or cared for lives
To share its fruits? – My time is past long since
And you stand waiting at the door! Good nurse,
I did not know that you had left the ward,
And I was merely talking to myself.
God bless this house and you! – The funeral,
Tomorrow, half past nine? Yes, I'll be here.

BEATRICE HASTINGS
(1879–1943)

Mind Pictures

A brown-skinned boy asleep beneath a clump
Of red-spiked aloe, red the flower;
   A mighty stream, moon-flooded, meeting ocean
   Between two crags which box the encounter
   Of the majestic waters.
What other have I seen in instant flashes?
A woman fleeing, shaking off the shame
Of the hounding dorp, trusting to alien aid,
Fleeing the pointing of the district finger;
   A beggar, catching shell-fish from a rock,
   With nought for all the world to covet,
Nor kith nor kin nor ox nor ass nor anything.

ISAAC ROSENBERG
(1890–1918)

On Receiving News of the War

Snow is a strange white word.
No ice or frost
Has asked of bud or bird
For Winter's cost.

Yet ice and frost and snow
From earth to sky
This Summer land doth know.
No man knows why.

In all men's hearts it is.
Some spirit old
Hath turned with malign kiss
Our lives to mould.

Red fangs have torn His face.
God's blood is shed.
He mourns from His lone place
His children dead.

O! ancient crimson curse!
Corrode, consume.
Give back this universe
Its pristine bloom.

(Cape Town, 1914)

The Lord's Prayer
Literal translation by Sol T. Plaatje (1916)

Prayer of-Lord
Father our, he-who is at-the-height, name Thy let-it-be-sanctified. Reign Thy let-it-come. Will Thy let-it-be-done, down-here on-earth as at-the-height. Give us today food our of-days all. Forgive-us faults our, as we-forgive those who-have faults towards-us. Draw-us-not into-temptation; but deliver-us from-wickedness. Because thine is reign, and power, and brilliance, with being-without end.

SAMUEL CRON CRONWRIGHT
(1863–1936)

A Song of the Wagon-whip

The great buck-wagon, our 'desert ship',
With its four-ton heavy load,
And its rooi-bont span and the Wagon-Whip,
Is coming along the road,
With its whip-stick light from the bamboo-brake,
Where the eyes of the tiger gleam,
And its whirling lash from the thick tough hide
Of the sea-cow by the stream.

In Indian thicket the whip-stick grew, where the Bengal tigers
prowl,
And the hooded cobra with angry hiss startles the jungle fowl;
Where the elephant crashes through steam-hot brakes rose the
springy, light bamboo:
It was cut and shipped for the Wagon-Whip to startle the wild
Karoo.

The lash was a length of the sea-cow's hide by the broad
    Limpopo stream,
Or where Zambesi breaks in foam o'er its great white falls
    agleam;
And the hardy Boer from the two-inch hide of the river-horse cut
    the strip,
And brei'd and rolled and hammered it round to make the
    Wagon-Whip.

The agterslag tough and the voorslag keen came from the royal
    koodoo,
With his glorious lyred horns laid back as he bounded the forest
    through;
But the hunter's deadly eye ran up the levelled, rifled gun –
And the antelope's hide was brei'd and stryk'd, and the
    Wagon-Whip was done.

Stand up! South Africa's son, with the Whip; stand up, if your
    arms be strong!
Toss up the snaky length in the blue; uncurl the writhing thong!
With foot advanced, swing up your arms; let the voorslag's
    crack resound,
Till the hills of Howison's Poort give back the echoing, rolling
    sound.

As adown the pass the wagon glides, let the Whip with its
    lightning crack,
Startle the buck from its lair in the kloof, while the baboons
    'borchem' back!
Let the rooi span trek as the voorslag's tongue is guiding the
    'desert ship',
And the pioneer comes with the heralding voice of the mighty
    Wagon-Whip.

Cronwright's prefatory note of 1922 reads: 'The lore of the transport
"bok-wa" (buck-wagon) is almost wholly in Afrikaans, as indeed might
be expected. Away from the coast there is hardly a town which this
"ship of the desert" has not helped largely to build up, feed and
populate. It was twenty-one feet long, its load was eight thousand
pounds, and it was pulled by a span of sixteen oxen, often of one colour.
What spans they were in the old "karwei" (transport) days! The

wagon-whip must have been some forty feet long over all – a beautiful weapon. It was a bit heavy, it required aptitude and practice, and not every man could even clap it; but, in a master's hands, it was a wonder; and it had a crack like the old muzzle-loading rifle ("roer"). When the oxen were outspanned at the end of the trek, the "leier" (leader, a boy who held the "voor-tou", the looped riem of the two front oxen) used to take them to graze; when it was time to inspan, the driver took the great whip and sent forth its reverberating signal, shot after shot, to "call the cattle home", however far away they might be. It was a favourite practice of the driver (often a Kafir: what lovers of cattle they are!) to lag a few yards behind when the back-wheels were "rem'd" (prevented from revolving by the "remschoen", a kind of grappling-iron: thus the verse speaks of the wagon "gliding") and clap the whip down the steep mountain sides, often to the accompaniment of a stentorian, joyous shout of his own, to awake the rolling echoes.'

FRANCIS CAREY SLATER
(1876–1958)

The Songless Land

How oft 'tis said, 'this is a songless Land.'
Song is not lacking – though blind and deaf neglect
And dumb indifference serve to stifle it.
Homely were Helen to a purblind lover,
And dull the Sirens' singing to deaf ears:
Thus those, who neither see nor hear, are dumb
In praise of those who can both hear and see.

Our heroes in this so-called songless Land
Are politicians, slim, sly criminals,
Prize-winning bulls, and sturdy footballers.
Portraits of these adorn our daily news-sheets:
But which are politicians, which criminals,
And which proud bulls, which brawny footballers
'Tis sometimes difficult to discriminate.

Stars in Sand

Sometimes I recall how, in the early eighteen-eighties,
Visiting farmers, while smoking, talked much about diamonds.
Thus the exciting talk of diamonds and the Diamond Fields
Frequently displaced such old familiar topics
As drought-ruined crops, the falling price of ostrich feathers,
Horse-sickness, stolen sheep, and some new disease in cattle.
In those far days I was a small but sturdy youngster,
Of an inquiring mind, wide open eyes and ears
And, maybe, mouth as well: so all this entrancing talk
Infected me with that terrible taint — diamond fever!

Diamonds at Kimberley! Why not diamonds on our farm,
    thought I!
So, spurred by splendid hope, I set out on one fine morning —
Armed with a rickety spade and a rust-rouged paraffin tin —
To a ravine near-by in search of a new Golconda.
In the ravine a sequence of glimmering pools —
Each estranged from its sister-pool by a reef of blue rock
Or a tawny-tinted sand-bank — met with silent disdain
My uncivil intrusion.
                        The pools were skirted and roofed
By evergreen trees of varied leafage and shape;
Some gladdened with blossom were haunted by birds and bees:
Sunbirds, outshining the tree-tangled wefts of a rainbow,
Busily stirred in the blooms — ruby breast to pink bird —
Digging their curved and delicate bills into the hidden
Depths of each blossom, those ardent diminutive miners
Gaily drew out the diamonds they avidly longed for —
Drops of bright honey — seekers who *found* were the birds.

But never so lucky was I, for although in my battered
And rusty old tin I sluiced, with eager persistence,
Handfuls and handfuls of sand, no glint of a gem did I see.
Sadly then did I learn that even as those diamonds, the stars,
In the vast mines of the sky are unattainable ever,
So were the stars I sought in the barren sands of the kloof.
No intuition had I, in those days, now mournfully distant,

That I was fated to be throughout all my lifetime a seeker –
Seeking ever for stars in the silent precipitate sands
Slipping ever remorselessly through my reluctant hands –
Seeking, yes, ever seeking for stars in escaping sands.

ROY CAMPBELL
(1901–57)

The Wayzgoose, Part I (1928)

Attend my fable if your ears be clean,
In fair Banana Land we lay our scene –
South Africa, renowned both far and wide
For politics and little else beside:
Where, having torn the land with shot and shell,
Our sturdy pioneers as farmers dwell,
And, 'twixt the hours of strenuous sleep, relax
To shear the fleeces or to fleece the blacks:
Where every year a fruitful increase bears
Of pumpkins, cattle, sheep, and millionaires –
A clime so prosperous both to men and kine
That which were which a sage could scarce define;[1]
Where fat white sheep upon the mountains bleat
And fatter politicians in the street;
Where lemons hang like yellow moons ashine
And grapes the size of apples load the vine;
Where apples to the weight of pumpkins go
And donkeys to the height of statesmen grow,
Where trouts the size of salmon throng the creeks
And worms the size of magistrates – the beaks;
Where the precocious tadpole, from his bog,
Becomes a journalist ere half a frog;
Where every shrimp his proud career may carve
And only brain and muscle have to starve.
The 'garden colony' they call our land,
And surely for a garden it was planned:

1. Example – 'Wanted: a good short-horn typist', S. A. paper.

What apter phrase with such a place could cope
Where vegetation has so fine a scope,
Where *weeds* in such variety are found
And all the rarest *parasites* abound,
Where pumpkins to professors are promoted
And turnips into Parliament are voted?
Where else do men by vegetating vie
And run to seed so long before they die?
In Eden long ere colonies took root
Knowledge was first delivered from a Fruit,
All Sciences from one poor Tree begin
And have a vegetable origin,
And to this day, as I have often seen,
It is accounted learned to be *green*.
What wonder then if fruits should still be found
Purveying wisdom to the world around.
What wonder if, assuming portly airs,
Beetroots should sit in editorial chairs,
Or any cabbage win the critics' praise
Who wears his own green leaves instead of bays!
What wonder then if, as the ages pass,
Our universities, with domes of glass,
Should to a higher charter prove their claims
And be exalted to tomato-frames,
Whose crystal roofs should hatch with genial ray
A hundred mushroom poets every day;
Where Brussels scientists should hourly sprout
And little shrubs as sages burgeon out;
Where odes from beds of guano should be sprung
And new philosophies from horses' dung?
Wisdom in stones some reverend poet found,
But here it is as common as the ground –
Behold our Vegetable Athens rise
Where all the *acres* in the Land are *wise*!

The Rising Sunset brightened on the scene
Somewhere around the coast of Karridene –
Seldom do suns such striking talent show

As when they set Natalian woods aglow,
And surely from the stir that this one made
He might have been a student at the Slade –
Save for his lack of frame and awkward size
He might have won the Gundelfinger Prize:[2]
A hundred guineas would have been his glow worth
Had it been signed by Goodman or by Roworth.[3]
Around him swam the mists of orange tint
And little cloudlets of boracic lint,
Beneath him puffed the waves (the tide was full)
As if they had been made of cotton-wool.
Never has dawned since Durban was a city
A sun so realistic or so pretty,
And now through mists that simmered with the dawn
His hard-boiled face had reddened like a prawn:
Beneath, the wild bananas waved about
And from the woods uprose a joyful shout –
For here, the fauns and dryads of the scene,
Did all the Learned of the Land convene
To solemnize with many a graceful rite
That sacred festival the Wayzgoose hight.[4]
Hither had flocked, with cushions and with tents,
The hoary prophets of Today's Events;
Behind them thronged the squadrons of the Press,
And many a doughty wight, in times of stress,
Whose typewriter like any maxim-gun
Had crackled deadly insults at 'the Hun':
Two Art Academies arrived in troops
And Durban sent its literary 'groups' –
All who upon the wings of 'uplift' rise

2. The Gundelfinger Prize is awarded annually to the most successful
   'painter' in Natal.
3. Two local popular painters.
4. This phenomenon occurs annually in South Africa. It appears to be a
   vast corroboree of journalists, and to judge from their own reports
   of it, it combines the functions of a bun-fight, an Eisteddfod and an
   Olympic contest. The Wayzgoose of this poem, however, is not only
   attended by those who celebrate the function *annually*, but by all the
   swarms of would-be poets, novelists, philosophers, etc., in South
   Africa, who should all be compelled to attend such functions *daily*.

To boost colonial culture to the skies,
All whom their own sarcastic fates pursue
To write for *Voorslag* or the *S. A. Q.* –
Statesmen-philosophers with earnest souls,
Whose lofty theories embrace the Poles,
Yet only prove their minds are full of Holes,[5]
And public orators, each one of whom
Had talked both Boer and Briton to their doom,
And slain, the feat of Samson to surpass,
Whole thousands with the jawbone of an ass –
The pale blue Naiads from their streams of ink
With pale blue stockings, such as never shrink,
With pale blue spectacles and pale blue stays,
And pale blue insight into human ways –
Nymphs of the novel, pert and picturesque,
And wooden hamadryads of the desk –
All these came flocking to the scene, and more
Whom to describe would only be a bore;
But this is true – deny it he who dare! –
That all the Lions of the Press were there.
They came grey-trousered, and they came tweed-capped,
And brought their food in their own writings wrapped:
Here Wodson's saws, transparent in the grease,
Wrapped a fat fowl with many a tasteful crease;
Here a whole *Mercury* with ample sheaf
Served as the trouser to a leg of beef;
And there 'Sundowner's' wit, turned outside in,
Served as the puttee to a turkey's shin –
Alas for 'Idler's' sayings, wise and neat,
Each for some sausage was the winding sheet!
'Words of the Wise' the yellow mustard stained,
'Temperance Notes' with beery froth were veined.
'Art Causeries' were littered far and near,
And 'Wesleyan Items' soaked in lager beer.
Rivers of gravy irrigate the sheet
That lately glowed with patriotic heat;
Here mental food with physical was pent

5. See *Holism and Evolution*, by General J. Smuts.

And mayonnaise with criticism blent.
With busy hands, in their own jokes and puns,
Their wives had wrapped the biscuits and the buns;
Blue-bottles, unabashed by Russel's rage,
Here skate in graceful circles o'er his page;
Over his text they skim with motions fleet,
Upon his climaxes they wipe their feet,
And here and there they pause – punctilious flies! –
To punctuate his text and dot his I's.
Under their fairy-gliding feet, in vain
The loud infinitive may split in twain –
They link the missing parts with greasy spoor
And prepositions to the verb restore.
Through mixing metaphors still unperplexed,
Betwixt colliding arguments, unvexed,
They weave their tracks, their hieroglyphs they score,
And leave it less a muddle than before!
But one poor cockroach halts with doleful mien,
Caught by 'Vermilion's' catchy style between
Two sentences of labyrinthine gyre,
And seems the way of exit to inquire:
Poor beast! in vain your hairy legs you hitch,
In vain your sensitive antennae twitch –
A vast abyss on either side is gapped:
Like Theseus in the Cretan mazes trapped,
Think you this awful darkness to escape
That never deviates into form or shape?
But stay! a rescuing fly with slender clue
Speeds to his aid like Ariadne true,
Unravelling a sinuous trail of germs
Along whose tracks the wretch to safety squirms.
Here good advice in anchovy is drenched
And patriotic fire in gravy quenched;
Here racialism in a martial ballad,
Spattered with oil, is turned into a salad;
And o'er some sad obituary, here,
The battered orange sheds an amber tear –

Such chaos lay for many acres round
And reams of greasy paper strewed the ground.

Storms in a teapot often have occurred,
But teapots in a storm are rarely heard;
Yet here, behold, a teapot they produce
Wrapped in a storm of scurrilous abuse
Levelled at Hertzog and at Tielman Roos,[6]
Yet it emerges with as little harm
As Roos or he have reason for alarm:
Unbroken, though by fierce invectives shot,
Uncracked by epithets, the fragile pot
From forth the tempest and the paper fray
Emerges with as little scathe as they.
What strange paralysis your wit must trammel
That cannot even crack this frail enamel!
Anger is but the powder, style the aim,
But Wit the shot that bags the wary game!
Ah, *Mercury* and *'Tiser*, my dear friends,
How much, alas, on hateful wit depends –
Wit, the irreverent, wit, the profane,
Wit, whom you shun with heart, and soul, and brain!
Yet without wit your anger has no point,
And when you strive to blister, you anoint;
You flatter to insult, you praise to shame,
And soar to panegyric when you blame.
Yea, without wit, you merely soothe and lull,
Both tamely fierce, and passionately dull!
I once was made the victim of your praise,
Your admiration withered up my bays,
Humbled and cowed I limped about the street,
Nor dared my image in the glass to meet.
Such damp humiliation weighed me down
When *'Tiser* sang my praises through the town,
And I – could anyone be deeper shamed? –
A laureate of the drapers was proclaimed.

6. Minister of Justice for South Africa.

But now I pass the Scylla of your praise,
The dread Charybdis of your love I graze –
With flying sails my vessel speeds elate
To reach the peaceful haven of your hate!
Bred on the bland senilities of *Punch*
How can you serve us save to wrap our lunch?
Think you the soul of Hertzog to perturb
Or Tielman from his rogueries to curb?
Restrain your rage, another method try,
Praise them but once – and both of them will die!
Lo, with your fulminations, drowsing deep,
Bland Tielman lullabies his babes to sleep;
And Taakhaar's children, round the cowdung fire,
Clamour for nightly readings from their sire.
See how his 'vrew' on nights of frost and sleet
Between her blankets folds the crackling sheet –
You serve from frost to guard her grimy toes,
By day you play the kerchief to her nose,
Or in the chill of dawn, with acrid fume,
Under her porridge-pot the sticks illume . . .
In vain, against your foes, this rage you spend,
Who only serve them as a Household Friend.
The chemist goes about with drooping lugs
For journalists monopolize the drugs.
What need of aspirin at two and six
When tuppence now will cure your sorest fix?
Read but a line – in drowsy slumber fall,
And wake tomorrow if you wake at all.
While Wodson demonstrates, to all who think,
The anaesthetic properties of ink,
While Russel chloroforms the land, and Hill
Continues strange emetics to distil,
What hope for Doctors – must they also starve
With no more carcasses to hack or carve?
Yet there's one strange disorder of the mind
For which the journalists no cure can find –
Wit, whom no vaccination can restrain,
Contagious wit, is quarantined in vain;

No sleeping draught can over Wit prevail
Which singes hoary critics in the tail.
Against this wild disorder of the brain
The *Mercury* may fulminate in vain –
It scalds like fire, it pierces every pore,
It bites as hard as Bolitho can bore.
It burns like small-box, it inflames the eyes,
And wipes out even journalists like flies;
And yet in spite of wit supreme they reign
And with their pens and rulers 'Rule the Main.'
Now water-seekers leave the land to Hill
Whose pen can bore more deeply than they drill,
White-ants and borers, turning boards to dust,
Give up their old professions in disgust,
Uncared for hangs the gimlet on the wall,
The Pen, the pen is mightier than the awl!
Shut in his shop, the ruined Butcher sighs
And o'er the hopeless prospect rolls his eyes,
For journalists are selling tripe too cheap,
And profiteering on the brains of sheep.
And Hill, at wholesale price, when all is said,
Can sell the contents of a whole calf's head.
Over the trades the journalists exult
And unemployment is the sad result.
You hoary sires, who send your sons to schools,
To learn good English and to keep its rules,
While deep into their wooden skulls, like tintacks,
The masters hammer in the rules of syntax –
What boots this weary labour and expense
Save to pervert them into common sense?
Save time and labour! teach them but to bore,
Cradle their youth in journalistic lore,
Teach them to walk in Dullness' narrow way,
And never from Tautology to stray,
Feed them on Kipling, nourish them on *Punch* –
And in their works the World will wrap its lunch!

Alas, good souls, with what dyspeptic ire
You boast your race and patriotic fire!
Show first that English blood you love to brag
And prove the spirit – if you claim the Flag.
Is yours the giant race in times of yore
That bred a Dryden, or a Marvell bore?
Are you the English, you, that groaning sit
Shot through and riddled by a Dutchman's wit?
Is it so English under Tielman's blows
To whine your impotence in feeble prose,
Your Pegasus a mule, your Muse a trull,
And is it to be English – to be dull?
What are your threats of battles that impend
And what would these avail you in the end?
Rush headlong forth for politics to die,
Go, sacrifice tame mutton for a lie,
Choose bricks and bats, choose anything but Wit,
The only thing that helps your cause a whit!
Rather with Tielman would I stand in yoke
Than rank with you in impotence and smoke,
For to his ignorance is wit suspended
Like an old Tomcat with its tail appended,
But your own ignorance is purely Manx
And has no stump to tally with its shanks.
(O Tielman, I will love thee evermore,
So thou their nationality restore
And *plague* them into Englishmen once more!)
What's that within your hands – is that the Pen,
Once sharp, and once the implement of Men –
Was this, ye gods, the dainty Whistler's foil
When he from Ruskin let a tun of oil,
And, like a swordfish round a whale astreak,
Deep through the yielding blubber shot his beak?
Was this the huge harpoon that Marvell bore
To fish the corpse of Holland to the shore?
Was this the boomerang that Dryden threw
To crumple Flecknoe as I crumple you?
Alas, and has it come to this strange use?

Its stem all rusty and its point obtuse.
In Wodson's hand it scratches like a pin –
So rasps the cricket with his horny shin,
And, wrapped around it like a woollen bib,
Lo! Jubb's soft hand, perspiring, plies the nib.

Over this rhyme in cafés you will nod,
Seem unconcerned when most you feel the rod,
Affect a yawn, pretend a weary smile,
Deplore the taste, and criticize the style.
Yet when at home and by the world unseen,
On senseless paper you will vent your spleen,
Claw forth with trembling hand my dainty page
And hurl it on the dustbin in your rage –
In vain you'll strive to hide the blows you catch
And only in my absence, dare to scratch.
For there is one in this most sacred place,
English in wit – whatever be my race –
In Durban here – unmentionable brute! –
Who dares the voice of Dullness to refute:
Behold, in naked blasphemy I stalk
And dare to prove I am not made of PORK!
Your small horizon, from Berea to Bluff,
Rings you with peace: you may be grim and gruff,
But out beyond – the World will laugh enough!
My words, O Durban, round the World are blown
Where I, alone, of all your sons am known:
I circle Tellus with an airy robe –
Thou art the smear I leave upon the globe!
Cobham outsoared, I sail on Satire's wings;
Satire, who dares to box the ears of kings,
And comes to statesmen as to roguish boys
To snatch from them their baubles and their toys.
In vain you'll strive to minimize my powers
Whose laughter will outlast your tallest towers.
I mock to last: you scold poor rats! to die
Save in my verse where you immortal lie –

Yea, when your grandsons bind my works in calf,
Your own unfeeling progeny will laugh
To see their grandsires pickled in my ink —
And Dullness will to future ages stink!

True poesy admits no curb at all
Though judges bellow, and though lawyers bawl;
Down on the gravest judge, as on a child,
My muse has looked, and as a parent, smiled:
For rhyme above the heads of monarchs sails
And wit outlasts the concrete of the gaols.
Then hear the damned sedition that I sing,
A poet, though in rags, is thrice a king,
Who dares the world, without an army, face
And kick a mongrel town into its place!
Jostling with emperors, an outlaw gay,
Shouldering paunchy statesmen from his way,
Along the sounding thoroughfares of time
He swaggers in the clashing spurs of rhyme,
And all around him throng, with forms divine,
His gay seraglio of Muses Nine,
Those strapping girls whose love, to say the least,
Would make a rabid Mormon of a priest.

Now do you groan when Tielman flays your backs —
You, who condone the bondage of the blacks?
The Lord, who sent the flies to Egypt's strand
Now sends a Tielman to Banana Land.
When you at poets hurl your venomed scrolls
And grudge us all the *riches* of our souls,
Why do you turn your envy, let me quizz,
To grudge poor Roos the *poverty* of his?
Alas, poor Tielman, what is he to blame? —
A Locust at the word of God he came,
With huge moustaches, like antennae curled,
And paper wings to swoop across the world.
He spares your gum-trees and he spares your crops,
But on your testimonials he drops,

He chews certificates, your chits he gnaws,
And plays the devil with your paper laws:
Your flagstaffs like banana-leaves are ripped,
Your noticeboards like mealie-stems are stripped,
Acres of paper desolated lie,
And groans of angered citizens reply.
Alas, poor Durbanites, which will you choose,
Which of the dread alternatives refuse,
This is the ultimatum that you shirk,
The awful question – Poverty or Work?
Work, that can turn a draper to a Man
And give a human accident a plan.
Work, that could make the sugar-planting race
Stand up and look a black man in the face!
Is it the sign of a 'superior race'
To whine to have 'the nigger kept in place'?
Where is his place save in his strength and sense,
And will he stand aside for impotence,
Does Evolution wait for those who lag
Or curtsy to a cheap colonial Flag?
Is this 'White Labour' – lolling on this stool,
Fed by a black with every needful tool,
The white man sits and uses but his hands,
The black man does the thinking while he stands:
Five years in long apprenticeship were passed
Ere, fit to loaf, the white emerged at last,
And yet in kicks and blows the black must pay
Unless he learns the business in a day.
And will they strive to teach you Afrikaans,
O'er lingual hurdles coax your tongues to prance –
You, through whose jaws the words with dismal hum
Like groans of dying pork from Liebig's come?
And how will you in foreign tongues advance
Who only learned your own by some mischance? –
Listen, how in the true Natalian twang
Your heathen tonsils meet with horrid clang,
And make your nose, as by deliberate choice,
A funnel for your all-too-frequent voice!

Plomer, 'twas you who, though a boy in age,
Awoke a sleepy continent to rage,
Who dared alone to thrash a craven race
And hold a mirror to its dirty face.
Praised in all countries where the Muse is known
But hunted like a felon from your own,
Whom shall I sacrifice, what blood infuse
On the neglected altar of your muse? –
Lo, his who took the name of 'Grub' in vain
Though he provides its wrapper with his brain,
Who thundered 'Grub Street!' from his paper throne
Though Grub Street was Olympus to his own[7] –
In vain would he recant the oaths he swore
And eat them back into his throat once more,
As frightened sharks, when sudden dangers loom,
Swallow their young ones back into their womb:
Caught in a puddle of his native ink,
Ere he could vanish down some friendly sink
To lie unnoticed in his destined drain
Where memory might fish for him in vain, –
Behold I haul him to the light displayed
To die the martyr of the scribbling trade!
Prone on the altar of your Muse he lies
And fatly in his own repentance fries,
As when Prime Hogs upon the embers twinge,
And the fat crackles, and the bristles singe,
The fusing limbs in their own blubber flare,
And up the chimney flies the reek of hair –
All that was mortal of him soars sublime
To reek for ever in the nose of Time.
You journalists with righteous wrath who swell
To see a brother turned into a smell –
Be warned by me and his own dreadful fate
Who dies your many sins to expiate –
Sooner with your own pens a lion assail
Or pick a sleeping mamba in the tail,

7. Field Street, Durban.

Than dare the great Apollo to abuse
Or squirt one drop of ink upon the Muse.
Sooner your own vile ink in buckets swill
And swallow both the paper and the quill –
Than dare, though journalists you be, our curse.
Which still can turn you into something *worse*.
We poets will forgive you all we can
With you the dog 'is father to the man';
'Tis Nature's whim that dogs, when taken short,
Still to the loftiest monument resort,
And oft we shrug and often we are mute
When you our sacred monuments pollute:
Dogs and colonials are in this alike –
One law suffices both for man and tyke –
But dogs are pleased with humble walls at times
And lift their legs unconscious of their crimes,
Yet what colonial would not run a mile
Might he some shining edifice defile?

EUGÈNE N. MARAIS
(1871–1936)

Deep River
Translated from the Afrikaans by Hugh Finn

O Deep River, O Dark Stream,
How long now must I wait, how long must dream,
And love's blade sharp in my heart without relief? –
In your embraces end my pain and grief;
Put out the flame of hate, O Deep River; –
The mighty longing which will leave me never.
I see far off the gleam of steel and gold,
I hear the quiet sound of waters deep and cold;
I hear your voice as whispering in a dream,
Come soon, O Deep River, O Dark Stream.

'Hier Hebben Wij Geen Vaste Verblijfplaats'

('Here We have No Firm Dwelling-place')
Translated from the Afrikaans by Hugh Finn

I built my house upon the solid rock;
I knew my workmen long as faithful stock;
A forest planted I, each tree that grows,
And made the desert blossom as the rose;
With flower and tree from regions near and far,
From the warm Tropic to the northern star,
I made it fairer still, unceasingly,
And looked up often from my work to see
The greatness which beneath my hands had grown,
Strengthened with bonds of steel and timeless stone.

When all was done, and I could rest, in pride,
That day I died.

Draadlose Wiegeliedjie

Slaap, Babetjie, doedoe gerus deur die nag,
Want om jou gedurig hou Engeltjies wag.
Slaap soet na die himne van draadloos J. B.:
,I want to be happy', en ,Take me to tea'.

Jou pappie speel brug en jou mammie probeer,
En Aia verjaar apostolies alweer,
Maar Babie, vir jou is die draadloos aan stoom:
,Bananas' en ,Show me the way to go home'.

Toe Mammie en Pappie nog babetjies was,
Had hulle geen keuse van Foxtrot en Jazz,
Nooit had hulle voorregte, Liefling, soos jy:
,Me and the Boy Friend' en ,Just for the day'.

Slaap soet, Lief' Kaboutertjie, soet deur die nag,
Jou ogies is toe, net jou lippies wat lag,
Want Pappie's 'n Jakkals en Mammie 'n ,Blaar',
Maar die program is ,J. B.' en ,C. T. Nujaar'.

Radio Cradle-song

Translated from the Afrikaans by Stephen Gray

Sleep, little Baby, kip in peace through the night,
Little Angels often guard you in your plight.
Sleep calmly to the hymns of Radio J. B.:
'I want to be happy' and 'Take me to tea'.

Your pa's playing bridge and your ma tries the same,
And it's Ayah's apostolic birthday yet again,
But for you, sweet Babe, the radio steams on:
'Bananas' and 'Show me the way to go home'.

When Mummy and Daddy were still little brats,
They had no choice between Foxtrots and Jazz,
Never your privileges, my Darling, had they:
'Me and the Boy Friend' and 'Just for the day'.

Sleep sweetly, Little Pixie, sweetly through the night,
Your little lips laugh, but your eyes are held tight;
Your Daddy is a prowler and Mum the kiss of death,
But the programme is J. B., so Happy New Year.

Translator's Note: 'On 1 July 1924 the first public broadcast service
opened in Southern Africa, Radio Johannesburg, hence J. B.'

PAULINE SMITH
(1882–1959)

Katisje's Patchwork Dress

When Sunday came and old Katis',
In patchwork dress and kapje,
Stood on the stoep to show herself
What ayah was more happy?

Of many a print the dress was made
 (All sizes were the pieces),
And starched so stiff she'd not sit down
 For fear of making creases.

And so she'd stand, our old Katis',
 With make-pretence of myst'ry,
And whisper low at our request
 Of every patch the hist'ry.

'Dis from de Predikant's wife came,
 It was her dochter's baby's;
An' dis de Jedge's cook give me,
 It was de Jedge's lady's.

'An' dese I got from Prince's store
 Dat time I do deir cleanin';
An' dese from oubaas Daanie's vrouw –
 His secon' one, I'm meanin'.'

And these had lain for years and years
 In some old chest, unheeded,
'Till yo' kin' Ma, she say, "Katis'
 Ar'n' dey jes' what you needed?"

'An' dis? Yo' Pa give me dis flag
 To show how I be loyal
At Jooblee time – look, here's de Queen,
 An' all her Fam'ly Royal.

'An' dis? Why chillen, dis same petch,
 So pink an' blue an' shiny,
It am de firs' doll's dress yo' Ma
 She make when she were tiny.

'An' dis – you see dis little rose?
 When she grow big she wore it,
And yo' own Pa he fall in love
 Mit her so soon's he saw it.

'An' dis one here's her weddin' gown –
 So sof' it is – you feel it!
Yo' Ma she give me dis herself,
 So don't t'ink dat I steal it.

'And this?' Katisje's voice grew soft
 As summer winds a-sighing,
'Dis am de dress she wore de night
 We watch her baby dyin'.'

And so she'd go from patch to patch
 Till 'Hark! De kerk bell's ringin'!
Dit's time for ole Katis to go
 An' praise de Lord mit singin'!'

And as she went we'd hear her croon
 'Oh bless de Lord! I'm happy
In dis here petchwork dress of mine
 An' dis here white-starched kapje!'

S. E. K. MQHAYI
(1875–1945)

The Pleiades

Translated from the Xhosa by Jeff Opland

Hail, Silimela!
The new Ndlambe,
Oh the new Ndlambe!
My chief's the son of Ndluzodaka,
He's a man born of two people,
He's born of Makinana and Nopasi.
Nopasi's the daughter of Moni, the light-skinned son of Ntshunqe,
The light-skinned son of Ntshunqe of Bomvanaland.
His name's Luhadi,
Whose chest expanded and contracted:
There's something dreadful under the stone,
For the young bucks and the loose women are there.

Who hasn't heard?
Who hasn't heard that the Pleiades appeared to the Ndlambe?
The Pleiades are great stars in the land of Phalo.

A letter came from Wright and Brownlee in Gqolonci,
It crossed the Kei and it crossed the Bashe,
And when it reached Mgazana it spoke.
It said, 'Return home, Makinana, your father is dead.
He died at Mthumane at the foot of Qangqalala,
Return home to serve the Ndlambe, who now lack a leader.'
Makinana said, 'I'm coming; I'm still reaping my corn.'
So saying he urged on the Nkanti to battle,
And Ntakamhlophe trotted in front.
Before Tyityaba Fynn's letter came, saying,
'Turn back, Makinana, the country's already disturbed.'
Makinana said, 'Oh no, it's not our custom to turn our backs.'
So saying he continued to press forward.
At Mpethu, Fynn arrived and said to his face, 'I say,
I say turn back, Makinana, you're looking for trouble.'
Makinana said, 'No-o-o-o!
It's not our custom to turn our backs.'
Just as he came into Draaibosch,
The Lisping English appeared with raised rifles.
That's when they first squared off at each other.
Bang went the arms of the whites;
Bang went the arms of the Xhosa:
Down dropped the warriors on both sides.
The Lispers retreated to Komga;
Off on his way went Ndluzodaka,
Until he linked up with Sandile.

Summon the nations, let's apportion the stars:
Let the stars be apportioned.
You Sotho,
Take Canopus,
To share with the Tswana and Chopi,
And all of those nations in loincloths.
You of KwaZulu,
Take Orion's Belt,

To share with the Swazi, the Chopi and Shangaan,
As well as uncircumcised nations.
You Britons, take Venus,
To divide with the Germans and Boers,
Though you're folk who don't know how to share.
We'll divide up the Pleiades, we peoples of Phalo,
That great group of stars,
For they're stars for counting off years,
For counting the years of manhood,
For counting the years of manhood,
The years of manhood.
I disappear!

An izibongo or eulogy by the oral bard, recorded on a Columbia disc in the early 1930s. Then Silimela was chief of the Ndlambes. Isilimela is also the name of the constellation by which the years of adulthood are measured. Draaibosch occurred during the Ninth Frontier War (1877). The distribution of the stars refers to the organization of land after the First World War.

ENOCH SONTONGA
(c. 1860–1904)

Lord Bless Africa
Translated from the Xhosa by D. D. T. Jabavu

Lord, bless Africa,
May her horn rise high up;
Hear Thou our prayers
And bless us.
> Descend, O Spirit
> Descend, O Holy Spirit.

Bless our chiefs;
May they remember their Creator,
Fear Him and revere Him,
That He may bless them.

Bless the public men,
Bless also the youth
That they may carry the land with patience,
And that Thou mayst bless them.

Bless the wives
And also all young women,
Lift up all the young girls
And bless them.

Bless the ministers
Of all the churches of this land;
Endue them with Thy Spirit
And bless them.

Bless agriculture and stock-raising;
Banish all famine and diseases;
Fill the land with good health
And bless it.

Bless our efforts
Of union and self-uplift,
Of education and mutual understanding,
And bless them.

Lord, bless Africa;
Blot out all its wickedness
And its transgressions and sins,
And bless it.

Composed in 1897 and first publicly sung in 1899 at the ordination of the Rev. M. Boweni, a Shangaan Methodist. Popularized in African day schools and by the Ohlange Zulu Choir. Adopted by the South African Native National Congress in 1912 as a closing anthem for meetings. Only the first stanza and the chorus is written by Sontonga, as follows:

> Nkosi, sikelel' i Afrika
> Malupakam' upondo lwayo;
> Yiva imitandazo yetu
> Usisikelele.
> > Yihla Moya, yihla Moya,
> > Yihla Moya Oyingcwele.

By 1927 new stanzas 2–8 had been provided by Mqhayi, and Lovedale published it with Jabavu's translation in 1934 as 'The Bantu National Anthem'.

J. J. R. JOLOBE
(1902–76)

The Making of a Servant

Translated from the Xhosa by Robert Kavanagh and Z. S. Qangule

I can no longer ask how it feels
To be choked by a yoke-rope
Because I have seen it for myself in the chained ox.
The blindness has left my eyes. I have become aware,
I have seen the making of a servant
In the young yoke-ox.

He was sleek, lovely, born for freedom,
Not asking anything from any one, simply priding himself on
    being a young ox.
Someone said: Let him be caught and trained and broken in,
Going about it as if he meant to help him.
I have seen the making of a servant
In the young yoke-ox.

He tried to resist, fighting for his freedom.
He was surrounded, fenced in with wisdom and experience.
They overcame him by trickery: 'He must be trained.'
A good piece of rationalisation can camouflage evil.
I have seen the making of a servant
In the young yoke-ox.

He was bound with ropes that cut into his head,
He was bullied, kicked, now and again petted,
But their aim was the same: to put a yoke on him.
Being trained in one's own interests is for the privileged.
I have seen the making of a servant
In the young yoke-ox.

The last stage. The yoke is set on him.
They tie the halter round his neck, slightly choking him.
They say the job's done, he'll be put out to work with the others
To obey the will of his owner and taskmaster.

I have seen the making of a servant
In the young yoke-ox.

He kicks out, trying to break away.
They speak with their whips. He turns backwards
Doing his best to resist but then they say: 'Hit him.'
A prisoner is a coward's plaything.
I have seen the making of a servant
In the young yoke-ox.

Though he stumbled and fell, he was bitten on the tail.
Sometimes I saw him raking at his yoke-mate
With his horns – his friend of a minute, his blood-brother.
The suffering under the yoke makes for bad blood.
I have seen the making of a servant
In the young yoke-ox.

The sky seemed black as soft rain fell.
I looked at his hump, it was red,
Dripping blood, the mark of resistance.
He yearns for his home, where he was free.
I have seen the making of a servant
In the young yoke-ox.

Stockstill, tired, there was no sympathy.
He bellowed notes of bitterness.
They loosened his halter a little – to let him breathe,
They tightened it again, snatching back his breath.
I have seen the making of a servant
In the young yoke-ox.

I saw him later, broken, trained,
Pulling a double-shared plough through deep soil,
Serving, struggling for breath, in pain.
To be driven is death. Life is doing things for yourself.
I have seen the making of a servant
In the young yoke-ox.

I saw him climb the steepest of roads.
He carried heavy loads, staggering –
The mud of sweat which wins profit for another.

The savour of working is a share in the harvest.
I have seen the making of a servant
In the young yoke-ox.

I saw him hungry with toil and sweat,
Eyes all tears, spirit crushed,
No longer able to resist. He was tame.
Hope lies in action aimed at freedom.
I have seen the making of a servant
In the young yoke-ox.

B. W. VILAKAZI
(1906–47)

Now I Will Only Believe

Translated from the Zulu by Cherie Maclean
(I remember father. He died in my hands on June 10, 1933, at um Voti)

I will now only believe that he has died
If the crying of the birds above
And the night which bursts into stars above;
If the star of dawn and the other stars
Which light up the blackness like moonlight itself –
If all these things disappear for ever and ever.

I will now only believe that he has died
If the mountains and the flowing rivers,
North and South (winds) which blow;
If frost of Winter and dew (of Summer)
Which cover the grass today and yesterday –
If they too are to disappear for ever and ever.

Just like a star which falls from high and far,
So did his body fall like the trees of the wild banana
Which surround the coast and the sands of the sea,
I saw it as if in a dream, it was covered up,
I waited with it until eventually it cooled.

At the time that the stars became obscure,
I saw that your bravery was coming to an end.

On top of this I cannot believe anything,
All of my vision is now a nothing of nothing.

I will now only believe that he has died
If the sun and moon die,
Fall down to the very earth of sods
Annihilated for ever and ever.

Now I Do Believe

Translated from the Zulu by Cherie Maclean
(Lament for my father – ten years later)

Now I do believe that he has died,
Because when the sun lights up the earth
I see animals grazing in the morning,
Whisking their hairy tails,
Which are white like the cows at umHlali,
Still however I sometimes see dusk at midday.

Now I do believe that he has died,
Because it also became dusk for me at midday with
    Mandlakayise.
When I asked them to take me to him,
They sorrowed with me,
I saw him lying down not yet covered up.
I saw a dream coming in the middle of the day.

And so it was also with Nomasomi.
The stars of her eyes were closed,
She became cold and failed to warm up again.
As for me, I could not stand and my arms shook
I took a quick look, her face became dusk,
And her astonishing beauty became obscured for me.

How can I not believe that you are dead
When your road is open in front of me?
I see all the years you have worn away.
It seems as if your own going opened the door

For others to go out when they were tired,
Indeed they are following you and not returning.

They don't return or you, hero of umZwangedwa.
They bade farewell and left me standing here alone.
Others I have buried at Groutville,
Where the darkness covers them up;
Others I have planted at Mariannhill,
There they are sheltered by the hens,
Because I hear the bell of angelus ringing,
It wakens them early to pray as it rings.
I see the red sunset,
I saw it turn the hills themselves red.

The red soils down at Mariannhill
I saw shining and competing.
I lay on the ground near a big fig tree
There where grandfather Frans lies,
I heard his words: 'Let us ring the angelus
Winter and summer it rings without grief!'

And so I am now satisfied that he is dead,
Because I see even in myself the falling
Out of the hair of youth, I am grey,
It gives me dignity, the mark of age
Which I saw with you when you were tiring.
After that you kept going until you came to nought,
I myself saw that you were slowly disappearing.

Today I do believe that he is dead,
Because in the place of Sleep I see you
You come with a cool heart,
You make me to cross over through gateways and fords
Of wisdom and awareness;
I can hear your guiding staff tapping
In front of me although I cannot see you.
I am like a blind person with my bodily eyes.
Yes, now I do believe that he is dead,
And that he has gone away for ever and ever.

WILLIAM PLOMER
(1903–73)

A Fall of Rock

Where not so long ago the breezes stirred
The summer grasses, now
A fat contralto gargles for applause
And bows in sequins when the curtain falls.

A sudden tremor shakes the theatre
And 'Oh!' cry two or three, while red and blue
Sparks fly from diamond earrings; several men
Are glad of an excuse to squeeze white hands
And murmur reassurance in small ears.
They say perhaps it was a fall of rock
In the deep mines below.

Perhaps it was a fall of rock. The city stands
On shafts and tunnels and a stinking void,
The bright enamel of a hollow tooth.
Where springbok bounded screams the tram,
And lawyer, politician, magnate sit
Where kite and vulture flew and fed.
Where the snake sunned itself, white children play;
Where wildebeest drank, a church is built.

Perhaps it was a fall of rock. Two kaffirs trapped
Up to the waist in dirty water. All the care
That went to keep them fit —!
Concrete bathrooms and carbolic soap,
A balanced diet and free hospitals
Made them efficient, but they die alone.
Half stunned, then drowned,
They might have lived in the sun
With miner's phthisis, silicosis,
A gradual petrifaction of the lungs.

If anybody imagines that ever
All this will come to an end,
That the jackal will howl on the ruined terraces
Of this city where science is applied for profit
And where the roar of machinery by night and day
Is louder than the beating of all the hearts of the inhabitants,
Far louder than the quiet voice of common sense;
If anybody should think that a mile below ground
The moling and maggoting will cease, or console himself
For his own failure to share the life of the city
With romantic hopes for its ruin,
He is wasting his time.

Do not let him suppose
That a bad future avenges the wrongs of now,
And let him remember
There is a fine gold to be won
By not always knowing best.

Namaqualand after Rain

Again the veld revives,
Imbued with lyric rains,
And sap re-sweetening dry stalks
Perfumes the quickening plains;

Small roots explode in strings of stars,
Each bulb gives up its dream,
Honey drips from orchid throats,
Jewels each raceme;

The desert sighs at dawn —
As in another hemisphere
The temple lotus breaks her buds
On the attentive air —

A frou-frou of new flowers,
Puff of unruffling petals,
While rods of sunlight strike pure streams
From rocks beveined with metals;

Far in the gaunt karroo
That winter dearth denudes,
Ironstone caves give back the burr
Of lambs in multitudes;

Grass waves again where drought
Bleached every upland kraal,
A peach tree shoots along the wind
Pink volleys through a broken wall,

And willows growing round the dam
May now be seen
With all their traceries of twigs
Just hesitating to be green,

Soon to be hung with colonies
All swaying with the leaves
Of pendent wicker love-nests
The pretty loxia weaves.

The Scorpion

Limpopo and Tugela churned
In flood for brown and angry miles
Melons, maize, domestic thatch,
The trunks of trees and crocodiles;

The swollen estuaries were thick
With flotsam, in the sun one saw
The corpse of a young negress bruised
By rocks, and rolling on the shore,

Pushed by the waves of morning, rolled
Impersonally among shells,
With lolling breasts and bleeding eyes,
And round her neck were beads and bells.

That was the Africa we knew,
Where, wandering alone,
We saw, heraldic in the heat,
A scorpion on a stone.

The Devil-dancers

In shantung suits we whites are cool,
Glasses and helmets censoring the glare;
Fever has made our anxious faces pale,
We stoop a little from the load we bear;

Grouped in the shadow of the compound wall
We get our cameras ready, sitting pensive;
Keeping our distance and our dignity
We talk and smile, though slightly apprehensive.

The heat strikes upward from the ground,
The ground the natives harden with their feet,
The flag is drooping on its bamboo pole,
The middle distance wavers in the heat.

Naked or gaudy, all agog the crowd
Buzzes and glistens in the sun; the sight
Dazzles the retina; we remark the smell,
The drums beginning, and the vibrant light.

Now the edge of the jungle rustles. In a hush
The crowd parts. Nothing happens. Then
The dancers stalk adroitly out on stilts,
Weirdly advancing, twice as high as men.

Sure as fate, strange as the mantis, cruel
As vengeance in a dream, four bodies hung
In cloaks of rasping grasses, turning
Their tiny heads, the masks besmeared with dung;

Each mops and mows, uttering no sound,
Each stately, awkward, giant marionette,
Each printed shadow frightful on the ground
Moving in small distorted silhouette;

The fretful pipes and thinly-crying strings,
The mounting expectation of the drums
Excite the nerves, and stretch the muscles taut
Against the climax — but it never comes;

It never comes because the dance must end
And soon the older dancers will be dead;
We leave by air tomorrow. How
Can ever these messages by us be read?

These bodies hung with viscera and horns
Move with an incomparable lightness,
And through the masks that run with bullocks' blood
Quick eyes aim out, dots of fanatic brightness.

Within the mask the face, and moulded
(As mask to face) within the face the ghost,
As in its chrysalis-case the foetus folded
Of leaf-light butterfly. What matters most

When it comes out and we admire its wings
Is to remember where its life began:
Let us take care – that flake of flame may be
A butterfly whose bite can kill a man.

Tugela River

I

The river's just beyond that hill:
Drive up that track!

Look, isn't that someone standing there?

Yes, someone old and thin,
Some old witch perching there,
Standing on one wasted leg
With scaly skin, and taking snuff.
Unwanted, old and thin,
And waiting for the end,
She'll smell of ashes, and have no good news.
The skimpy rag she wears,
A cotton blanket once,
Protects her with its colour, not with warmth;
It has the dusty, ashen look
Of winter, scarcity, and drought.
Bones in a blanket, with a spark of life

Nothing by now can fan to flame,
Old hag, why don't you move?

It's not a woman, after all –
Only a thorn bush all disguised with dust!
Ah well, in this clear light
Things often are not what they seem,
Persons are often things,
Fear takes on form,
Delusions seem to have
The density of facts:
Kick one, and see!

It's just a thorn bush in a web of dust,
A statue of powder in this windless glare.
But, all the same, I shouldn't speak to it:
It might reply.
Silence itself might crack
Into an eerie cackle, dry and thin
As all this sapless winter grass,
Deriding us out of the lost past and out
Of what will be the past, when we are lost.

We've passed her now – or rather, *it*.
There, down the hill, the river in its bed,
Tugela River, seems as quiet
As this dead pythoness in her dusty fur.

White light, dry air, an even warmth
Make for well-being, tone and calm
The nerves, the blood.
No cloud, no breeze;
Clear as the focus of a burning-glass
But wholly bearable, the sun
Is fixed upon us like an eye.
We seem enclosed inside a vast
And flawless plastic dome
As for some new experiment.
We shall not know if we have passed the test,
We don't know what it is.

I feel we cannot fail.
The river in this still
Gold morning will renew our strength;
Reduced by drought
It does not show its own,
Only its constancy.
Look, turn off here, and park above that rock.

2

Tugela River! Thirty years ago
These same eyes saw you at this very place
Just at this time
Of winter, scarcity, and drought:
Not that you know or care;
But nothing is unrelated, wasted, lost.
There is a link
Between this river and that boy,
A boy obliged to learn
Subjects not mastered all at once –
Patience, and energy, and rage.

The hard earth cracked, the river shrank,
The boy came here because the river knew
Answers to questions.

Juiceless as straw, the glistening grass
Brittle and faintly gold
Waited for fire.

Then came the time of burning of the grass:
At night the veld-fires drew
Their mile-long arcs of jerking flame
Under the smoky stars.
Fences of dancing fire
Crackled like pistol shots,
Pricking new frontiers out
Into the passive dark.

It seemed the field by night
Of one of those miscalled
Decisive battles of the world,

With cannon smoke and musket fire,
A master plan, and screams of pain
As some to-be-renowned outflanking move
Destroyed a long-established power
With crowns and crosses on its ancient pinnacles.
Morning revealed the hills mapped out
(Yesterday's straw-pale hills)
With empires painted black!

Burnt veld-grass had a sad and bitter smell
Like letters kept, then burnt,
Like battles fought, and lost —
No, battles fought and won!

3

Eastward and constant as a creed
Tugela swam,
The winter river, much reduced,
Past shaped alluvial clean white sand,
Past stalks of maize upright but dead
In hillside patches poorly tilled
By dwellers under domes of reeds
Who by their poverty seemed to expiate
Their furious past.

Cool, cool Tugela slid
Haunted with unwritten myth,
Swam like a noble savage, dark
And muscular in shade, or clear
In the sun an emerald angel swam.

As sleek as oil Tugela poured,
And paused in pools,
And narrowing lapsed
Below the rigid erythrina trees
That held their carved and coral flowers
Like artifacts against the arid sky.

And farther down, down there,
Funnelled through channelled rocks
To rapids and cascades, kept up

A white roar of applause
In the still brightness of an empty day.

4

Rivers of Europe with a cross of gold
In liquefaction at the inverted point
Of wavering dome or undulating spire,
Printed with dimnesses of trees
And redolent of mist and moss,
Reflect what looks like peace.

There, seated idols in a row,
The anglers on the bank
Catch something less than peace.
They never catch the gold reflected cross:
It ripples, breaks, re-forms, and melts.
No anglers here, fishing for peace.
Look at that pool, a glass
For nothing but the shadow of a rock.

It was a glass once for a Zulu youth —
I saw him standing on that rock
His fighting-sticks put by —
Who on a concertina improvised
A slow recurrent tune, subdued
By want of hope, yet with the stamping feet
The drums of hope
Beyond the horizon, and its just-heard song.

I know his family. They tell me he was found
Dying of inanition in the sun
On a road verge, while new cars
Hissed past like rockets
Loaded with white men hurrying like mad,
While he lay on the dark red earth
With all his youth subdued.

5

It is to be misled
To think his death was final, as to think

The river that you see, the dried-up grass,
Will stay like that;

Or that a race of men locked up and ruled
In a delusion built by psychopaths,
Locked up and staring at the floor
Between their patient feet,
Are there for good.

If, after thirty years, in winter calm
Tugela gliding as before might seem
Merely an unnavigable stream
Idling for ever in the gold
Dry atmosphere, remember this:
Patience erodes.

Here where we stand
Through the rich grass of summer there will pour
A press and pride of senseless force,
Roar like a mob, a tidal wave
Shaking its mane, and overturning rocks
Fulfil the promise of catastrophe.

When patience breaks, the sinews act,
Rage generates energy without end:
Tugela River, in the time of drums
And shouting of the war-dance flood
Will break a trance, as revolutions do,
Will promise order, and a future time
Of honey, beer, and milk.

White Gloves

Reading some Russian novel
    far on a Transvaal steppe,
blue hills near in the clean sky's lens
    and Russia brought quite as near
in the focus of prose, the place I was in
    and was not were strangely merged.

Straight as a caryatid
　　a brown girl held on her head
a brown girl's burden of white things washed
　　for whites, of whom I was one:
she knew she was graceful, I knew
　　her life was the life of a serf.

Now, with half a century gone,
　　a letter that comes from those parts
shows by its turn and tone of phrase
　　it comes from a Tolstoi-time,
from a sun-dried Russia where even now
　　the serfs have not yet been freed.

A terrace in lilied shade,
　　ice clinks in glasses there,
white gloves disguise black hands that offer
　　a tray – untouchable hands.
Cars race to a feast. On the burning veld
　　slow peasants stand apart.

The scene dissolves to Kazan:
　　the snowy versts race past,
wrapped snug in furs we chatter in French
　　as with clinking harness-bells
we drive to a feast. On the frozen road
　　slow peasants step aside.

Some other caryatid
　　no doubt, after all these years,
barefoot and slow, with patient steps
　　in the place I knew upholds
with her strength what has to be done:
　　the serfs are not yet freed.

Not of them the letter brings news
　　but of a picnic, a bride,
white bride of the son of a millionaire,
　　and of pleasures bought. It implies
that a usual social round
　　runs on its inbuilt power,

runs by itself, by right;
    will last; must drive, not walk.
Alone and apart, more alone and apart
    it floats, floats high, that world
with the tinted oiliness
    of a bubble's tensile skin:

but inside the bubble a serf,
    black serf, peels off his gloves,
white gloves. With naked hands
    he opens a door FOR WHITES ALONE
and salutes in a mirror the self
    he is destined at last to meet.

FERNANDO PESSOA
(1888–1935)

The Blighter

Translated from the Portuguese by Charles Eglington

The blighter that is at the end of the sea
On the pitch-black night raised itself flying;
Round the vessel it flew three times,
Three times it flew creaking,
And said, 'Who dared pierce
Into my dens that I do not reveal,
My black ceilings of the end of the world?'
And the helmsman said, trembling,
'His Majesty King John the Second!'

'Whose sails are these then which I rub against?
Whose the keels I see and hear?'
Said the blighter, and rolled three times,
Three times it rolled filthy and bulky,
'Who attempts what is solely my power,
I who abide where no one ever could see me
And who drip the fears of the depthless sea?'

And the helmsman trembled, and said,
'His Majesty King John the Second!'

Three times he raised his hands from the helm,
Three times he had them rooted on the helm,
And said after trembling three times,
'Here at the helm I am more than myself:
I am a People who wants the sea that is yours;
And more than the blighter, that my soul fears
And rolls on the darkness of the end of the world,
Orders the will, that ties me at the helm,
Of His Majesty King John the Second!'

The Ascent of Vasco da Gama
Translated from the Portuguese by F. E. G. Quintanilha

The Gods of the storm and the giants of the earth
Suddenly stop the fury of their arms
And they stare amazed. Throughout the valley where one
    ascends to heaven
A silence arises and it keeps swaying the veils of the mist,

First a movement then a wonder.
Fears, side by side, escort it while it lasts,
And in the distance the wake thunders in clouds and in glaring
    radiance

Down below, where the earth lies, the shepherd is stunned and
    his flute
Falls out of his hand and in ecstasy he sees, at the light of a
    thousand thunders,
The sky opening its abyss to the soul of the Argonaut.

The Portuguese Sea

Translated from the Portuguese by F. E. G. Quintanilha

O salty sea, how much of your salt
Are tears of Portugal!
For us to sail you, how many mothers cried,
How many sons prayed in vain!
How many brides stayed unmarried
Just for you to be ours, oh sea!

Was it worth it? Everything is worthwhile
If the soul is not mean.
Whoever wants to sail beyond the Bojador
Must go beyond anguish.
God gave the sea danger and depth
But in it mirrored the sky.

If, after I Die

Translated from the Portuguese by Jonathan Griffin

If, after I die, they should want to write my biography,
There's nothing simpler.
I've just two dates — of my birth, and of my death.
In between the one thing and the other all the days are mine.

I am easy to describe.
I lived like mad.
I loved things without any sentimentality.
I never had a desire I could not fulfil, because I never went blind.
Even hearing was to me never more than an accompaniment of
    seeing.
I understood that things are real and all different from each
    other;
I understood it with the eyes, never with thinking.
To understand it with thinking would be to find them all equal.

One day I felt sleepy like a child.
I closed my eyes and slept.
And by the way, I was the only Nature poet.

Azure, or Green, or Purple
Translated from the Portuguese by Jonathan Griffin

Azure, or green, or purple when the sun
Goldens it with a false wash of vermilion,
The sea forbids, or idles, or leads on,
Is at times the abyss, at others mirror.
I summon up, as age moves in,
That in me which would want more than the sea
Now that nothing's there for discovery.

The great sea-captains and the crews with whom
They did the navigation of solitude
Lie far away, their reward in their gloom
Is our forgetting, our ingratitude.
Only the sea, when in storm mood
The waves are great and it is truly sea,
Seems remembering them uncertainly.

But I am dreaming . . . Sea is water, mere
Nude water, slave to the force, darkly felt,
Which, like poetry, comes from the moon
And at times will let fall, at others lift.
And yet, whatever descants float
Above the natural ignorance of the sea,
I still forefeel its murmur, oozily.

Who knows what the soul is? Who can make out
What soul there is in things which appear dead –
How much, in earth or nothing, can't forget?
Who knows whether space, the empty, is doored?
O dream, who thrust on me this duty
To meditate so on the voice of the sea,
How meditate on you? Teach that to me.

Captains, quartermasters – all argonauts
Of every day's landfall on unbelief –
Perhaps you heard, calling you, unknown flutes,
Their tune, elusive, unattainable.
Did your hearing perhaps follow

A being of the sea yet not the sea –
Sirens of hearing, not of victory?

One who beyond oceans without end
Has called you out towards the distance, or
One who knows there is, in our hearts of men,
Desire for good, natural, yet also more
Elusive, subtle – to the core
A thing which demands the sound of the sea,
And not to stop – far from all things still be.

If it is so, if the vast sea and you
Are something (you because you perceive, and
The sea by being) of this which I think true;
If, in existence's unknown profound,
There's more soul than can reach the vain
Surface of us, as though that of the sea, –
Make me, to unknow it, in the end, free.

Give me a soul transposed, an argonaut's,
And make me have, as the old sea-captain had,
Or his quartermaster, ears for the flute's
Call out of the distance to our heart, –
Make me hear, like a pardon, part
Remembrance of a teaching sunk in me,
The ancient Portuguese speech of the sea.

(9 June 1935)

VINCENT SWART
(1911–62)

Convict

Your ankle wrapped in iron, yourself encased
In stone and rolled aside to die aside.
Your pain can gather round that chain and tears
Have there to fall and sorrows there to cling.
Yourself intent upon the iron becomes

The iron. You thought to steal a something how
To live and stole instead a greater, stole,
A concrete reason why to die.
Needing the iron . . .
Needing the iron the spider spins his entrails
Out, the moth's wings chafe and tatter, the bee
His own drum beats, the silkworm lays her death.

This is Not a Poem but a Proem

This is not a poem but a proem. I want to be in the wide
Country of outspoken language, among the bits and pieces
Of life left out; slough rhyme, line and logic, three
Suppurating sores from the poet's procrustes' bed.
In an ordinary gulp of words I want to tell you
How I got up this morning and every morning.
I am always drunk but old enough not to be dizzy.
Drink no longer even proves that the world is round.
In fact it is altogether flat, and to walk on a flat surface
Is far more tricky than on a modulate, yielding globe.
So it was that when I stepped out of bed this morning I fell.
But what a terrible fall. Have you ever been over a precipice?
My body burnt like a thousand candles, my hair stood up like
    grass
Newly rained on, my hands were in a flutter as if
Catching butterflies. Lips numb as if stunned by a stone.
Let the last word of that line, in spite of protestations,
Rhyme with bone. For life goes very near the bone.
Wives, mistresses, booze, and discussion from sharp minds,
Friends' gleam and the glum look of creditors.
Minutes wasted as I am wasting these minutes. Waste time with
    me.
Doubtless, and surely, we must put out our wandering arms
Around the ambient and beautiful years, look out of great
    windows
Onto long meadows. But to come back, back to you my friend.
Shake my hand and you shake not only exasperated blossom

But you shake sap. You take me in to put me out –
The diastole and sistole of life anywhere.
When I was really up and dressed I fell over a beam
And discovered as Keats once said that wood is wooden.

N. P. VAN WYK LOUW
(1906–70)

Dedication
Translated from the Afrikaans by Hugh Finn

You were my youth, you gave to me
all that I know of joy and pain;
and of the fullness that was ours
these wordless silences remain.

I had to find then words all new
of hard conjecture, prayers no less,
for one whose passion strove to save
their life in youth and loveliness; –

take these for yours; but I, who go
where higher, colder paths may lead; –
little the comfort, prayers none,
and few but pure the words I need.

Oh Wide and Sad Land
Translated from the Afrikaans by Adam Small

Oh wide and sad land, alone
under the mighty southern stars
will never a happiness break through
your silent sadness
You know the pain and lonesome suffering
of ordinary men each on his own
the unreported dying on the veld
the small man's burial

the simple people who devotedly
do singularly bitter things
and singularly fall like grains of corn
the silent deed, devotion small, and undevotion small
of those who, for some other service, like serfs
would part with you

Raka, Part I

The Coming of Raka
Translated from the Afrikaans by Guy Butler

The women were first to catch sight of him
in the drowsy afternoon when their work was done –
at the wooden mortar, in the young green fields –
when by threes and fours in slender files
with jar and yellow, wind-light calabash
on hip and shoulder through the clutching grasses
they strolled at ease to the cool hippo-pools
to loiter there until the brown, late
twilight and the early stars, with moist sand
and softer mud about their ankles and their hands,
laughing a great deal and talking for hours
or sometimes wading singly and timid
through the tough water plants, naked and gleaming –
Raka, the ape-man, he who cannot think,
black and obscure, a supple bow
of bone and muscle, a mere beast.

Across the water, out of the broken reeds he came
and like a child who silently, toothlessly laughs
at the strangeness of a piebald calabash,
grinned whitely, and squatting, waited.

Nervous, the women moved closer together
and stared across the still stream.
Had he somehow come through the great swamps
where many waters swirl in shallowing circles
in foul scum and lie gleaming under the sun

day-journeys broad, and the flotsam stinks
rotting among rushes and warm reeds?
He was no child of the spacious worlds
of giant forests and great, green streams.

And then with a ripple of his muscles
he stood erect, and on the grey sand
performed a strange dance from his place of birth —
rank with desire, with frantic flight and rape
mating and yelling under compulsion
of urges blind and beyond the reach of speech;
and then like a sprinter spurting towards the tape
dived into the water and disappeared
where the distant bushes make blue corridors —
only to return while the women were still
motionless with wonder — one had shivered
as if the pools were suddenly colder
between the small canes — with a young buck
over his shoulder, its throat freshly
torn out by hand and the fawn hide
still full of twitchings, smeared
with blood; this he shyly let slip
on to the sand across the stream
and laughed engagingly, with eye and teeth
and pink tongue like a dog's; and added
fruit and nuts and sweet cane
plucked with a rough wrench from branches
or ripped up by the pale roots —
but did not utter a single word.

Then the women abandoned the gifts
and through the twilight took the path to the kraal,
the cruses on their heads, slow and slender
and taller now in the meagre light,
rocking on hip and foot, in supple poise;
but said little, for each was disturbed
by the beautiful beast and the strange desire
she felt stirring deep and strong in her heart —
as a playing child who stares down

into the eye of an arid fountain perhaps
might glimpse black water and silver frogs —
his heart stays restless in sunlight and at play
troubled by the surmise of a weird land —
so in the early night they emerged
from the reeds. And that night round the fires
riddle and song were dumb, but the darkness
was living and loud with talk till late.
The children sat wide-eyed and shy
awake until the white ash
of the last logs fell . . .

                The following day
when the blue kingfisher was quiet after hunting
over the smooth warm hippo pools
and slept small on a twig above the water,
the children saw him – Raka, the black beast:
this time he tumbled for their amusement
over the sand, rolled like a horse, grinned, leapt,
hobbled with a lame dance round in a ring —
then suddenly splashed from sight into the water
in which he was quick and otter-smooth.
On to the sand he tossed a shining fish
long as a man's shin and red
and yellow above the white belly . . .
but more than their fear his mad capers
pleased them; laughing they fled
out of the reeds, but laughing looked back
because he was so odd; and back at the kraal
with laughter and fear they told it all.
After this the men perceived his power
from the clues in the great forests: his work
it must be when the black buffalo
who fills the bush tracks and thickets of grass
with hoarse sniffings and lowings, lay stiff in the morning
in the footpath where his heavy body
had snapped in the knees; when the crocodile
lay far out, high on the sand, quivering
like a little lizard children had struck

with a stick; or when the old fencer, the oryx, lay
doubled up, broken, motionless among tussocks –
when the warthog with its white tusks
lay in the grass, with its eyes,
like a fish's, fixed. The hunters knew
what strength was and they were afraid.
But in the red night at the wild feast
with beer and blood and dance and drum
each one felt the new hunt coming
like fire to his feet –
blind were the eyes, white with the vanity of a new power
and a new dance; and obscure words
frothed up through the strangely disturbed
chanting, like murky water that mushrooms to the top
when a huge hippo gets under way
in the dark depths of a whirlpool . . .

                                          Only one was silent
and stood in the night far removed
from the dense throng and the red glare –
Koki, swiftest of foot in the hunt,
the lithe juggler with the javelin, he
who lifts a bullock on his sloping shoulders
and carries it off like a dog – he did not partake
of the dark song that rose out of the ring
through the dust and the smoke – but thought
of the ancient clean desolation that rings
through the older, starker songs, and feared
great evil to be rampant in the blood
of his obsessed people . . .

                                    And now
Raka hung about the kraal like a dog –
During the day no one could take the small footpaths
that twist in and out of the labyrinth
of blue bushes or grass thickets or rushes
without glimpsing his black body moving among the reeds
or the brushwood, or set like a sentry somewhere –
but at night when the bush apes complain
shrill in the dark he wandered about the kraal

like a rustling of small nocturnal beasts;
when the white mist rises off the water
and in the darkness along the damp paths
blends grass and leaf and twig to a single greyness
that sways like long wires in the wind,
Raka would come from his lair and glare
at the glow and the red ribbons of fire
between the stakes; and then they heard
far and sad, lost in the mist,
his cry like that of a beast, or suddenly close
and sharp, his hyena laugh, then wails again
and soft snortings, and late
when the coals were cold and the small smoke wreath
clung close to the ground because of the mist
and smothered kraal and hut with its bitterness, they heard him
sniff loudly at the thin posts in the dark.

Then a woman would move on her mats
restless, pregnant with dreams, and in the quiet hut
suddenly, clearly, would scream
with terror and ecstasy, and half-awake thereafter knew
that the great beast naked and restless
was outside in the dark.

UYS KRIGE
(1910–87)

The Taking of the Koppie

No, it was only a touch of dysentery, he said. He was doing fine
    now thank you . . . What the hell were the chaps grousing
    about anyhow?
He was sitting on the edge of his hospital cot clad only in a slip
    with both his feet on the floor,
his strong young body straight and graceful as a tree, golden as
    any pomegranate but only firmer,
its smooth surface uncracked, gashed with no fissure by the
    burning blazing sun of war;

and with his muscles rippling lightly
like a vlei's shallows by the reeds touched by the first breath of
   the wind of dawn,
as he swung his one leg over onto the other.

He was telling us about the death of the colonel and the major
whom all the men, especially the younger ones, worshipped.
'The colonel copped it from a stray bullet. It must have been a
   sniper . . .
just a neat little hole in the middle of his forehead, no bigger than
   a tickey, and he dropped dead in his tracks.
The major was leading us over some rough open ground
   between the gully and the far koppie
when a burst of machine-gun bullets smacked from the kloof,
   tearing him open;
he was a long way ahead of us all and as he fell he shouted:
"Stop! Stay where you are! Don't come near me! Look out for
   those machine-guns! There's one in the antheap and one on
   the ledge . . . Bring up the mortars! The rest take cover!"
Then he rolled over on his back, blood streaming all over his
   body, and with a dabble of blood on his lips he died – Christ,
   what a man he was!'

The boy reached for a match box, then lighting a cigarette, he
   continued:
'We came on them about ten minutes later, three Ities curled up
   on some straw in a sort of dugout
– as snug as a bug in a rug – and they were sleeping . . .
The two on the outside were young, I noticed. They were all
   unshaven. The bloke in the middle had a dirty grey stubble of
   beard – and that's all I noticed . . .'

As the boy stopped talking he moved, his hair falling in thick
   yellow curls over his forehead, his eyes.
And as I caught the soft gleam of blue behind the strands of gold
I was suddenly reminded of quiet pools of water after rain
among the golden gorse that mantle in early summer
the browning hills of Provence.

'Then I put my bayonet through each of them in turn, just in the
   right place, and they did not even grunt or murmur . . .'

There was no sadism in his voice, no savagery, no brutal pride or
    perverse eagerness to impress,
no joy, no exultation.
He spoke as if he were telling of a rugby match
in which he wasn't much interested
and in which he took no sides.

And as I looked at his eyes again
I was struck with wonderment
at their bigness, their blueness, their clarity
and how young they were, how innocent.

(Addis Ababa, May 1941)

NONGEJENI ZUMA
(c. 1870–1942)

The Praises of Field-marshal J. C. Smuts
Translated from the Zulu by Harry C. Lugg

Gasa, the aggressive one,
Famed for his armoured chariots
Heading for far distant Kenya;
He who fights like a lion brought to bay;
Hustler amongst hustlers.
He whose head baffled the bullets of his foes,
And famous for his buffaloes and Springboks
Vying with each other to reach the North;
He who fights with the weapon of his brother Louis;
The elusive one who slips from the grasp of his enemies,
The whirling whirlwind.

Listen ye upon the mountain tops,
Report to those below,
For great is that which is to come,
Snow-drifts fall and so do men,
And men discuss the news with awe;
Even the heavens become o'ershadowed

And the sun hidden from view;
The fire burns fiercely,
It is the Flame of the Unquenchables.

The red and white bull
Thundered at Cape Town and Pretoria,
His lightning flash struck Mgungundlovu,
And the glitter of it was seen in Bloemfontein.

The cloud which rose from above the Union
To hail its leaden rain upon Somaliland, Libya, Eritrea,
And Abyssinia,
And make men gaze in wonderment.

His snarling teeth were those of lions and tigers,
Fangs of a serpent striking at those who hate him,
For it struck the armoured hosts of Italy.
His helpful hands are clean in the Island Fortress
Where those in London's sequestered places
Laugh with confidence.

He marshalled his volunteers; Springboks answered the call,
And the young men of Mussolini trembled with fear.

He whose innumerable horns are guns
Crowding the skies;
He whose descent to earth destroyed men,
He is the spear that pierced the forts of his enemies:
So that –
In Somaliland fell the shields of men,
In Libya fell the shields of men,
In Keren fell the shields of men,
In Harar fell the shields of men,
In Asmara fell the shields of men,
In Diredawa fell the shields of men.

Thunder which peals over Addis Ababa,
Peals which will soon be felt.

Recorded by the translator shortly before Zuma's retirement in 1942
and translated with assistance from the Rev. J. M. Mpanza and Charles
Mpanza of Mahlabatini. The original is quoted in Vilakazi's thesis, *The
Oral and Written Literature of the Nguni* (1946).

CALVIN MAKABO
(d. 1943)

————— ⌣ —————

Desert Conflict

Translated from the Southern Sotho by Sgt Alexander Qoboshane

Cast your eyes and look over to the ocean and see ships.
It is far, you cannot see with your naked eyes.
Had it not been so, you could see the track of a big sea snake.
It is dusty, it is where the sea dogs play.
Raise the waves and hide yourselves, for you see the country has
    changed.
England and Berlin are in confliction.
It is where we saw bulls in a rage,
Each one being proud of its equipment.

A woman left the baby and ran away,
The women up north are crying,
They cry facing towards the east,
And say 'There our husbands have disappeared'.
Keep silent and listen to the war affairs.
Year before last in September,
There were great flashes towards the west.
It is there the enemy were troublesome.
The Resident Commissioner heard from home,
He heard about great deeds done by Africans,
He heard they were victorious.
Rommel neglected his duties.
The son of Makabo has taken part in those deeds.
The Chiefs at home heard – Chiefs Theko, Litingoana, Seele
    Tane and Mahabe.

You always deceive us and say that
His Majesty King George VI is not seen.
A telegraphic message was sent from England to Tripoli.
It was received in the morning,
And delivered to the companies on Saturday, 21st June.

All Companies according to their race and colour
Coming to cheer the King.
There were those with three stars on their shoulder,
And those who had a crown in their hands.

The General Lyon went down by the main road being silent.
There was wireless round his motor car,
And cannons guarding him on all sides;
Then the soldiers cheered the King as he passed and shouted
  Hurrah!

From *Return to Oasis: War Poems and Recollections from the Middle
East (1940–1946)* where it appears as previously unpublished, with the
following note: 'Written by Sgt Calvin Makabo 1946 Coy. A. A. P. C.
(Basuto), on the occasion of King George VI's visit to the Western
Desert in 1943 after the defeat of Rommel. Sgt Makabo was drowned
west of Tripoli later in 1943. "General Lyon" was the codename for the
King.'

GUY BUTLER
(b. 1918)

Stranger to Europe

Stranger to Europe, waiting release,
My heart a torn-up, drying root
I breathed the rain of an Irish peace
That afternoon when a bird or a tree,
Long known as an exiled name, could cease
As such, take wing and trembling shoot
Green light and shade through the heart of me.

Near a knotty hedge we had stopped.
'This is an aspen.' 'Tell me more.'
Customary veils and masks had dropped.
Each looked at the hidden other in each.
Sure, we who could never kiss had leapt
To living conclusions long before
Golden chestnut or copper beech.

So, as the wind drove sapless leaves
Into the bonfire of the sun,
As thunderclouds made giant graves
Of the black, bare hills of Kerry,
In a swirl of shadow, words, one by one
Fell on the stubble and the sheaves;
'Wild dogrose this; this, hawthorn berry.'

But there was something more you meant,
As if the trees and clouds had grown
Into a timeless flame that burnt
All worlds of words and left them dust
Through stubble and sedge by the late wind blown:
A love not born and not to be learnt
But given and taken, an ultimate trust.

Now, between my restless eyes
And the scribbled wisdom of the ages
Black hills meet moving skies
And through rough hedges a late wind blows;
And in my palm through all the rages
Of lust and love now, always, lie
Brown hawthorn berry, red dogrose.

Great-great-grandmother

Bolt upright, reading her Bible for hours
in a wicker chair on the front stoep in the winter,
in summer under the pepper trees whose lacy shadows
wavered over the lacy shawl,
drawn tight across her little brittle shoulders.

When her sight grew dim someone might read to her –
but deafness following shut that door.
So then she'd sit, there, crocheting for hours
by a remnant of sight and what sense of touch
was left in fingers as dry and shiny as silver leaves
freckled gold and brown.
But mostly her hands lay limp in her lap

except for occasional desperate twitches
which shook the shawl round her shoulders,
the shawl with which she seemed to shelter
her loneliness like a deformity
from a frightened and frightening world.

Alone. Husband and all her own children gone:
living among the noise of children's children
who found it hard to come near the awful
weak-eyed eagle of a race now almost extinct.
Sometimes, though, one of the wives in fumbling compassion
would make a child ask the old, old lady for a story.
She seldom obliged, reluctant to switch her mind
from her beginnings and endings to theirs.

But when she did her stories were mostly biblical
where the miraculous burst into the matter-of-fact
and the weirdly wonderful was all mixed up
with things a child could see at once
were as they always are.

Or sometimes she'd talk of pioneer days, long treks,
locusts darkening the sky, assegai wounds
that would only heal to herbs that the Bushmen knew,
the coffin always ready in the loft, the frequent
births, betrothals, burials.

But rarely of her childhood over the water, among
hills called the Cotswolds, of things we never knew, like snow,
like chestnuts, and nightingales, whole hillsides
deep in perpetual lawn with not a stone to be seen,
trees, without thorns, as high as the house, things
as lovely, strange and barely credible
as chapters in the Bible.

Each sundown her custom was to go for a slow, slow walk
along the selfsame track that had brought her there
three score and all but ten years before,
her long mauve gown trailing a whiff of lavender
through miles of heady mimosa groves,

her cheek far softer and smoother
than any wild petal or fruit.

I was a young savage then, forever
chasing rats and lizards with my catty.
Springtime it was – what passes for spring up there –
that gradual crescendo of heat with little change or colour,
that thorough desiccation of air
before the great clouds stride across the sky
meet growling, and sighing fall.

The blue-headed lizard flicked his tail
and my futile pebble clicked on his purple boulder.
Released from their fatal focus, my eyes drifted up
and there she was, not fifty yards away, stock-still, black,
next to a wild pomegranate, flaming yellow, intense
against the funereal mauves of the scrub.

Was she resting, or dreaming, or peering with lashless eyes
at that annual but always surprising outburst of yellow?
And then, behind her, I saw the whirlwind coming;
now lurching like an inspired dancer
who snatches a beautiful moment
from the verge of a hideous fall,
now stalking straight and poised
like the holy pillar of smoke that led the Israelites
into the Promised Land.

She did not hear or see it come.

It struck her and she was gone.

For a dizzy split-second I thought:
She's been taken up to heaven, like Elijah!
And her shawl spun out of the sky and settled beside me.
Was I Elisha, inheriting
her mantle of powerful pain?

But then I saw her dress like a gnarled old branch
black in the flame of the bush.

I ran up crying, trying to help her.
But she'd sized things up, as always;
she never lost her head.
'Go to the house. Fetch Thomas.'

In her fall she had clutched at the thorny branches.
That's how the palms of her hands were pierced.

She was three long weeks a-dying.

There were times when she struggled to speak,
but it was too late, tetanus being what it is.

They buried her between two thunderstorms.
The scent the damp earth breathed
from the parted lips of her grave
was neither bitter nor sweet.

I did not weep then;
it is now that I weep.

In Memoriam, J. A. R., Drowned, East London

This brilliant boy was stupidly drowned
while his parents watched from the beach,
his special body never recovered
from the indiscriminate sea.

Shrug your shoulders, sigh, say
accidents will happen; try
a little compassionate speech:
it's hardest on those who have to stay.

He was going into the Church.
And there's such a shortage of priests.
Then Who left whom in the lurch?

God loves
in such a mysterious way
sigh, say:
we can't understand His moves.

This boy was here on holiday
from Cambridge, where they say
he disciplined his tongue
to most incisive acts of prayer;
in agony for us here
where light after light is dowsed
he gathered a group of friends
to intercede for his and our land.

What on earth has this to do
with this butterfly-brilliant holiday crowd
drowsing near-naked in salty sand?

It's not much use to look wry, to say
we didn't ask for his impudent prayers;
whether we like it or not, forget or remember,
each Friday across this indiscriminate sea
his friends still pray for us, pray,
lift this landscape of separate beaches
into the indiscriminate light of heaven,
and hold it there.

For one who never set much store
by the efficacy of prayer
this legacy left to a drowsy country
blind in its easy dreams, left
by a dead boy, stupidly drowned,
wrings the mouth from its usual clinch
to tremble at the corners.
Staring at the indiscriminate sea
the eyelids blink to dismiss the impertinent tears.

Boy, young man, even
if there is no heaven
(I stand where your parents stood that day upon the beach)
continue to lift our drowning forgetfulness up,
teach us to look twice at every sea,
to discipline our speech,
to cry, to pray
incisively.

CHARLES EGLINGTON
(1918–71)

Lourenço Marques

Once, grave laodicean profiteer,
This harbour welcomed neutral ships
And warring secrets: enemies,
Remote from where fierce, fatal loyalties
Strode armed with death, strolled casually
And mingled with shut faces and tight hearts
In this pacific city, open then
To an ocean menaced by their conflict.
In still blue waters of flamboyant shade
Intrigue and treason, treachery and hate
Fermented like paludal slime. In febrile dreams
The city shared the strangers' destiny.

Yet, in that tense neutrality
There was a brooding innocence:
The war was far away and though the sea
Might wash a blaze of fire from the night,
The city knew the probabilities;
Its lassitude was old and wise;
The ocean it confronted was
(As backward-looking, sad Pessoa knew)
Salt with the tears of Portugal;
The mother-country's wars had all been fought –
How could there ever come a time
For guilt, expatiation and remorse?

Now (many years have passed) I sit
In still blue waters of flamboyant shade
And muse as sad Pessoa never could:
I lack blood knowledge of those bitter tears,
Those centuries when caravels
Caught storms of hazard in their sails
And left, in spastic writing on all maps

189

Directions to the unknown worlds of earth;
The city, grown and prosperous,
Exalts in me no backward-looking thoughts –
It has the future's brooding innocence.
I sense another taut neutrality.

Its world, though growing old, is young,
Its rooted heritage is germinal:
Behind its tall, proud back a continent
Throws out a challenge, like the oceans once.

RUTH MILLER
(1919–69)

Sterkfontein

Our caves do not go Boom! and make one nervy,
For they are underground, and dark and hard,
And high up near a Scot a Van der Merwe
Has notched his name, and left the crystal scarred.

Our caves say nothing in aggressive manner.
The skulls are dumb, and who would dare say less?
We throw away a flag to flaunt a banner;
Our caves have echoes which say No to Yes.

In India the smooth sides make one shiver,
But here the walls have teeth, the roof is low;
And suddenly a deep and silent river
Looms out of nothing, and into nothing flows.

Some of the time we walk upright, though slowly,
Often we have to stoop and crouch beneath
A craggy corridor, where aching, lowly,
We reach a cavern strewn with ancient teeth.

And when we reach the light – bare veld and boulder
Hard as the hidden bones within the caves
Stand in the wind, that wind which, growing colder,
Will blow us to the kingdom of shared graves.

Poet's note: 'The Sterkfontein caves, Transvaal, were the scene of Dr
Broom's famous discovery of the skeletal remains of prehistoric man.'

Mantis

He lifts his small hands
To god of nothingness.
Jagged legs stand
On pale green crutches.
The pear-shaped pod
Flanged for flight
All dainty lines
Except the head:
Except the triangle terrible as death.

Responding to his hands, I touched him once.
His minute mouth roared
In such a horror of silence that I saw;
I saw his face grow large as mine
The tender spring green blades of him
Thrust like vengeance. His vicious eyes
Glared. His mouth was red
As hell, the pointed face
Filling with knowledgeable malice.
His hands –
Came for me, crept for me, felt for me through the space
Of cosmic distances that make an inch.

Now that I am brittle as a twig
Time having squeezed the sap and wrung me dry
To the bone, to the outdistancing brain,
Being careful to be quiet and restrained,
Would the terrible triangle of my face
Make *him* afraid?

ELISABETH EYBERS
(b. 1915)

Narrative
Translated from the Afrikaans by the poet

A woman grew, with waiting, over-quiet.
The earth along its spiralled path was spun
through many a day and night, now green, now dun;
at times she laughed, and then, at times, she cried.

The years went by. By turns she woke and slept
through the long hours of night, but every day
she went, as women go, her casual way,
and no one knew what patient tryst she kept.

Hope and despair tread their alternate round
and merge into acceptance, till at length
the years have only quietness in store.

And so at last the narrative has found
in her its happy end: this tranquil strength
is better than the thing she's waiting for.

Reflection
Translated from the Afrikaans by the poet

Two moving figures flow together: see,
the glossy wavering of watered serge
has caused their fainting images to merge
and reconciled all incongruity.

But when the rocking copulative bliss
is ruffled from the lake, how can they last
against a rigorous and bitter blast
to blend once more in gentle wantonness?

Snail
Translated from the Afrikaans by the poet

My softness heaves its spiralled canopy:
another roof would be too much to bear.
At home I'm sunk, abroad I'm still at sea,
awkward antennae fumble everywhere.

Hermaphrodite the ruttish ocean spewed
up from the ooze, on dry land I endure
a living thirst by day and night renewed,
and know, except slow death, no certain cure.

Confrontation with an Artist
(for Jean Welz)

His vast frame splayed on an uneasy chair,
he takes me in and I return the stare,
claiming from this antithesis my share.

He punches home the trembling sheet and grips
the ardent charcoal. Hoisting heavy lids,
the bright eyes bore. The pursed lips fire squibs

of approbation. Suddenly distress
as some miscalculation intercepts . . .
He pauses, groans bilingually, reflects,

starts ambling drunkenly around the room,
veers back and sits down squarely to resume
this patient scrimmage with creative doom.

Prepared for his ferocity, I find
him circumspect and eloquent and kind
and marvel at the dartings of his mind.

He has the lead on me for he can trace
immediately the sensuous evidence.

I grapple dumbly with that prow-nosed face.

WALTER BATTISS
(1906–82)

Limpopo

Above my head, as I sleep, are
not stars but names lit up and
the Limpopo is calling them out:
Koo She and Aldebaran,
Dschubba and Saiph,
Kursa and Izar,
Phakt and Minkar,
Zozma and Spika;
The Scorpion's claws:
Zubenelchemale and
Zubenelgenubi.
The Limpopo is
calling their names like
lost children,
calling over the rocks,
Al Suhail, al Wazn,
in the pools, Han and
Yed Prior,
in the rushes, calling for
Nunki and Diphda . . .
Holding hands are three,
Alnilam, Alnitak and Mintaka.
Call again quickly,
Alnilam, Alnitak, Mintaka
walking across the Hunter's Belt.
Whispered as in a dream,
Tsih, Shedir, Chaph.
Call loudly, Menkarlina,
            Menkarlina,
            Menkarlina!
occulted by the moon?
Call again.

Where is Wei?
Hiding and seeking behind clouds
Sing-song names:
Tejat, Mirphak,
Alphekka and Minkar . . .
Alcyone . . . Alcyone! . . .
Alpheratz and Alrischa,
Matar,
Mirach,
Hamal . . .
Unukalhai,
Achernar and Acamar,
Tureis and Turais,
Menkent and Shaula,
Lesath and Girtab . . .
In the Crux Australis,
Mimosa and Mira . . .
The names of the stars
sing me to sleep.

JOHN DRONSFIELD
(1900–51)

Visitation
(for Gwen Ffrangcon-Davies, in memory of 16th March 1951)

Nearly a twelvemonth we had laboured to complete our house,
And labour –
Even though love's labour –
Too long protracted
Wears down the pristine keenness of the mind's teeth,
Dries up the sap of the spirit.

We were tired,
And the house, a prepared stage as yet unlighted,
Awaited the players' entrance,
Breathing uneasily, swaddled in twilight.

Then you came.

Late night, late summer, you chose,
(Gracious, experienced mummer,
With your unerring sense of timing!)
With the applause of an enravished audience still in your ears,
For whom you had made rise
From the chilled cinders of the *Collected Works*
A refulgence of phoenixes,
A baker's dozen of Shakespeare's women.

There you stood,
Framed in the indigo gap of the door,
The lights of Belmont winking for your backcloth,
Smiling, though with Gioconda eyelids a little weary,
Amply costumed as a Cinquecento goddess,
Your flame-shot skirt weed wide enough
To enwrap Nerissa-René too;
Puck, your invisible linkboy, at your elbow
To suffuse at your command
The houses of these latter-day Athenians
With glimmering light.

You entered.

Our long-awaited illumination was here.

One hand outstretched to unhood Puck's lanthorn,
One hand upraised as if to bless our threshold,
One smile that uttered your pleasure, your approval,
One veil-enstifled word — a whispered name —

And the hall was Portia.

Now you must see everything, you said,
And Puck, your captive fire-drake, going before us,
The Petty Tour began.

First, the little sitting-room, the Blue Room.
Here, between walls hung with flamboyant banners,
Weapons of war, and ceremonial double axes,
That might have been plundered from dim Knossian temples

By your black warrior-husband in the Cretan wars,
You shuddered at the sinister carved toys of Africa
And begged your gossip, Emilia-René,
To mark the painted Zodiac on the wall.

And the room was Desdemona.

Now to the dining-room, Puck going before
To light the model theatres, set the puppets frisking.
Dear masque-loving mayfly, did I need Sir Oracle
To tell me how this chamber should be called?
No sooner were you inside, your cousin Hero-René following
    you,
Than through an infinitesimal chink of glass
A star escaped from a picture at your back,
Danced like a marsh-light over your lilting head,
And as we passed into the adjoining yard
Exploded in a merry death of tinkling sparks.

And the room was Beatrice.

Cocking a housewifely eye over the moonlit washing-lines
Hanging from the green rails of the galleried yard,
You turned to the kitchen, nodded grudging approval;
To the broom-cupboard, coal-shed, and 'usual offices'
(To which our liberal servants give a grosser name);
Then crossed to the door of the sleeping-maid's room,
    restraining Puck
Lest he nip through the keyhole and pinch her i' th' bum,
Mumbling the while into your warted dewlap,
'I wash, wring, brew, bake, scour, and do all myself,'
Shaking a wimpled, disapproving head
Over the fecklessness of modern wenches.

And the yard was Quickly.

Next, up the stairway to the Lilliputian garden,
I your donzel bearing your turbulent train;
Pink-fleshed amoretti staring in mute surprise from the walls.
Your fingers touched the heartsblood flags of hibiscus;
You peered through moonstreaked branches, a phoenix,

A smouldering firebird, encaged in the sole Arabian tree.
(O Flower of the middle summer,
What gifts you brought to these men of middle age!)

And the garden was Perdita.

Round the lamplit catwalk you rustled to the upper landing,
Bidding gawping Peter drop your train and take your fan.
A nod told us bathrooms and privies had passed muster.
We followed in your bustling wake to the dressing-room
(Were the wardrobes tidy? The linen folded and lavendered?
Heaven forfend you should not spy that cobweb!);
Through to the guest-room, a very pouncet-box of a chamber,
Fit for that proper gentleman the County Paris himself.
Would that censorious, sparrow-hawk eye commend or
    condemn?
You smiled: your three chins wagged approval. Sweet Jesu! We
    breathed again.

And these rooms were Juliet's Nurse.

Our bedroom was in darkness and dark we kept it,
Puck leaving his lanthorn hooded, the better to see
From the high window the city's thousand-and-one lights,
A bushel of sequins tricked out on an indigo cape.
We, behind you, saw your arm circle Celia-René,
Both gazing beyond the mountain to the biding forest:
'Sweet coz, tomorrow we shall be in Arden. The less fools we;
If we were at home we were in a worser place!'
Ganymede and Aliena, silent against the spangled glass,
Half thrilled, half scared, at banishment and metamorphosis.
Then Puck unleashed his light, the present slid back,

And the room was Rosalind.

Crossing the landing you entered my untidy work-room,
Glanced around, then softly commanded Puck
To summon his domestick fairies, when the house was abed,
To set in decent order the riot of objects —
Spilt pigments, jumbled canvases, scattered brushes —

And come, with brooms before, to sweep the dust behind the
    door.
(Lord, what hogs these artists be!) Then, the spiced African air
Reminding you, you fell to thinking of that dark, dead girl,
Your erstwhile playmate, and of her blackamoor son, your
    darling charge,
But the shallow fairy grief as quickly turned to laughter,
And waving an invisible wand in benison you were gone.

And the room was Titania.

Through Antony's bedroom you passed to the inner room,
Green-painted, raftered chamber of the Garter Inn;
Pausing in the doorway to hear the Windsor bell strike twelve;
On either hand a bed. Which, i' th' dickens, you wondered,
Housed nightly the Fat Knight? for, by cock and pie,
Five such, pushed together like the great bed of Ware,
Could scarce encompass that monstrous conglobation of bum
    and belly.
But you could muse no further. Was it not midnight by Windsor
    clock?
You turned to Alice-René at your side: 'Sweet Gossip Ford,
Is not this a pretty, cleanly lodging?' Then: 'Good Master
    Clarke,
Heaven give you many, many merry days of it.'

And the rooms were Mistress Page.

Descending the staircase, I your Boyet, your trainbearer,
Your doting courtiers pomaded spaniels at your heels,
You became for a moment the Princess of France
And your laughter rang out as Rosaline-René called to mind
The incident of the discomfited mess of Russians;
And your silken progress brought you, laughing still, to the last
    room.

You had scarcely crossed the threshold ere I guessed its name.

But I will draw the curtain and show the picture:
Framed by the floreated carving of the window-seat
You sat, as gracious a piece of Eve's flesh as any in Illyria.

We brought you coffee and you talked – of plays and players,
Of friends and places in England, whence you had lately
    returned.
At length you rose to go, but lingered awhile,
Wandering from wall to wall of the high-ceilinged room,
Paying graceful tribute to our Lares and Penates,
Begging Maria-René to notice that and this.
That strange, unnameable quality you possess
Seemed to have entered a little into all of us.
Our spirits were quickened, our senses heightened: we were your
    bondsmen.
Oh, I would not have given my part of this night
For a pension of thousands to be paid from the Sophy!

And this last room was Olivia.

Puck lighting the way, you went to your waiting car,
But the glow of your presence remained behind in the house;
An effulgence, an inspiration, a thing not to be quenched.
Kisses exchanged, we waved you into the darkness.

Good-night, ladies;
Good-night, sweet ladies; good night, good night.

> Morgan le Fay, ageless Welsh sorceress,
> Protean portrayer of evil and of good,
> The play is over now; the actors go:
> We to our beds; you to Broceliande Wood.

N. H. BRETTELL
(b. 1908)

— ❧ —

African Student
(Shakespeare for A-level)

The pressure lamp hisses into the silence
The narrow radius of sufficiency.
Mousefoot, moth-flutter, batswing, fumble and twitch
The foolscap shadows of the thatch.

Black scholar, intent, impassive still, you have no place
In time or language: as, pages rapidly flicking,
You turn from text to gloss to commentary,
Or now, as one listening to music might
Stare through the face of a friend,
You with poised pencil point look up, question the night,
Midnight, Twelfth Night, or what you will.

Or what you will: Illyria or Arcady,
The polity that never was but could be now,
Built with the measureless cubes of want and wit;
After the wit-weary exit of the courtiers,
The lonely envoi of the clown's last song
Leaves questions hung like cobwebs. Can you then
Sort out the faceless fragments into place,
Print on the dark your projects' clean impress,
With ridge and furrow the uncouth landscape combing,
To every Hodge his acre, every Jack his mistress —
O mistress mine where are you roaming?

Roaming: keep your wild hills for roaming; rest
Within the enormous solace of their thighs.
Still pick your ditties out of the wind's teeth,
Wind and the rain, the clean and bitter east
That shakes the bright drops from the flinching leaves
To twitch and fall like notes of harpsichord
To the nimble tissues of the cricket's fiddle:
Each untouched thing that still is but a toy;
The land is innocent still: so, keep innocency,
Keep the half-naked thing you were
When that you were and a little tiny boy.

Boy now no longer. Eye for eye we stare
Into the dark that tilts towards some dawn.
Can we accept these half-surmised replies,
That benign irony that still could make
Its chorus of the necessary clown,
Strolling aloof through knot-garden and gallery,
Accosting duke and dunce indifferently —

Accept the final self-withdrawn surrender,
The grim staff snap, the ruthless hands recall,
The god-like hands that jerked the puppet strings;
Could you, or I, with honesty endure
That golden franchise that embraced them all —
The knave, the gull, the Jew, the blackamoor?

On an Inyanga Road
(for Edward Thomas)

Up the dark avenue, leading to no end,
We both plod on, he thirty years ahead,
Leaving the circled hearth, the book, the friend,
Seeking a word no friend or book has said:

Leaving the hearth, although the cruel rain
Claws the blind pane, and the casement stay
Yelps at the cuff of the wind. The counterpane
Is smooth with sleep. It was his way

To clench up his joy as tight as bud or fist
And think as straight as ploughboy throws a stone.
The blue scythe of his eyes would slice the mist
The Merlin's isle I've sought in an alien sun,

And, like him, never found, losing my way, myself.
On we go, on and up. The track is harsh with flint,
Diamonds but quartz and turquoise scraps of delf,
His the edged splinter, mine
The agate's curious grain of serpentine.
Through the black pines the constellations glint
And scrawl their heartless theorems on the sky.

His long stride never falters left or right:
Even at eighty-odd you can go far in a night.

The final hills arch their enormous crests,
Stretch their black necks up to the steepest pitch
Of the world's utmost gable: to Sheba's Breasts
Or Mother Dunch's Buttocks — which?

JOSEPH KUMBIRAI
(1922–86)

Dawn

Translated from the Shona by Douglas Livingstone

Cock-crow and early-rise!
Venus, the morning star, appears,
a first light, growing.

The sky is a blood-orange;
the first zestful breeze delights the heart
but shrivels up the morning star.

The roosters' voices fade
while the light gets brighter;
the elephants of dawn have finished washing.

The first dew steams
along with smoking hearths;
birds awaken, chirruping.

Brilliantly, pristine,
the great sun appears
like a large and glittering forehead.

Children warm their backs,
shouting: The sun,
the sun is King!

Their little polished heads
shimmer and glitter
like leaves turning from the west.

As the sun sets, so we set;
as the sun rises, so we rise:
the sun, the sun is King!

SOLOMON MUTSWAIRO
(b. 1924)

My Birds

Translated from the Shona by the poet and Donald E. Herdeck

All birds that swim are mine:
The ducks that drink neck-arched are mine,
The kingfisher – he is mine,
The pondfowl is also mine.

All birds that fly are mine:
The dove, the drongo-shrike are mine,
The black bird and the turtle-dove are mine,
The hornbill, the hammerhead and the honey-bird are mine.

And all birds that run are mine:
The ground hornbills, the korhaans are mine,
The secretary-birds – these are mine,
Turkeys and ostriches are also mine.

Birds that crouch in running are mine:
The bush partridges, the giant-breasted bustards are mine,
Francolins, spurfowls and partridges are mine,
The quail, the fowl and the guinea-hen are mine.

All birds that sing are mine:
The starling and the waxbill,
The hoopoe and the skylark are mine,
The widow-bird and the Go'way bird are mine.

Birds that eat birds are not mine:
The lizard buzzard is not mine,
The eagle and the falcon are not mine,
The hawk and the kite are not mine.

Nocturnal birds are not mine:
The pennant-winged nightjar is not mine,
And the owlet, and the house-owl are not mine,
All the large owl species, no, these witches are not mine!

Day or night, wet or dry, hawk or dove,
There is one better; indeed, the finest,
Silent singer in carven stone – the symbol of peace,
Remnant, hope, love – the unruined bird of Zimbabwe.

AARON HODZA
(1924–83)

The Slighted Wife
Translated from the Shona by George Fortune

My husband, our opened home has broken my heart.
Did I not say a second marriage would destroy us!
It is destroying a home that once stood firm.
Did I not say again a new marriage would consume it!
See where it has brought us today,
The second home you wanted has destroyed our peace.

While we were two, we would eat warm food together,
Night and day like the ladle and the water-pot.
Grindstone and grinder envied our intimacy.
Like children waiting for their share of the fowl we waited for
 each other.
But today I am a fowl feeding among refuse of your lack of care.

My husband, before this other came into our home,
You and I were squirrels, squabbling but in one hole,
Eating porridge stirred by a single whisk alone,
Served into our single dish, we were two,
Seasoning our morsels from a porringer without partition,
Each an invitation to the other as a pair of doves.

Before love learned to splinter into branches,
There was always love and laughter in our home.
Today I feel naked of affection like a witch.
Thought and reflections burden my heart.
All the joy and laughter that there once was
Seems like a story now.

Your new love is given pride of place today.
It is I who am made to seem the second wife.
The place of your first wife is taken by your favourite
Not even your footprints do I see more at my door.
I may not even tell you what distresses me.
You have forgotten that it was for you that I came here
Had it been for food, I would have long gone.

GERALDO BESSA VICTOR
(b. 1917)

That Old Mulemba
Translated from the Portuguese by Donald Burness

That old mulemba . . .

Men armed with machetes
and axes came,
hardened in body and soul
(where goodness is not sown)
ordered by someone with a heart of stone
– and thus, in the name of the law,
they demolished and killed
that old mulemba,
old queen without a king.

They did not suffer, they did not cry;
I alone cried;

My old mulemba . . .
Under its shade (I was a kid),
playing with other children,
I tried a step of the massemba . . .
So many times I stretched out my mat
and there did sums
under the shade of the mulemba.

Alone I cried from nostalgic yearning,
when today I saw it fallen,
dead. It was as if
it were the death of my own life!

You, reader, who are reading me,
you are going to tell me with surprise:
Why do you suffer? I do not understand
The cause of your weeping.
They cut down a cashew-tree,
where you ate so many good cashew nuts;
they cut down a baobab,
where you savoured many mucuas;
they also cut down a tamarind-tree
where you ate the tasty tamarind.
They cut down those trees
that provided you shade and fruit;
and you remained like a beast,
you did not feel then the compassion
that you now have for the old mulemba,
that gave you nothing but shade!

No one can understand
the grief of my longing,
which causes me to suffer!

You, reader who are reading me,
please note this truth
which I can never forget.

– Once as a boy
I tugged at the moustaches of my old grandfather;
he gave a slap,
so that my black face turned red.
So, for many years, day after day,
I used to pull the branches of the old mulemba,
out of them I made a swing to play;
and the old mulemba never became angry,
never did anything to me,
not a single slap, not a single lament,

other than the strokings of the long beard
on my face, on my body, when the wind
was kissing and shaking it . . .

My old mulemba . . .
Ah! I alone know what makes me suffer!

Note on a Shop in the Muceque

Translated from the Portuguese by Don Burness

In the shop in the muceque
of S. Paulo de Luanda,
a black child is sucking sherbet,
a white child is eating quitaba,
both smiling, both singing,
the first 'Maria Candimba', the second 'April in Portugal'.

And my poet's soul
– a hybrid soul, luso-tropical –
discerns signs of Africa
in the gesture of the white child
and visions of Europe
in the look of the black child.

JOAQUIM PAÇO D'ARCOS
(1906–81)

Re-encounter

Translated from the Portuguese by Roy Campbell

The jetty with its old wormeaten planks,
The cheerless sand-dunes and the ancient fort,
The desert that advances on the sea
Peppering the poor city with its yellow dust
And burying it in sand.

The vegetable gardens of Giraul,
A timid streak of green in sandy wastes,
The withered flowerbeds, burnt and dried,
By the fierce sun of Africa,
Destroy, when re-encountered thus, the image
Of the lush park which memory retained.
The little garden in the city,
Without its bandstand now,
But with its filing spectres,
Its long, interminable files of spectres . . .
Miss Blond out walking with her childish charges.
'Tiger', the dog, so mute and mild and sleepy.
The Negroes with submissive, startled looks,
Walking with fettered feet
Through a street of mud-built huts and yielding earth.
Miss Blond no longer takes the children walking,
Tall, noble 'Tiger' died of ripe old age,
The natives long ago destroyed their fetters,
Only the spectres have remained
Where they were left. They, only, populate
The memory and inhabit the town,
With their faint, beloved voices,
With their lost voices
In the deserted house, which now the desert
Covers with dust, and in this life, which time
Is covering with its dust,
In death, in memory, in death . . .

(Moçamedes, 8 December 1950)

AGOSTINHO NETO
(1922–79)

We Must Return

Translated from the Portuguese by Michael Wolfers

To our homes, to our labours
to the beaches, to our fields
we must return

To our lands
red with coffee
white with cotton
green with maize
we must return

To our diggings of diamonds
gold, copper and petroleum
we must return

To our rivers, and our lakes
to the mountains and forests
we must return

To the freshness of the fig tree
to our legends
our rhythms and fires
we must return

To drum and thumb piano
to the throb of carnival
we must return

To the fair Angolan country
to our land, our mother
we must return

We must return
to liberated Angola –
Angola independent

(Aljube Prison, October 1960)

ANTONIO JACINTO
(b. 1924)

Poem of Alienation
Translated from the Portuguese by Michael Wolfers

This is not yet my poem
the poem of my soul and of my blood
no
I still lack knowledge and power to write my poem
the great poem I feel already turning in me

My poem wanders aimlessly
in the bush or in the city
in the voice of the wind
in the surge of the sea
in the Aspect and the Being

My poem steps outside
wrapped in showy cloths
selling itself
selling
   'lemons, buy my le-e-e-emons'

My poem runs through the streets
with a putrid cloth pad on its head
offering itself
offering
   'mackerel, sardine, sprats
   fine fish, fine fi-i-i-sh . . .'

My poem trudges the streets
'here J'urnal' 'Dai-i-i-ly'
and no newspaper yet carries my poem

My poem goes into the cafés
'lott'ry draw-a tomorra lott'ry draw-a tomorra'
and the draw of my poem
wheel as it wheels

whirl as it whirls
never changes
   'lott'ry draw-a tomorra
   lott'ry draw-a tomorra'

My poem comes from the township
on Saturdays bring the washing
on Mondays take the washing
on Saturdays surrender the washing and surrender self
on Mondays surrender self and take the washing

My poem is in the suffering
of the laundress's daughter
shyly
in the closed room
of a worthless boss idling
to build up an appetite for the violation

My poem is the prostitute
in the township at the broken door of her hut
   'hurry hurry
   pay your money
   come and sleep with me'

My poem lightheartedly plays at ball
in a crowd where everyone is a servant
and shouts
   'offside goal goal'

My poem is a contract worker
goes to the coffee fields to work
the contract is a burden
that is hard to load
   'contract wor-r-r-ker'

My poem walks barefoot in the street

My poem loads sacks in the port
fills holds
empties holds
and finds strength in singing

'tué tué tué trr
arrimbuim puim puim'

My poem goes tied in ropes
met a policeman
paid a fine, the boss
forgot to sign the pass
goes on the roadwork
with hair shorn
  'head shaved
  chicken braised
  o Zé'

a goad that weighs
a whip that plays

My poem goes to market works in the kitchen
goes to the workbench
fills the tavern and the gaol
is poor ragged and dirty
lives in benighted ignorance
my poem knows nothing of itself
nor how to plead

My poem was made to give itself
to surrender itself
without asking for anything

But my poem is not fatalist
my poem is a poem that already wants
and already knows
my poem is I-white
mounted on me-black
riding through life.

D. J. OPPERMAN
(1914–85)

Fable
Translated from the Afrikaans by Jack Cope

Under a dung-cake
with the rain in spate
two earthworms held
a terse debate

on 'you' and 'me'
and 'my native land',
on 'my mud-hut
was first to stand.'

A casual spade
by chance sank through,
the earthworms both
were chopped in two:

Four earthworms now
jerk slimily along
the 'I's' and the 'you's'
doubt where they belong.

In the next thick mush
of a meeting place
politely each
greets his own face.

Christmas Carol
Translated from the Afrikaans by Anthony Delius

Three outas from the High Karoo
saw the star, believed the angel true,

took knob-sticks, and three bundles with
and set forth along a jackal path,

following that bright and moving thing
that shone on shanty, rock and spring,

on zinc and sacking of District Six –
in a broken bottle a candle flicks

where salt fish hangs and donkeys jib,
and lights them kneeling by the crib.

Biltong, sheep fat, and eggs they've piled
humbly before God's small brown child.

With hymn and prayer for thanks, they tell
That a child will save *this* folk as well . . .

And on her nest, throughout the whole affair
a bantam clucks with a suspicious stare.

ADAM SMALL
(b. 1936)

Brown Lullaby

They call your mama girl
love
they call your mama girl
all places that she go
they call your mama girl
they see to all the white man first
your mama she must wait
your mama she must wait very long
afore they call her girl
but your mama she come home
love
your mama she come home
for nothin' but to love you
your mama she come home

an' she love you more than she got to wait
aye even more
an' more today than yesterday
more everyday

There's Somethin'

You can stop me
drinking a coke
at the café
in the Avenue
or goin' to
an Old Nic revue,
you can stop me doin'
some silly thing like that
but o
there's somethin' you can
never never do;
you can stop me
boarding a coach
on the Jo'burg run
white class
or sittin' in front
of the X-line
on the Claremont bus,
you can stop me doin'
some silly thing like that
but o
there's somethin' you can
never never do;
you can stop me
goin' to Groote Schuur
in the same ambulance
as you
or tryin' gettin' to Heaven
from a Groote Kerk pew,
you can stop me doin'

some silly thing like that
but o
there's somethin' you can
never never do;
true's God
you can stop me doin'
all silly things of the sort
and to think of it
if it comes to that
you can even stop me hatin'
but o
there's somethin' you can
never never do —
you can't
ever
ever
ever stop me
loving
even you!

What abou' de Law?

Translated from the Afrikaans by Carrol Lasker

Diana was a white girl
Martin was a black boy

they fell in love
they fell in love
they fell in love

Said Diana's folks
What abou' de law
Said Martin's folks
What abou' de law
said everyone's folks
What abou' de law

Said Diana, said Martin
What law?
God's law
man's law
devil's law
what law

But the folks just said
de law
de law
de law
de law
what abou' de law
what abou' de law

Diana was a white girl
Martin was a black boy

they go to jail
they go to jail
they go to jail

Said Diana's folks
See, we told you mos
Said Martin's folks
See, we told you mos
said everyone's folks
see, we told you mos

Said Diana, said Martin
what you tell
what God tell
what man tell
what devil tell
what you tell?

But the folks just said
de law
de law
de law
de law

what abou' de law, huh
what abou' de law?

Diana was a white girl
Martin was a black boy

Diana commit suicide
Martin commit suicide
Diana and Martin commit suicide

Say Diana's folks
O God protect
Say Martin's folks
O God protect
Say everyone's folks
O God protect

Diana and Martin they died for de law
God's law
man's law
devil's law
what law?

And the folks just said
de law
de law
de law
de law
What abou' de law
What abou' de law?

Second Coming

Translated from the Afrikaans by Carrol Lasker

I

Lord, I also want to meet you, see
Surely I've not been singing
'Jesus be with me' all this time
for nothing.

So Lord, when you've climbed out of your limo
and each and every big guy is finished with his speech
and shaking the hands
All the VIP's who've prayed so much
for our society and our land
Before you climb back into your private car
ay, with your bodyguard
before the motorcycles with their sirens
escort you away to the reception of his honour, the mayor,
and his excellency, the President
I ask you, Lord Jesus,
Please lift your head and turn this way
just once and notice me back here
and smile.
Please.

II

When the Lord
stepped off the jet
at the airport
between the streamers on the tarmac
and gave the V-sign
to the Lord Jesus fan club,
there wasn't even room for a mouse.

In the press conference
which followed
He apologized
and expressed sincere regrets
that he was forced to delay this assignment for so long
He had really tried His best, He explained
but like He also explained,
a superstar always
follows His Manager's Will,
never His own.

Then He kindly agreed
to pose with the teenagers
before a whole battery of

media people – press photographers, whatnot
The groupies screamed
and spontaneously broke into dance
(picture on page three) –

and they all warmly applauded the Lord
when He revealed He was to hold a personal appearance show
for his non-white fans, a special at the Gem.

DENNIS BRUTUS
(b. 1924)

Cold

the clammy cement
sucks our naked feet

a rheumy yellow bulb
lights a damp grey wall

the stubbled grass
wet with three o'clock dew
is black with glittery edges;

we sit on the concrete,
stuff with our fingers
the sugarless pap
into our mouths

then labour erect;

form lines;

steel ourselves into fortitude
or accept an image of ourselves
numb with resigned acceptance;

the grizzled senior warder comments:
'Things like these
I have no time for;

they are worse than rats;
you can only shoot them.'

Overhead
the large frosty glitter of the stars
the Southern Cross flowering low;

the chains on our ankles
and wrists
that pair us together
jangle

glitter.

We begin to move
    awkwardly.

(Colesberg)

Letters to Martha, 1 and 2

1

After the sentence
mingled feelings:
sick relief,
the load of the approaching days
apprehension –
the hints of brutality
have a depth of personal meaning;

exultation –
the sense of challenge,
of confrontation,
vague heroism
mixed with self-pity
and tempered by the knowledge of those
who endure much more
and endure . . .

2

One learns quite soon
that nails and screws
and other sizeable bits of metal
must be handed in;

and seeing them shaped and sharpened
one is chilled, appalled
to see how vicious it can be
– this simple, useful bit of steel:

and when these knives suddenly flash
– produced perhaps from some disciplined anus –
one grasps at once the steel-bright horror
in the morning air
and how soft and vulnerable is naked flesh.

MAZISI KUNENE
(b. 1930)

A Meeting with Vilakazi, the Great Zulu Poet
Translated from the Zulu by the poet

Sleep tried to split us apart
But the great dream created a new sun.
Through its towering rays two worlds emerged
And our twin planets opened to each other.
I saw you descending from a dazzling hill,
Your presence filled the whole world.
I heard the drums beat behind your footsteps
And the children of the south began to sing.
They walked on the ancient path of the goddess
    Nomkhubulwane
And the old dancing arena was filled with festival crowds.
Your great songs echoed to the accompaniment of the festival
    horn.
It was the beginning of our ancient new year

Before the foreigners came, before they planted their own
    emblems.
I came to the arena and you held my hand.
Together we danced the boast-dance of our forefathers
We sang the great anthems of the uLundi mountains.

When My Poems were Lost
Translated from the Zulu by the poet

Where is the arbiter of a thousand languages?
Where is the narrator of the traveller's tales?
Where is the hunter of the beautiful words?
Where is the patient one whose visions are the stars?
Where is the magic lover whose hands carry the season's secrets?
Where is the stranger who walked through the mist?
Where is the granddaughter of the first sea-mountains?
Where is the one who created a feast of song in the wilderness?
Where is the one who gave milk to the children?
Where is the one who no longer sang the songs of the birds?
Where is the one whose hair was white like the waterfalls?

'Advice' to a Young Poet
Translated from the Zulu by the poet

O Meliwa, I come, a messenger of the Beautiful Ones.
Intermediate between man and beast, I,
A cousin of the roaring elephant and the rhinoceros.
I have had my own share of hunters
I still bear the scar of my youth, their fun;
But I gored the little pest, trampled him under foot.
So I confess I am not innocent or noble
But I am chosen for my experience.
I bring before you, our cousin the cow, for sacrifice.
After the feast, after the festival, after the drunkenness
I shall give then the Message.
I shall say:

'Take from me this dagger, their gift,
It cannot kill but mankind prefers fear to love.
Because of it many will bow down their heads.
They will sing of you and say:
"My god of plenty, my god of power
Grant that I may rule the earth for all time."
Take heed do not yield
Or begin to tell the truths of your secrets.
Imagination feeds only on future promises
Man follows those who shall produce a harvest.
Yes for a while say a few wise things
Yet know: all dreams, and all visions are suspect
Not yours, not theirs, do they contain the truth
Not even these words.
Search then from all things
Search for the message that is yours.'
I have obeyed their commands
Not that I believe in all they said
Nor do I think they are fair to humankind
But then that is my own truth and ecstasy.

Nozizwe

Translated from the Zulu by the poet

You were to be the centre of our dream
To give life to all that is abandoned.
You were to heal the wound
To restore the bones that were broken.
But you betrayed us!
You chose a lover from the enemy
You paraded him before us like a sin.
You dared embrace the killer of your father
You led your clans to the gallows.
You mocked the gods of our Forefathers.
You shouted our secrets before the little strangers
You mocked the sacred heads of our elders
You cast down their grey hair before the children

Their lips that hold the ancient truths were sealed.
By their sunken eyes your body was cursed
The moving river shall swallow it!

Nozizwe – a traitor who served the South African police.

Death of the Miners
or, The Widows of the Earth
Translated from the Zulu by the poet

We waited in silence for our children
Their voices wounded the earth.
It was as if our very footsteps
Crushed their last breath of life

The final day came . . .
Our village was a forest of new comers and goers
Decorations were suspended on high poles of the village.
Men with polished shoes and women with high pitched voices
Paraded the streets like some freshly fed peacocks
Yes! Bells, voices, sirens:
'THE LEADER has arrived'
Proclaimed the carefully woven banners
Only then and only then did we know the fate of our men . . .

Life continues unchanged in our village
Men still leave early at dawn.
Silence walks where once was the pomp of yesterday.
Old tattered flags hang on the side-streets
Only us and the memory of pain remain
We are the widows of the earth
We are the orphans of stone
Insanity stares unblinkingly through the broken windows.

Those who waited in the night of the earth
Until their eyes succumbed to the darkness
Until they bellowed with mocking laughter,
Until they lived the illusion of escape;
They were our fathers, our husbands and our children.

On that day, on that morning
The last words were spoken softly on the doorsteps
The air was cold
The farewells were long.

News travels fast these days
Suddenly our village was invaded by whiskered men
By those who spoke for us to yet others
Who spoke for us.
They clucked in a language that was foreign to us.

These were Publicmen and Writers
And men of substance who make money and interviews.
Some spoke casually to us
Until told we were the wives and children of 'Them'.
Then they came closer to us to dissect our feelings
To know how we had spent the night.

They did not remember
We had seen them that very day
Talking wisely for us in those boxes.
From their words you would have thought
They knew all the buried truths of our husbands' terrors
In truth to know so much is a gift of divining.

ARTHUR NORTJE
(1942–70)

Cosmos in London

Leaning over the wall at Trafalgar Square
we watch the spray through sun-drenched eyes,
eyes that are gay as Yeats has it:
the day suggests a photograph.
Pigeons perch on our shoulders as we pose
against the backdrop of a placid embassy,
South Africa House, a monument of granite.
The seeds of peace are eaten from our brown palms.

My friend in drama, his beady black eyes
in the Tally Ho saloon at Kentish Town:
we are exchanging golden syllables
between ensembles. I break off to applaud
a bourgeois horn-man. A fellow in a yellow
shirt shows thumbs up: men are demonstrative.
While big-eyed girls with half-pints stand
our minds echo sonorities of elsewhere.

One time he did Macbeth
loping across like a beast in Bloemfontein
(Othello being banned along with Black Beauty).
The crowd cheered, they cheered also
the witches, ghosts: that moment you could feel
illiteracy drop off them like a scab.
O come back Africa! But tears may now
extinguish even the embers under the ash.

There was a man who broke stone
next to a man who whistled Bach.
The khaki thread of the music emerged
in little explosions from the wiry bodies.
Entranced by the counterpoint
the man in the helmet rubbed his jaw
with one blond hand, and with the other
pinned the blue sky up under his rifle.

Tobias should be in London. I could name
Brutus, Mandela, Luthuli — but that memory
disturbs the order of the song, and whose
tongue can stir in such a distant city?
The world informs her seasons, and she,
solid with a kind of grey security,
selects and shapes her own strong tendencies.
We are here, nameless, staring at ourselves.

It seems at times as if I am
this island's lover, and can sing her soul,
away from the stuporing wilderness where
I wanted the wind to terrify the leaves.

Peach aura of faces without recognition,
voices that blossom and die bring need for death.
The rat-toothed sea eats rock, and who escapes
a lover's quarrel will never rest his roots.

(London, 1966)

Immigrant

Don't travel beyond
Acton at noon in the intimate summer light
of England

to Tuskaloosa, Medicine Hat, preparing
for flight

dismissing the blond aura of the past
at Durban or Johannesburg
no more chewing roots or brewing riots

Bitter costs exorbitantly at London
airport in the neon heat
waiting for the gates to open

Big boy breaking out of the masturbatory
era goes
like eros over atlantis (sunk
in the time-repeating seas, admire our
tenacity)
jetting into the bulldozer civilization
of Fraser and Mackenzie
which is the furthest west that man has gone

A maple leaf is in my pocket.
X-rayed, doctored at Immigration
weighed in at the Embassy
measured as to passport, smallpox, visa
at last the efficient official informs me
I am an acceptable soldier of fortune, don't

tell the Commissioner
I have Oxford poetry in the satchel
propped between my army surplus boots
for as I consider Western Arrow's
pumpkin pancake buttered peas and chicken canadian style
in my mind's customs office
questions fester that turn the menu
into a visceral whirlpool. You can see
that sick bags are supplied.

Out portholes beyond the invisible propellers
snow mantles the ground peaks over Greenland.
What ice island of the heart has weaned
you away from the known white kingdom
first encountered at Giant's Castle?
You walked through the proteas nooked in the sun rocks
I approached you under the silver trees.
I was cauterized in the granite glare
on the slopes of Table Mountain, I was baffled
by the gold dumps of the vast Witwatersrand
when you dredged me from the sea like a recent fossil.

Where are the mineworkers, the compound Africans,
your Zulu ancestors, where are
the root-eating, bead-charmed Bushmen, the Hottentot
    sufferers?
Where are the governors and sailors of the
Dutch East India Company, where are
Eva and the women who laboured in the castle?
You are required as an explanation.

Glaciers sprawl in their jagged valleys,
cool in the heights, there are mountains and mountains.
My prairie beloved, you whose eyes are
less forgetful, whose fingers are less oblivious
must write out chits for the physiotherapy customers
must fill out forms for federal tax.

Consolatory, the air whiskies my veins.
The metal engines beetle on to further destinations.

Pilot's voice reports over Saskatchewan
the safety of this route, the use of exits,
facility of gas masks, Western Arrow's
miraculous record. The flat sea washes
in Vancouver bay. As we taxi in
I find I can read the road signs.

Maybe she is like you, maybe most women
deeply resemble you, all of them are
all things to all poets: the cigarette girl
in velvet with mink nipples, fishnet thighs,
whose womb is full of tobacco.
Have a B. C. apple in the A. D. city of the saviour,
and sing the centennial song.

(1967)

Native's Letter

Habitable planets are unknown or too
far away from us to be
of consequence. To be of
value to his homeland must the wanderer
not weep by northern waters, but love
his own bitter clay
roaming through the hard cities, tough
himself as coffin nails.

Harping on the nettles of his melancholy,
keening on the blue strings of the blood,
he will delve into mythologies perhaps
call up spirits through the night.

Or carry memories apocryphal
of Tshaka, Hendrik Witbooi, Adam Kok,
of the Xhosa nation's dream
as he moonlights in another country:

231

but he shall also have
cycles of history
outnumbering the guns of supremacy.

Now and wherever he arrives
extending feelers into foreign scenes
exploring times and lives,
equally may he stand and laugh,
explode with a paper bag of poems,
burst upon a million televisions
with a face as in a Karsh photograph,
slave voluntarily in some siberia
to earn the salt of victory.

Darksome, whoever dies
in the malaise of my dear land
remember me at swim,
the moving waters spilling through my eyes:
and let no amnesia
attack at fire hour:
for some of us must storm the castles
some define the happening.

(Toronto, May 1970)

NOÉMIA DE SOUSA
(b. 1927)

——— ~ ———

The Poem of João

Translated from the Portuguese by Margaret Dickinson

João was young like us
João had wide awake eyes
and alert ears
hands reaching forwards
a mind cast for tomorrow
a mouth to cry an eternal 'no'
João was young like us.

João enjoyed art and literature

enjoyed poetry and Jorge Amado
enjoyed books of meat and soul
which breathe life, struggle, sweat and hope
João dreamt of Zambezi's flowing books spreading culture
for mankind, for the young, our brothers
João fought that books might be for all
João loved literature
João was young like us.

João was the father, the mother, the brother of multitudes
João was the blood and the sweat of multitudes
and suffered and was happy like the multitudes
He smiled that same tired smile of shop girls leaving work
he suffered with the passivity of the peasant women
he felt the sun piercing like a thorn in the Arabs' midday
he bargained on bazaar benches with the Chinese
he sold tired green vegetables with the Asian traders
he howled spirituals from Harlem with Marion Anderson
he swayed to the Chope marimbas on a Sunday
he cried out with the rebels their cry of blood
he was happy in the caress of the manioc-white moon
he sang with the shibalos their songs of homesick longing
and he hoped with the same intensity of all
for dazzling dawns with open mouths
to sing
João was the blood and sweat of multitudes
João was young like us.

João and Mozambique were intermingled
João would not have been João without Mozambique
João was like a palm tree, a coconut palm
a piece of rock, a Lake Niassa, a mountain
an Incomati, a forest, a maçala tree
a beach, a Maputo, an Indian Ocean
João was an integral and deep-rooted part of Mozambique
João was young like us.

João longed to live and longed to conquer life
that is why he loathed prisons, cages, bars

and loathed the men who make them.
For João was free
João was an eagle born to fly
João loathed prisons and the men who make them
João was young like us.

And because João was young like us
and had wide awake eyes
and enjoyed art and poetry and Jorge Amado
and was the blood and sweat of multitudes
and was intermingled with Mozambique
and was an eagle born to fly
and hated prisons and the men who make them
Ah, because of all this we have lost João
We have lost João.

Ah, this is why we have lost João
why we weep night and day for João
for João whom they have stolen from us.

And we ask
But why have they taken João,
João who was young and ardent like us
João who thirsted for life
João who was brother to us all
why have they stolen from us João
who spoke of hope and dawning days
João whose glance was like a brother's hug
João who always had somewhere for one of us to stay
João who was our mother and our father
João who would have been our saviour
João whom we loved and love
João who belongs so surely to us
oh, why have they stolen João from us?
and no one answers
indifferent, no one answers.

But we know
why they took João from us
João, so truly our brother.

But what does it matter?
They think they have stolen him but João is here with us
is here in others who will come
in others who have come.
For João is not alone
João is a multitude
João is the blood and the sweat of multitudes
and João, in being João, is also Joaquim, José
Abdullah, Fang, Mussumbuluco, is Mascarenhas
Omar, Yutang, Fabião
João is the multitude, the blood and sweat of multitudes.

And who will take José, Joaquim, Abdullah
Fang, Mussumbuluco, Mascarenhas, Omar, Fabião?
Who?
Who will take us all and lock us in a cage?
Ah, they have stolen João from us
But João is us all
Because of this João hasn't left us
and João 'was' not, he 'is' and 'will be'
For João is us all, we are a multitude
and the multitude
who can take the multitude and lock it in a cage?

MALANGATANA NGWENYA
(b. 1936)

Woman
Translated from the Portuguese by Philippa Rumsey

In the cool waters of the river
we shall have fish that are huge
which shall give the sign of
the end of the world perhaps
because they will make an end of woman
woman who adorns the fields
woman who is the fruit of man.

The flying fish makes an end of searching
because woman is the gold of man
when she sings she even seems
like the fado-singer's well-tuned guitar
when she dies, I shall cut off
her hair to deliver me from sin.

Woman's hair shall be the blanket
over my coffin when another Artist
calls me to Heaven to paint me
Woman's breasts shall be my pillow
woman's eye shall open up for me the way to heaven
woman's belly shall give birth to me up there
and woman's glance shall watch me
as I go up to heaven.

RUI KNOPFLI
(b. 1932)

Kwela for Tomorrow

Translated from the Portuguese by the poet
(for José Craveirinha)

A thousand and more negro children
play with mud toys
in the heart of the slum.
A thousand and more athletic boys,
blond, red-cheeked, dressed in khaki,
raise up in the air the glinting gun breeches
at the Union Grounds.
Precisely two minutes ago, the Mayfair bus
knocked out a miner
and blood breaks out a net of paths
over the sooty skin face.
A million people
at the early morning rush

moving automatically
on the tarmac thread
under the automatic command
of electric robots.
Last night there were
four hold ups,
three bloody street fights
and a woman killed her husband
striking him with an axe
because he had raped their daughter.
Moenie du Preez attends a meeting
with Moenie Potgieter and the stock prices
of the Diamond Co. (Pty.) Ltd. go up.
Since dawn at the General Hospital
one hundred and two casualties
have already been cared for
and the Youth in blue jeans
dreams in the morning a dagga-
nourished nightmare.

Birds pass along
refusing the concrete and the tarmac
of a hostile town.
The few that stop by the wooded silence
of the Joubert Park
are neurotic,
stare with a silly look at the Museum
and stain the alley benches.
People's faces
are stout and inscrutable
like the Voortrekker Monument.

In spite of this

an astounding sound soars
arabesques in the morning.

In spite of the concrete, of the figures,
of the useless blood,
of the chromium-plated motor-cars,

astounding, a sound soars through
the morning air.

In spite of this,
with the longing green of the veld,
and of the herds in the mountain,
Spokes Mashiyane, from a piece of tin,
makes a kwela for tomorrow.

(1959)

Death Certificate
Translated from the Portuguese by the author

A time of naked spears
awaits us, evil laughter
from protruding jaws.
However, life blossoms
tender and tepid,
flower and fruit in the aged longing
of someone that has waited in vain.
Yet, to us,
it is a time of pitiless spears,
of blades in whose whiteness
one can foretell already a sign
of our blood. From this time
we inherited the sharpness of the spears;
this is the sour share that has fallen to us
and that we patiently chew.
However, in a leavening of tenderness,
frail and beautiful, life sprouts
from the dark pulp of different fingers.
To us, the prize of steel,
the star of powder, the badge of fire.
To us the solace of the sad smile
and of a well-known bitterness. We talk
to each other and in every common word

there is a rite of farewell. We talk
and the words we say
say goodbye.

(1964)

F. T. PRINCE
(b. 1912)

from Memoirs in Oxford

Somewhere in Mauriac a girl
   Sees the young man (the so-recurring
Young man in Mauriac) as 'preserved',
That is to say untouched, reserved;
   And wonders to herself, demurring,

'For what? . . .' All things are preparations:
   Our birth and parentage – when, where –
And the ups and downs of foreign nations;
Sunsets and pets and railway-stations;
   The nursery frieze, an old Scotch air.

And English and French novelists
   Once dwelt on home as preparation
Through good plain love. If asked 'For what?'
They might have said at least 'Why not
   To live again in our narration?'

It was a wide blue British sky
   That arched above deep seas in foam,
Where ships in glossy paint went by
To India, China and Shanghai
   And back to England, back to 'home'.

And liners and hotels had *Punch*
   And *Ideal Homes*, the *Tatler*, *Sphere*

And the *Illustrated London News*;
Cartoons by H. M. Bateman; views
  From the Matopos to Kashmir.

That world was ours, no matter where;
  So brave and staid it stretched away
Through the unthinking pastimes of
Colonial England, bridge and golf,
  Tea-parties – tea four times a day –

Saturday racing, drives on Sunday . . .
  Yet through those acres of dry thorn
And sun and dust and boulders ran –
Not quite a ghost – a thought of man
  And God and law; not quite outworn.

Trophies and scars of faded wars,
  A hillside grave seen from the train;
An empty blockhouse by the bridge
And granite needle on the ridge,
  Might tell of greed and pride and pain.

And the other, further war (of course
  We won) was worse – incomprehensible!
But reason surely must increase
And what was left of hatred cease;
  That would be only sensible.

My father from the time I claim
  Remembrance, on his mantel-shelf
Had standing always in the same
Silver and dark-blue velvet frame
  A small old photograph of himself:

At twenty, at his most beautiful –
  Long-jacketed, pale-faced, dark-eyed.
Like a young moon that nears the full
And gazes on a twilight pool,
  His head was tilted to one side.

I had left home before he died,
　　Young as the picture showed him then.
Afterwards — sore, unsatisfied,
I begged it and was not denied;
　　But it had gone, no one knew when

Or where! And I recall the room,
　　The silence. No one spoke because
Everyone saw the question loom
'He had given it — but to whom?'
　　We held our breath and left the pause.

My mother blamed his education
　　For faults and lessons never learned:
His puns and self-depreciation,
Wrong choice of friends, and speculation —
　　Gambling with money so well-earned.

Thinking himself a common man
　　He gave himself with too much trust.
Stubborn in weakness, dumb in pride —
His deepest hopes unsatisfied
　　Were apt to end in self-disgust.

I had adored then hatefully
　　Rejected him, in an immense
Hard rage and boyish misery.
Yet now in all he was I see
　　A strange and saving innocence.

I grieve that we were never friends.
　　It hurts; but neither would know how.
What that I say can make amends?
I leave it, knowing how it ends,
　　And love him as I see him now.

For now he is beyond our reach
　　I share and understand too well —

And let his love of music teach
Me, like a touch not needing speech –
  Things he could never tell.

But I must thank my mother's mind,
  Her fiery rational sense of right
And love of all things well-designed,
Books, furniture and people – signed
  With logic, courage, wit and light.

She gave us pictures and adventures,
  Ballads and stories by the fire,
Echoes of Ruskin and Carlyle,
The notion that there could be 'style';
  But most herself and her desire.

She *was* Jane Eyre and Maggie Tulliver,
  Those ardent women! only free,
After such hardships – childhood scrapes,
Young visions, efforts and escapes –
  As in the mind's eye we could see.

And we were Oliver and Jim
  Hawkins and David Copperfield;
And Absalom with gold hair in
The Bible, and young Benjamin
  And Jairus' daughter that was healed.

I owe her my delight in verse
  But some part too of misery –
Were that for better or for worse:
Fear of 'the body' like a curse,
  That so long would bewilder me.

She had wished that she could believe;
  Said once 'the basis of our lives
Is wrong'; and once that she could feel
Something mysterious, an appeal
  That 'opens like a flower – revives'.

For he died early, she lived on,
   Through all the latter part of life
Bitter, but gradually less,
And chafing yet not comfortless.
   But now, the thought is like a knife,

That they could have such confidence
   And win so far, but be defeated!
Nothing be left of it at length,
Their hope, young arrogance and strength –
   Their work undone or uncompleted.

But – childhood, music in the summer
   Garden and the first fire lit
On a cold sunny afternoon;
Apricot blossom – bees in tune –
   Butterflies that alight and sit

And sun themselves and wag their wings! . . .
   Our moderate greatness went awry,
But not before we had these things,
Fenced with their love; and if it wrings
   The memory, that all went by –

Yet they were lucky all the same,
   Both he and she, and those who live
Have far more to regret or blame.
We only took, but they can claim
   They taught the way to give.

SYDNEY CLOUTS
(1926–82)

Firebowl

Kalahari Bushman fires flowing
in the hollows of the desert
click all night

stick stuck upright
click
click
of starlight
bowstring
toes of the eland
thk thk the big raindrops
tk tk tk the sandgrains
drinking.

Sssskla!
sparks of honey
arrowheads
we who dance
around the circle
around the circle
spoor him
find him

my arrow clings to the thick thick
grunt of darkness
my arrow sings through fire

we who dance we find
the
fire
of the fire.

After the Poem

After the poem the coastline took
its place with a forward look
toughly disputing the right of a poem to possess it

It was not a coast that couldn't yet be made
the subject of a poem don't mistake me
nothing to do with 'literary history'

But the coast flashed up – flashed, say, like objections
up to the rocky summit of the Sentinel

that sloped into the sea
such force in it that every line was broken

     and the sea came by
     the breaking sea came by

Roy Kloof

'Such a little king's eye,' said my mother
who still had the kind imperial look.
'He'll command. Dear cherry-bright boy!'
Her faded English blood ran strong,
she dreamt of the shires all night long,
rose in the morning and called me, Roy.

That was the beginning. My father who came
raw from the veld with a rocky name,
though a mild man, frequently dreamt
that Circumstance galloped with him riding,
that History was thatched into his roof.
It hurt him to hear me christened, Roy Kloof.

Up behind father with little bright spurs
I dreamt I was galloping, bravely horsed.
I dreamt of a sceptre, I cried and I cried
till rock and shire were divorced.
Division incarnate! An unhappy role!
My country has given me flint for a soul.

DOUGLAS LIVINGSTONE
(b. 1932)

On Clouds

Disturbed, the kudu are running:
five cows, one pregnant, and in
the lead, ducking under branches,
a bull, 5 feet at the shoulder, a blanched
lance-corporal's chevron between his eyes,

muzzle out-thrust and the long spirals
of horn laid along his back
to meet, curled forward and similarly stacked,
his tail; rocking up the hill, fleeing
but with an air of tall dignity;
surefooted as small grey clouds slide
scudding up a wooded hillside.

It is impossible to punch a small hole,
grease- and cordite-stained, into all
this cloudy elegance: impossible I say – they
tame so easily – and pulsing now, grey
like clouds, repulse the sort of vaporization
known, among others, to the Sonderkommando.

Of course, these clouds are but kudu, true;
those other clouds only Jews.

The Sleep of My Lions

O, Mare Atlanticum,
Mare Arabicum et Indicum,
Oceanus Orientalis,
Oceanus Aethiopicus
      save me
            from civilization,
      my pastory
            from further violation.

Leave me my magics
and tribes;
to the quagga, the dodo,
the sleep of my lions.

Rust me barbed fences.
Patrol what remains.
Accept bricks, hunting rifles
and realists, telephones
and diesels
to your antiseptic main.

Grant me a day of
moon-rites and rain-dances;
when rhinoceros
root in trained hibiscus borders;
when hippo flatten, with a smile,
deck-chairs at the beach resorts.

Accord me a time
of stick-insect gods, and impala
no longer crushed by concrete;
when love poems like this
can again be written in beads.

Vanderdecken

Sometimes alone at night
lying upon your surf-ski
far beyond the sharknet

drifting on the salt-wet belly
of your mistress the black ocean,
cool under a windless moonless sky

your dangling toes you hope
not luminous from below,
dozing to the sleepy remote

mutter of shorelusting breakers
you start hearing the thrash
of bone, foam and wake;

splintering yardage and thrumming
cords; creak, groan and rattle
of blocks – and, trembling

as you lie, wet from your own death-
salt, you hear the solitary
hopeless steady cursing in Dutch.

Bateleur

All night he craned with an unbending neck
like, some nights, the statue of Jan van Riebeeck.
Indifferent to suffering, to valour;
   obsessive, consequently fathomless,
he fared most of his life a speck in the air.

He knew thermals like an old hypochondriac
her pulse or the phosphates cementing her back.
He suspected gods, but harshly ignored them.
   He knew much, without reason. At the last,
it was reason of sorts that floored him.

The curved beak disdained; the alert cruel eyes
vigilant for prey drilled from the skies;
the big profile evoked Roman sunlight.
   His kills were unerring, suddenly fierce:
he razored his beheadings in midflight.

Aerobatic: clouds below him earth above;
a celestial gymnast: he mock-fumbled
   eddies, bouncing through invisible hoops
or in quick controlled somersaults tumbled
jousting gravity in a sinuous glove.

His world of survival: that awareness
which thins fatally in time and with space.
   While reason gets by, just, threadbarely,
reason's proving the more durable race.
And the wind was his solitary mistress.

Stiff-necked in his terminal disaster,
he tore shot from his chest. All resistance
   – jib bloodied, eyes glazing, slumped – he glared
away ventured human assistance:
bateleur-eagles will brook no master.

On still white wings held aloft in a V
above the slow rocking of his black-hulled craft,
his beat tacked the Drakensberg to the sea.
   When his sails were struck, he fell like a spike,
a great feathered fist clenched on its haft.

A Piece of Earth

The blue duiker, left hindleg
in a poacher's noose held
to a piece of earth by an iron peg,
stands, heart jumping, puzzled;
his scared velvet ears spread
to the sly rustle of leaves and stems;
huge tired eyes probing
the recesses of his epoch's dusk.

He has been snared three days
of sleepless terror; throat scorched with thirst,
tongue thick from rust, dust and blood,
one tiny horn broken from his first
fight with the iron in the earth's skin.
The footloose poacher, long gone
for weeks, has moved on,
will not be returning.

At lengthening intervals
the hare-sized buck gathers himself
for bounding, mouth wide and whistling,
to tow the piece of earth with him.
The wire bites tighter.
Blood flows, clots, runs, congeals
until metal wholly rings on bone.
The earth remains unmoving.

He stops aghast at his noise;
quivering, pants quietly;
resumes his frenzied leaping.
Soon, small herbivorous teeth
will have to grit to gnaw through pain.
Water lies a doubtful day
away: a three-legged stumble through
hyena-patrolled terrain.

Bad Run at King's Rest

Clanking past the crest of a dune:
in the foreground, a group of urchins
straighten up, yelling. They scatter and run.

The big loggerhead turtle lay
swimming among human footprints, beached;
shell split by an errant propeller-blade.

Its flippers bloody where some lout's
hacking had ripped nails for medicines
or trophies. Both its eyes stabbed or pecked out.

It raised its beak to scream or pant,
the exhalations making no sound.
Dumping my bottles on the heaving sand,

I moved – lifelong stand-in for thought –
avoiding the still dangerous beak,
asking pardon, cut the leathery throat.

Rinse off queasily. Circle wide,
back, past that inert, spread-eagled mound.
Call dumbly on gulls, on incoming tides.

(1981)

INGRID JONKER
(1933–65)

The Child who was Shot Dead by Soldiers in Nyanga
Translated from the Afrikaans by Jack Cope and William Plomer

The child is not dead
the child lifts his fists against his mother
who screams Afrika shouts the scent
of freedom and the veld
in the locations of the cordoned heart

The child lifts his fists against his father
in the march of the generations
who are shouting Afrika shout the scent
of righteousness and blood
in the streets of his warrior pride

The child is not dead
not at Langa not at Nyanga
not at Orlando not at Sharpeville
not at the police station in Philippi
where he lies with a bullet through his brain

The child is the shadow of the soldiers
on guard with rifles saracens and batons
the child is present at all gatherings and law-giving
the child peers through house windows and into the hearts of
    mothers
the child who wanted just to play in the sun at Nyanga is
    everywhere
the child grown to a man treks all over Africa
the child grown to a giant travels through the whole world

Without a pass

(1961)

Bitterberry Daybreak

Translated from the Afrikaans by Cherry Clayton

Bitterberry daybreak
bitterberry sun
a mirror has broken
between me and him.

If I look for the highway
where I can flee
his words make the tracks
twist away from me.

Pinewood of memory
pinewood lost again
if I wander from the highway
I stumble into pain.

Parrot-loud echo
cheating with his fun
till I turn around deceived
to see the teaser run.

Echo is no answer
he answers everyone
bitterberry daybreak
bitterberry sun.

BREYTEN BREYTENBACH
(b. 1939)

Sleep My Little Love
Translated from the Afrikaans by Stephen Gray and A. J. Coetzee

sleep my little love
sleep well sleep dark
wet as sugar in coffee
be happy in your dreams
blow on flutes
buy a big house
eat the oldest pears –
those that grow sweeter growing old –
sleep sweeter than pears

keep away the threats
away the bastard wind
the bursts of rain the plundering sun
away hunger and court cases
away the lack of money
away all cancer
and toothache and narcosis

and blind dogs
away the whole of idiotdom
except for you
        and if you wish
please me too

I'll watch over your dreams
I pin the flies to the wall
I wait armed against the sun
        and the wind
        and the rain
if you laugh I'll laugh
and if you cry
little love . . .
don't cry
look I'll buy a hat for you
and fresh bread so dark, new eyes and a coach
like pears in trays
and music for your hours
and crutches for your complaints
        and if you wish
America and the moon
I'll cut my beautiful country
free for you,

but that's for tomorrow, mañana
sleep now my love
sleep soon, sleep far
sleep sweeter than nights
and higher, lighter, more loved
freer, longer
and happier than a feather

Menace of the Sick

Translated from the Afrikaans by Stephen Gray and A. J. Coetzee
(for B. Breytenbach)

Ladies and gentlemen, let me introduce you to Breyten
*   Breytenbach*
the thin man with the green sweater; he is devout
and holds and hammers at his long-drawn head to
fabricate a poem for you   for example
I'm afraid to close my eyes
I don't want to live in the dark *and* see what's going on
the hospitals of Paris are crammed with pale people
standing at the windows with menacing gestures
like the angels in the furnace
the streets are slaughtered with rain and slippery

my eyes are starched
on such a wet day they/you will bury me
when the soil is raw black flesh
and the leaves and over-ripe flowers are coloured and cracked
    with wet
before the light can gnaw at them,   the air sweats white
    blood
but I shall refuse to imprison my eyes

rip off my bony wings
the mouth is too secret not to feel pain
put your boots on for my funeral so that I can hear
the mud kissing at your feet
the sparrows droop their shiny leaking heads, black blossoms
the green trees are muttering monks

plant me on a hill near a dam with snapdragons
let the cunning bitter ducks crap on my grave
in the rain
the souls of insane but clever women are possessed by cats
fears fears fears with saturated colourless heads
and I won't have my black tongue comforted (calmed)

Look how harmless he is, have mercy on him.

Eavesdropper

Translated from the Afrikaans by Ernst van Heerden
(for Stephen L.)

you ask me how it is living in exile, friend —
what can I say?
that I'm too young for bitter protest
and too old for wisdom or acceptance
of my Destiny?
that I'm only one of many,
the maladjusted,
the hosts of expatriates, deserters,
citizens of the guts of darkness
one of the 'Frenchmen with a speech defect'
or even that here I feel at home?

yes, but that I now also know the rooms of loneliness,
the desecration of dreams, the remains of memories,
a violin's thin wailing
where eyes look far and always further,
ears listen quietly inward
— that I too like a beggar
pray for the alms of 'news from home',
for the mercy of 'do you remember',
for the compassion of 'one of these days'

but I do not remember,
songs have faded,
faces say nothing,
dreams have been dreamt
    and as if you're searching for love in a woman's seaweed hair
you forget yourself in a shuffling nameless mass
of early-ageing revolutionaries,
of poets without language and blind painters,
of letters without tidings like seas without tides,
of those who choke on the childishness of longing,
of those who call up spirits from the incense,
conjure up landscapes on their tongues,
throwing up the knowledge of self

– must I too give a deeper meaning?
that all of us are only exiles from Death
soon to be allowed to 'go home'?

no, for now I begin, groping with hands rotted off
to understand those who were here before us
and all I ask of you
in the name of what you want to know
        be good to those who come after us

(Paris, Easter 1968)

We Shall Overcome

Translated from the Afrikaans by Ernst van Heerden
(for Yousef Omar)
'John Brown's body lies a-rotting in his grave'

a man walks calmly on his legs in the grass
in a negative exposed too long
                        in the light
but he knows the land, his land, lies under snow,
                        rich with worms and black

he wraps a drop of blood tightly in a rag
somewhere between all the vomit and the crap
he will keep it
for later

his heart is a clot of fear
the man is not a hero,
he knows he'll have to hang
for he is stupid
and wanted to believe

in front of the wall he bids farewell
to his legs in the grass,
he gives his hands to his executioner
his brains to a dead heap

at six when the day is aborted
the gallows will strip him
and true to the yellow trinity
of two dangling legs
and a bird without feathers

fortunately this is only a swinging verse
stiff words
in a book

Testament of a Rebel

Translated from the Afrikaans by André P. Brink

give me a pen
so that I may sing
that life is not in vain

give me a season
to look openly into the eyes of the sky
when the peach-tree vomits its fullness in white
a tyranny goes down to earth

let mothers lament
let breasts dry up
and wombs shrivel
when at last the stake weans its offspring

give me a love
that will never rot between the fingers
give me a love
like this love I want to give you

give me a heart
that will go on beating
beating more strongly beating than the white beat
of a terrified dove in the dark
beating more loudly than bitter bullets

give me a heart, a small blood-factory
to spout

blossoms of bliss
for blood is sweet is beautiful
is never needless or in vain

I want to die before I'm dead
while my heart is still fertile
and red
undarkened by the black sediment of doubt

give me two lips
and clear ink for my tongue
to cover the earth one vast love-letter
inscribed in milk

becoming sweeter day by day
exorcizing all bitterness
burning more sweetly, summer-like

let summer come then
without blindfolds or ravens
let the pillory of the peach-tree be content
to yield its red fruit

and grant me a song of love
of doves of satisfaction
so that I may sing from my udder
that life has not been in vain

for as I'm dying into open eyes
my deep red song will never die

C. J. DRIVER
(b. 1939)

A Ballad of Hunters

My great-grandfather hunted elephants,
Shot four hundred in a year,
Till one day his death turned round
And sniggered in his ear.

The theme's the same, the method changes —
Time has planned the ending,
Has turned the hunter to the hunted
And bred the next from nothing.

My great-great-uncle farmed alone,
Made next to nothing from his land,
Till at last the cancer took him,
Eating from his living hand.

The theme's the same, the method changes —
Time has planned the ending,
Has turned the farmer to the harvest
And bred the next from nothing.

Cousins and cousins in their dozens
Were killed in their mission churches
By the tribes whose heads they broke
To teach them the Christian virtues.

The theme's the same, the method changes —
Time has planned the ending,
Has turned the clergy to the converts
And bred the next from nothing.

My father's father died at Delville Wood,
Shooting Germans for his British past —
Left his wife a private's pension
And children to make it last.

The theme's the same, the method changes —
Time has planned the ending,
Has turned the sniper to the target
And bred the next from nothing.

Both my uncles fought the war,
Like lovers died a year apart —
Left some letters and a flag or two
And silence to be their art.

The theme's the same, the method changes —
Time has planned the ending,

Has turned the fighters to the dying
And bred the next from nothing.

Now I'm my subject, a sort of hunter
Stalking the blood of my family —
But hunted too by time's revenge
For all they made of my history.

The theme's the same, the method changes —
Time will plan the ending,
Will turn the hunter to the hunted
And breed the last from nothing.

Letter to Breyten Breytenbach from Hong Kong

Another holiday.
    The kids away,
My wife, the dogs; I here, alone at home,
Working, as always, with words, while they play
Sporadic games on a beach, and miss me
To catch the high ones, or fetch the picnic
From the car-park.
    Musing on you, I write
With my head still buried in Africa,
Which I abandoned, when I was younger,
Before it abandoned me, or stranded
Somebody a little bit like me then,
For the years I did not care to barter
For my own or someone else's freedom.

Now in front of my window a blank wall
And coils of wire — conditional enterprise
To keep the felons out, to keep me in,
In a great city on the edge of China;
And I remember you in gaol, whom no one
Trusts any more, not entirely.
    The police,
Called 'special', have obviously learned by now
How to fish for poets, both thin and tall —

You catch them with words, a little bit bent
And baited with action. They are too trusting
For words. You pull the buggers in like eels.
They pant under the lights.
      In Pollsmoor Gaol
You joke with the warders — a traitor, true,
But still their kind, the volk. The prison governor,
Whose mind is almost his own, commissions
(Not too abstract!) paintings. Poems are harder;
You can't be always sure that what they say
They really mean: they might be in a code
Or tell your readers what is best concealed.
It must be hard to try to represent
A revolution when you want to be
A revelation. Out of words we make
Sporadic fictions, now and sometimes then.

Since I am hardly what I seem to be
What seems to me may not be you at all —

For self-concealing me, read you, romantic:
Your France, my England; your Pollsmoor Gaol,
My Asian exile. Yet we must be shared . . .
The world feasts on writers, especially
When they're wrong. You cannot mean those lies.
And yet you meant them, just as I mean mine.

Oh Breyten Breytenbach, we take our gaols
On our backs like pilgrims, and Giant Despair
Inhabits cities anywhere airlines
Care to dump us and our lame histories.
The choices that we make are not so sure
As policemen think, and what we make ourselves
Flickers like gunfire over the borders.
Traitors are traitors, even our own kind;
We gave away our futures long ago.

CHRISTOPHER HOPE
(b. 1944)

The Flight of the White South Africans

I

Kinshasa, we feel, is not the place to reach
At noon and leave the plane to endure inspection
By a hostile ground-hostess, observing the bleach
On her face, her cap tacked with leopard skin,
Faked, and far too tired for the erection
A good bristle requires. We make no fuss,
However, knowing why she snarls at us;
But proffer our transit cards, and march in

To stand at the urinal complaining aloud
Of filth, flies and spit, amazed that this
Is it, an Africa the white man bowed
Before, growling outside the walls of the Gents:
We fumble uncomfortably, unable to piss
Till a soldier, bursting from a booth, clodhops
Past, still buckling up, and the talking stops.
Steady yellow stains white marble in silence.

II

Perhaps, Nongquase, you have your revenge. Tell me
Why, when surf rides like skirts up a thigh, we bare
Ourselves, blind behind black glass, bellies
Up, navels gaping at the sun? We lie
Near ice-cream boys, purveyors of canvas chairs:
While they and the fishermen who stand
Off-shore, shooting seine, busily cram
Their granaries: we gasp, straining to fly:

While in the upstairs lounge, our waiting wives
Caress expensive ivory souvenirs;
By rights, white hunters' spoil; and home-made knives.
We flounder about, flying fish that fail,

Staring with the glazed eyes of seers
At our plane, hauled from the sky, lying like dead
Silver on the tarmac, feeling hooks bed
Deep in our mouths, sand heavy in our scales.

III

Our sojourn: what might dear Milne have made of it
Or Crompton, Farnol, even the later James,
Who promised homely endings, magi who lit
The lamp we wished to read by, gave us The Queen,
A Nanny we almost kissed, our English names?
We blink and are blinded by the Congo sun
Overhead, as flagrant as a raped nun.
Such light embarrasses too late. We've seen

So little in the little time spent coming
To choke on this beach of unbreathable air
Beyond the guns' safety, the good plumbing;
Prey of gulls and gaffs. We go to the wall
But Mowgli, Biggles and Alice are not there:
Nongquase, heaven unhoods its bloodshot eye
Above a displaced people; our demise
Is near, and we'll be gutted where we fall.

The writer's note, quoted from *The Encyclopaedia of Southern Africa*:
'In 1856 a young Xhosa woman, named Nongquase, preached that the
day was approaching when Europeans in their country would be driven
into the sea.'

Lines on a Boer War Pin-up Girl
Seen in the Falcon Hotel, Bude

Demure you are over your left shoulder,
Above the great embankment of your back;
Buttocks and thighs heavy as sandbags;
Shapely ankles bolting you
Beside your pennyfarthing:
Fortress Britannia; Boadicea on a bike.

Flesh sweetly stripped and posed before
Steel frame and exciting leather saddle:
How well you have withstood your rucksack days,
Their sieges and reliefs,
Your lovers fallen below.

Perhaps in his backyard *kia*,
Some old black veteran has his copy, too,
Which he touches with a dirty fingernail and laughs,
Showing his gums:
Who else remembers you?

JENI COUZYN
(b. 1942)

World War II

In Egypt we had the best time
on a table under the sun
the children kiss
a ragged cloth displays their wrinkled brown skin
the small penis grows pink with fine blue veins
the girl, her rotting teeth jagged
slips a scarlet tongue around its rim
her brother giggles wearily
feeling it stiffen

now he twists her half formed nipples with his
nails till the pores prick upwards
I feel the prickle sliding down my thighs
the sergeant is running his yellow tongue across
dried, sun-cracked lips

and now the boy bites into the swell of her buttocks
drawing blood to get a laugh
darts his tongue into her small red chasm
and spits loudly

the rest wasn't so good
the usual thing except for the spurting, the way she
cried and clawed receiving the
white stink from his small brown body

and then the way they leapt up
pawing us for the coppers we slung into a filthy
leather pouch their vermin crawling heads
below the level of our shining gun belts.

There were side-shows too
elephantiasis of the vagina
natives doing donkeys
donkeys doing natives
and the pretty adolescent youths who would
bring you off for sixpence –
but nothing could quite beat those bloody kids
performing on that table stranded in that
bloody vast desert where we were fighting
searching for an enemy through dry months
cursing the sand and flies and constant thirst
through mile after mile of nothing
nothing ever happening, at best now and then
a skirmish losing a few guns a few men.

My wife thinks me a hero
for getting out of that war
alive.

My Father's Hands

My father's hands
are beautiful, they can
fix this moth's wing and make
machines
they can mend the fuse when the world
goes dark
can make light swim and walls jump
in around me again
I can see my mother's face again.

You must take good care of them with
your finest creams
never let the nails break or
skin go dry, only those wise fingers
know how to fix the thing
that makes my doll cry and they make
small animals out of clay.

Never let blades or anything sharp
and hurtful near them
don't let bees or nettles
sting them don't let fire or burning oil
try them

My father's hands are beautiful, take
good care of them

DAVID WRIGHT
(b. 1920)

A Funeral Oration

Composed at thirty, my funeral oration: Here lies
David John Murray Wright, 6′ 2″, myopic blue eyes;
Hair grey (very distinguished looking, so I am told);
Shabbily dressed as a rule; susceptible to cold;
Acquainted with what are known as the normal vices;
Perpetually short of cash; useless in a crisis;
Preferring cats, hated dogs; drank (when he could) too much;
Was deaf as a tombstone; and extremely hard to touch.
Academic achievements: B. A., Oxon. (2nd class);
Poetic: the publication of one volume of verse,
Which in his thirtieth year attained him no fame at all
Except among intractable poets, and a small
Lunatic fringe congregating in Soho pubs.
He could roll himself cigarettes from discarded stubs,
Assume the first position of Yoga; sail, row, swim;

And though deaf, in church appear to be joining a hymn.
Often arrested for being without a permit,
Starved on his talents as much as he dined on his wit,
Born in a dominion to which he hoped not to go back
Since predisposed to imagine white possibly black:
His life, like his times, was appalling; his conduct odd;
He hoped to write one good line; died believing in God.

from *A Peripatetic Letter to Isabella Fey*
(January 1974)

This was as far as I had got
One winter day, November 8,
Two months ago, while on the way
From Cumberland to Africa.
For when the London suburbs ran
To meet me, I laid down my pen
(That is, I closed the typewriter),
To watch grimy, and grimier,
Victorian backyard plots flit by,
Then cuttings, until, quietly,
The engine halted at Euston.

Twenty-four hours of London,
The peculiar bit I love and know
(That dingy littoral of Soho
– Now pasture where dinosaur heads
Of power-shovels dip and feed –)
Then, full of grief and Guinness, I
Boarded a plane to Italy:
From whence, from Rome, a jumbo-jet
Carried me southwards through the night
And further from the ego who
Began, but could not continue,
As he approached his other home
And other self, his letter-poem.

What had brought me flying over
To Africa was my mother,
Living in, and older than,
Johannesburg, where I was born;
Eternal, maternal love
Returning me to Orange Grove.

How recreate the glassed-in stoep
Where my bed was, four floors up,
That overlooked a bioscope,
A golf-course, and Voortrekkerhoogte
(One of the hills whose thin blue line
Edges the horizon like a stain),
And the green tree-tops which hid
Corrugated iron red
Roofs of Norwood bungalows?
Or, when the sun dropped below,
Slid like a penny in its slot
Under the highveld's rim, and brought
The white stars out, and the white moon,
And the Lido Café's neon,
Revive those moments of being
In a familiar, alien
Environment, which absence from
Underscores, at each return,
After half a life elsewhere,
That will or nill my roots are there?

Still living there, my mother, born
In Dumfriesshire in '81
When klipspringers used to haunt
The kopjes of Witwatersrand;
Born when that glass and concrete flower
Of Langlaagte and cheap labour,
Those withered hills of yellow spoil,
The Jameson Raid, and Treason Trial,
The fractured lives, and fractured hearts,
Lay implicit in the quartz.
It's strange that everything around,

Crumbling suburban mansions, drowned
In their own gardens, under tall
Oaks already memorial
To a way of life half gone,
That all things there I look upon,
Growth or artefact, should be
Younger than her living eye.

A spacious view, and full of clouds,
At evening, from her high windows:
Below, above the summer green,
There's a blue smoke of blossoming
Jacaranda through the tree-tops threading;
Vague curtains of unfallen rain.
I watch her blue and fading eyes
Look inward, reminisce;
Histories not of this land.

She talks to me of Henry Lamb,
A wicked wit, a wicked eye,
A Strachey portrait still half-dry;
Of a tide flooding Solway sand,
Two children running hand in hand –
Their deliverer, unknown.
'My father gave him half-a-crown.'
Like that sea long ago, the dark
Wells up below Magalicsberg,
And washes over veld and trees.
'He never showed affection to us,
And so I never got enough,'
She says, who gave me too much love.
Then back to Henry Lamb again.

And were there not the mornings when
Like a Jo'bourgeois, bright and early,
I'd catch a doubledecker trolley
(City-Stadt), pull up the hill,
Pass the cracked cement of Yeoville,
Look for St John's low red-brown tower

Remembering those lost and other
Selves that time and change have killed,
The man, the schoolboy, and the child,
Who saw the same yet not the same
Prospects; for and because of whom
These constructs, mediocre, tatty,
Possess, as now I concede, beauty.
Though outside the O.K. Bazaar
The mutilated, as before,
Are squatting, patient, black, and humble,
I miss the Pioneer Hotel,
Ornate and pinchbeck and decayed;
The glassed, voluminous Arcade's
Overblown and plaintive
Grandiosity of 1890.
Most of the old stuff's coming down;
You'd not think, in so new a town,
The current fashion to erase
Could so affect the sense of place,
And as in London or Paris,
Effacing more than history,
Erect the outworks of Nowhere
Here, there, and everywhere.

But I best of all remember
A green summery December
Afternoon, when from the shade
Of the old Pretoria road
We turned off, where a painted sign
As in my boyhood, read: IRENE.
I'd often passed it as a boy,
But that was in the general's day.
The once I saw the general,
He was driving down the Mall,
Apple cheeks, white dagger beard,
At the Victory Parade.
No great tactician, so they say,
No De Wet, no De la Rey;

Yet his commando took the war
From Stormberg to Concordia;
Smuts for my generation was
Take it or leave it, the Ou'Baas.
Along side-roads, no longer tar,
But blood-rust dirt of Africa,
We sought the old dead general's farm
Hedged and edged with heavy green
Huge eucalypti towering
Over fields where browsed oxen,
Patriarchic, biblical
As Exodus or Samuel;
And found, down in a wooded hollow,
His tin-walled, tin-roofed bungalow
Grateful for bougainvillaea and
Grassblades that pricked through the red sand,
Tall trees above, a vlei below.

The whole anachronism so
Irrelevant as to be a dream,
To be the Africa we mean.

Under boulders, on a hill
Above Irene, his bones lie still;
To the north, syncretic, bland
As polythene, highrisers stand
Witness to Pretoria.
And if you look the other way
Over the water-broken highveld
Dome, you see against its rifled
And enormous monotones
The lumpy soil, and brittle bones
Of a meretricious city.

Yet to say that is too easy.
Their own history has made
Dumb ox politicians afraid,
Subverters of truth and sense,
Polyhistors of the shade of skins;

And Oppenheimer rings a bell
As Eugène Marais never will.
A consolation is, that here
Culture does not spell Career:
Between indifference and police
The real, the gay and serious
Makers would appear to thrive
Unflattered, unacademized,
Pro tem at least. There was the night
Two days before my homeward flight,
When Barney Simon took me round
To Lionel Abrahams's, and I found
With him and Nadine Gordimer
A rapport that seems seldomer
To happen, but the kind I'd know
In Fitzrovia, long ago.
And these were friends of two good men,
Of Nat Nakasa, and Bosman,
Dead men I had wished to meet,
Masters of the ironic
Throwaway, the smile that stings
Where indignation wastes in weeping.
Ill-bodied Lionel, if I
Who also am a cripple, may
So apostrophize, I see
In you a human victory:
Not a heroic, but human,
That says, 'If he can, then I can.'
I mean not only what you are
But what you did with *Renoster*.
I am not to forget your room
That held so much, shadowed and warm;
Its glass wall, where a dark garden
Looked with the moon and sadness in;
What we said, and did not say.

I sign off: *desunt cetera*:
And leave Johannesburg behind

And that ill country where no wind
Blows good, though it be blowing change:
Dear Isabella, I must end
This desultory and octo-
Syllabic letter to a friend.
What has been said in it is true
But of no moment; in the end
A way to record truth is to
Preserve the unimportant and
Personal, so be it moves:
The what, to find the why one loves.

LIONEL ABRAHAMS
(b. 1928)

The Whiteman Blues

Two cars, three loos, a swimming pool,
Investment paintings, kids at a private school . . .
we entertain with shows or gourmet food –
and yet we don't feel right, we don't feel good.

Why doesn't the having help?
Why doesn't the spending save?
Why doesn't the fun –
Why doesn't the culture –
Why don't the ads add up to something?

We can afford to say we know
the blacks are really given hell,
Big Boss is harsh and stupid and must go:
we say it – and it helps like one Aspro.
We still feel jumpy, mixed up, not quite well.

Which specialist can cure the thing we've got –
the got-it, gotta-get-it blues,
the deep-freeze, cheaper wholesale, world excursion blues?
We're high on the know-all-about-it booze.

We're bursting with kwashiorkor of the bank.
We're depressed by the whiteman blues.

In the backyards they pray for us.
In Soweto they see our plight.
In the border areas they understand.
In the Bantustans they wait
to pat our shoulder, hold our hand.
They know, they know,
to them it isn't news:
we've got these lost-man, late-man,
money-man, superman,
whiteman blues.

Thresholds of Identity

Visitors, indignant, didactic, pronounce
their solutions or dooms.
A home poet comments: 'They speak and go back.
In this place it is you and me.'
I apprehend the challenge in his thought:
inhabitants, we are alone
and the difference that still lies between us
may shatter the land.
Yet he and I agree enough
to discount the old divides
of pigmentation, culture, class;
nor would he or I endorse
the use of blood spilt on the street
or silence of the blackened cell.
In this we are joined. So far have we come.
But as I calmly sorrow
over acts of years that grind
his feeling small and his thought narrow
or sputter anger over days
that smash him into terror, grief and rage –
so he would deplore, merely deplore
the ferocity that in its turn
could make the children of my race bleed.

WOPKO JENSMA
(b. 1939)

———— ～ ————

In Memoriam Akbar Babool

you introduced me to my first goddess
    'dis towns full a bitches
    ya wanna try one?'
afterwards we saw your home
    'loaded w'mosquitoes hea
    dey nibble ya ta pieces 'tnight'
creaky floor, a gauze door,
backyard of sand
in the middle a dagga plant
    'lets've suppa'n onion'n egg
    drive down dry bread a drop a wine'
next day the glittering town
prêgo and café com leite

me without cash later some day
you flogged the camera i stole
    'ya got trouble w'ya gal?
    listen boy, go home, juss go home'
a room in ho ling, a room at least
one with the broads, one with them
    'listen boy, go home an see ya dad
    dis place's not f'ya 't all'

sudden cash from nowhere and billy
we paint the town all bloody red
    'now prawns, boy, we a' square w'all
    square as da patten on a makapulan'
a flat in alto mae, all of it
clean bath, polished floor, wide bed
    'ya sudden luck's gonna change
    an ya laurentina'll juss be water'

for sure it happened as bad luck wanted
this time a reed hut in xipamanine

'palish'n makov evry day
dis reed hut, ma love, a pit walk'
sometimes akbar, sometimes billy, always i
a walk to the beach a relief, the open sea
'ya kid gro's up, wants grub
da kid wants ta learn letters'

yes, i remember home and drone living
cash and 8 to 5 till you are not you
'stop dreamin, look, a'm real
billy's sax's lost long ago'
i love my big love, my cry
the thorn bush, my life an open plain
'akbar, 's ya, ya rotten —
'strue, all ya said, akbar, 'strue'

sometimes now i remember you said
someone called you bloody coolie
when you asked for help
with your first heart attack
up the steps of casa elefante

In Memoriam Ben Zwane
(for Paula)

ma people, come an get ready
train's a comin
aint no room fo' sinners
we're goin all da way

i heard a word, ben
but i fear t' say 't here
tell azania
i only say 't soft, not loud

did you tumble down steps?
did you slip on a piece 'f soap?
what da hell did you do?
tell me you died 'f tb

ma people, god got ya covered
let's rail away, all stoned
'f winin 'n dinin all day
gonna be great in south africa

A Beggar Named Mokopi

One day the big hand of a spirit caught a boy named Nonyane because he could sing like a bird. The spirit changed Nonyane into a bird and put him into a cage.

The spirit then changed himself into a human and entered a village as a beggar, Mokopi. He called the people together at the market place and made Nonyane sing. The people were so charmed by the songs of Nonyane that they gave Mokopi money for they felt sorry for the beggar.

Mokopi went to village after village and made Nonyane sing for the people. Soon Mokopi became very rich, but he kept on pretending he was a beggar.

Then one day they visited Nonyane's home village and Nonyane's mother recognized her son's voice. Secretly she told everybody.

They gave Mokopi a lot of beer and, as spirits are always greedy, he drank it all. He became so drunk that he fell asleep.

The people took Nonyane from the cage and asked their moruti to pray to the Great One so that Nonyane could become human again. The moruti read the Great Book of Prayer and, almost immediately, Nonyane became a boy again.

They then caught an ordinary bird and put it in Mokopi's cage. Later Mokopi woke up with an enormous headache, took his bird and left.

It was only at the next village that Mokopi discovered that he had been tricked. He got so cross that he changed himself into a cloud of dust and disappeared over the horizon.

MBUYISENI MTSHALI
(b. 1940)

—————— ～ ——————

Farewell to My Scooter
(for Alan and Derryl, my friends)

Round the streets of this city I rode you,
As proud as a rider on a thoroughbred.

Through streets reeking with petrol fumes
Sometimes I slithered and fell on the grease-stained tarmac,
Nearly dislocating my shoulderblade
And bruising my limbs.

Passers-by stared, some laughed at your twisted
Handlebars, others came to our aid and lifted
You and collected scattered letters and parcels.

Then I would jump on you again
And off we would zoom at breakneck speed
Dodging jaywalkers, dicing through
The endless stream of cars.
We became inseparable partners
In this seething mass of man and machines.

Oh! dear friend, remember the cold days
When I sprang on you and felt you
Quiver under my scrotum like
A virgin bride on the first night.
How can you forget those sweltering summer
Days when we sweated and gasped for
Air, and when the rain came in
Heavenly buckets your single spark plug
Chortled and spluttered like an overfed baby.

Beloved bastard that you are
You would not budge an inch
Though I cajoled and patted you.
Man! I had to shove you to the basement

After exhausting myself giving you
Many vicious kickstarts. No response.

Hey man, overnight we became celebrities
We hit the limelight with a bang,
Much sought after by pressmen
We posed for photographers,
I complete in my messenger's regalia
A crash helmet, goggles and a dust coat.

Goodbye my friend.
To me you were not just a piece of machine
You were my winged steed
Carrying me like Pegasus
To the dizzying heights of success.

Three cheers chum as you lie forlorn
In that basement corner collecting dust.
Believe me, I loved you.

Column in the *Rand Daily Mail*, Johannesburg, 11 March 1972.

The Day We Buried Our Bully

Through years and years
of harassment
we tolerated his hideous deeds:
    girls abducted,
    women molested,
    boys assaulted,
    and men robbed.

Our fear made him our master.

One day
old warrior Death
whipped out his .38 special
from his holster
and felled our tormentor with a single shot.

We turned his corpse
into a piece of meat
tucked in between
the sandwich of soil
black like burnt toast
ready for ants and worms
to eat for breakfast,
and excrete as manure.

We laid wreaths
of withered flowers
to fill his grave
with an odour of decay
wafted by the wind,

As mourners smiled
through tears of relief,
'Lord! take care of his soul –
though he was but a bully.'

The Removal of Our Village, KwaBhanya
Translated from the Zulu by the poet

O, I remember you,
my tiny little village of KwaBhanya
where my umbilical cord was cut with a reed knife;
where I yelled a scream of horror at being brought into this
    world,
where I inhaled the herbs burnt to banish the evil spirits,
that choked every infant born to the black mothers,
where my forefathers and my parents were masters of their lives,
and owners of their plots,
where they lived without paying any rent to mlungu,
where we tilled the ground,
harvested a bountiful crop,
fresh mielie corn, large pumpkins
which we squashed into pulp
to make pumpkin broth and melon porridge;
and ate juicy calabashes, luscious peaches, plums and pears.

Mlungu came from the town of Vryheid (Freedom)
to deprive us of our liberty by his endless decrees
and pompous proclamations,
'All Bantu people of this slum and black spot must move.'

We went on milking our cows,
Heleyisi and Batata.
I drank milk straight from the cow's udder
by squeezing the teats into my mouth;
we ladled rich cream in our claypots
and mixed the sour milk
together with fresh corn bread;
we stuffed ourselves full like piglets.

It was a blissful life.

It was an existence we savoured more than
Christians hanker for their Jesu and Heaven in the clouds;
we had our feet in the soil of our ancestors,
and we salted the soil with our tears during the drought,
and watered the crops with our sweat.

Alas, the sunshine of our happiness was short-lived;
dark clouds marched across the sky carrying guns,
and took up menacing positions above our heads.

And when I think of my boyhood
I feel I am bashing my head against a rock.
The rock is stone deaf to my cries;
I wish I could pinch it once
and make it wince with pain.

I see myself in short pants and khaki shirt,
running a race with my shadow,
trying to catch the tail of Gugu, our fluffy cat;
and then collide with my many friends –
Sikobho, Fabiyana, Thami, Jimisoni;
they are all dead now.
I will follow them
when crabs and frogs have grown horns.

I feel a million arrows pass through my heart,
my eyes turn into a stream of salty water,
I page through the flimsy salinity,
I see the broken graves of my grandfather and grandmother.

I hear their voices calling,
'Buya, light the lantern,
the stars are hidden in the sea cave,
the rain has gone to fetch them,
the sea is sorry it lashed the earth with thunderclaps.'

I grope in the dark in the feeble light of my lantern,
the grave is ablaze,
the tombstones are smiling ghosts,
they are singing to me a valedictory hymn!
'Hhayi usizi lomunti omnyama e-Afrika . . .
O, the black man's sorrow in Africa.'

I know the time is near,
Mlungu is coming to our village,
KwaBhanya will soon be dead;
the voices from the ghostly graves are warning me
to tell the villagers;
I dare not.

Then it was morning again,
as all mornings come in the morning
never at noon nor in the evening nor at night.
The morning brings the word from Pretoria,
as words come from Pretoria,
because only Pretoria has a mouth;
Cape Town has the brain to think
what the mouth has to say.
Only Johannesburg has the heart;
they say it has a heart of gold, maybe for whites,
and a clay heart for us blacks,
and of course Durban has a banana heart.

And the word was this . . .
'Bantu people of Bestersspruit, you must move . . . Julle moet
    trek.'

Villagers gathered in clusters,
they called meeting after meeting,
and decided in unison to defy the word from Pretoria;
'Mlungu is mad, his head is full of shit, asihambi.'

Then it was Monday morning,
as Monday mornings are ominous everywhere,
when army trucks trundled to a stop,
raising an acrid dust and petrol fumes
that filled our eyes with tears
and our mouths with unvomited puke.

Police in battle dress jumped out from the trucks,
they were armed to the teeth,
and as grim-faced as the white man
who hangs people in Pretoria.

'We told you to move . . . so trek nou.'

We pleaded for an extension of time.

We wanted to harvest our crop,
we wanted to transfer our children to other schools,
we waited for the return of our husbands
and sons from the mines in Johannesburg.

We were taken by force
and put in row upon row of tents,
like prisoners of war in a camp,
while bulldozers razed our houses to the ground.

'Mlungu, how can you do this to us?
Look at what Mlungu the Christian is doing to us;
Mlungu, wait for our days of vengeance,
Mlungu, we are Zulus, born fighters,
we will take our spears and fight for our lands.'

THEMBINKOSI NDLOVU

Elegy for the Dead of Soweto
Translated from the Zulu by Chris Mann

Rest in peace, warriors of Soweto.
I pity the souls of the departed,
I weep for the orphans left without care,
And I mourn for you, the women
Who gave these heroes birth.
Alas, what sorrows there are
For you the younger generation!
But you in the end will be heroic,
As Nozishada the warrior was.

Take your rest, heroes who like me are black.
Where you are now, we are also going.
Open the earth for others to enter,
Who are already entering it
Like raindrops, in great numbers together.

Make sure you tell the shades
About the sorrow you've seen.
We ourselves still weep for them,
We who survived the battle of Isandhlwana.
Your sweat like theirs became drops of blood,
Your corpses the proof of heroism,
And our weeping was your applause.

Young men may die, but their praise-poems remain.
Warriors, we will live remembering you,
Though in the end you did not change
This land of black heroism.
All of us say, Warriors, rest in peace,
This most beautiful country is dead.

Measure for Measure

go measure the distance from cape town to pretoria
and tell me the prescribed area i can work in

count the number of days in a year
and say how many of them i can be contracted around

calculate the size of house you think good for me
and ensure the shape suits tribal tastes

measure the amount of light into the window
known to guarantee my traditional ways

count me enough wages to make certain that i
grovel in the mud for more food

teach me just so much of the world that i
can fit into certain types of labour

show me only those kinds of love
which will make me aware of my place at all times

and when all that is done
let me tell you this
you'll never know how far i stand from you

When I Lost Slum Life

I will have to ask for my slum location again
I feel a lot went wrong when I was moved from it
a lot died in the process
I lost my stance for standing up straight
I lost the rhythm of walking right
I lost my sense of humour
I lost the feel for loving
I lost my sense of smell

I lost the sense of discriminating
I lost my pride of not caring for smart things
I lost that heart for sharing
I lost Sofasonke Mpanza's guts
but to understand my real plight you've got to know
I lost the gum-tree which was my shade
my lean-to and a lovers' lean-on
I began to grasp for real all illusions
I began to love charity
I began to think comfort was real
I began to worry about the hygiene of toothpaste
I began to wear clean clothes as if that's wearing a golden watch
I began to seek a light complexion as if that was a reality
I began to despise the smell of life
I went in for imitations
I bought second-hand as if that wasn't paying for cheap class
I need to hold on to something
like the shine of corrugated-iron roofs or the rusted coating
I need to take in something
less obnoxious than the billowing smoke from
nearby factories
I need a big wide yard
in which to dance in prayer or do the jive
I need a roofing that can resound
with hard hand-clapping soulful singing and foot-stamping
or just the thud of drunken brawls

I know I don't just want fresh air
I need the smell of sweaty life
oh yes I want to live colourfully once more

If

If you still have bacon and eggs for breakfast
If you donate freely to welfare societies that serve the needy and
    underprivileged
If your standards are such that they are measured by the number
    of servants you keep

If you believe in granting to others opportunities open to you
If you have once said: it is madness to separate people on colour
    lines
If you kneel down hands cupped for the body and blood of
    Christ
If you travel to Kenya and other places for conferences on
    Christian fellowship
If you sometimes take a plane from Jan Smuts to European and
    American cities for dinner and conversations
If you have sat at table with servants of other people to talk of
    building bridges
If you have once said: I don't believe in being unjust to anyone
If you insist that you are of the 20th century
Then for God's sake match word with deed always

MONGANE SEROTE
(b. 1944)

A Poem

The gasp sounded
bubbled through the broken mouth
and rang like a yelp of a dog on his lips
when his eyes shot out
staring at the nightmare
his wife
having packed her dresses and petticoats neat in her heart
and her long hidden manhood,
emerged
in her eyes which were as bold as defiance
her face
folded shadows cold as gathered clouds
as her voice pierced him
he bled
fear dripping down his trousers
and when his frail hand went up his mind fell in
like the heap of soil on the grave

Death Survey

i had a dream
true like i'm black like this
conflict.
a dream fell on my head that sleeps still like a stone
my head on the bed
the stone in the donga
i had a dream last night
it fell like a feather into my sleep.
a friend came running into the yard and his face was like a
                                            horror
a death running wildly loose
when some guys i know came running after him
charging
like dogs so vicious
barking and chasing a cow from a dustbin
my friend came rushing into my house
i ran
could not keep my eyes off from the sparkling knives
dangling over my shoulders
and bricks flying over my head like this
we ran
i was calling my friend's name
he called mine too
and we could not keep off from that gaping donga
which was swallowing my scream and desperately needed
                                            my life
why did gatsha come
because there he was holding some meeting with the old leg
                                            of the past
sitting in a circle.
i saw them take a kerrie and try to beat out some brain
out of a boy who was kneeling and trying to scream
frightened
i ran loose
to frank's place at ninth avenue and found that the bulldozer
                                            had been there

before me
i stumbled over bricks
they bit my toes like hungry rats
and something was in my ear
a cockroach
desperately wanting to hide inside my ear
its long legs frantic
its sharp small head digging right through
cruel
even screams don't come in a dream like this
why
this bloody bulldozer had done a good job and its teeth
                              dripped blood;
bricks-pillars-hunks-of-concrete-zincs-broken-steps-doors-
    broken-glasses-crooked window-panes-broken-flower-
                        pots-planks-twisted-shoes
lay all over the show
like a complete story,
i ran
my toes bleeding
and i held my heart in my right hand
like a jacket.

Another Alexandra

the skies and god's mystery look on
the blood flows
the tears dry
the screams are mute
and the mothers now depart
their doeks falling awkwardly over their faces
and their heads are bowed
the slaughter sheep hangs from a tree red like the setting sun
here,
it is only children who still laugh and play and jump
as they play on the rubble heap;
Alexandra,

the streets are now closed
the doors
windows
poked out while the little girl stands there licking her lips
scratching her grey thigh
dazed by her child and adult experiences locked so tight in her
                                                    little head
where her innocence has been snatched;
Alexandra,
this little girl clutched a crying child in her arms and heard its
                                    heart beat on her back
and tricked into sleep
while she was playing with rag-dolls
and longed to be held by the hand and told stories,
and the men sit on the stoep staring straight into space
wearing blank expressions
not even noticing women passing
Alexandra,
it is true that women have come to know
they know that graves are not only below the earth
where worms are so well informed, wearing mocking smiles
                            everytime they hear us sing hymns
these women –
they sweat
their sweat drips in thick dart-drops big as their staring eyes
where sweet smiles still appear;
Alexandra,
if love is pain
this i have carried inside my loins
as i walked
fell
intoxicated
and fucked-up right inside the pitch of all that's me
watching
listening
even to concubines conspiring in secrets with husbands
and

i have heard a murder declared while we sat on a broken sofa
drinking
while i slept drunk, my heart shook like a tornado-uprooted
tree
as the whore's scream whirled in the dark
and i heard a man weep like a woman giving birth
while he pleaded for his life;
Alexandra,
i have seen what i have seen
for
me, i was born with open eyes
to bleed my heart like a licking tin
and the blood is messy on my lap where i wring my hands
absent mindedly
while your streets fade
and your houses tumble like that
your face is twisted like a woman's riddled with bloody pain
for now,
the graves gape —
Alexandra,
i give you my back now, the secrets are in my heart and on
my lap
i cannot look
for your legs are chained apart
and your dirty petticoat is soaked in blood
blood from your ravaged wound.

The Breezing Dawn of the New Day

Many things have come and gone
come with the night of silent footsteps which stole some children
who went and left us with empty spaces which are full of noises
noises which ring and ring
yet some day has gone and left some children here
who ask and ask and so teach us how to talk and fix an eye on
   any other eye

so things go –
sometimes as if a wink of an eye
at times as if thick darts of tear droplets
time –
that movement of people
the dark and the daylight, we do what we do with them –
so with trees
or the sky
and the earth
it could have been so with our lives
it is not
since we have sense thought and memory
also
since we have hands and legs
also
since we have come to know what we want
since we know that the mind and nature are god
and that indeed we are our god
we keep the record:

> isandhlwana. bulhoek. sharpeville. are milestones of
> which the latest is soweto; as most travellers know,
> people who walk the road do now and then come to
> junctions. if they know the road, they walk on without
> stop, if they don't they wait around and ask around until
> they find their way or the night comes or the daylight
> goes, which is to say, ah, how much do you know about
> yourself and where you are and where you are going to:
> blood river. cato manor. or another type of soweto?

we keep the record here
and give the report straight
since
so many people have gone
so many things have gone
the heat
the fire
swept all that was then
some saw the smoke and some saw the smotherings

some even —
left their footprints on the cold cold ashes
and day by day one by one we come still
and the new paths are begun
when those of us, whose falling was like a pebble in the pond,
hit the bottom of the grave
or by night jump fences feeling footsteps rearing them
of some of us in jails whose cells howl like empty graves
we keep in our hands, as if a fresh hot coal from the fire
our memory
this is when we keep choosing the weapons
and like a storm
keeping calm before it emerges
we gather force
we *are* here
betrayed by everything else but ourselves
and our best ally is our clarity about who we are
where we come from
who our enemy is
where we want to go to
and these begin to define our natural allies
as we gather force
as we create the storm
since here, we are
talking about a land of many colours and sounds
we sing here, for we can sing still, about a national life
which will be chiselled by the long long gone time
by the long gone lives of some of us
and by what we do now,
what we do now
is that we say we cannot work and be exploited
we refuse too to be oppressed
some don't like to hear this, but we say it, not only that,
we are fighting now
did you hear
how some people, god's children, talk
about us
all we can say or sing now

is that
many things have come and gone
come with footsteps which have no sound
gone with some of our children –
we keep the record:

> nothing stays forever, even our oppression or our op-
> pressor. and we know that it is us who must make this
> true. since we were once conquered, we have lost too
> many things, that is, we have had to do with nothing at
> times. now we look into that, and find that we need our
> country, also, that our country needs us to fight; and then
> we find out that we are ready, all this time, of having
> nothing, has prepared us. which is to pitch the price of
> our country at the height of our life – nothing less.

who, who we ask, does not know our story
the story of our country
if you lift your hands and say you know it
listen,
we sing here, for we can sing still, about our national life
a life
which must grow now,
like a child
a child looked after and taught well
that is our future,
we keep the record:

> africa needs south africa. not america or europe. because
> these two have no manners, know nothing about being
> guests; we give them the full fury of our wrath. they will
> leave our land. and those inside the country, black or
> white, who own the south african army and money, or
> who want to defend these, at the expense of the lot of the
> people, we count down on them.

and day by day one by one we will come
and the new paths will be started
and the old will turn to chaos
the house of law will turn mute

the house of reigns will turn limp
and their security will go blind
something terrible for them will be around, without sound
    stalking everything
the old days dying
and some child somewhere in the mist of this death will know
the breezing dawn of the new day —
they will put brick on brick
and build, a new country.

MTUTUZELI MATSHOBA
(b. 1950)

The Mantatee Horde

Fifty thousand people uprooted by mfecane,
led by that formidable chieftainess Mantatisi,
rolling aimlessly in a circle of destruction and pillage across the
    plains.
Tracks marked by human and animal skeletons;
cattle penned inside a constantly moving, circular human wall;
council held on the move: to destroy is to survive.

Clouds of dust and doubt during the day,
glowing campfires dotting the still hillsides at night.
Whither tomorrow?
Whither, to sow fear and death?

When the first rays of the sun pour over the eastern margin,
they shall move;
theirs is a policy of motion aimless and doubtful.
They believe in the swift, rash decision for survival.
Why?
Regina belli, Mantatisi believes so,
so they move like a juggernaut, mixed and stirred black clans.
They kill and they die.
Regina belli is dead,

Sikonyela now leads the Horde.
Later there is an implosion;
the Horde crumbles under its own weight,
its own strain.
How much like a laager!

NJABULO S. NDEBELE
(b. 1948)

The Revolution of the Aged

my voice is the measure of my life
it cannot travel far now,
small mounds of earth already bead my open grave,
so come close
     lest you miss the dream.

grey hair has placed on my brow
the verdict of wisdom
and the skin-folds of age
bear tales wooled in the truth of proverbs:
if you cannot master the wind,
flow with it
letting know all the time that you are resisting.

that is how i have lived
quietly
swallowing both the fresh and foul
from the mouth of my masters;
yet i watched and listened.

i have listened too
to the condemnations of the young
who burned with scorn
     loaded with revolutionary maxims
        hot for quick results.

they did not know
that their anger
was born in the meekness
with which i whipped my self:
it is a blind progeny
that acts without indebtedness to the past.

listen now,
the dream:
i was playing music on my flute
when a man came and asked to see my flute
and i gave it to him,
but he took my flute and walked away.
i followed this man, asking for my flute;
he would not give it back to me.
how i planted vegetables in his garden!
      cooked his food!
how i cleaned his house!
how i washed his clothes
      and polished his shoes!
but he would not give me back my flute,
yet in my humiliation
i felt the growth of strength in me
for i had a goal
as firm as life is endless,
while he lived in the darkness of his wrong

now he has grown hollow from the grin of his cruelty
he kisses death through my flute
which has grown heavy, too heavy
for his withered hands,
and now i should smite him:
in my hand is the weapon of youth.

do not eat an unripe apple
its bitterness is a tingling knife.
suffer yourself to wait
and the ripeness will come
and the apple will fall down at your feet.

now is the time
    pluck the apple
and feed the future with its ripeness.

HAROLD FARMER
(b. 1943)

Lost City

Travellers have seen it, uncovered
for a moment, like an ostrich egg
white and perfectly domed
in the stretches of the desert –
the lost city of the Kalahari
belonging to a forgotten people.
What tools they used no one knows.
How they survived in that arid place,
a matter of conjecture, slavers
it could be, or miners
of precious minerals, but I think
that what preserved them
was the visits of travellers,
not tourists exactly, but
accretions of dream which at last
congealed into that pearl,
covered and again uncovered
by the winds of the desert
to a few in every generation.

CHARLES MUNGOSHI
(b. 1947)

A Letter to a Son

Now the pumpkin is ripe.
We are only a few days from
the year's first mealie cob.
The cows are giving us lots of milk.
Taken in the round it isn't a bad year at all –
if it weren't for your father.
Your father's back is back again
and all the work has fallen on my shoulders.
Your little brothers and sisters are doing
fine at the day-school. Only Rindai
is becoming a problem. You will remember
we wrote you – did you get our letter? –
you didn't answer – you see, since your
father's back started we haven't been able
to raise enough to send your sister Rindai
to secondary school. She spends most of the time
crying by the well. It's mainly because of her
that I am writing this letter.
I had thought you would be with us last Christmas
then I thought maybe you were too busy
and you would make it at Easter –
it was then your father nearly left us, son.
Then I thought I would come to you some time
before the cold season settled in – you know how
I simply hate that time of year –
but then your father went down again
and this time worse than any other time before.
We were beginning to think he would never see
another sowing season. I asked your sister Rindai
to write you but your father would have none of it
– you know how stubborn he can get when
he has to lie in bed all day or gets

299

one of those queer notions of his that
everybody is deserting him!
Now, Tambu, don't think I am asking for money —
although we had to borrow a little from
those who have it to get your father to hospital
and you know how he hates having to borrow!
That is all I wanted to tell you.
I do hope that you will be with us this July.
It's so long ago since we last heard from you —
I hope this letter finds you still at the old address.
It is the only address we know.

Your Mother

Dotito is Our Brother

Dotito is our brother.
He is strange.
He will not play with us on the streets.
He doesn't want to go with us to the Community Centre.
He doesn't want to play the hula-hoop.
He likes sitting under the mango tree
all day long all alone drawing strange things
that look like people but aren't really people
on any scrap of paper. He is at the bottom
of his class and he disappears each time
we go for games in the playground.
He loves the rain. He could walk for hours
in a heavy downpour and never notice.
Father caned him for it once and now when
it rains he just sits by the window looking out;
sometimes talking — opening his mouth
and saying strange noises to the rain.
When he is tired of talking to the rain
he blows breath onto the glass pane
and draws the same weird things as on the scraps of paper.
People who don't know him think he is deaf —
but he isn't although we aren't sure he won't be — soon.

Behind a closed door in their bedroom father and mother
whisper about him in the dark.
Although we aren't supposed to hear it
we know what they have begun to think
about Dotito. We are a little afraid.
Strange people point and stare at us in the street
even when Dotito isn't with us. We know what they
are saying too even when we don't see them open their mouths.
We can't go anywhere without meeting them.
They are talking about how we are Dotito's people.

JULIUS CHINGONO
(b. 1949)

An Epitaph

Here lies Stephen Pwanya
A renowned gentleman
who lived to forty-five
he is survived by his pipe
the smoke could not wait
took to the wind.

(1974)

N. C. G. MATHEMA
(b. 1949)

A Maze of Blood

A Shona married a Ndebele,
Children were born.
A Ndebele married a Khalanga
Children were born.
A Suthu married a Shona,

Children were born.
A Tonga-Ndebele child
Married a Shona-Ndebele child,
Children were born.
A Shona-English child
Married a Shona-Ndebele child
Who married a Tonga-Suthu child
Who married a Khalanga-English child
Who married a Shona-Ndebele-Suthu child
Who married a Tonga child
Who married a Ndebele child
Who married a Khalanga child
Who married an English-Ndebele-Nyanja-Tonga child
Who married a Ndebele-Shona-Khalanga child
Who married a Shona child
Who married a Tonga-Khalanga child
And Zimbabwe was born.

MUSAEMURA ZIMUNYA
(b. 1949)

White Poetess

She saw Africa as a continent
with festering sores
bleeding and clotting
in defiance of western therapy.

Something ghoulish from the north
of the Zambezi river offended
those who, like her, were civilised
although there was no end to the prospect
of titillating tattle about Africans.

So, she stepped into the sun
and into the smell of tangible haze
which you could peel with your fingernails
to see the virgin Zimbabwe spring

courting the rains of the summer
and embracing the mountains.

Close to tears,
she clutched them close to her heart
and surrendered to the intoxication
of endless safari dreaming.

But she couldn't see that beneath
the mountain, a shadow with living eyes
and witching black lips, beard, body and legs,
her own servant, was thrusting roots around her.

She had no dreams that night,
merely sat on the typewriter
and composed a romantic piece
about the Rhodesian veld in which
the shadow of the servant had no place,
save for a grudging vernacular word, wrongly spelt,
making wild reference.

After the Massacre

There was a row in the pub,
and, frankly speaking, the English landlord
was, to say the least, quite shaken.

But then we were customers,
exiles haunting every green place,
and so there was no bouncer in evidence
to pick up the pieces.

We castrated the regime,
we prophesied doom for the puppets
we praised the work of the peasants,
managed to smash the capitalists,
and with a gulp the size and noise of a cataract
we cried, '*A luta continua.*'

Somewhere the CIA and BOSS got a roasting
and a guerrilla leader was picked up

in the same bed as Lonrho,
and a hell of a rage ensued,
enough to demonstrate that
we have more righteousness than Livingstone had rated us.

And, once more, '*A luta continua.*'

The pilgrims from Denda
proclaimed themselves the future leaders
because no one could deny they had suffered the most
who would deny that they had fought the most
who would deny that they were the most educated
and in a most accomplished stroke of genius
every tribe and clan was given the Anglo-Saxon equivalent –
Welsh, English, Scottish, Irish –
and our pyrrhic nature was complete.

The following morning
we considered the post mortem positive:
hadn't we talked about the wounds of the people,
hadn't you talked about their sore backs,
hadn't I talked about their deaths for our freedom,
I did mention their burning huts and that typhoid, didn't I?

Brother, well brother,
even with a hangover negotiating the head
like a koggelmander what we did not talk about
comes bleeding through the heat like a deep gangrene.

SHEILA CUSSONS
(b. 1922)

Yellow Gramophone
Translated from the Afrikaans by the poet

Hello, daffodil, saffron-yellow exclamation,
whirligig, little windmill,
an old-fashioned gramophone horn.

And I feel my mama dancing again
to the swing of twenty-two,
and I, through membrane,
conscious of a submarine glow —
the lamps glitter — the pulsation
and mermaid song of drums and saxophone,
until, exhilarated, I let go
and race my little feet along with mama.

You are beautiful, daffodil, out of
the dark earth, the silent, cold dark earth —

Hello, goodbye, yellow gramophone.

The Barn-yard

Translated from the Afrikaans by Johann de Lange

The pigsty did not reek:
it smelled pleasantly crass-sour-rotten,
and the gluttonous snouts in hogwash and gourd
and the unmentionable mud was the most wonderful
most daring bad manners imaginable —
I loved the pigsty far removed
at the lower end of the barn-yard,
behind a row of cypresses, and liked to sit on its wall
and sniff in deeply the feral scent
and be amazed at animals so shamelessly
gluttonous they even guzzle with their snouts;
and their ugly heavy mugs with the stupid
white-lashed eyelets like something from Grimm
or Andersen. Indeed, the pigs were Somebodies,
like princes disguised by withered old witches
or Circe's swine-sailors —
Nearly sun-blind I dreamt about them,
until mud-mellow, so strong and richly-sweet
saturated my young veins, the magical enchantment
of all the summers of my youth —

Back in the house:
Good Lord one really can't bear this
Grandmother piously complained of the heat
and, hell but it's hot, bluntly
from my slightly more carnal mother:
how could they understand that the scorching day
and the pigsty
was a heaven to me, a fable unrivalled –
Also the lost paradise was just outside the house:
a big old plum-tree with sinful fruit
which fell from above just like us,
and if you picked one up you could still see in time
how the evil quickly recoiled
back into the injured flesh –
O lost barn-yard, in you I could find the whole Old Testament
and the Greek legends and Andersen.

WILMA STOCKENSTRÖM
(b. 1933)

On the Suicide of Young Writers
Translated from the Afrikaans by Stephen Gray

Because when they die
no flights in formation are necessary
crying starlings accompany them and the macabre gulls
there's no need for a gun-carriage to be towed past
poems carry them
sketches tell small intimate details
long after the last report about the dead politician.

But when they die too young
– branch of a radiant peach-tree torn down –
it's an arm wrenched off

the blood drips on our breakfast table
the houses crouch, the palaces of gods cringe
a bitter smoke blows through the land from endless caves.

Stockenström's note: 'Written to commemorate the death by suicide
in July 1965 of two young South African writers, one white (Ingrid
Jonker), one black (Nat Nakasa). The poem also refers to the grandiose
funeral of the politician, H. F. Verwoerd, assassinated in 1966.'

The Rank Harvest of Betrayal
Translated from the Afrikaans by Rosa Keet

On the rank harvest of betrayal they feed
with their pinched mouths
the ruddy righteous upright burghers
of my country. And it is sweet fare.

Their prating makes the printer's ink spatter
across the Hansard pages; and let's not overlook
the publications of mining interests
that delve up cocopans of liberal ideas

for very profitable sale.
Ah, the servile and shameless ants
earnestly tugging carcasses and rubbing their hands
with puritan complacency. Wiselings!

These, gentlemen, are the years that distort,
that take the pink mouth by its corners
and pull it into a thin-lipped grin,
like a graveyard angel's set idiocy.

These, gentlemen, are the monstrous times
when parents are weaned from their children,
when children start eating their mothers with small, straight
white milk teeth, brought by the mouse.

Look, the sewage gurgles on the pavement.
Cracks in the road gape darkly.
The last flight is being announced, gentlemen.
The seven four seven slides sharply into the air.

L'Agulhas, a Walk

Translated from the Afrikaans by Rosa Keet

I collide with sun and foam, a fierce
meeting my walk with wind and sea. Striding on
shelly sand I hear it slosh,
gulp and eddy. The bright tide
is thick with plankton, dense with mineral
and odes and omens of wrecks
caught undetectably on rocks.

Beside me the black-winged gull, his garb
like a pilot, fisher, expert, his eye
on me upon this soft-sieved verge between
beach and plant where I go cloven, he webbed,
where I stroke sandflowers and he
skips and skirts the bumptious wave,
still his eye on me, my comrade.

He rises into the evening. He leaves me behind
with no defence against his sudden-shown
indifference. I had wanted to question him,
thought we were companions at least for one
vacation. I had still wished to hear and chronicle
a history sailing by. Had wished to tinker,
and lay bare, a tidal zone of monsters.

I feel the sweep of the lighthouse beam
that brackets me with leaky shells and saluting crab,
with ebb and flow and primal links,
me and the houses and the gathered waters
in one brief proposition: this then,
cape of needles, is the beginning of an africa
which ever so friendly forfeits nothing.

Prayer for a Thief

Translated from the Afrikaans by the poet

While I am praying
you close your eyes
while I eagerly look at my hand
charting your body

you are barricaded
against my reconnaissance beyond the skin
against any invasion
inside your fortress your eyes your forehead

in an unguarded moment
I'll have to penetrate your battlements
drive in with a furtive rite
and desecrate the holy trifles you hoard

I shall have to be a thief
I shall have to give up my honour
and the right
to worship you

I shall actually be the victim
in my search for icons
while you as your own avatar
continue to grow as your own sanctuary

you grow from your feet
like a tree of godly flesh
to the hair around your neck and shoulders
where my hands want to nest like mating birds

don't shut your eyes again
there remains for me for my sins
no merciful shelter
no inn
no shrine along the way

Neocolonialism

Above all, define standards
prescribe values
set limits; impose boundaries

and even if you have no satellites
in space
and no weapons of any value
you will rule the world

Whatever tune you sing
they will dance
whatever bilge you spill
they will lick
and you may well pick
and choose
their rare minerals
and their rich forests

They will come to you
in fear and trembling
for the game will be played
according to your rules
and therefore the game will be played
only when you can win

Above all,
prescribe values
and define standards
and then sit back
to allow the third world
to fall into your lap.

To the Writers' Workshop in Zomba

Comparisons will be made;
contrasts will be drawn
and conclusions reached –
but never mind us
unholy parasites who resemble you to a hair,
save for the anguish in your heart
and the music upon your lips.

Write as the spirit moves you
and as the spirit moves
tell us about
the fire next time;
and about skulls filled with wind
in our own valley of dry bones.

Tell us also about that louse
in the arm-pit of the elephant;
tell us, brothers, tell us all
about that elegant T-shirt
on the chest of a well-endowed
undergraduate
above whose breasts hang
like an ad at a trade-fair the words
'Her Majesty's Treasury'.

Yes, brothers, tell it like it is
for comparisons will be made
and conclusions reached
on how you who are
part of the elite anywhere on earth!
though dressed in faded jeans and
with very open-necked shirts
fluttering in the wind
like the sails of a dhow on Lake Chirwa
met your souls one fine morning
and gathered from them
that you could tell us
about the world to come

and tell it like it is
about our lot on planet earth.

Comparisons will be made
and contrasts drawn
between your world
and the times and places
of seers and prophets
for profane writ has it
that angels have departed
and miraculous conversions
become
mere convulsions
in our sterilised
and banal age

Do your thing
brothers and sisters
though comparisons will be made

Contrasts drawn
and conclusions reached.

Sizeline

It means everything
that you float above these waves
buoyed by my fingers;
winding your arms around my neck
you chuckle and giggle
like a child in a bath-tub.

Secular saint to a mocking generation
in an indifferent universe
here I stand
grinning at the elements
but mesmerised by the giggles at my back
and the hands around my neck.

'A new kind of joy,'
did you say?
sadness, too,
a lingering and gnawing sadness
from the vast eternity
of remembered time –
life's unfinished business
is a day in the sun
while conventions and usages
precedence and successors
minutes and memoranda
colleagues and superiors
officers and their batmen
keep this earth on its axis
and tomorrow in its groove.

And so, Sizeline, my friend,
'Let Rome in Tiber melt!'
while we joke with the clear skies above us
and the blue mountains across the lake
and leap above the waves
like demented dolphins
adding our sound-track
to the movie of your smile
and the glow of your birth-mark.

No, no,
I am no Mark Antony
forfeiting his third of imperial Rome
to cling to the warmth of Cleopatra
still less an Octavius Caesar
freezing his emotions
to pursue the 'Pax Romana'
no, no portion of the world now known to man
will ever be thrust upon my shoulders.

I have never seen Cleopatra
except in your eyes
never touched her skin

except in your arms
but as I lift you whole
and stare into these eyes
weighing your dangling legs
on the sighing scale
of this murmuring breeze
a brand-new world opens its arms
though no portion of the globe now known to man
will ever be thrust upon my shoulders
and I may well cry,
'Let Rome in Tiber melt'

For Sizeline, my friend
in these waters and on these sands
we are no longer cockroaches
trapped in the glare of artificial light
but glistering black submarines
entering the lake from one end
and coming out at the other.

You are woman and
I am man.

FRANK CHIPASULA
(b. 1949)

Tramp

He trudges the streets of Blantyre
weighed down by his KAR 'medals':
pierced Coca-Cola bottle tops,
funeral bands and decorations, shouting:
Africa for the Africans! before tourists
their cameras clicking incessantly as
he recounts memories of the dark bomb shelters
in the last battle of Tanganyika:
cycling a stationary bicycle tied

to the roof to keep the lamp burning
the boys singing for morale and how
with phangas, bayonets and muscle
they 'trounced' the Germans for their masters.

He tramps from bar to bar, sack over shoulder,
gathering half-drunk bottles of Carlsberg beer
and cigarette butts from rich people's ashtrays
for the victory party that he will hold
with the spirits of his slain colleagues
whom he salutes in his solitary minute of silence
remembering Burma and cheap women in eastern brothels,
Zomba and Nyasa camps, cannon and thunder
on the wooded banks of the yellow river.

And when we shower him with tambala coins
for a thrill, he smiles, his glassy eyes smarting
and like a khaki robot he drills stiffly
for another war he only knows, fingers
his stars, black stripes, and softly weeps
for a wife violated in absence, his land gone,
the promised compensation he will not see.

We watch him burn into ash like a cigarette
as he talks of blood in the red strip of the banner,
the setting sun casting darkness over his lost land
all so green, all so green, yet gone, going;
And he sulks, murmuring of the blood spilt in the struggle,
of the bullets turned into bees in *Operation Dawn*
human targets melting into lakes and mirages in Mulanje
and the fifty innocents massacred mercilessly at Nkhata Bay.

And when we query him about the contents
of his sticky soiled sack, he answers: 'Promises'
and embraces his silence again.

Warrior
(for David, and Derek Walcott)

Imitation warrior
in synthetic monkey skins

over a three-piece suit
inevitable overcoat, stick,

homburg hat, dark glassed
and false toothed smiles,

he clutched horse-hair
flywhisk and plastic spears

at conference tables in Whitehall
fighting with words only

begging his masters for a new name,
a flag and a new anthem.

'Out of your people's skins
fashion a flag, their bones a flagpole;

Their laments shall be your anthem;
Rename the country and it shall be.'

That is the recipe of his rule
sincere to the last instruction.

Meanwhile, the settlers massacred
his people with volleys

of bullets, littering their
mangled bodies like trash

all over our country. Over them
he preached non-violence, forgiveness

and the masters, relieved, curled up
in bed and slept without headaches.

Now he prances clumsily among survivors
mourning their kin at his rallies

as he samples the men for export
to the deep dungeons of Joni

on loan and Aid agreements
for the bribe of blood rands.

He demands handclaps
everywhere he turns he confronts

his inflated portraits
nailed and hoisted on flagpoles

whose blood-drenched banners
are birds straining at ropes.

Corrugated mist like fish scales
covers the eyes of the praise

dancers round him dancing for
the war lost to the settlers.

Then the songs shore up his lofty
platform as he leaves his people

at its foot, steeled with spears
and shields praising the deserter.

They hail him Messiah, Saviour
as he fattens on larceny.

A Hanging, Zomba Central Prison

His pendulous body tolled
its own death knell from the rope
yet refused obstinately
to die, clinging desperately
to the last thread
of his condemned life.

That morning oh!
his body sang until it could not
stand its own song;

Like a guitar it hummed
and they could not but listen, stunned.
Every part of his body
opened its mouth and sang
death songs, Orphic heartsongs
shrill and sweet pent-up
songs of freedom or sad and solemn
as the national anthem.

The heartstrings raised their harp
in a flood of insistent rhythm
and a slow drumming dance:
All his blood stood up and sang,
twisting towards the throat.

All the silent mouths raised their voices
and cried out their chorus.
No one could gag or stop the prison
walls from singing;
No one could muzzle or shield the ringing
echoes of Zomba mountain.
And the whispering pines on Queens Point,
witnesses to the sordid deed
raised their frosty mourning.

His heart was a cube of golden light,
a nest of incense where weaver-
birds had made their welcome permanent
weaving a wall of thin silken tears
that sang with the lips of broken earth,
rolled waves, resistant and durable wind.

From every pore on his body a river of song
or wail sprang and poured out.
His feet opened out like dark petals and chirped;
His fingers bloomed and plucked his heartstrings.
The song twined into the makako and jammed it;
The looped noose would not close, numbed.

Being political, he was not entitled
to the miraculous luck of the criminals.

So they called in the prison doctor
to administer the *coup de grâce*.
He stabbed the chest with a thick
syringe and pumped the poison
into the heart with orgasmic release.

The heart made a sudden excited leap,
missed only one deceptive beat
and resumed its journey as usual.
Slowly he turned into a deep emerald green
and covered the whole country.

Like a stone he would not die.
They summoned a hardcore life prisoner,
placed a rock hammer in his hand
and ordered him to locate the victim's heart.
He bashed in the chest completely
and left a wide yawning gap. Not murder
technically, only routine execution.

Then a waterfall of blood! There was no one
that the blood did not touch and baptise.
Pilate searched vainly for water
to cleanse his hands of the *business*.

The song gushed out in a steady jet.
The body tolled its final knell
and then momentarily froze, then in a futile
move to cross the dark river before him,
he spread out his legs and kicked
and tried to rip the darkness that cloaked him.

Then . . . ah, this is *it*
The final parting moment, the end, the last
wisp of breath escaping from his gaping mouth
again with the song rising like smoke.
He wanted the last swing, the final
expression of his freedom arrested and preserved

before the sandbags dragged his compressed body
into the dark hole, into total oblivion.

JACK MAPANJE
(b. 1944)

—————— ❧ ——————

The Cheerful Girls at Smiller's Bar, 1971

The prostitutes at Smiller's Bar beside the dusty road
Were only girls once in tremulous mini-skirts and oriental
Beads, cheerfully swigging Carlsbergs and bouncing to
Rusty simanje-manje and rumba booming in the juke-box.
They were striking virgins bored by our Presbyterian
Prudes until a true Presbyterian came one night. And like
To us all the girls offered him a seat on cheap planks
In the dark backyard room choked with diesel-oil clouds
From a tin-can lamp. Touched the official rolled his eyes
To one in style. She said no. Most girls only wanted
A husband to hook or the fruits of Independence to taste
But since then mini-skirts were banned and the girls
Of Smiller's Bar became 'ugly prostitutes to boot!'

Today the girls still giggle about what came through
The megaphones: the preservation of our traditional
Et cetera . . .

On African Writing (1971)

You've rocked at many passage rites, at drums
Mothers clapping their admiration of your
Initiation voices – now praises of decay
That still mesmerize some; at times you've
Yodelled like you'd never become men gallant
Hunting, marrying, hating, killing. But
In your masks you've sung on one praise
After another. You have sung mouth-songs!
Men struggling to justify what you touched
Only, heard merely! Empty men! Do you realise
You are still singing initiation tunes?
You have not chimed hunting-marrying-

Fighting-killing praises until you've
Stopped all this nonsense about drinking
Palm wine from plastic tumblers!
And these doggerels, these sexual-tribal
Anthropological-political doggerels!
Don't you think even mothers will stop
Quaking some day? Don't you realise
Mothers also ache to see their grand-
Children at home playing bau on sofas?
Why do you always suppose mothers
Never want to see you at these conferences
They are for ever hearing about?
Why do you imagine they never understand
Things? They too can be alert to all this
Absurdity about what you think they think!
You've sung many songs, some superb
But these lip-songs are most despicable!

Steve Biko is Dead

The Boers have poked another
Human's sparkling eyes
With electric tongs
Soldering his sharp brain to metal

Steve Biko is dead
The most liberal of Western
Papers will probably
Report his death thus:

'The duffers have wafted
Biko with another poisonous wand
Of a gorgeous apartheid peacock
Ogling sanity into slumber . . .'

That Biko was another Man
With a wife, a child, a conscience
And the right to live ordinarily
Fighting in peace,

Of the restive ship behind,
Why or for how long
Steve Bikos will waste
We'll not bother to ask.

Who dares to budge
These precious days
And give evidence
For hope bereft?

After Wiriyamu Village Massacre by Portuguese

No, go back into your exile, go back quick.
When those Portuguese soldiers abducted
Falencha's baby quietly strapped on her back
And scattered its precious brain on Falencha's
Own maize grinding stone, when those soldiers
Grabbed and hacked Dinyero's only son
With Dinyero herself stubbornly watching
Or when they burnt down Faranando in his own
Hut as he tried to save Alefa his senile wife –
Where, where was your hand? Tell me that!
And if you helped Adrian Hastings report
The Portuguese atrocities to humans, where,
Where is your verse? You have no shame!
No, go back until our anger has simmered.

Baobab Fruit Picking
(or Development in Monkey Bay)
(for Mary and David Kerr)

'We've fought before, but this is worse than rape!'
In the semi-Sahara October haze, the raw jokes

Of Balamanja women are remarkable. The vision
We revel in has sent their husbands to the mines

Of Jo'burg, to buy us large farms, she insists.
But here, the wives survive by their wits & sweat:

Shoving dead cassava stalks into rocks, catching
Fish in tired chitenje cloths with kids, picking

Baobab fruit & whoring. The bark from the baobab
They strip into strings for their reed wattle,

The fruit they crack, scoop out the white, mix with
Goat milk, 'there's porridge for today, children!'

The shell is drinking gourd or firewood split
(They used to grate the hard cores into girls'

Initiation oil once). 'But you imported the Boers,
Who visited our Chief at dawn, promising boreholes!'

These pine cottages on the beach shot up instead, some
With barbed wire fences fifty yards into the lake!

(What cheek!) Now each weekend, the 'blighted-tomato-
thighs in reeking loin-cloths' come, boating, grinning

At them baobab fruit picking. 'My house was right
Here!' Whoever dares check these Balamanja dreamers?

TIMOTHY HOLMES
(b. 1936)

Room for All

When the storm passed away
The weather prophets were puzzled
By its mildness. Compared
To hurricanes in other parts, at other
Times, it made no more than ripples
On the lake: in one or two
Places though, side eddies had
Caused damage not yet repaired.

In the days that followed
Benefits flowed in its wake:
Rivers had a scour-out,
Fishing improved: crops of corn, cotton,
Sugar, nuts, fruit, shot up; cattle
Flourished. For the better was any difference
In the season.
              No thing despaired;
Not even the underlings of farm
And factory; nor the gnawers, borers,
Chewers of growth, who in the springing
Upshoot had ample staple for lean bellies:
Cutworm, weevil and wilddog
Did well: there was room for all.

Deep

A cold spot on the heart repeats
The klink-klink of a blacksmith plover's cry,
    Over lake waters
    Goodbye goodbye.

Purple heron's doubled neck and wings
Unfold, fold, change, become the sedge;
    Cold wavelets lap
    The false shore's edge.

Stonechat, fish eagle, jacana, coucal, hawk,
Egret, pied crow, names that catch the eye;
    Words with more meaning
    Less confidently fly.

The cold spot on the heart repeats
Malignant fears of tadpole, beetle, bream;
    Deep in all that beauty
    The predator's gleam a-gleam.

SWIDI-NONKAMFELA MHLONGO
(b. 1948)

His Praises

Translated from the Zulu by Elizabeth Gunner

Sweet-tied-tight-in-the-middle.
The Sought-after Bachelor.
Tree trunk that drips water,
here is the broad-shouldered fellow, the Smeller-out,
because he smelt out those of other nations.
The Strange Noise of the Whites 'tokking Ingleesh'.
He is a 'dog', the White man, he defecates in a bucket!
So say I the Stump of the thorn tree – He Drips and dries.
The Broad-shouldered fellow, the Smeller-out
because he smelt out those of other nations.
Scatterer of the embers but they do not burn him.
    So say I –
The Swallower of something burning but it's cool in his insides.
Body that never tires of blows.
Terrible are the places, it is difficult, it is frightening.
As for the older men some are not here and some are here –
[*He breaks off*]
I am stopping now, the child of Mhlongo.
[*There is a general hubbub and then he goes on*]
I am He-who-stands-with-his-legs-wide-apart and out come the
        young girls and maidens.
Sweet-tied-tight-in-the-middle, the Sought-after bachelor.
It is I Maize-please-blossom so we can eat the ripe fruit.
It is I the Shadow of the hills.
It is I Sheyi the (draughts) game the Basotho play.
Hotso – only his eyes were seen on the stairs.
I met a rock-rabbit from up-country. Oh what trouble I had in
        those parts.
[*Sounds of sympathy from the female listeners*]
I was without Mother and without Father, whom did I have?

And then when I returned home I returned sick at heart.
. . . Then I went . . .
[*He pauses*]
Then I thought the mountains were tumbling down because . . .
It was then that I found maize still to be had in our own place of
      KwaDlangezwa and I ate.
Then once more I spoke and I said, 'It is I, I have come back,'
Sweet-tied-in-the-middle.
Bachelor-among-bachelors.

Recorded by the translator in Zululand in 1976, and transcribed with this literal rendering. His praise-name, 'Swidi-nonkamfela', means 'Sweet-tied-in-the-middle'.

MATSEMELA MANAKA
(b. 1956)

Two Choruses from Pula

I

In the name of the people,
let peace prevail
amongst all people and parties.
Let oneness
be the path to happiness.
In the name of the people,
let us not allow our differences
to stand against our national aspirations.
Let us all agree
that people are people.
Be they 'maPantsula'
      'maHieppie'
      'maCat'
      'maIntellectual'
      'maIlliterate',
people are people.
Be they in the bantustans

or urban areas,
people are people.
In the name of the people,
let oneness
be the path to happiness.
Let us not call each other
by ugly names.
Be they Bagoshedi Congress Party
or the People's Congress Party,
don't call them names.
In the name of the people,
ask yourself why our people
spend sleepless nights
drinking Babylon waters
and dancing to Babylon rhythms.
In the name of the people,
ask yourself why our people
rob one another,
rape one another
and kill one another.
In the name of the people,
ask yourself why
can't we be one.
In the name of the people,
let us all sing for the rain.
Let oneness
be the path to happiness.

Give back our happiness
Give back our happiness
Give back our blood
Give back our sweat

We need bread we need meat
We need bread we need meat
  We have been barking
  it's enough
We must teeth ourselves
  and go for the meat

People beautiful people
People beautiful people
> This day has long begun
> Let it be done and be gone

People beautiful people
People beautiful people
> Give this day some feathers
> And let it fly away!

2

Babylon, I did not come to you for the sake of coming.
I am here in search of my happiness.
Did you hear the cries of my children who died of hunger?
When my wife delivered my child into this earth,
I sang a melody and my people celebrated.
We sang, beat the drum and did the dancing.
For a while we forgot about the immediate future of the child.
> She sucked the last milk from her mother's breast, then she
> joined our song of hunger.

Now do you remember me?
I come from that land that bleeds of nothing but gold and
> diamond.

That land that smells of the sweat of our disunity.
Remember, I saw the death of my child.
By Shaka I swear!
There was no milk, no water, no food for my child.
I let her rest in my own arms.
And with my own arms,
I let her soul part from her body.
What could I have done?
There was no water for the poor
but for the rich to wash their feet and feed their pigs.
Milk was for cats and dogs.
Babylon, you know more about the cause of our agony.
You have destroyed our souls and divided us.

We all know the truth.
We all know that we are fragments
of a common segment.

Cemented by the blood of a common struggle.
We are a people with a common destination.
We are the children of Shaka.

Shakarra
  Shakarra
    Shakarra
Let the rain
come down to wet our souls
Let it rain
for us to reap the harvest
of our times
Let it rain
for us to enjoy the beauty
of being born
Let the rain come down.
Pula
Shhhhhhhhhhhhhh
Pula
Shhhhhhhhhhhhhh.

CHRIS VAN WYK
(b. 1957)

The Reason

The reason why
murderers and thieves
so easily
become statues
are made into monuments
is
already their eyes are granite
their hearts
are made
of stone.

The Ballot and the Bullet

The ballot.
This means voting.
There's this big box.
It has a slot.
Ja, like a money box.
You're given options.
Do you want a cruel government
or a kind one?
A lazy one
or one that works?
You have to make an X
on a square sheet of paper
to decide who is to be
the custodian of the people.
But first you have to identify yourself.
This is easy.
All you need is an I.D.
This looks like a passbook;
It has your photo and signature.
Only difference is
you can leave it at home
and not get caught.
That's a ballot.
Now a bullet.
Ag now, surely you know
what a bullet is.

DON MATTERA
(b. 1935)

―――――― ·~· ――――――

The Day They Came for Our House
(Sophiatown, 1962)

The sun stood still
in the sullen wintry sky
a witness
to the impending destruction.

Armed with bulldozers
they came
to do a job
nothing more
just hired killers.

We gave way
there was nothing we could do
although the bitterness stung in us,
in the place we knew to be part of us
and in the earth around,

We stood.
    Slow, painfully slow
    clumsy crushers crawled
    over the firm pillars
    into the rooms that held us
    and the roof that covered our heads,

    We stood.
Dust clouded our vision
We held back our tears
It was over in minutes,
Done.

Bulldozers have power.
They can take apart in a few minutes
all that had been built up over the years

and raised over generations
and generations of children.

The power of destroying
the pain of being destroyed,

Dust . . .

Giovanni Azania
(On the birth of my son)

Yesterday,
  You were but a thought in our minds
  A clot of life
  In your sweet mother's womb
  Touched by my spark
  Nourished by my flame.

  Today a child in our arms
  Feeling the nipple
  Drinking the milk of our twilight
  Carrying the mark of our slavery.

  Tomorrow a warrior
  Burning the bush with your blood;
  Azanian son
  Carrying along a nation's song
  A singing tree
  Fighting tyranny
  For the right to be free . . .

(13 March 1981)

MAFIKA GWALA
(b. 1946)

In Defence of Poetry

What's poetic
about Defence Bonds and Armscor?
What's poetic
about long-term sentences and
deaths in detention
for those who 'threaten state security'?
Tell me,
what's poetic
about shooting defenceless kids
in a Soweto street?
Can there be poetry
in fostering Plural Relations?
Can there be poetry
in the Immorality Act?
What's poetic
about deciding other people's lives?
Tell me brother,
what's poetic
about defending herrenvolkish rights?

As long as
this land, my country
is unpoetic in its doings
it'll be poetic to disagree.

My House is Bugged

my house is bugged
since i was mc at a student's funeral
another june 16 victim
my house is bugged
since i told my senior economics students

not to shun karl marx for their assignment
references
my house is bugged
since i preached a sermon condemning
mass removals and job reservation
– i can still see that sellout eye
from a member of my congregation
my house is bugged
since i invited sherita maharaj
to our kwamashu youth braai
my house is bugged
since i've been organizing bursaries
& improved reading for black highschool kids
my house is bugged
since that security policeman
called my Hillbrow pad a den for kaffirs
and communists
my house is bugged
since customs officials withheld literature
sent by friends overseas and said the stuff was red
my house is bugged
since my daughter came out of 200 days' detention
to a banning order and house arrest

oh, my house is bugged.

The New Dawn
(for Ngoye students, present and past)

There's talk of a New Dawn for Blacks
As if hauling the monkey off their backs;
It's a New Dawn
With a Tri-cameral Dispensation,
Pronouncing Blacks to utter damnation.

Our youth are burning themselves
Cane, Vodka, Espirit, Castello and
grind session for squeezer

It's open season for the gym Caesar;
It's days of humble handshakes
Ganja with the Rastas on Jah blues,
Only a hand grenade to choose.

This New Dawn
When people are no longer people
By their smiles, jokes or laughters drawn
As if chasing on Summerveld's Polo steeple
We know people by the cars they drive
Their frustration scars to hide
We know people by the houses they've built
Perpetuating class madness to the hilt.

It's a New Dawn
That gets you rusticated
For wanting to know East from West,
Days are not ours
As we lithe through the polkadot hours
With hippoes roaming the ghetto streets
– waddling like prehistoric beasts;
In this New Dawn we slip our lives
– kicking the Muse in the backside.
They say in '36 some of our parents
nurtured dreams of Berlin jazz
          and Vienna orchestras
They too had sidles into the labyrinths
of a false dawn.

In this New Dawn
Cynics are laughing themselves to jerry blush
Holding the dawn darkness to a seary hush;
During the evenings there's claim
to powerful vibrations at exclusive braais
The women gyrating to break dance
Breaking
          Curling
               Bending
Vibrators between their thighs;

The men priding themselves in BMs
And latest makes from Nippon;
Mitsubishi, Nissan and Toyota
never had it better on African soil.
Occasionally there'll be a push-push play
on the Black Power slogans of yesterday
Then the stones will start falling:
'Detentions brought us nothing
Some of us were playing heroes
Not wanting to settle on basic issues
Let us face reality
Get to know what's priority.'
The get down quips go on and on
into the New Dawn.

In this New Dawn
Some of us will kill their old selves
Shunting here and there for discotheques
Shuffling on stage floors
with a tornado go on the tiles-gloss
Warped in pocketless, bottomless tight pants;
There'll be permed heads
For men graduating into women.

The other side watches on
with apple-care anxiety
engaging on constructively
for its own fun to jog on;
A New Dawn cowboy in a dollar printed shirt
rides along to
'The Rand is total!
Power has no fraction!
Let there be a black nouveau riche,
Bastions against the red menace from the East.
We Westerners shall never go down!
Not when our terrestrial dreams
are centred in astronautic geography
and a Star Wars program.'
The cowboy swings his Ten Gallon hat

For the passing of Halley's Comet
Our hopes are being blessed with the Rand to Dollar jive
Giving our Black boys some bit of shine.

It's a New Dawn
As we claw
Like roaches up the academic crawl
Displaying an innate passion for words and scrawls
with the avid longing of a green-winged shitfly
our piggish fed and carrot-programmed computers
Exhibiting a ringworm itch for swinishness.

This New Dawn
Giving us pep and bliksem vim
To peck through all those webbed streets
with the shrivelled disconcern of a city park pigeon
Shopping Game and gaming clicks
with the pollen scoop of a bee
blended with the ferocious chew of the piranha.

It's a New Dawn
where public urinals and shrubs
are like butter and cheese
in ghetto townships
– stretching on the wound's rub
for Heil Hitler cries
rotten-egg engagements sighs.

This New Dawn
the Führer wears a black mask.

(22 July 1985)

ESSOP PATEL
(b. 1943)

Haanetjie's Morning Dialogue

'. . . is jy klaar
met die koerant?'

'nee, die newspaper
is te moeilik.'

'Boet, daar is nix
intellektual –
Die newspaper is mos
sommer 'n pampier
met die news, luister
my stupid,
die story is die same
maar die style is different
altyd dit is this or that
but stroes die story is the same:
     'n terrorist daar
     en
     'n murder hier
     en
     'n revolution daar
     en
     'n rape in 'n bossie . . .
wat is swaar met die news?'

'my brainpower, my Haanetjie
tog, jy, is clevah, then
wat is die try-camera parlormint . . . ?'

'that my dear Boet is simple, kyk,
daar is three cameras
vir d(r)ie bioscopes:
     een vir die wit mense

ander vir die Bushies
one for the Mememes.'

'jus, sus, jy is slim
jy het al die answers
my plaatland/Fietas
Aristotal.'

'Ja Boet dit is die analesis
van die new dream.'

'jy weet Haanie
ek gedink dit was
something like
spearment-pepperment-X X Xment.'

'tog Boet jy is stupid.'

'hoekom?'

die tricameral parliament is
APARTHEID 1983 STYLE.

PATRICK CULLINAN
(b. 1932)

1818. M. François le Vaillant Recalls His Travels to the Interior Parts of Africa (1780–1795)

I

At home in the damp hills of Champagne
I take my warmth at the fire. Official
And unofficial birds stare glassy-eyed
From cabinets, uncurious now
And oddly meditative. As flames rise a glow
Lightens their wing feathers;
They seem to move but stand rock still.
They are not and I am not
In Africa now; yet we remain, we are
The artefacts of that long journey,

Survivors of a narrative:
A story that I chose to tell, solid
In parts, deliberately vague
In others. I had no choice, I found
A normal country, rather like paradise
In places, a garden
Camouflaged by scandal,
Darkened by a kind of history.

So from the very start, exploring,
Plume-hatted among the hordes,
I sought what had been lost and what I found
I made my own: birds, animals, a cave of leaves,
And men. My friends became the fearful tribes,
Unwanted half-breeds, and, by letters
From the wilderness
A lonely savant at the Cape. Only
The Colonists were not to be endured:
Vicious at times or just plain boring, sly;
Certainly not schooled enough
To leave the wild unploughed,
Brandy-sots who could not comprehend
Rare Sensibility, true Pride.

But I was clever, had a way
Of getting what I wanted; that trick . . .
Of loading my fusee
With powder, wax and water
To bring a warbler down,
Immaculate
And flat on earth . . .
Before I broke its neck
I named the bird
And it was mine.

I had a method, yes, because I found
Buffon's stale categories a bore.
My method was to educate,
Delight, attract:
As in the breed of *Drongos*

The species multiply. *Drongri,*
Drongear, Drongo Moustache,
Drongo Fingah, and finest of them all
Disporting on a bough
Le Drongo à Raquettes.

To crawl to no god, command no slave:
This was the ordinary
Guide of my life; but given a want
Of Civility, common
To that land, good manners helped:
Narina stank of grease but liked
A buckle, most of my toys
And understood the gallantry,
The camouflage of teasing which
Hid the method. Item:
For the King of France. The Pelt
Of one Giraffe or Cameleopard.
Chased in the Canton of the Boshmen.
Beyond the Gariep.

II

So, in the end, it all went well enough.
A King and an Emperor both
Admired my great bird book.
The one has lost his head, the other
Studies seagulls on a lonely rock . . .
And walking in this room today
A true Apostle of Jean Jacques,
By private conversation,
Step by step, deferring, said
What I have written nicely balances
The Good with Evil, Nature with the Perfidy
Of Man.
          Is that enough, is that
What I was looking for?
I said and say again:
The Fabulous was quite destroyed

And in its place I set the truth.
I made a country real, a normal place.
Romantic, I agree, and odd but
Savage the right way at last. I showed
There were no Giants, club-footed or one-eyed.
Who now denies that Pigmies are small men?
Monomotapa, Vigite Magna have disappeared
From the maps; and where I travelled
That continent it is not dark.
I say the best minds of the age
Have made my Africa their own: my truth
Feeds their imagination. I have shown
That men in skins move in a certain
Landscape, are men like us, have names:
Confused, they love and hate.
          Is that the truth,
Is that what I see now?
There was a night, when wandering from my tent
At the stream of the Gonaquas,
I saw the moon had covered all
That forest, all the mountains with its light.
It flowed as bland as milk, the normal landscape
Seemed to shift, to alter . . . what I saw
Remained authentic yet I knew
It was not real.
          And here much later,
Here by the fire tonight my Africa
Is dark again. Stuffed Drongos, Trogons,
Shrikes will not flap their wings;
They sit as still as rocks. Nothing
Moves but firelight closed
In the long high room.
The world is what it seems
Always, but it can flow beneath the moon
And change, alter the staid
Sequences of vision.
          Half blind amid
The humdrum panic of the herd

Or camouflage of predator and prey
I saw only what I was made to see,
Could comprehend.
            Do all
Travellers into darkness know,
Their eyes half closed,
Exploring they betray themselves,
Betray what they have found?

STEPHEN GRAY
(b. 1941)

Hottentot Venus

My name is Saartjie Baartman and I come from Kat Rivier
        they called me the Hottentot Venus
they rang up the curtains on a classy peepshow two pennies
        two pennies in the slot and I'd wind up
shift a fan and roll my rolypoly bum
        and rock the capitals of Europe into mirth
I was a special voluptuary a squealing passion
        they had never seen anything like it before
Little Sarah twenty six born on the vlei past Grahamstown
        bought for a song and a clap of the hands
a speculative sketch come to life a curiosity
        of natural science weighed measured
exported on show two pennies two pennies
        in the Gallery of Man I am unique

I am lonely now I always was out here
        my deathbed a New Year's eve
a salon couch girdled with reporters and I turned
        my complexion to the wall and dreamed
of a knife cutting deep in a springbok's hide
        and they woke me with brandy for smelling salts
and I wouldn't wake again in their august company
        my soul creeps under cairns where

wayside travellers throw another stone in my memory
    two pennies two pennies dropped on my eyes
they laid me in state in my crinoline robe
    my hands folded coyly as they always were
and I let them bury my body so celebrated so sensational
    they could never do while I was alive
what they wanted to do sink me in wax and decant my brain
    and put me in a case in the Museum of Man

I stare out at the Eiffel Tower my hands covering
    my vaginal flaps my own anomaly
the kneebone connected to the thighbone connected to
    the hipbone connected to the spine and the skull
they mounted me without beads or skins or quivers
    Saartjie Baartman is my name and I know
my place I know my rights I put down my foot
    and the Tuileries Gardens shake I put down
my foot and the Seine changes course I put
    down my foot and the globe turns upside down
I rattle my handful of bones and the dead arise.

Apollo Café

Always I have meant to write of Apollo Café
Apollo Café has everything you need
Open on Sundays at 9.00 for the news
Open after-hours for bread and milk
On the corner-stand at 6th and Church
Johannesburg S.A. below the ridge
Always I have meant to write of Apollo Café

There are many Apollo Cafés in this poem
Each has his own with blue awnings
And moustaches smoke Winston and Good and Clean
And a catalogue of newslines and braaiwood
And the greased-over windows of curiosity
Packed with last-minute supergoods
Each has his own with overpainted frames

And prams and banana-peels and the City Council bin
And the leak of paraffin from a silver pump
Siphoning the poor juice of a spirit-stove
Between nets of bulbs and a shaking fridge
A necklace of cardboard Outspan oranges
And the sawdust of sandals and boots and straws
Each has his or her own Apollo Café

The corner of commerce in a sluggish suburb
Meeting-place of caught-out consumers
Eggs in design boxes soap soup Coke
Crackers and Mars Bars dope racing forms
Crinkle chips sliced polony biltong and sweat
Condensed milk rusks biscuits instant balloons
Always I have meant to write of Apollo Café

And in this purple city of Johannesburg S.A.
When the jacarandas refine the air with sap
And the roots swell under tarmac pavements
Ready to bunch up the stones for bare feet
And the lethargic cleaner in a wide straw hat
Sweeps blood into a municipal bag that's when
It's time to write about your or my Apollo Café

When the secret life of things can no longer be hidden
When minedust in the eye-duct generates pain
The grass instead of waving and shining crawls forth
And the railway borders tumble up to billboards
And shunting and connected the cattletrucks bellow with heat
Christmas beetles bring down the thunder
That is the time to write of Apollo Café

When the blue Fords of the Brixton Murder and Robbery
Crackle with rape and disaster and greetings
And Allied Publishing drops Sarie and Huisgenoot in bundles
And the butcher's delivery swings a calf's head
And the black poet's BMW stops for ginger beer
At the refreshment station on a hot afternoon
That is what Apollo Café is there for for ever

Yours or mine it stays while we go by
Apollo Café is a fixture needs a face-lift
Probably isn't even called Apollo Café
Tram Terminus or Springbok or Madeira
Boland or Vyfster or Mixolodeon
On five thousand South African corner plots
But always Apollo Café is what I remember

In Johannesburg S.A. this purple city
Which feeds the hungry and cares for the poor
Which balances the GNP almost daily
Which emanates mercy over the wide land
Which stays a people town and loves the lame and halt
In which I live save my soul
There is always a special Apollo Café

Its yellow-framed door is always open
For pawpaws and lichees and watermelon
For catfood and iced suckers and Marmite
And drinking yoghurt and bubblegum and lard
And cheddar cheese and mousetraps and brooms
Tuna peas bacon butter carrots chops
Matches candles fittings jelly Doom

And despite the reign of avarice and greed
Despite the sweepstakes and the price of gold
The rampant dollar and the declining rand
The pegging of the fuel-line and the ANC
The boycott of arms and sports and plays
Despite the ministers on TV with faces like frogs
At Apollo Café necessity holds sway

For a coin that's devaluing at Apollo Café
You can buy comic books and make a call
Buy liquorice and vetkoek and the wing
Of Farmer Brown and Dreyer's ice-cream
And milkshakes and coconut and samp
And return the empties and collect the tops
For a coin you can insert a silver jukebox tune.

CHRIS MANN
(b. 1948)

―――――― ― ――――――

The Comrades Marathon
Burn not the house of Pindar the poet!

1

The City Hall of Maritzburg, one silver-misted dawn.
Thousands of men, their chests thumping, throng the square.
They flex and jog a little, to keep their muscles fluent,
As night with liquid fingers lingers coolly among them.
Their destination's a city on the distant coast, Durban,
Hours and hours of tendon-jarring toil ahead.
My task, to mould their marathon in verse, is also tough,
For poets and athletes no longer praise each other's purpose.
I ask the god of love to grace this small creation
With lines that breathe and leap, and will continue to,
When we, who cheered or raced that day, are changed to dust,
And hear the steps of others thud above our heads.

2

With mock groans, the runners merge and mass the start.
They sense the same fervour as autumn swifts and swallows,
Which twitter in the cold cliffs, or twitch across the skies
Reluctant to risk the long journey, but eager to leave.
The starter climbs the steps, and as the custom, crows.
Slowly the black and bronze, blonde and rosy beings
Surge between the silent, unheroic suburbs,
Then find beneath their feet, the highway's endless hyphens.
Burly and red, the sun ahead of them bulges.
They look like upright, hornless buck with nylon hooves,
Trotting down tar, where once the tawny bushveld sloped,
Where herds migrated past, in search of greener grass.

3

The leaders, alert with pride and fear, lope ahead.
The favourites smoothly pad behind biding their time.

347

A metal bird, which hovers above, transmits their names:
Tobias Thembu, tiny, prancing, a teacher from the Cape;
And Derek Wilson dawdling by him, a farmer from De Doorns;
With red-haired Sean le Roux nearby, a miner on the Reef.
Their souls, the race's soul, is set on the road ahead.
The fame for most lies not in winning, but finishing.
Gangboss and grocer, clerk and cleric seek it together,
Have chucked their shoes and shirts aside, and changed to
    athletes.
They seek a glory which neither money nor power possess,
And hurry onwards, like warriors on some ritual hunt.

4

Le Roux, by Umlaas Road, slightly speeds his rhythm.
The favourites are already drifting up the field.
They glide past others crouched with cramps, or globuled with
    sweat,
Whose mental iron the sun has melted with the mist.
The road steepens, and squiggles along the rim of a ridge,
The world beside it shimmers with sugar and shiny cars,
The valley below is packed with people in shabby shacks.
It languishes there like Lazarus, lying at Dives' gate.
Some rich, some ragged line the route and jubilantly cheer,
As if their class and colour neither counted nor clashed.
Just so the feuds in Greece were for a moment forgotten.
The Games were called Gifts of Peace, ordained by gods.

5

At Botha's Hill, the red-haired miner moves ahead,
He doesn't wish to, not there, the leaders have let him down,
The hills destroyed them, his stride and strategy falter.
The pace of the pair behind is deliberate, they don't even pant.
More and more spectators cluster the corners and clap.
Their gaiety's a passage, an airy annual passage.
The smooth and wrinkled run it, the bearded, bandy and bald,
Short legs, spindly ones, shufflers, striders, one showman with a
    cigar.
Their skins sparkle with drops of water and spent sweat.

Like wandering Boers and Britons, or weary Zulu troops,
Who reached a river, and rubbed its wetness round their heads,
They splutter in the cool they splosh from paper cups.

6

If lungs were radios, which draw their rhythms from the air,
Then Sean le Roux, out front, would surely turn his up.
Alas for him, the voltage in his veins was low.
Beside the pines of Kloof, the others patter past,
Patches of plaster, across their nipples, peeking out pinkly,
Their popeyed faces so fierce and solemn they look ridiculous.
Madness! Thousands of grown-up men and women groaning
    along,
Without a cent, though maybe a medal, to claim at the end!
But that is their secret, their partial death to daily essentials.
They sense the same strange exhilaration as astronauts,
Who watch the world, its snowcaps and seas, shrinking away,
Yet journey onward, drawn towards the star-specked deep.

7

Deftly, daintily, Thembu has drifted a minute ahead.
From Westville Ridge, the freeway sweeps towards the bay.
He sees the ships, the smart and smoggy city-blocks.
Transistor radios, beside the road are roaring his name,
Wilson's as well, so frequently, he fears to look behind.
May after May, the athletes make this pilgrimage.
Unless the poet or painter anoint his brush or pen,
There'll be no lasting tribute, worthy of their travail.
On barren rock, Bushmen painters embellished their hunts,
And Zulu bards, in whirls of words, preserved their warriors.
Their motive is mine, to fix a moment which merits praise,
To place its image in wide perspectives of purpose and time.

8

Inside the tar and concrete bowels of the inner city,
Oblivious to the office-blocks and blustering wind,
Derek the Dawdler, step by step, drew up behind.
A string between two poles, a strident gasping ache

349

Consumed each calory of both, until with wobbling steps
They entered the stadium, Wilson struggled past, and won.
And yet, who finished means much more than who came first,
The sweaty stream of striders, shufflers, the limp and lame,
For marathons are like a life that's lived by peaceful faith,
A chance within the bitter aimlessness of things, to choose
A route, to find a reason and reward for suffering,
Before the god of love gathers his grizzled athletes in.

The Poet's Progress

Plain verse to start, no tricky stuff,
he wrote to reach his countrymen,
in all the heat of youth believed
they hungered after poetry,
if only written fresh and strong.

A pinch of seed that fell like dust:
night after night, those countrymen
anaesthetized their officed hearts
before a Punch and Judy box.

Romantic still, he slung the words
across the easy beat of song,
and let his privileged fingers dance
a peasant dance along the strings
to melt the stiffness of his caste.

Some hands were clapped, some people swayed,
but still the rusty shacks went up,
the nouveaux riches became the old
and Greenwich ticked their days around.

A dream more fanciful than false,
an adolescent craze, to think
this strict and passionate affair
could stay its complex rainbow self
and set the hurrying world to rights.

So he is where he dreaded to be,
writing for poets, scholars, friends,
aware his truest merit comes
in shaping language from the soul.

Fellow craftsmen, lovers of form,
who let the shades within you sing,
but strip their utterance of its guff,
strength to our solitary art:
let's mock simplistic creeds, make acts

not words the servants of the poor;
and may our sturdy soulsongs make
their readers yelp in scared delight,
their deepest selves dragged up to life.

JOSÉ CRAVEIRINHA
(b. 1922)

Ode to a Lost Cargo in a Ship Called Save
Translated from the Portuguese by Chris Searle

How many died in the holds?
Those who were there, and us.

I

The ship was large
The ship was large, but not large enough.
The holds were enormous
The holds were enormous, but not enormous enough.

The berths were many
The berths were many, but there were not enough.
And the cargo ship ran aground.

But the disciplined merchandise was in there
And when the great company boat ran aground
A cargo of khaki uniforms and golden buttons
Relinquished all.

But don't despair, mothers,
Don't be sad, fathers, friends and brothers,
Don't soak your white handkerchiefs with tears of goodbye,
Idyllic widows and saddened sisters,
The ship was safe
And the lost cargo was insured
On the salty erotic breasts of the sea.
Don't be sad, widows of mourning,
Don't despair, old ones, fathers, friends and brothers,
The company's damages were covered,
The shipowner arrived for three days
On the front page of the newspapers
And never came again.

Under the hatchways
The company's cotton was the insured cargo
And the cargo that had no history of escudos
Or no mention in the lists of the ship's inventory
Were the sons and brothers and sisters,
Black, white, Chinese and mulatto,
Widowers, unemployed, football players without contracts,
All of them now recruits and nearly soldiers
With photographs of the type you put in numbered passes,
Khaki jackets and yellow buttons,
Eyes devoid of metaphysical questions,
Mouths without dialectic,
Singers, unfortunately, of only 'Rock 'n Roll',
All of them beautiful with youth, absurd and incoherent,
Almost men, setting off together for the destiny of shell sounds
Dressed in the same unkind uniform
Purple in its Portuguese heat for ammunition

II

Who cried out?
It was the cargo.
Who burned?
It was the cargo.
Who was it that exploded?
It was the cargo.

Who disappeared?
It was the cargo.
It was the cargo which consumed its strengths,
The last of the burned arms and the burned legs
The last of the glassy eyes and the burned hands
The last of the cries devoured by the flames
The last marijuana in military service
The last of the Mozambicans in a hiatus of agony.

Oh! The cargo freed the strengths in all the holds.
Oh! The cargo freed the holds of the burdens of cotton and
    youth.
Oh! The Company's cargo freed itself to the undulant sound of
    the waves
And the breeze of the palm trees crying over the waters of
    Quelimane
With the hull biting the hard rocks under the sea
And the rhythm of the marvellous crowd of living people on the
    decks,
The cargo of youth broke its nails
Bloodied their hands on the gangway's mirage
And gave themselves up without even seeing
The imagined green landscape of the promised land.

III

The young men came in the berths
The young men came in the bunks
The owners of the men came in the cabins
But the cargo which burned in the old mornings of the Indian
    Ocean
Was the cargo of the berths
Was the cargo of the bunks
Was all the merchandise that cried out in vain
In the horror of the grave of salt and burning iron
With the mothers and sisters
The widows and the brothers
The widows and the friends, all travelling
On the left side of the soldiers' khaki uniforms

And their yellow buttons with false golden stars in the night
Of the fatal, bloody route of the slavetraders in the sea.

They came in the berths and the bunks
The sad passengers
Almost soldiers
Almost husbands
Almost widowers and almost men
And almost children too, in their living memories of the hunting
Still hunting lizards
And pressing together like brothers
Against the burning hot vertical walls
Of the tropical zodiac of death freeing them in the holds
And together uniting their last voices
In the last understanding.
And together they spat out the same scorn for the smoke and the
        fire
And gnashed their teeth in the same physical happiness
Clear of the extinct love, burned without connection.

They came in the berths and the bunks
And cotton and young recruits together asked for peace
And they disembarked together on the quays of absolute silence,
Recruits without leather belts girding their kidneys
Mixed in the white gold with ashes and insurance policies
And only with the assurance of the misty eyes of old mothers
Of old fathers and old friends of their recent infancy
And the insurance policy of the misty eyes of their mothers and
        beautiful widows
In the tragic, infinite minutes of longing
In the enigmatic hour of burning sticks of arms and cries
With the beautiful yellow buttons of the shining uniforms,
Single metal flowers blooming in their zenith
Of gunpowder and bursting ammunition
In the common grave of the holds.

IV

They came in the berths
In the sumptuous bunks of the holds,

Beautiful examples of boys nearly men
Who filled the misty eyes of the old mothers
Who dug deeper the wrinkles of the old fathers,
The old friends of twenty years
And the widows and the brothers
The mourning in the newspapers' headlines
And typographically clear photographs on the front pages
Looking at us with the same absorbed stares
Of free adolescents, dead
Who won't grow old any more.

It didn't have a history,
The cargo that burned in the bowels of the monster *Save*
In the vengeful liquid forests of the sea.
White faces
Dark and brown faces
Curly hair and straight hair
On the same terrible day were in that foundered ship
The same mythic colour of the poppies
And the exact total dimension,
The same sated death
In the cargo of insured cotton
And the cargo of young people, uninsured but liberated
From the hellish hold of the burned boat.

Translator's note: 'The poem takes its theme from the foundering
and sinking of a ship called the *Save* (the name of a major river which
has its estuary in southern Mozambique). The ship was lost in the
Mozambique Channel off Quelimane, the port and capital city of
Zambesia Province, in 1962. It was carrying two main cargoes: new
recruits for the Portuguese colonial army, and cotton.'

The Tasty 'Tanjarines' of Inhambane
Translated from the Portuguese by Michael Wolfers

I

Is the applause always plausible that applauds the bosses'
    speeches?
Are certain over-exuberant panegyrics to be trusted?

Let us heed carefully the shouts bawled at the rallies.
Isn't there something odd in the secretive whispering in the
  queues?

Let us leave the dreamers at peace in their epics of humility.
It is sabotage to demote a genuine poet into a functionary.
Aren't there enough incompetents in offices?
Still more carpets and air conditioners?

Let us leave for those at the top the intricate charts.
How ingenious are the reports of those state enterprises
happily in deficit either because of drought
or because it said in the newspaper there was too much rain
or because of the sun or because the tractor had lost a screw
or perhaps because the traffic police had not fined Vasco da
  Gama
for traffic offences on the Calcutta spice run.

In our eardrums the ambient murmurs?
Isn't it ideologically sound to spot undeniable rumours at their
  birth?
Isn't a silent population dangerous? Where will it hide the
  burden of its voice?
As for the muteness of versifiers? If no poetry emerges, will there
  be
rose-coloured images of the twilight summers in the townships?
Who is the tops at forecasting from bad tidings?
Who reads the signals in the wind before the gale and issues a
  warning?

II

At the side of highways paved with litter we gaze in wonderment
at the mocking apartment blocks we are smashing up. Isn't it a
  heartbreak?
Is it so much more fun to break the school desks and study on
  the floor?
And in the factories what are these hands, our proletarian hands
  that unmake?
But in this beehive, watch out for the honey of the fawning bees.

What's going on here with the well-padded director
for ever sending himself on duty to the best hotels in Europe?
Or in the spoils of a night on watch and a full bag
national shortages are worth more than having been a PIDE
what do you think our crafty militiaman Fakir?

III

Let the heroic truck drivers of trucks raked by ambushes en
    route
bring the tasty 'tanjarines' from Inhambane, at their ambushed
    cost,
but unload first at hospitals, creches and schools,
as our country's future too lies in the toothsome sweetness of
    Inhambane's 'tanjarines'
and power survives in the strength of a people with catalogues of
    love not price lists.
But the promising ripeness of crimson cashew no longer gives us
    fruit – and why?
Isn't it gambling away the country to run a new vehicle against a
    wall or a pillar?
Is unlawfulness only unlawfulness in others? Is the hyena only
    the hyena in the bush?
So I vow that 'tanjarines' of Inhambane are 'tanjarines' of
    Inhambane!

I love to bite sensuously into the juicy segments of Inhambane's
    'tanjarines'.
And from east to west who does not delight in the tasty
    'tanjarines' of Inhambane?
So let those who abjure the sacred fruits of the soil find their wife
    and children.
Find a father and mother. Find uncles and nephews. Find a
    family.
Find brothers and sisters. Find friends. Find colleagues and
    comrades.
Unwittingly find tenderness, love and tranquillity if they can!

IV

The guidance of some directors turns heads . . . (theirs too).
But who says I don't care about the safari suits enfolding them
spankingly and without the sweats that come from this
   unreliable tropical climate?
Who says that I'm not sorry to see them easing themselves from
   the Ladas with their airs and graces
and uncalloused hands scarce able to open a door
as they sit and wait for the chauffeur inevitably
to go around the world of destiny and fulfil his hereditary task?
Who says I don't care? Who says I don't feel the drama?

V

Quickly Madalena, you get in the firewood queue, give up the
   fish queue.
Granny, stand in the 'comparative' queue, there's rice
   tomorrow.
Auntie, leave the clothes queue, line up for the bread.
Tony and Querestina, you queue for water.

Last Friday, mama Julia slept there.
She queued all night at John Orr's but when her turn came . . .
   nothing!
As for a cup of tea yesterday, there was none . . . went to work.
If you don't drink today you'll drink tomorrow.
If you don't drink tomorrow you'll drink some other day.
Or if you find something, you drink at night.
And if you don't drink at night you just sleep.
But if you dream of groundnuts you've already drunk your tea
   and had something to eat.

VI

People want the pleasure of digging into the peel of Inhambane's
   'tanjarines'.
Look here! Are you tired of your country? Hop over the wire . . .
   get going . . .
You don't fancy the flag? Take your papers . . . scram!!!
In the old days you went hungrier but didn't you stay put?

In the old days there were beatings. Didn't you hold on? Or
   weren't you in the hold?
In the old days weren't you shod with iron chains? Now all you
   want is 'Adidas', am I right?
In the old days you sat under forced labour. Now you sit in the
   seats at the Scala, don't you? But who gave them to you?
In the old days could you write your name? Where? Could you?
   Now you write to the newspapers to complain about the
   bread.
In the old days could you have a passport? Now when you don't
   score a passport you're upset.
Really angry. Huge fuss. In the old days was there more than the
   passbook?
Yes? Now you eat mackerel. Isn't that fish? Aren't sweet potato
   and cassava food?
Our stomachs remember beef with fried spuds and olives.
   Remember cod
with sprouts and that olive oil and red wine from a sealed bottle.
But did we have that when we felt like it or just the leftovers?
   Was it our house? What house?
In that house were we pulling the chain for our own backside or
   someone else's? Away with you! Tell the truth! Weren't we
   squatting in a hole? What else did we have?

VII

It's true there's no rain for the fields. But be patient. The rain will
   come.
It's true that we eat cabbage on cabbage, mackerel on mackerel,
   mealies on mealies.
But we sit at our own table. The whole family is at home in the
   apartment block. Our friends are seated too.
To leave for good and all? Impossible. Leave here. For where?
   Could you do that!
Change from Mozambican and remain what? Change your face
   and what are you left with?
Running away is for someone else. A real Mozambican doesn't
   run away.
When a man's a man he has one heart. Not two.

VIII

Even if you've no petrol coupons it doesn't matter. No harm
    done. There's petrol on the black market.
But who says those tasty 'tanjarines' of Inhambane aren't
    around any more?
Is it necessary? We are going to use the strategy of maestro Lenin
and go forward with two dialectical backward somersaults
objectively in the most Mozambican of styles
and Mozambican in the most concrete of senses.

IX

So attention comrade Control. Here comes the truck with the
    Inhambane 'tanjarines'.
Take your finger from the trigger and make a joyful bow to the
    stoic driver.
He's earning money but driving from Inhambane, from
    Chai-Chai, from Manhica
without knowing if he'll arrive until he's there.
Comrade Control: the village is a village not a town.
Comrade Control: the town is a town not a city.
Comrade Control: the city is a city not a district.
Comrade Control: the district is a district not a province.
Comrade Control: the province is a province not a nation.
Comrade Control: the control is a control not a government.
Comrade Control: our national territory runs from the first
    speck
of sand in Cabo Delgado to the last inch of Ponta d'Ouro.
Comrade Control: put on your most brotherly smile in the
    middle of the road
and wave through from within to within Mozambique
our precious 'tanjarines' of Inhambane.
Now peel a 'tanjarine' and taste it bit by bit.
Isn't it sweet comrade Control?
Right!
Thank you very much comrade Control?
And long live the tasty 'tanjarines' of Inhambane!!!
VIVA!!!

(1982–4)

NGUNO WAKOLELE

Southern Africa

You know the world how big it is,
You know the continents all around,
You know the people within those parts,
Can you tell me one secret only?

A week is as long as a year,
A day is as long as a month,
Not even a second can pass without
Hearing news about me all over the world.

Am I the most important part,
In comparison with others?
Am I the news-giving medium?
To those who don't have anything to say?

In the heat of the day,
In the cold of the night,
In rainy seasons — no shelter provided,
Ask no question about mosquitoes.

Across full rivers — through forests and bushes,
My children are walking — armed to the teeth,
They are determined — they are committed,
They are prepared to suffer and sacrifice.

They are prepared to suffer and sacrifice,
They are dedicated to my cause,
They'll fight the enemy to the bitter end,
To liberate me — their mother,
And put an end to foreign domination.

Now you can see why the world talks,
And I assure you
That time is now —

My children will walk – my children will play,
They will cultivate wherever they wish,
Enjoy the wealth that I provide,
When I am free – I will be free!

JEREMY CRONIN
(b. 1949)

Group Photo from Pretoria Local
on the Occasion of a Fourth Anniversary
(Never Taken)

An uprooted tree leaves
       behind it a hole in the ground
But after a few months
You would have to have known
       that something grew here once.
And a person's uprooted?
Leaves a gap too, I suppose, but then
       after some years . . .
There we are
       seated in a circle,
Mostly in short pants, some of us barefoot,
Around the spot where four years before
When South African troops were repulsed before Luanda
Our fig tree got chopped
       down in reprisal. – That's Raymond
Nudging me, he's pointing
At Dave K who looks bemusedly
Up at the camera. Denis sits on an upturned
Paraffin tin. When this shot was taken
He must have completed
       17 years of his first
Life sentence.
       David R at the back is saying
Something to John, who looks at Tony who
Jerks his hand

So it's partly blurred.
There we are, seven of us
        (but why the grinning?)
Seven of us, seated in a circle,
The unoccupied place in the centre
        stands for what happened
Way outside the frame of this photo.
So SMILE now, hold still and
        click
            I name it: Luanda.
For sure an uprooted tree
        leaves behind a hole in the ground.
After a few years
You would have to have known
        it was here once. And a person?
There we are
        seated in our circle, grinning,
        mostly in short pants,
        some of us barefoot.

Lullaby

    But who killed Johannes, mama . . . ?
Sssssssshhh! now close your eyes.
    Mama . . . ?
Only a bar of soap, they said.
So *thula, thula,* now quiet my child.

    But who killed Solomon, mama . . . ?
Sssssssshhh! your blanket's tucked in.
    Who?
Only a length of rope, I suppose.
So *thula, thula,* now quiet my child.

    But who killed Ahmed, mama . . . ?
Sssssssshhh! we must get up early.
    Please?
Only the tenth floor, I heard.
So *thula, thula,* now quiet my child.

But who killed Joseph, mama . . . ?
Sssssssshhh! tomorrow's work is hard.
    Mama . . . ?
Only a flight of stairs, I read.
So *thula, thula*, now quiet my child.

    But who killed Steve, mama . . . ?
Sssssssshhh! it's a long walk to the bus.
    Mama . . . ?
A brick wall, the magistrate said.
So *thula, thula*, now quiet my child.

    But who killed Looksmart, mama . . . ?
Sssssssshhh! sleep and grow strong.
    Who, mama . . . ?
His own belt, that's what was blamed.
So *thula, thula*, now quiet my child.

    But who . . .
Thula! Thula! Thula! my child.

The River That Flows through Our Land

A swift stream in the high mountains, dropping dental, lateral
Clicking in its palate like the flaking of stone tools;
And a wide river that grazes the plains,
Lows like the wind in summer maize.
And a waterfall that hums through a turbine
And is whirled into light.

A river that carries many tongues in its mouth.

And a river that flows from times of peace,
And times of war when its fords became slippery,
A river that has bathed spears and bridal parties.

And a river that trickles
Down the worker's face.
The salt river that welds tomorrow forward,
Steel girder on girder and concrete.

This is the river that flows through this land.

To learn how to speak

To learn how to speak
With the voices of the land,
To parse the speech in its rivers,
To catch in the inarticulate grunt,
Stammer, call, cry, babble, tongue's knot
A sense of the stoneness of these stones
From which all words are cut.
To trace with the tongue wagon-trails
Saying the suffix of their aches in -kuil, -pan, -fontein,
In watery names that confirm
The dryness of their ways.
To visit the places of occlusion, or the lick
In a vlei-bank dawn.
To bury my mouth in the pit of your arm,
In that planetarium,
Pectoral beginning to the nub of time
Down there close to the water-table, to feel
The full moon as it drums
At the back of my throat
Its cow-skinned vowel.
To write a poem with words like:
I'm telling you,
Stompie, stickfast, golovan,
Songololo, just boombang, just
To understand the least inflections,
To voice without swallowing
Syllables born in tin shacks, or catch
The 5.15 ikwata bust fife
Chwannisberg train, to reach
The low chant of the mine gang's
Mineral glow of our people's unbreakable resolve.

To learn how to speak
With the voices of this land.

ALFRED TEMBA QABULA
(b. 1942)

Migrant's Lament: A Song

If I have wronged you Lord forgive me
All my cattle were dead
My goats and sheep were dead
And
I did not know what to do
O Creator forgive me
If I had done wrong to you
My children: out of school
Out of uniforms and books
My wife and I were naked – naked . . .
Short of clothing

If I have wronged you Lord forgive me
I went to WENELA
To get recruited for the mines
I went to SILO
To work at sugarcane
O Creator forgive me
If I had done wrong to you
But they chased me away
They needed those with experience
With long service tickets and no one more

If I have wronged you Lord
Forgive me
I left my wife and children
To look for work alone
I had to find a job
O Creator forgive me
If I had done wrong to you
I was despairing in Egoli
After months searching for this job

And when I found one
I lost it
For I didn't have a 'Special'

If I have wronged you Lord
Forgive me
I found a casual job
I felt that my children would be happy
With my earnings
Oh how happy I was!
O Creator forgive me
If I had done wrong to you
Yes, as my children were happy
And as I was working
The blackjacks arrived to arrest me
So again I lost my job

If I have wronged you Lord
Forgive me
When out of jail I searched again –
Another casual job, happy again
The boss was happy too
And he gave me a letter
To fetch a permit from back home
O Creator forgive me
If I had done wrong to you
But the clerk said: 'I can't see the paper'
And added, 'You must go in peace my man'
So I had to buy him beer, meat and brandy
For him to 'learn' to read my piece of paper

If I have wronged you Lord
Forgive me
I was working again
But I realized so far for nothing
O Creator forgive me
If I had done wrong to you
So I joined the union to fight my boss

For I realized: there was no other way Lord
But to fight with the employer
There was no other way
Now go trouble maker go.

(MAWU AGM, Curries Fountain Stadium, 1984)

NISE MALANGE
(b. 1960)

This Poem is Dedicated to Brother Andries Raditsela

Your death has come to me over hundreds of miles away
It has shocked me but did not surprise me
It has shocked the workers but did not surprise them.

I have a few words to say – my mouth is a grave without flowers
My mouth is the empty coffin when the corpse is gone
It is like a river without water
But it has faith in your death.

If I had strength enough I would go and avenge your blood
Our blood
I would carry a bazooka and go straight for the murderers
I would go to the murderers' Concrete Capitals and shoot

Comrade, I did not come here to open a wound nor to mourn
I am here to challenge the minister of law and order
I am here to condemn death in detention
And I am here to say: 'qinani basebenzi lomthwalo unzima'.

Your blood, Andries, will not be in vain
Your blood will be a moral lesson for us to punish oppressors,
Treason, detention and murders
Your blood will give power to your comrades,
To the workers, to your family and to us all.

Andries asikhali ngawe ufe okwe qhawe ezandleni zamagwala.

(Raditsela Commemoration, May 1985)

OSWALD BASIZE DUBE
(b. 1957)

He was a Man of Jokes outside Office

Fellow countrymen —
there's a white proverb
about not letting the left hand know
what the right hand's doing.
Could be
they take it far more seriously
than we will ever know
or understand.
Having learned it from one's mother
and one's mother's mother
we
find it strange
that they don't know —
and refuse to see —
that in this land,
here in the whole of Africa,
where every man is the other's brother,
one hand washes the other.

Written in memory of King Sobhuza II of Swaziland, who ruled from
1921 to 1982, and on the occasion of the coronation of his successor,
Crown Prince Makhosetive, in 1986.

ZIM MNOTOZA
(b. 1961)

Still There's No Trace

The sunheat was equivalent
to the scandalous sun of Barberton Farm Prison.
It was not overheating we did not die
Perhaps we were too many to die of it.

In a dusty Karoo Town
from all walks of life
we converged,
different types of people
from trench diggers to bishops
left radicals moderates christians
and of course iimpimpi were there –
young hopeful blood singing amadumo
tapping and dancing to Toyi-Toyi
and this was the burial of the men of peace
Matthew Goniwe, Fort Calata,
Sparrow Mkonto and Sicelo Mhlawuli.

The banners made the dusty stadium colourful
even more than Olympic Games stadium,
yes those were the progressive forces of the soil
expressing their grief and loss.

The coffins of the fallen
decently entered the stadium
led by Red Soviet Union flag
with its symbolic hammer and sickle,
behind it a Green Black and Gold
the one that had been a threat
to South Africa's security.

The service continued with
speeches that taught us
not to mourn
speeches that challenged us
to assume our responsibilities,
to find the assailants.
There was no medical report
to tell us whether these deaths
were 'accidental' or 'natural'.
A few days earlier police
were 'investigating'
all peace-loving people.

We laid the bodies
in their places
still there was no trace
of the assailants.

A day later
after the country's government
had declared a state of emergency
the police were trying to trace
the Red Flag and its origins
but there's still no trace of the assailants.

NOTES ON CONTRIBUTORS

ABRAHAMS, LIONEL; born in Johannesburg; studied at the University of the Witwatersrand. Editor of *The Purple Renoster* (1957–72) and publisher of black poets who found no outlet elsewhere in the early seventies. Critic and poet with two volumes; 'The Whiteman Blues' is dated 1974, and 'Thresholds of Identity', 1984.

ARBOUSSET, JEAN THOMAS (1810–77); born near Montpellier; for the Paris Missionary Society head of the Morija station in Basutoland (Lesotho). With F. Daumas he published his *Narrative of an Exploratory Tour of the Cape of Good Hope* (1836), which appeared in English subsequently. A Southern Sotho linguist and familiar of King Moshesh, he is credited with having named the Mont-aux-Sources.

BAIN, ANDREW GEDDES; born in Scotland; set up as a saddler in the Eastern Province in 1816, lived as an explorer, notably as in his *Journey to the North* of 1826, military man and farmer, until pass-building became his way of life – Bain's Kloof being named after him. Known as the father of South African geology, he amassed fossil collections from the Karoo which contributed evidence to the evolutionary debate on Darwinism. His sketch, 'Kaatje Kekkelbek', is usually remembered for its recording of vernacular speech, particularly of pidgin Dutch, but his linguistic interests embraced all varieties of frontier and marketplace usages. Bain composed and performed copious war-songs, drinking-songs, patter-pieces and epigrams, many of which were published only in colonial newspapers and satirical reviews and are uncollected.

BATTISS, WALTER; born in Somerset East, Cape Province, doyen of the fine arts in South Africa as a painter who often incorporated prehistoric motifs into abstract expressionism; not primarily a poet, he often included the written word in his canvases, and in his books, as in this list from his collection of sketches and photographs, *Limpopo* (1965).

BESSA VICTOR, GERALDO; born in Luanda, Angola, of an assimilated black African family; trained as a lawyer in Lisbon; critic, short-story writer and poet whose collections started appearing in Lisbon in the 1940s. These translations first appeared in *Okike* in 1974, as an interest in early Lusophone poetry and its origins in Negritude developed.

373

BLEEK, W. H. I. (1827–75); philologist, who for the South African Library systematically collected San and Khoikhoi poetry and narratives. A selection appears in his *Specimens of Bushman Folklore*, edited by his daughter and published in London in 1911, from which 'The Broken String' is taken. The animal poems are from *Reynard the Fox in South Africa; or Hottentot Fables and Tales* (London, 1864).

BOKWE, JOHN KNOX (1855–1922); a Presbyterian minister and the first composer of written Xhosa music. He also wrote the earliest black hagiography, *Ntsikana: The Story of an African Convert* (Lovedale, 1914).

BRETTELL, NOEL H.; born in Worcestershire, educated at Birmingham; arrived at Marandellas, Southern Rhodesia, in 1930 as a teacher, and retired to the Eastern Highlands of Inyanga. His *Bronze Frieze* collection was published in 1950. His essay in autobiography, *Side-gate and Stile*, was published by Books of Zimbabwe in 1981.

BREYTENBACH, BREYTEN; born in the Western Cape, studied in Cape Town; artist, novelist, autobiographer and poet. Settled in Paris in 1961; returned to South Africa in disguise in 1975 and was arrested, sentenced to nine years for terrorism. The translations here were made by fellow writers in South Africa in 1978 to pay tribute to the liberating power of his poetry. Since his release in 1982 he has published voluminously in Afrikaans in South Africa, and in his own English versions elsewhere. Certainly the best-known Afrikaans-language writer of his generation.

BRODRICK, ALBERT; versifier of Yorkshire stock, a merchant and bar-keeper in Church Square, Pretoria, Transvaal Republic, from 1859, where he was nicknamed 'Albertus Broodryk', and an inveterate prospector. His *Fifty Fugitive Fancies in Verse* (Pretoria, 1875) was the first volume of poetry to be published north of the Orange River. His later *A Wanderer's Rhymes* (London, 1893) – from which these items are taken – was twice reprinted. Opposed to the British annexation of the Transvaal in 1877, his publications nevertheless served to guide diggers to the Eastern Transvaal for the Pilgrim's Rest goldrush, which is the background of 'Shu' Shu' of Delgo' (Delagoa). 'Joe's Luck' dates from later, when the goldstrikers were displacing farmers on the Witwatersrand.

BROOKS, FREDERIC; various researchers have deduced South Africa's first burlesque pamphleteer, 'Q. in the Corner', to have been Frederic Brooks, who operated in Cape Town from 1820 to 1825. A disciple of Momus and familiar of Hogarth, his 'choice doggerel' is prolifically descriptive of that slave-holding society. Obviously a Londoner, he directed his wit at 'Caper' backwardness, using the strategy of writing open letters home.

BROWN, JOHN CROUMBIE (1808–95); Scottish Presbyterian minister, Colonial Botanist at the Cape, who was the first to advocate soil, water and forestry conservation in Southern Africa.

BRUTUS, DENNIS; born in Harare (then Salisbury, Rhodesia); educated at the University of the Witwatersrand; left South Africa in 1966 after imprisonment with hard labour for his opposition to apartheid. A noted campaigner, resident in the United States. His poetry includes *Sirens, Knuckles, Boots* (1963) through to *Stubborn Hope* (1978), and has been widely translated. From *Letters to Martha* (1968), written to his sister-in-law.

BUTLER, FREDERICK GUY; born in Cradock, educated at Rhodes and Oxford universities and until his retirement Professor of English at Rhodes University, Grahamstown. Autobiographer, playwright and poet, whose *Stranger to Europe* (1952) set much of the tone of post-World War II English-language poetry in South Africa. Editor of the influential *A Book of South African Verse* (1959), which superseded Slater as a standard text (revised, 1979). Spokesman for liberal values and historian of the Eastern Cape.

CAMOENS, LUIS VAZ DE. Born of a noble family and related to his epic hero, Vasco da Gama, he was a classical scholar at Coimbra University during the flowering of the brief Portuguese Renaissance, which occurred roughly between Da Gama's death and Portugal's loss of independence to the Spanish at the time of his own death. Fighting the Moors, he lost an eye, and his portraits are striking for this feature. Banished in 1553 to the Indies, he sailed the route described in Canto V with Cabral's expedition. Legend maintains that he completed his poem towards the end of his enforced exile in Mozambique. On the publication of *The Lusiads* in 1572 he was pardoned and awarded a modest pension. He died of the plague in Lisbon in 1580, on 10 June, which date is commemorated annually as Portuguese national day.

CAMPBELL, JOHN; a director of the London Missionary Society, whose *Travels in South Africa* (1815) served to open up the hinterland for missionary and subsequent commercial endeavour.

CAMPBELL, ROY (IGNATIUS ROYSTON DUNACHIE); born in Durban. His book-length poem, *The Flaming Terrapin* (1924), launched his distinguished career as a British modernist poet. Back in Natal in 1926 he briefly edited the literary and cultural review, *Voorslag*, with Plomer; his dismissal from it largely gives rise to his attack in Augustan style on the 'Garden Colony' Philistines in *The Wayzgoose*. He later displayed his animus against Bloomsbury in *The Georgiad* in similar vein. Probably the best known South-African-born man of letters. His lyrics, particularly from *Adamastor* (1930), endure. Here Campbell is also featured for another facet of his career apart from his satire – his skill and dedication as a translator, whose quest was to admit the work of many writers of the Mediterranean, where he usually resided, in French, Spanish and Portuguese, into English. His *Collected Poems* first appeared in 1949, and in 1955 was updated shortly before his death in an accident near his final home in Portugal. Currently a definitive edition of his *Complete Works* in four volumes is being published.

CHINGONO, JULIUS; born in Rusape; journalist whose poems in English and Shona, *Flags of Love*, appeared in 1980.

CHIPASULA, FRANK MKALAWILE; Malawian-born scholar who studied at Chancellor College and the University of Zambia. A founder and organizer of the Zomba Writers' Group. One of his collections as a poet, *O Earth, Wait for Me*, appeared in Johannesburg in 1984. He is the editor of *When my Brothers Come Home: Poems from Central and Southern Africa* (Wesleyan University Press, 1985), which has a similar reach to this collection. He lives in exile and teaches in the United States.

CLOUTS, SYDNEY; born in Cape Town; after serving in World War II he studied at the University of Cape Town. He emigrated to Britain in 1961 where he worked as a librarian. His volume, *One Life* (1966), was followed by his *Collected Poems*, published posthumously in 1984.

COLVIN, IAN DUNCAN; Inverness-born and Edinburgh-educated, he arrived after a shipwreck in the Maldives at the Cape in 1903, aged twenty-six, as leader-writer of the *Cape Times*. As Rip van Winkle (pseud.) he produced *The Parliament of Beasts* (1905), from which these poems come. Although he left South Africa in 1907, in London in 1910 to commemorate Union he produced his Introduction to Sidney Mendelssohn's *South African Bibliography* which, by summarizing the literature to that date, acts as the threshold of all modern South African letters.

COUZYN, JENI; born and educated in Johannesburg; she left for London in 1966, and has lived there as well as for some years in Canada, where her selected poems (*Life by Drowning*, 1983) is published. Her earlier volumes include *Christmas in Africa* (1975) and *House of Changes* (1978).

CRAVEIRINHA, JOSÉ; born in Lourenço Marques (Maputo); journalist whose long career began in the fifties. Foremost poet of Mozambique. Under the colonial regime along with other intellectuals he was imprisoned for political dissent (1966–9). He has published only four collections (1964, 1966, 1974, 1980). His vision of post-independence Mozambique, 'The Tasty "Tanjarines" of Inhambane', was published in this translation and for the first time in *Portuguese Studies* (1987).

CRONIN, JEREMY; born in the Cape, educated at the University of Cape Town and the Sorbonne; sentenced to imprisonment under the Terrorism Act in 1976. On his release in 1983 his first volume of poems, *Inside*, was published in Johannesburg (enlarged edition, London, 1987). Co-compiler of *30 Years of the Freedom Charter* (1986).

CRONWRIGHT, SAMUEL CRON; farmer whose *The Angora Goat* (1898) became the standard manual; born inland in the Cape Karoo, he was a sportsman and free-thinker. A progressive politician, he married Olive Schreiner in 1894, and together the Cronwright-Schreiners opposed the Second Anglo-Boer War. After Schreiner's death he published her *Life*, edited her letters, and issued several other works by her. 'The Song of the Wagon-whip' appeared as a piece of nostalgia first in *The Waste Paper Basket of the Owl Club* (1922).

CULLINAN, PATRICK ROLAND; born in Pretoria and educated at Oxford; lectures in the Cape; during 1980–81 the editor of *The Bloody Horse*, a literary review. Translator, and as a poet he has produced three volumes, including *Today is Not Different* (1978), in the Mantis Poets series.

CUSSONS, SHEILA; born of Afrikaans-Irish stock, trained as an artist, she has published slim volumes consistently since 1970. For many years before she returned to South Africa in 1982, she lived in Spain. In 1985 she produced a selection of her work in her own English translation, entitled *Poems*.

DALE, SIR LANGHAM; English-born superintendent-general and professor of education in the Cape Colony, who virtually single-handed established a modern English-language educational system. This poem seems unique in his writing, which is otherwise on educational or archaeological topics. From Roderick Noble (ed.), *The Cape and its People* (1869).

DE SOUSA, NOÉMIA; born in Maputo, and schooled there and in Brazil; politically active in Lisbon in the 1950s before the armed struggle for Mozambique, she went into exile permanently in France in 1964. Published in many Portuguese-language journals, she is the first African woman to have achieved a reputation as a poet. From *When Bullets Begin to Flower*, the anthology of 1972.

DRIVER, CHARLES JONATHAN (JONTY); born in Cape Town, educated at the University of Cape Town and Oxford; principal of a school in Hong Kong for a period from 1978; currently the same in England. Exiled from South Africa in 1965. Biographer and novelist, whose *Elegy for a Revolutionary* (1969) was released in South Africa only recently. A contributor to the anthology of South African poets in exile, *Seven South African Poets* (1971), from which 'A Ballad of Hunters' is taken.

DRONSFIELD, JOHN; born in Lancashire; settled in Cape Town in 1939; artist and stage-designer who first worked with Ffrangcon-Davies on a production of *The Merry Wives of Windsor* in 1945. Died by his own hand. His only volume, *Satires and Verses*, was published posthumously in 1955.

DUBE, OSWALD BASIZE; born in Swaziland and a school-teacher; musician and poet often billed as Swaziland's foremost, whose book of poems and tributes, recounting the praises, documents and oral records of King Sobhuza's reign was dedicated to his successor (Mbabane, 1986).

DU PLESSIS, PHIL; born in Fouriesburg, qualified as a doctor in Pretoria. Lives in Cape Town, where he has facilitated the publication of much avant-garde poetry. He has produced four volumes of poetry in Afrikaans since 1971.

EGLINGTON, CHARLES; born in Johannesburg; journalist and editor, particularly prominent after World War II and noted for his animal verse. This poem, recalling Lourenço Marques (now Maputo), the capital of Mozambique, is from a sequence of the 1960s called 'Homage to Fernando Pessoa'. He died by his own hand, leaving his complete poems to be published posthumously (*Under the Horizon*, 1977).

EYBERS, ELISABETH; brought up in Johannesburg, one of the generation of 'Dertigers', who in 1948 issued her selected poems with her own English translations as *The Quiet Adventure*. In the 1960s she emigrated to Holland; 'Confrontation with an Artist' was written in the seventies after sittings for well-known drawings of her by Welz. She has continued publishing in Afrikaans in the eighties.

FAIRBRIDGE, KINGSLEY; colonial-born of British parents, his *Auto-biography* of 1927 tells of a Rhodesian pioneer's life. His *Veld Verse* was first published in London in 1909, updated in 1929. A Rhodes scholar and something of a visionary, he created a child emigration scheme to populate the hinterland, although his first farm school to effect this was not established until shortly before his early death, and in Western Australia.

FANSHAWE, SIR RICHARD (1608–66); Royalist and Restoration poet, occasionally diplomat to Iberia. His translation of *The Lusiads* was made during his detention under Cromwell, and before he returned to Lisbon to negotiate Charles II's marriage to Catherine of Braganza. He died in Madrid, attempting a commercial treaty with Spain.

FARMER, HAROLD; born in Windhoek, Namibia; lawyer and recently lecturer in English at the University of Zimbabwe. This poem first appeared in *Meanjin* when he was on leave in Australia in 1983.

FYNN, HENRY FRANCIS; pioneer-trader, whose *Diary* is one of the main sources of contact-history in Natal in the 1820s. Landing in Port Natal in 1824, aged twenty-one, he obtained land and barter concessions from King Shaka of the Zulus and built up his own tribe, the 'Locusts'. His nickname, Mbuyazi, means 'he who comes back with the whole thing summed up'. Of the few dozen early Natal settlers, Fynn is the only one to have remained beyond Shaka's death in 1828, becoming among other things a magistrate for the colonial administration. The Fynn papers in the Pietermaritzburg archives, from which his only poem is transcribed, are a trove of early Nguni lore.

GARDINER, ALLEN F.; English midshipman and missionary who treated unsuccessfully with King Dingane in 1835, and who advocated the colonization of Natal. Always a flamboyant wanderer, he was finally martyred in Tierra del Fuego.

GIBBON, PERCEVAL; Welsh-born short-story writer and novelist who, like Wallace, arrived in South Africa shortly before the Second Anglo-Boer War. As a correspondent he wrote the collection, *African Items* (London, 1903), the first volume of verse to establish and analyse reconciliation and a composite white African personality. After leaving in 1903, he produced a trilogy of novels, including *Margaret Harding* (1911), which offers a materialist scrutiny of colonized Africa typical of Edwardian radicalism. He is one of the few English-language writers on the war to give voice to the colonial-born white South African.

GRAY, STEPHEN; born in Cape Town; lectures in English in Johannesburg. He has published four volumes of poetry, including *Hottentot Venus and Other Poems* (1979). 'Apollo Café' first appeared in *Ariel* in 1985.

GREENE, ALICE M.; suffragist; born near Cambridge, arrived at the Cape in 1887, vice-principal of Collegiate Girls' School, Port Elizabeth, until 1900; friend of Betty Molteno, Schreiner, Emily Hobhouse and others, passionate anti-Boer War crusaders who subsequently fought for women's rights. From *Songs of the Veld and Other Poems* (London, 1902), an anthology of mostly anonymous poems first printed in support of the Pro-Boer movement in the reformist *New Age*.

GWALA, MAFIKA PASCAL; born in Verulam, Natal, and matriculated at Vryheid; leading exponent of Black Consciousness in the early 1970s, and a cultural worker in Hammarsdale, Natal. His first volume of poems appeared in 1977, followed by *No More Lullabies* (1982). His 'The New Dawn' first appeared in an anthology of the Writers Forum, Johannesburg, in 1986.

HASTINGS, BEATRICE (pseud. of EMILY ALICE HAIGH). Feminist, brought up in Port Elizabeth, and in her teens sent to Europe on remittance; Bohemian friend of Mansfield and literary editor of *The New Age* at the time this poem was published there (1909). Novelist and intimate of Modigliani in Paris, she became a socialist in the 1930s and wrote extensively of the colonial woman's links with oppressed black women. One of the first South African 'psychological' writers.

HENRY, WILLIAM. No more is known of this writer than is revealed by his 'Verses', published on 4 October 1842, in *De Verzamelaar* newspaper, Cape Town.

HODZA, AARON C.; born in Mazoe; taught Shona linguistics in the Department of African Languages at the University of Zimbabwe. Co-author of *Shona Praise Poetry* (1979).

HOLMES, TIMOTHY; born in Johannesburg, where his father was a mine engineer; grew up in the Natal Drakensberg. He has lived and worked in Zambia since 1963 as a teacher and journalist. His *Double Element* – one of the few volumes produced in Zambia – appeared from Wordsmiths, Lusaka, in 1985; these poems are from there.

HOPE, CHRISTOPHER; graduated from the universities of the Witwatersrand and Natal; editor in the early 1970s in Durban of the literary review, *Bolt*; his volumes include *Cape Drives* (1974) from which these poems come. He is also an award-winning novelist, and lives in London.

HUNTER, WILLIAM ELIJAH; Somerset-born, he was ordained by Bishop Colenso and served on the diamond fields and at Alice, where he retired. Published *The Nightingale and Other Poems* (1908). His 'Monologue in a Rand Hospital', a fine example of a work on the theme of mateship, appeared in *The South African Bookman* in 1913.

JABAVU, DAVIDSON DON TENGO (1885–1959); son of John Tengo Jabavu and father of Noni. Teacher at Fort Hare and principal, prolific author and editor, who at the time of this translation called into being the first All-Africa Convention.

JACINTO, ANTONIO; born in Luanda, energizer of Angolan resistance to Portuguese imperialism and of cultural nationalism. After lengthy imprisonment, from 1975 he has been Minister of Education and Culture, and held other posts in the MPLA government of Angola.

JENSMA, WOPKO PIETER; born in the Cape of Dutch and Afrikaner parentage; graphic artist, whose mixed-media books of the early seventies hold a unique place in South African poetry. In the late sixties he lived in Lourenço Marques ('In Memoriam Akbar Babool'), and taught art in Botswana – 'A Beggar Named Mokopi' is neither an indigenous nor a Setswana tale, but his own, and first appeared with other fables set in Africa in *English in Africa* (March 1978).

JOLOBE, JAMES JAMES RANISI; preacher, novelist, playwright and translator, born in the Eastern Cape; taught at Lovedale from the thirties, where his own translations of his Xhosa poems, notably on historical themes, were published as *Poems of an African* in 1946. He became a moderator of the Presbyterian Church, and in 1952 was awarded the Vilakazi Memorial Prize for his creative work.

JONKER, INGRID; born in Douglas, Cape Province, whose first volume appeared in 1956. Lived mostly in Cape Town. She suicided by drowning, aged thirty-three. Her *Selected Poems* has been translated by Jack Cope and William Plomer (1968). These two poems first appeared in the literary journal, *Contrast*, in 1961. While 'Bitterberry Daybreak' has become an Afrikaans classic, her 'The Child Who was Shot Dead by Soldiers in Nyanga' – one of the first Afrikaans anti-apartheid protest poems – is not included in her *Collected Works* (1975).

KIPLING, RUDYARD; novelist, short-story writer and imperialist; author of *Just So Stories* (1902). As a guest of Rhodes he occasionally summered at the Cape, and covered some of the action of the Second Anglo-Boer War from the frontline, notably for the *Friend* in Bloemfontein in 1900, during the invasion of the Orange Free State. These are two lesser known 'Barrack-room Ballads'. The first introduced the place-name, Stellenbosch, as a verb into English. The second dates from the last guerrilla phase of Boer resistance, with its notorious mopping-up operations, which included the last battles of Watervalboven and Onder in 1901. In both he uses his favourite mouthpiece, Tommy Atkins.

KNOPFLI, RUI; born in Inhambane, schooled in Maputo where he lived through to the seventies, and where he co-edited a poetry journal, *Caliban*. As a photographer he recorded, among other aspects of colonial life, the island of Mozambique. Resident in London. He published slim volumes in the fifties and sixties in Lisbon.

KRIGE, UYS; born in the Cape, educated at Stellenbosch University. During the 1930s he lived on the Mediterranean, the poetry of which he subsequently translated copiously into Afrikaans. As a war correspondent with the South African forces during World War II he was captured; *The Way Out* (1946), his classic autobiography, describes his escape. Maverick belletrist who wrote verse and short stories with equal facility in English and Afrikaans; for a while from 1946 he edited *Vandag*, a review which enacted his lifelong bilingual policy. Noted as a playwright and translator of Shakespeare. In 1968 he was co-editor with Jack Cope of *The Penguin Book of South African Verse*.

KUMBIRAI, JOSEPH C.; born at Driefontein Mission, Mvuma; Catholic priest and teacher; lecturer in African languages at the University of Zimbabwe; leading Shona-language poet who occasionally translated his own published work into English.

KUNENE, (RAYMOND) MAZISI; born in Durban; acclaimed lecturer in African languages and literature in London and for many years in the United States, after going into exile from South Africa in 1959. He has produced a revival of the use of Zulu poetry, with his own translations, maintaining a clan-voice. His book-length epic, *Emperor Shaka the Great* (1979), is surely one of the greatest contemporary African poems. From *The Ancestors and the Sacred Mountain* (1982), which contains short pieces.

LEIPOLDT, C. LOUIS; born of Rhenish missionary parents in the Cedarberg, Western Cape, the setting of this poem. As a young journalist and circuit-court recorder he witnessed events such as are dramatized here. From 1903 to 1907 at Guy's Hospital, London, and then South Africa's first paediatrician. His first volume of poems, *Oom Gert Vertel en Ander Gedigte* (1911), began a prolific career as poet, dramatist (in Afrikaans) and novelist (in English), and established him as one of the founders of modern Afrikaans literature. His memoir, *Bushveld Doctor* (1937), shows him to have been a concerned humanitarian, whose attitudes were polymath and wisely polemical. The figure of Uncle Gert, the first rounded character in Afrikaans literature, is a rich colloquial invention, despite the Browningesque form of his dramatic monologue. His posthumously published novel, *Stormwrack* (1980), further analyses the conflict presented in this piece.

LINDSAY, LADY ANNE. Daughter of James Lindsay, fifth earl of Balcarres; familiar in literary circles of Edinburgh and London; married Andrew Barnard, colonial secretary to the governor in the British occupation of the Cape during the wars with France. Her letters, journals and sketches of court and peasant life at the Cape (1797–1801) have been frequently printed. The Scottish ballad, 'Auld Robin Gray', published anonymously, dates from her youth and was set to music and sung popularly. This is the earliest version.

LIVINGSTONE, DOUGLAS; born in Kuala Lumpur, lived in Southern Africa from 1942, latterly as a marine bacteriologist in Durban. Since the mid-sixties with *Sjambok*, his slim volumes have brought metaphysical exactness to bear on romantic and satirical themes, culminating in his *Selected Poems* (1984). He is also the author of radio plays and a translator.

LOUW, N. P. VAN WYK; leading Afrikaans-language poet, playwright, essayist and academic, born in Sutherland in the Karoo; prominent from the thirties in the Dertiger movement which released Afrikaans from parochialism, and founder of *Standpunte* in 1945. After establishing a chair of Afrikaans in Amsterdam, professor of the same at the University of the Witwatersrand until his death. A versatile and prodigious worker in all literary fields, a nationalist frequently critical of unthinking patriotism, he launched his epic *Raka* in 1941 as an allegorical warning against the collapse of civilization – this extract is the opening sequence, one of five parts. Many English-language poets have translated his work as a homage to his stature.

MAKABO, CALVIN. No further details available beyond the note. His poem and his tragic death symbolize the black African contribution to the British war effort in both the First and Second World Wars.

MALANGE, NISE; born in Clovelly, Cape Town, and of the generation of schoolchildren protesters; organizer for the Transport and General Workers' Union in Durban. A member of the Workers' Cultural Locals there, with whom she has written and performed occasional and commemorative poems for union gatherings.

MALCOLM, DANIEL McK. The praises of Henry Francis Fynn, collected by James Stuart, are in the Stuart Archives, Killie Campbell Africana Library, Durban. Malcolm translated these into English, as well as completing Stuart's editing of the Fynn *Diary*. From Trevor Cope (ed.), *Izibongo: Zulu Praise-poems* (Oxford, 1968).

MANAKA, MATSEMELA CAIN; poet, artist and playwright, founder member and director of the Soyikwa African Theatre group, based in Diepkloof, Soweto, where he was born. Several of his plays, involving group improvisations, use mime, dance, song and incantatory choruses such as these from *Pula*, first performed by a group of four in Johannesburg in 1982.

MANN, CHRIS ZITHULELE; born in Port Elizabeth; educated in South Africa and at Oxford. He works for a medical and agricultural project at Botha's Hill outside Durban. Co-editor of *A New Book of South African Verse in English* (1979). His poetry collections include *New Shades* (1982). Both these poems were written subsequently.

MAPANJE, JACK; born in the Mangochi District, Southern Malawi; completed his education at the University of Malawi and at London University. Head of the English Department at Chancellor College, Zomba, and a founder of the influential Zomba Writers' Workshop. His collection, *Of Chameleons and Gods*, appeared in the African Writers Series (London, 1981). The last poem here was first published in 1986.

MARAIS, EUGÈNE NIELEN; advocate, journalist and poet, whose 'Winternag' ('Winter Night') (1905) is commonly held to have commenced the writing of lyric poetry in Afrikaans. Although after the recognition of Afrikaans as an official language in South Africa in 1925, and when he assembled his *Versamelde Gedigte* in 1933 it comprised only thirty items, his collected poems have had a disproportionate influence, particularly on the post-Georgian strain of personal testimony and on writing for children in Afrikaans. A naturalist whose works like *The Soul of the White Ant* (in English translation, 1971) have given rise to often inaccurate theories of the origins of aggression. Consumed by his morphine addiction, in his later life he excelled in bitter and dark uses of the lyric impulse. Died by suicide.

MATHEMA, NDABAZEKHAYA CAIN GINYILITSHE; born in Tjolotjo, schooled in Zimbabwe, Britain and the USSR. He has published a collection of Ndebele poems as well as other poems and stories in Zimbabwe. Works for the Ministry of Public Services in Harare. This poem, which names all the language groups in Zimbabwe, first appeared in *And Now the Poets Speak* (Mambo Press) in 1981.

MATSHOBA, MTUTUZELI; born in Orlando East, Soweto; educated there and at Fort Hare. 'The Mantatee Horde' first appeared in his short story, 'Three Days in the Land of a Dying Illusion', in 1979 in *Staffrider*, published by Ravan Press, who issued his story collection, *Call Me Not a Man*, in the same year.

MATTERA, DON; born in Western Township, Johannesburg; once a gang-leader and political spokesman, banned for many years. His much delayed first collection, *Azanian Love Song*, appeared as the first of the Skotaville Series in 1983. His autobiography, *Gone with the Twilight*, appeared from Zed Press in 1987.

MHLONGO, SWIDI-NONKAMFELA; his izibongo was recited by Mr Mhlongo in the Sihuzu section of Mthunzini district on 16 May 1976, on the occasion of a wedding between the Mthethwa and Sikhakhane families; he was a cousin of the bride.

MILLER, RUTH; born in Uitenhage, worked in Johannesburg as an English teacher until her death from cancer. Her first volume, *Floating Island* (1965), was followed by her much acclaimed *Selected Poems* (1968).

MNOTOZA, MZIMKHULU; born and educated in Grahamstown, active in the Young Christian Workers movement. A founder member of the Chumani Writers group. 'Since There's No Trace' is about the funeral in Cradock in 1985 of the four community leaders mentioned, murdered by unknown people. The following day the first state of emergency was declared in South Africa.

MNTHALI, FELIX; born in Zimbabwe of Malawian parents, he was educated there and in Lesotho and Canada. Professor of English at the University of Malawi and latterly at the University of Botswana, Gaborone. His collection of poetry, *When Sunset Comes to Sapitwa*, is published in the Longman Drumbeat series (1982).

MOTHIBI; head of the Tlhaping clan of Tswana-speakers around Kuruman in the 1820s. A full account of the picho at which this speech was delivered, together with a summary of many other leaders' speeches, with a description of their performance, is given in previous numbers of *The South African Commercial Advertiser*, edited by John Fairbairn. Mothibi was soon to be dispossessed by the invasion of Mzilikazi.

MQHAYI, SAMUEL EDWARD KRUNE; greatest of Xhosa poets, novelist, historian, translator and autobiographer; a teacher among the Ndlambes, much of whose history is encoded in this praise-poem. For detailed annotations, see the translator's 'Two Unpublished Poems by S. E. K. Mqhayi', *Research in African Literatures*, Austin, Texas, Vol. 8, No. 1 (Spring, 1977), from which this is taken.

MTSHALI, MBUYISENI OSWALD JOSEPH; born at KwaBhanya, near Vryheid, northern Natal; in the late 1960s his poetry began appearing in journals and, collected as *Sounds of a Cowhide Drum*, first published in Johannesburg in 1971, became an international bestseller. In 1980 his second volume, *Fireflames*, which contained several translations of his own poems from the Zulu, was banned in South Africa. Journalist, theatre critic and teacher, the first of the so-called 'Soweto' poets.

MUNGOSHI, CHARLES L.; born at Manyene near Enkeldoorn; Shona-English poet, novelist (*Waiting for the Rain*, 1975) and author of selected short stories (*The Setting Sun and the Rolling World*, 1987). He is literary editor of Zimbabwe Publishing House.

MUTSWAIRO, SOLOMON M.; born in Mazoe; obtained his doctorate from Howard University, Washington, DC, where translations of his long-suppressed historical novel, *Feso* (1959), and of his Shona (Zezuru) poems were published. The first writer in residence at the University of Zimbabwe after independence.

NDEBELE, NJABULO SIMAKAHLE; grew up in Western Township, Johannesburg, and Charterston Location, Nigel; educated at Cambridge and Denver; head of the Department of English at Roma, Lesotho. Better known as a critic and short-story writer (*Fools*, 1983), his poetry first appeared in the anthology, *To Whom it May Concern* (1973), which launched the South African black poetry revival. From *Staffrider* magazine (1981), which has served to maintain it.

NDLOVU, THEMBINKOSI. Written in the Zulu traditional style of lament, his poem first appeared in *Ilanga Lase Natal*, the newspaper, on 28 October 1976.

NETO, AGOSTINHO. Poet-president; born near Luanda; qualified as a doctor in Portugal and back in Angola became underground leader of the MPLA; held in Aljube Prison, Lisbon. After his escape from restricted residence, head of the liberation movement – and President of the People's Republic of Angola from 1975 until his untimely death. Perhaps the best known literary figure of Angola, his work is much translated (for example, in English as *Sacred Hope*, 1974).

NGWENYA, MALANGATANA VALENTE; born in Marracuene, Southern Mozambique, renowned painter whose works hang in many collections; his verse in the Lusophone negritudinist style first appeared in *Présence Africaine* in the 1960s. First anthologized by Langston Hughes. In contemporary Mozambique his art enjoys high favour and has recently toured Europe.

NORTJE, ARTHUR; born in Oudtshoorn, and educated at the University College of the Western Cape; after a scholarship at Oxford, he taught in Canada, returned to Oxford for a doctorate and died of an overdose. Perhaps in all of South African poetry his work catches most personally the erosion of confidence and alienation of the exile. From *Dead Roots* (posthumous, 1973).

NTSIKANA; son of Gaba of the Cira clan and councillor of King Ngquika. Converted by vision to Christianity in about 1815, Ntsikana as a preacher and prophet is held to be the founder of black theology. His 'Great Hymn', the first to be composed in the vernacular, dramatizes the familiar Biblical message through traditional African imagery. After his death, the hymn was heard performed at Glen-Lynden in 1825 by Pringle, who translated it into English with assistance from frontier missionaries. Bokwe's literal translation of a later version was published at Lovedale.

OPPERMAN, D. J.; Afrikaans poet and dramatist, born of humble parents in Natal; professor of Afrikaans literature at Cape Town and at Stellenbosch universities. Influential editor of *Groot Verseboek* – a survey of Afrikaans poetry from its origins – frequently updated. With nine volumes to his credit, he maintained a guiding influence on the literary scene throughout his distinguished life.

PAÇO D'ARCOS, JOAQUIM; Portuguese novelist, whose only volume of poems, *Poemas Imperfeitos* (1952), was translated by Campbell into English as *Nostalgia* in 1960. According to the translator the collection is imbued with the spirit of 'saudades', or melancholy and regret, typical of fados. The poet was a diplomat who visited Angola more than once.

PATEL, ESSOP JOE; born in Ladysmith; qualified as a lawyer in London and at the University of the Witwatersrand and practises in Johannesburg and Botswana. He has published three volumes of poetry, including *The Bullet and the Bronze Lady* (1987) from which this poem is taken. The satirical comments of his character, Haanetjie, were first heard in 1980.

PESSOA, FERNANDO; born in Lisbon, educated in Durban (1899–1905) while his step-father was Portuguese consul, where he began to write poetry in English. From 1915 in Lisbon he introduced futurist and modernist poetry in Portuguese. Although he published little apart from in literary reviews, and led an apparently uneventful, reclusive life, he is considered one of the greatest modern European poets. His *Selected Poems* have been translated into English (1974, 1982). The first examples here – 'The Blighter' ('O Mostrengo'), 'The Ascent of Vasco da Gama' and 'The Portuguese Sea' are Nos. 27, 29 and 30 respectively of the patriotic *Mensagem*, the only book collection he published in his lifetime. He adopted several heteronyms under which he composed poetry, and 'If, after I Die' is delivered in the voice of the sceptical Alberto Caeiro. 'Azure, or Green, or Purple' is from his last poems in his own voice, issued for the first time only in 1973.

PHIPSON, THOMAS; Londoner, settled in Natal from 1849 and for many years the colony's sheriff. His letters portraying aspects of life in Natal, collected by his great-grandson, the poet R. N. Currey, include many items contributed to the early British press. This poem was included in the first number of *The Natal Standard* (2 March 1852).

PLAATJE, SOLOMON TSHEKISHO (1876–1932); mission-educated of the Barolong group of Tswana-speakers; editor and translator who, during World War I in London, prepared with the phonetician, Daniel Jones, *A Sechuana Reader* (1916). Founder member of the South African Native National Congress (now ANC), his novel *Mhudi* – the first by a black South African – was written at the same time. Since his days as a court interpreter at Mafikeng during the siege, he was a versatile translator, from Tswana and Dutch into English and vice versa, especially of Shakespeare into Tswana.

PLOMER, WILLIAM; born in the Northern Transvaal, educated in England and Johannesburg. Novelist, autobiographer, broadcaster and editor. This selection from his large corpus ranges over a considerable span of his career – 'A Fall of Rock', 'Namaqualand after Rain' and the frequently anthologized 'The Scorpion' were included in his third collection, *The Fivefold Screen* (1932), published after he left South Africa in 1926; 'The Devil-dancers' is from *Visiting the Caves* (1936); and 'Tugela River' dates from after his brief return visit in 1956, and was published under the sub-heading 'After Thirty Years' in his *Collected Poems* of 1960. 'White Gloves' dates from his last slim volume, *Celebrations* (1972). With the publication of his first novel, *Turbott Wolfe* in 1926, Plomer began a lifelong monitoring of the issue of race and class in South Africa, which has caused him, together with Campbell, to be called the father of modern poetry in Southern Africa.

PRINCE, FRANK TEMPLETON; born in Kimberley, educated at the University of the Witwatersrand in the 1930s and at Oxford; until recently Professor of English at the University of Southampton; scholar of Shakespeare and Milton. His *Poems* of 1938 contains some South African pieces; *Soldiers Bathing* of 1954 contains the title poem, which is one of the most anthologized of World War II. *Memoirs in Oxford*, published as a single work in 1970, is in five parts, of which this extract is the second. From the reshaped version included in his *Collected Poems* (1979).

PRINGLE, THOMAS; Scottish poet who, before emigrating to the Cape as an 1820 Settler party leader, co-edited the *Edinburgh Monthly Magazine* (which later became *Blackwood's*). 'The Emigrant's Cabin', written when he was thirty-three, is precisely autobiographical. His addressee, John Fairbairn, did indeed join the Pringles once they had left the Eastern Cape (see *Narrative of a Residence in South Africa*, published posthumously in 1835). In Cape Town, Pringle and Fairbairn founded the brief-lived *South African Journal* (1824), and fought for freedom of the press. Pringle was also first librarian of what would become the South African Library. His *African Sketches* (1834) collects together many poems of his African experience and has been frequently reprinted. Dissatisfied with autocratic rule and slaveholding policy, he left for London in 1826 to become secretary of the Anti-Slavery Society. He died of tuberculosis, one day after the abolition of slavery throughout the British Empire was announced. Commonly held to be the father of South African poetry, his 'Afar in the Desert' has opened many anthologies of the English strand of it.

QABULA, ALFRED TEMBA; born at Flagstaff, Transkei, in a community controlled by migrancy laws; a factory worker at Dunlop in Durban, and member of MAWU (the Metal and Allied Workers' Union), where he has initiated a revival of imbongi praise-poetry, performed in costume at meetings and rallies. He has become known as a leading 'worker poet'.

REITZ, FRANCIS WILLIAM. Poet-president. Born in the Cape of a farming family, called to the bar in Westminster in 1867; president of the Orange Free State republic from 1889 to 1895, and thereafter state secretary to President Kruger of the Transvaal republic. From the 1870s and into his eighties, he translated and adapted many works from English, including some of Pringle's and particularly ballads, into 'Kaapsch-Hollandsch', within the First Afrikaans Language Movement, creating Afrikaans as a literary language, particularly by catching the idiom and wit of rural speech. His war polemics, widely distributed on postcards and in the press, were collected in 1910. With Union he became the president of the Senate.

ROSENBERG, ISAAC; Bristol-born, trained at the Slade School as a printmaker and artist; in 1912 he circulated his first pamphlet of poems. In 1914 he sailed for South Africa to recover from lung trouble and taught art in Cape Town. One of the generation of First World War poets, he enlisted in 1916, and was killed in action in 1918. From his *Collected Poems* (1977).

RUNCIE, JOHN; on the staff of the *Cape Times*, he widely published poems in newspapers; his collection of 1905, *Songs by the Stoep*, is one of the few examples of Decadent verse in South Africa. Little else is known of him, other than that he retired to Scotland.

SCHREINER, OLIVE. Influential Victorian author of *The Story of an African Farm* (1883) and other fiction, including dream allegories; spokesperson and essayist, who at the turn of the century represented the anti-imperial intelligentsia in South Africa. Confined to various Karoo villages for most of the war years, she presented her protest in this, one of her few poems; it was not published until after her death in the collection, *Stories, Dreams and Allegories* (1923), and is akin in sentiment to her long short story, 'Eighteen-ninety-nine'. This line of thinking about war and peace in relation to the status and suffering of women is much expanded in her *Woman and Labour* (1911). Her *Thoughts on South Africa* (1923) gives the most reliable analysis of South Africa during the period of her lifetime.

SCULLY, WILLIAM CHARLES; Dubliner, emigrated to the Cape in 1867, rover, civil commissioner for Namaqualand, and magistrate; short-story writer of the Transkei and early novelist. *His Reminiscences of a South African Pioneer* (1913) is an important writer's autobiography. In 1886 he published his *Wreck of the Grosvenor and Other Poems* at Lovedale – one of the earliest volumes of 'serious' poetry, indebted to Pringle – and *Poems* (1892) in London. ''Nkongane' is one of several 'Zulu Pictures' and the speaker is Scully himself.

SEPAMLA, SIPHO SYDNEY; born in Krugersdorp on the Rand and trained as a teacher; lives in Wattville, Benoni. Director of Federated Union of Black Arts (Fuba) Centre, Johannesburg, founded to provide an alternative education after the Soweto '76 uprising. Novelist and a prolific poet whose four volumes produced his *Selected Poems* (1984). These pieces are all from his *The Soweto I Love* (London, 1977).

SEROTE, MONGANE WALLY; born in Sophiatown, educated in Alexandra and Soweto; after a fine arts degree at Columbia, returned to Gaborone, Botswana; now resident as a cultural worker in London. His second volume, *Tsetlo* (1974), from which all but the last of these poems come, appeared in Johannesburg as a key text of the black poetry revival of the 1970s. 'The Breezing Dawn of the New Day' dates from his later exile; from *Selected Poems* (Johannesburg, 1982).

SHAKA; son of Senzangakona and Nandi, first King of the Zulus, who in his short life converted Nguniland, South East Africa, from a clan-based agricultural region into the Zulu military empire. The first nineteenth century African paramount to achieve legendary fame in Europe. Hospitable towards early whites like Fynn, whom he used as advisers, he was always open to innovation and an alliance with Britain. Many travellers who were entertained at his court testify to his ability as a poet, both of battle-hymns and domestic lyrics.

SLATER, FRANCIS CAREY; Eastern-Province-born of 1820 Settler stock, manager of various Standard Banks (1899–1930); novelist and prolific writer of patriotic verse. As editor of *The Centenary Book of South African Verse* (1925; extensively revised 1945), he fostered an English-only, white tradition of sometimes academic lyrics, frequently confessional of the individual sensibility, eschewing outside influences. His own *Collected Poems* of 1957 is more varied, using narrative and dramatic techniques extensively.

SMALL, ADAM; born in Wellington in the Cape, philosopher and social worker, who has introduced the use of the mixed-race Kaaps language into written literature. A dramatist of great power, his *Kanna Hy Kô Hystoe* had over a decade's battle to find a staging before unsegregated audiences. He has written much in English and is a translator.

SMITH, PAULINE; born in the Little Karoo which she uniquely celebrated in her stories, *The Little Karoo* (1925) and her novel, *The Beadle* (1926). In 1935 she published *Platkops Children*, her children's book strongly based on her own childhood reminiscences of the Victorian 1890s. Her reconstruction of the dialect here is undertaken with an archaeologist's care.

SONTONGA, MANKAYI ENOCH; of the Tembu people, northern Transkei. A teacher in Methodist mission schools who, while at Nancefield on the Rand, wrote songs for his pupils in tonic sol-fa notation. His other compositions have become lost.

STOCKENSTRÖM, WILMA; born in Napier in the Cape; playwright and actress. Since 1954 she has lived in Pretoria. One of her novels, *The Expedition to the Baobab Tree* (1981), has been widely translated. Her 'On the Suicide of Young Writers' was first published in 1968. To date she has published five collections of poetry.

SWART, EDWARD VINCENT; Free-State-born, in the 1930s as a student at the universities of the Witwatersrand and Cambridge he published imagist poems. Later jailed and banned for his Communist Party activities, he died in Bohemian squalor in Johannesburg. His ashes were scattered over Alexandra Township. His *Collected Poems* appeared for the first time only in 1981.

VAN WYK, CHRISTOPHER; born and educated in Riverlea, Johannesburg; his first collection of poems, *It is Time to Go Home* (Johannesburg, 1979), contained several key items of 'post-Soweto' black poetry in South Africa. Until recently he was editor of *Staffrider*.

VILAKAZI, BENEDICT WALLET BAMBATHA; born at Groutville Mission Station of convert parents, Zulu novelist, poet and founding scholar. Studied there, and at the Roman Catholic Mariannhill near Durban, and at the University of South Africa. His *Inkondlo ka Zulu* (1935) was the first published collection of Western-influenced poetry in Zulu. Co-compiler of the standard Zulu–English dictionary while lecturing at the University of the Witwatersrand, where he obtained his doctorate. He was also associated with the African Languages Department of Roma, Lesotho, before his early death. His 'In the Gold Mines', first published in *Africa South* in 1945 in an English translation by A. C. Jordan, is frequently taken as a definitive protest against urban-industrial conditions for blacks.

WAKOLELE, NGUNO; born in Namibia; in 1982 in exile in Zambia; a student at the United Nations Institute for Namibia in Lusaka. This poem was included in the UNIN's Creative Writers' Club collection of 'Young Namibian Poetry', expanded as *It is No More a Cry: Namibian Poetry in Exile* (1982).

WALLACE, EDGAR; the Cockney newspaper seller who arrived with the army at Simonstown in 1896; his first poems appeared in the Cape press (like this one, in *The Owl* on 20 November 1897) before he became a war-correspondent and founder-editor of the *Rand Daily Mail* in Johannesburg. Bestselling author of crime thrillers and the Sanders African romances, he also scripted the original film of *King Kong*.

WHEATLEY, JOHN. According to his obituary in *The Cape of Good Hope Literary Gazette*, author of *Remarks on Currency and Commerce* (London, 1803), *Thoughts on the Objects of the Foreign Subsidy* (London, 1805), *An Essay on the Theory of Money and the Principles of Commerce*, 2 vols (London, 1807, 1822), *A Letter to His Grace the Duke of Devonshire, on the State of Ireland and the General Effects of Colonization* (Calcutta, 1824) and *Tempora Praeterita: or More Currency and More Corn* (Cape Town, 1828). His familiarity with Camoens and Milton is overshadowed by his knowledge of the recent deaths of Shelley and of Byron particularly, the latter in the cause of liberty. Wheatley presents the extraordinary case of a political economist turned Romantic poet, who published his known poems while wintering at the Cape.

WRIGHT, DAVID; born in Johannesburg, but moved to England early, educated at Oxford; translator of *Beowulf* and *The Canterbury Tales* and a noted anthologizer (for example, *The Penguin Book of Everyday Verse*, 1976). His *Deafness: A Personal Account* appeared in 1969. Some ten volumes of poems include *To the Gods the Shades* (1976), the new and collected poems from which these are taken; both were included in his *Selected Poems* (1980). He lives in the Lake District.

XAA-TTIN. See notes to 'The Broken String'. Nothing further is known of this San poet, although photographs of his associates are preserved in the South African Library, Cape Town.

ZIMUNYA, MUSAEMURA BONAS; born in Mutare, lectures in English at the University of Zimbabwe. Co-editor of *And Now the Poets Speak* (1981), an anthology of poems inspired by the liberation struggle in Zimbabwe. He has published several volumes, including *Thought Tracks* (1982), from which these poems come.

ZUMA, NONGEJENI; born in Zululand, as a youth he stabled Sir Theophilus Shepstone's horses; in the Natal police and between the World Wars 'induna' at the Chief Native Commissioner's office in Pietermaritzburg. Appointed to act as chief of the Bokvus of Umvoti, he was tragically killed by a passing car.

ACKNOWLEDGEMENTS

———— ~ ————

For permission to include copyright items in this anthology, acknowledgement is made to the following copyright-holders:

Ad. Donker (Pty), Ltd, P. O. Box 41021, Craighall, 2024, South Africa, for Roy Campbell's translation of Luis de Camoen's 'On a Shipmate, Pero Moniz, Dying at Sea' and of Joaquim Paço d'Arcos' 'Re-encounter' from *Nostalgia* (Sylvan Press, London, 1960); and for Roy Campbell's *The Wayzgoose*, Part I; for Vincent Swart's two poems from *Collected Poems* (1981); for Guy Butler's three poems from *Selected Poems* (1975); for Douglas Livingstone's 'Vanderdecken' from *Selected Poems* (1984) and 'Bateleur' and 'A Piece of Earth' from *The Anvil's Undertone* (1978); for Lionel Abrahams' 'Thresholds of Identity' from *Journal of a New Man* (1984); and for Mbuyiseni Mtshali's 'The Day We Buried Our Bully' from *Sounds of a Cowhide Drum* (1982); for Mongane Serote's 'A Poem', 'Death Survey' and 'Another Alexandra' from *Tsetlo* (1974) and 'The Breezing Dawn of a New Day' from *Selected Poems* (1982); Oxford University Press, Oxford, for Daniel Malcolm's translation of 'Mbuyazi', reprinted from Trevor Cope (ed.), *Izibongo: Zulu Praise Poems*, © Oxford University Press, 1968, and for Daniel P. Kunene's translation of 'A War Song of the Basotho', reprinted form Daniel P. Kunene's *Heroic Poetry of the Basotho*, © Oxford University Press, 1971;
Stephen Gray for his translation of 'The Concert', Eugène N. Marais' 'Radio Cradle-song' and Wilma Stockenström's 'On the Suicide of Young Writers' and for his poems, 'Hottentot Venus' from *Hottentot Venus and Other Poems* (1979) and 'Apollo Café';
F. M. C. Scully for the Estate of W. C. Scully for his ''Nkongane' (1892);
Oxford University Press, Cape Town, for the following from A. P. Grové and C. J. D. Harvey (eds), *Afrikaans Poems with English Translations* (1962): C. J. D. Harvey's translation of C. Louis Leipoldt's 'Oom Gert's Story'; Guy Butler's translation of N. P. van Wyk Louw's *Raka*, Part I; and Anthony Delius' translation of D. J. Opperman's 'Christmas Carol';
Peter Shields for the Estate of C. Louis Leipoldt for the original of his 'Oom Gert's Story';

A. A. Slater for the Estate of Francis Carey Slater for his two poems;
Hugh Finn for his translations of Eugène N. Marais' 'Deep River' and
'Here We have No Firm Dwelling-place' and of N. P. van Wyk Louw's
'Dedication';
the University of Cape Town for Pauline Smith's 'Katisje's Patchwork
Dress' from *Platkops Children* (1935);
Jeff Opland for his revised translation of, and the original of, S. E. K.
Mqhayi's 'The Pleiades';
Witwatersrand University Press, Johannesburg, for the original Xhosa of
J. J. R. Jolobe's 'The Making of a Servant', from *Umyezo*, No. 2 of the
Bantu Treasury Series (Witwatersrand University Press, 1936), and for
B. W. Vilakazi's 'Sengiyokholwa-ke' from *Inkondlo kaZulu* (Bantu
Treasury Series, No. 1, 1935) and 'Sengiyakholwa' from *Amal'ezulu*
(Bantu Treasury Series, No. 8, 1945);
Robert Kavanagh for his part in the translation of Jolobe's 'The
Making of a Servant';
Cherie Maclean for her translations of the two Vilakazi poems above;
Jonathan Cape, Ltd, London, on behalf of the Estate of William Plomer,
for his 'A Fall of Rock', 'Namaqualand after Rain', 'The Scorpion', 'The
Devil-dancers', 'Tugela River' and 'White Gloves' from his *Collected
Poems* (1973);
Hope Eglington for the Estate of Charles Eglington for his translation of
Fernando Pessoa's 'O Mostrengo' as 'The Blighter' and for his 'Lourenço
Marques' from *Under the Horizon* (1977); the University of Wales Press,
Cardiff, for F. E. G. Quintanilha's translations of 'The Ascent of Vasco da
Gama' and 'The Portuguese Sea' from *Sixty Portuguese Poems of Fernando Pessoa* (1971); and Jonathan Griffin for his translations of 'If, After I
Die' and 'Azure, or Green, or Purple' from *Fernando Pessoa, Selected
Poems* (2nd edn) (Penguin, 1982);
Tafelberg Publishers (Ltd), Cape Town, for N. P. van Wyk Louw's
'Opdrag' ('Dedication') from *Die Halwe Kring*, 'O Wye en Droewe Land'
('Oh Wide and Sad Land') from *Die Dieper Reg*, and *Raka*, Part I; for
Elisabeth Eybers' 'Verhaal' ('Narrative') from *Die Ander Dors*; for D. J.
Opperman's 'Fabel' ('Fable') from *Dolosse* (1963) and 'Kersliedjie'
('Christmas Carol') from *Blom en Baaierd* (1956); and for Sheila Cussons' 'Yellow Gramophone' from *Poems* (1985) and the original of 'The
Barn-yard';
Adam Small for his translation of 'Oh Wide and Sad Land' (Maskew
Miller, 1975) and for the original of his 'Second Coming, I and II' from *Sê
Sjibbolet* (1978);
the Estate of Uys Krige for his 'The Taking of the Koppie';

Lionel Abrahams for the Estate of Ruth Miller for her 'Sterkfontein' from *Floating Island* (1965), and 'Mantis' from *Selected Poems* (1968), and for his 'The Whiteman Blues', *Bateleur Poets* (1975);

Human and Rousseau (Pty), Ltd, Cape Town, for Elisabeth Eybers' 'Refleksie' ('Reflection'), 'Slak' ('Snail') and 'Confrontation with an Artist' from *Gedigte (1962–1982)*, 1985; and for Wilma Stockenström's 'The Rank Harvest of Betrayal' ('Die Wulpse Oes van Verraad') from *Spieël van Water* (1973), and 'L'Agulhas, a Walk' ('By L'Agulhas 'n Wandeling') from *Van Vergetelheid en van Glans* (1976);

Giles Battiss for the Estate of Walter Battiss for his 'Limpopo';

Denis Hatfield Bullough for John Dronsfield's 'Visitation';

Noël H. Brettell for his two poems;

Mambo Press, Gweru, for the original of Joseph Kumbirai's 'Chedza' ('Dawn'); the original and translation of Aaron Hodza's 'The Slighted Wife'; Charles Mungoshi's 'A Letter to a Son' and 'Dotito is Our Brother'; Julius Chingono's 'An Epitaph'; and N. C. G. Mathema's 'A Maze of Blood';

Douglas Livingstone for his translation of Kumbirai's 'Dawn' and for his 'On Clouds' from *Sjambok* (1964), 'The Sleep of my Lions' from *Eyes Closed against the Sun* (1970) and 'Bad Run at King's Rest' (first published in *The London Magazine*, 1983);

Three Continents Press, Inc., Washington, D.C., for Solomon Mutswairo's 'My Birds' from his *Zimbabwean Prose and Poetry* (1974) and for Geraldo Bessa Victor's 'That Old Mulemba' and 'Note on a Shop in the Muceque' from Don Burness, *Fire: Six Writers from Angola, Mozambique and Cape Verde* (1971);

Heinemann Educational Books (Ltd), London, for the originals and Michael Wolfers' translations of Agostinho Neto's 'We Must Return' and Antonio Jacinto's 'Poem of Alienation' from *Poems from Angola* (1979); for Dennis Brutus' 'Cold' and 'Letters to Martha, 1 and 2' from *Letters to Martha* (1968); for Jack Mapanje's 'The Cheerful Girls at Smiller's Bar, 1971', 'On African Writing (1971)', 'Steve Biko is Dead' and 'After Wiriyamu Village Massacre by Portuguese' from *Of Chameleons and Gods* (1981) and for his 'Baobab Fruit Picking' (first published in *Kunapipi*, 1986);

Jack Cope for his translation of D. J. Opperman's 'Fable', and as trustee of the Ingrid Jonker Trust for the originals of her 'The Child who was Shot Dead by Soldiers in Nyanga', translated by himself and William Plomer, and her 'Bitterberry Daybreak';

HAUM Publishers, Pretoria, for Adam Small's 'Brown Lullaby' and 'There's Somethin'', and the original of 'What abou' de Law?', from

Kitaar my Kruis, 1962, and Carrol Lasker for her translation of the latter and of 'Second Coming, I and II';

Mazisi Kunene for his five poems;

Cecilia Potgieter for the Estate of Arthur Nortje for his three poems;

Malangatana Ngwenya for the original of his 'Woman' and Dorothy Guedes for Philippa Rumsey's translation;

Rui Knopfli for his 'Kwela for Tomorrow' and 'Death Certificate', both first published in *Ophir* (September, 1968);

Anvil Press Poetry (Ltd), London, for an extract from F. T. Prince's *Memoirs in Oxford*, from his *Collected Poems* (1979);

David Philip, Publisher (Pty), Ltd, P. O. Box 23408, Claremont, 7735, South Africa, for Sydney Clouts' three poems from *Collected Poems* (1984), and for Patrick Cullinan's poem from *Today is Not Different* (1978);

Cherry Clayton for her translation of Ingrid Jonker's 'Bitterberry Daybreak';

Rex Collings (Ltd), London, for the five translations of poems by Breyten Breytenbach, from *And Death White as Words* (1978), and for the three poems by Sipho Sepamla from *The Soweto I Love* (1977);

John Johnson (Authors' Agent) (Ltd), London, for C. J. Driver's two poems;

A. P. Watt (Ltd), London, for Christopher Hope's two poems;

House of Anansi Press (Ltd), Toronto, for Jeni Couzyn's two poems from *Life by Drowning* (Anansi, 1983). Reprinted by permission;

Carcanet Press (Ltd), Manchester, publisher of David Wright's 'A Funeral Oration' and an extract from 'A Peripatetic Letter to Isabella Fey', from *To the Gods the Shades* (1976);

Ravan Press (Pty), Ltd, P. O. Box 31134, Braamfontein, 2017, South Africa, for two poems and the prose-poem, 'A Beggar Named Mokopi', by Wopko Jensma; for Mtutuzeli Matshoba's 'The Mantatee Horde' from *Call Me Not a Man* (1979); for Frank Chipasula's three poems from *O Earth, Wait for Me* (1984); for Mafika Gwala's 'In Defence of Poetry' and 'My House is Bugged' from *No More Lullabies* (1982); and for four poems by Jeremy Cronin from his *Inside* (1983);

Shuter and Shooter (Pty), Ltd, Pietermaritzburg, for Mbuyiseni Mtshali's 'The Removal of Our Village, KwaBhanya' from *Fireflames* (1980) and the poet himself for his 'Farewell to My Scooter';

Chris Mann for Thembinkosi Ndlovu's 'Elegy for the Dead of Soweto' and his translation of it, and for his 'The Comrades Marathon' and 'The Poet's Progress';

Njabulo S. Ndebele for his poem;

Harold Farmer for his poem;

Longman Group, U. K. (Ltd), Harlow, for 'White Poetess' and 'After the Massacre' from *Thought Tracks* (1982), © Musaemura Zimunya, and for 'Neocolonialism', 'To the Writers' Workshop in Zomba' and 'Sizeline' from *When Sunset Comes to Sapitwa*, (1982), © Felix Mnthali;

Johann de Lange for his translation of Sheila Cussons' 'The Barnyard';

W. Kirsipuu for the original of Wilma Stockenström's 'On the Suicide of Young Writers' and Rosa Keet for her translations of her 'The Rank Harvest of Betrayal' and 'L'Agulhas, a Walk';

Phil du Plessis for his poem;

Wordsmiths, Zambia (Ltd), Lusaka, for Timothy Holmes's two poems from *Double Element* (1985);

Elizabeth Gunner for the original and her translation of Swidi-Nonkamfela Mhlongo's poem;

Matsemela Manaka for his two choruses;

Chris van Wyk for his two poems;

Skotaville Publishers, P. O. Box 32483, Braamfontein, 2017, South Africa, for 'The Day They Came for Our House' and 'Giovanni Azania' from Don Mattera's *Azanian Love Song* (1983) and for 'Haanetjie's Morning Dialogue' from Essop Patel's *The Bullet and the Bronze Lady* (1987);

Writers Forum, P. O. Box 11046, Johannesburg, 2000, South Africa, for Mafika Gwala's 'The New Dawn' from *Exiles Within* (1986);

Allison and Busby (Ltd), London, for the original and Chris Searle's translation of 'Ode to a Lost Cargo in a Ship Called *Save*' by José Craveirinha, from *The Sunflower of Hope* (1982);

José Craveirinha for the original of his 'The Tasty "Tanjarines" of Inhambane' and Michael Wolfers for his translation of it (1987);

Basler Afrika Bibliographien, Basle, for Nguno Wakolele's 'Southern Africa';

Alfred Temba Qabula for his poem, and Nise Malange for her poem, both from *Black Mamba Rising* (Culture and Working Life Project, Durban, 1986);

Oswald Basize Dube for his poem;

and Mzimkhulu Mnotoza for his poem.

Some copyright-holders of work included here, despite repeated efforts to make contact with them, have proved untraceable. The publishers would be pleased to hear from them.

The publisher and editor are also grateful to the following for the use of material:

Geoffrey Bullough, editor of the Centaur Press edition (London, 1963), for an extract from Fanshawe's translation of Luis de Camoens, *The Lusiads*;

the Estate of W. H. I. Bleek for 'The Broken String' material from *Specimens of Bushman Folklore* (1911) and the Khoikhoi Animal Poems from *Reynard the Fox in South Africa* (1864);

Janet Hodgson for John Knox Bokwe's translation from *Ntsikana's Great Hymn* (1980);

Shuter and Shooter (Pty), Ltd, for King Shaka's 'Battle Song' with notes from *The Diary of Henry Francis Fynn* (Pietermaritzburg, 1969);

the South African Library, Cape Town, for access to the original of Andrew Geddes Bain's 'Polyglot Medley' and to them and the National English Literary Museum, Grahamstown, for supplying copies of many other early texts;

R. N. Currey, editor of *Letters of a Natal Sheriff* (Oxford University Press, Cape Town, 1968), for Thomas Phipson's 'The Press';

also especially Rosa Keet for supplying many translations of Afrikaans poems, and many scholars, poets and translators, librarians and archivists, without whose friendly assistance and advice over a long period this anthology could not have been assembled.

INDEX OF POETS

INDEX OF TRANSLATORS

FOR THE BEST IN PAPERBACKS, LOOK FOR THE

In every corner of the world, on every subject under the sun, Penguin represents quality and variety – the very best in publishing today.

For complete information about books available from Penguin – including Pelicans, Puffins, Peregrines and Penguin Classics – and how to order them, write to us at the appropriate address below. Please note that for copyright reasons the selection of books varies from country to country.

In the United Kingdom: Please write to *Dept E.P., Penguin Books Ltd, Harmondsworth, Middlesex, UB7 0DA*

If you have any difficulty in obtaining a title, please send your order with the correct money, plus ten per cent for postage and packaging, to *PO Box No 11, West Drayton, Middlesex*

In the United States: Please write to *Dept BA, Penguin, 299 Murray Hill Parkway, East Rutherford, New Jersey 07073*

In Canada: Please write to *Penguin Books Canada Ltd, 2801 John Street, Markham, Ontario L3R 1B4*

In Australia: Please write to the *Marketing Department, Penguin Books Australia Ltd, P.O. Box 257, Ringwood, Victoria 3134*

In New Zealand: Please write to the *Marketing Department, Penguin Books (NZ) Ltd, Private Bag, Takapuna, Auckland 9*

In India: Please write to *Penguin Overseas Ltd, 706 Eros Apartments, 56 Nehru Place, New Delhi, 110019*

In Holland: Please write to *Penguin Books Nederland B.V., Postbus 195, NL–1380AD Weesp, Netherlands*

In Germany: Please write to *Penguin Books Ltd, Friedrichstrasse 10–12, D–6000 Frankfurt Main 1, Federal Republic of Germany*

In Spain: Please write to *Longman Penguin España, Calle San Nicolas 15, E–28013 Madrid, Spain*

In France: Please write to *Penguin Books Ltd, 39 Rue de Montmorency, F–75003, Paris, France*

In Japan: Please write to *Longman Penguin Japan Co Ltd, Yamaguchi Building, 2–12–9 Kanda Jimbocho, Chiyoda-Ku, Tokyo 101, Japan*

Also edited by Stephen Gray

The Penguin Book of Southern African Stories

In this remarkable anthology – a companion volume to *The Penguin Book of Southern African Verse* – the different voices of South Africa are linked into a unique pattern.

From the pre-Christian African legends, full of people, animals and death, to the arrival of the white settlers settling in a land both beautiful and inhospitable, to the later stories of a civilization that had established itself, the stories reflect a thriving, diverse and colourful tradition.

Including material from Botswana, Lesotho, Malawi, Namibia, Swaziland and Zimbabwe, as well as South Africa, this collection offers the authentic voice (many of the stories have been previously unknown) of an extraordinary experience.